Book 2 Divination of Jezebel

Book 2 Divination of Jezebel

Jessie Craig

authorHOUSE®

AuthorHouse™ LLC
1663 Liberty Drive
Bloomington, IN 47403
www.authorhouse.com
Phone: 1-800-839-8640

Published by AuthorHouse 04/30/2014

ISBN: 978-1-4969-1024-0 (sc)
ISBN: 978-1-4969-1025-7 (e)

Library of Congress Control Number: 2014908253

Contents

I would like to dedicate this book to my
parents for being so supportive.

I would also like to dedicate this book to my Aunt Missy. You are a
strong and vibrant woman, God loves you very much and so do I.

Love you guys.

In Memory of
Harrison E. Denham
October 20, 1936—November 5, 2009

Illustrated by: Martin Geppert
Edited by: Angie Boone

Oh sweet Tristan,

It's so simple. It seems as though your grip on Jessie is vanishing. But let's be honest, we both knew that you were incapable of winning this game. I will give you credit for one thing though . . . . Your ability to sit on the sidelines is impeccable. Like the fleeting sands in an hour glass pouring through your fingertips, you are losing her. But don't you worry my dear . . . I've been salivating to commandeer the reigns. Time is escaping Tristan, but once I've gained full control, my influence will overwhelm her.

—Jezebel

CHAPTER I

Metamorphosis

I sat at the end of Jessie's bed. The moonlight is casting a faint shadow upon her face. She's sleeping peacefully for the first time in a while. I watch her body rise rhythmically up and down as she breathes. Every so often, I hear her sigh. I wonder what she's dreaming about— probably the first day of school since it's tomorrow. Tomorrow, Jessie will be starting her senior year of high school. I can't believe how time has passed us by. I've seen it all. I miss when she was little. She was dependent, but she isn't too much anymore. It's the little things, not the really big thing, that I miss. For example, she walks through the halls of her high school saying hi to her lifelong friends and new ones. She puts in the combination to the locker that was assigned to her. When she drives, it all sends a flood of emotion. She's growing up and, like a parent, it hurts but it's also a happy feeling. Bittersweet. The sun is starting to peek through. The moon tells us goodbye as the sun enters to say hello. I hear a bird chirp. It's that mockingbird that I heard the morning before. I think it has a nest in the tree that resides next to Jessie's window. It sings as the sun comes up, welcoming a new day—a day that the Lord has made. Jessie's eyes opens suddenly and looks at her clock that is revealing the time in large green numbers—6:00 a.m. Jessie would have to be up in thirty minutes. She squints her eyes, yawns, and then drifts back to sleep. I pray to Jehovah that she has an amazing day and for His protection.

My train of thought is broken when Jessie's alarm screams at her to wake up. Jssie sits up in her bed and turns the alarm off. Her hair falls freely down her back. She yawns and then reaches over to turn on her lamp. At that moment, her cell phone rings. It's Karla. Jessie and Karla haven't hung out or talked all that much since Jessie's deliverance. Jessie stares at the phone and then answers.

"Hey, Karla."

Jessie slaps on a fake smile, as if Karla can see it. I can hear Karla talking on the other line. I didn't understand why teenagers had to have everything so loud—their phones, music, or television. It was all just . . . loud.

"Are you ready for our first day as seniors?!" Karla exclaimed. Jessie pulled the phone away from her ear shaking her head.

"Karla, it is 6:35 a.m." Jessie put the phone back to her ear. "Be dull and grouchy like the rest of us normal students." Jessie moaned.

"Oh, Jessie, it's senior year! Then we're out and off to Florida!"

I could just feel Karla smile as she said that. Jessie and Karla had made plans to move to Florida and become bartenders. Jessie knows she has other plans. Karla has her heart set on the previous plans. Jessie grabbed her hairbrush from the nightstand and began to brush her hair, holding her phone between her ear and shoulder. Then she headed to her closet.

"Yo, Karla, what are you going to wear?" Jessie said changing the "Florida" subject.

"I'm going to wear jeans and my Slipknot t-shirt. You?" Karla said.

"Um, I'm thinking I'm going to wear jeans and my Chicago Cubs shirt and put my hair in a pony tail." Jessie shrugged.

"Oh, I thought you were going to wear Mudvayne and I was going to wear Slipknot?" Karla's tone changed to disappointment.

"I can't find my Mudvayne shirt." Jessie lied as she stared at it hanging in her closet.

"Oh . . . Chicago Cubs. You a tomboy again?" Karla asked in disgust.

"Yeah, well, people change."

"Yeah, I know." Karla huffed.

"Okay. I'm going to get ready. I will be at your house at 7:15." Jessie said loudly through the phone.

"I got you. See you then." Karla said and then hung up.

I heard the phone click and the dial tone hum through the phone. Jessie shut her phone and tossed it on her bed. She went back and stared at her Mudvayne shirt. Her face filled with emotion at the memory of buying the shirt with Karla. I knew she missed being who she was. This metamorphosis was an amazing thing—one she would never forget or want to forget. Jessie ripped her gaze from the shirt and filtered through the others till she found her light blue Chicago Cubs shirt. Jessie smiled at the shirt. Her dad had bought it for her when she went from a fun-loving tomboy to a God-hating rebel. Her dad tried so hard to cheer he up, so he bought her a Chicago Cubs shirt to try and get her back into sports and away from drinking and smoking. Jessie looked from the shirt to herself and then back up to the shirt. Her long, blond hair bounced against her long-sleeved black shirt. Her beige and black plaid pajama bottoms swayed with the movement of her body. She pulled the shirt off of the hanger and tossed it on the bed. She looked at the clock—6:45. Even I panicked. It took her ten minutes to get to Karla's house and that gave her thirty minutes to get dressed and put on make-up. It was a good thing that she took a shower last night. When I knew she had her outfit picked out, I exited her room and stood by the door. The only time I am ever in a room when she is undressed is when there are evil spirits in the room with her. In this case, they are not, so I am free to exit the room. When there are evil spirits in the room, I cannot see Jessie as naked human being. She is like a white shadow and I can see her skeleton, her ribs, legs, arms, and skull. Every bone in her body is dark gray in color with a white transparent skin. It's a blessing for it to happen this way. Our humans deserve their privacy, but there are occasions where we see the human in its naked form. For example, we see them when they are beaten and bruised so badly by an evil spirit. That happens rarely, but it can happen. It hasn't happened with me and Jessie, and she's been through a lot with evil spirits. I personally choose to see Jessie as a white, shadowy yet transparent skeleton. I feel more comfortable.

Jessie and I jumped into her truck. I sat in the passenger's seat as she started the engine. She turned on the CD player that blared Casting Crowns' "Life Song". Good song. Jessie put her truck into reverse and we headed to Karla's.

"Let my life song sing to you . . . let my life song sing to you. I want to sing your name to the end of this day, knowing that my heart was true . . . ." Jessie sang.

We rounded the corner onto Karla's street. Jessie zoomed past a stop sign.

"Oops," Jessie snickered. I just smiled. We reached Karla's house and found her sitting on the swing that hung from her porch ceiling. She bounded down the steps. I moved to half cab.

"Jessie, you look so different," Karla said as she pulled her earphone from her ear and shut her MP3 player off.

"Really? Thanks." Jessie smiled.

"You look kind preppy." Karla stared at Jessie.

"Labels suck." Jessie sighed.

"I haven't changed." Karla looked herself up and down.

"I haven't either." Jessie smiled as she put her truck into drive and sped away from Karla's house to school.

"Yes, you have."

Karla looked out the passenger side of the window. The ride to the school was silent until we came up to the school.

"You ready?" Jessie let out a big sigh.

"As ready as I'll ever be." Karla let out a nervous chuckle.

"Senior year, here we come."

Jessie pulled into the senior parking lot. All the rich kids are parked at the front, and the nobodies were in the back. Ridiculous. Jessie found a parking spot between Jeremy McDaniel's car and Carrie's. Jessie turned off the engine and looked at Karla.

"We got this." Jessie reached for her purse that was in the back cab where I sat.

"We the biggest bad ass chicks in here," Karla yelled. Jessie closed her eyes and sighed.

"Well, let's go."

Karla and I exited the truck. A swarm of students walked to the double doors.

"Lord, be with us as we enter the Abyss," Jessie said in a low satanic voice. Then she smiled.

"Ha! No kidding," Karla laughed.

Jessie, Karla, and I entered through the double doors. Demons were everywhere, crawling on the ceiling, hanging on students' backs, walking next to students like they were guarding them. The white brick walls seemed to close in on us. Demons ran down the hallway or stood still up against the wall observing. Their lean, scraggly features set on the student. They growled as I passed. I also saw some fellow angels. They walked by their humans closely. The floors squeaked beneath the students' shoes and the halls smelled of textbooks and oppression.

"I hate this place." Jessie looked over to Karla who was mean-mugging a preppy girl named Grace. Grace surprisingly came up to us.

"Jessie! You look so pretty." Grace hugged Jessie.

"Hi, Grace, and thank you," Jessie nodded.

"Hope we have a class," Grace said.

Her long eyelashes brushed against her high cheek bones. Her plump lips wore a big smile reveling pearl white teeth.

"Me, too," Jessie replied.

"I got to get to class, Karla."

Grace's face grew cold with hatred as she turned to greet Karla. Her long brown hair swayed as she walked to her class.

"Bitch." Karla mumbled.

"Hey." Jessie shot Karla a dirty look.

"You guys never even talked." Karla huffed as we walked up the ramp.

"We both need to make new friends," Jessie said as they made it to building 2 stairs.

"I don't want a new best friend," Karla spat as they reached the top of the stairs.

"I didn't say best friend. I said friend." Jessie made her way to her and Karla's first class.

"Algebra 2," Karla moaned.

"We got this." Jessie linked her arm into Karla's and we entered the classroom.

The school day went by rather fast. We got through most of the day with no problems. Jessie and Karla had one class together. Jessie had classes with all her friends—three with Carrie, two with Shelby, two with Shane, four with Eric, and the list went on. We are now on our way to the last period of the day—English. There is one person I haven't seen—Leo Gutierrez, Jessie's old best friend.

"Jessie!" the teacher exclaimed.

"Mrs. Lazarus!" Jessie hugged her teacher.

"You look amazing, like refreshed, Jessie." Mrs. Lazarus held Jessie at arm's length.

"I've been getting that a lot," Jessie smiled. She looked at her English teacher. Mrs. Nancy Lazarus was tall, slender, and had blonde hair. She wore librarian-type glasses, loose t-shirts, jeans, and crocs. I looked around the room at some other students who were in their seat and I spotted Leo Gutierrez looking up at Jessie. Jessie finally got away from Mrs. Lazarus and turned toward the seat and spotted Leo. She froze. Leo and she locked eyes and held each other's gaze. I could just see the wheels in Jessie's mind spinning on what to do. Should she be mean or should she be nice? I hope she picks the latter.

"Leo, how have you been?" she asked as she approached.

Leo got up and greeted her with a hug. Jessie's face beamed with happiness. She hoped that Leo would see the difference in her.

"Jessie, I'm glad we have a class together. You look great." Leo smiled.

"Oh, thank you. So do you." Jessie smiled and hugged him again. She sat in the desk in front of Leo and turned to speak to him.

"How was your summer?" Jessie beamed.

Jessie was overjoyed to see Leo again. I decided to take a seat in the desk in front of Jessie.

"There's something different about you, but I can't put my finger on it. Mrs. Lazarus was right. There's something different about you. Your smile is bigger and more real." Leo smiled. "Your eyes have a brightness to them. Your voice is even more clear. I guess that's what summer will do for you." Leo looked hesitantly at Jessie. "You're even dressed better and your hair is . . . ." Leo cut himself off.

Jessie looked at him with surprise. He was seeing Jessie as a new and improved child of Jehovah. I am so proud. Words cannot explain. Other students filed in and started talking but, to Jessie and Leo, they were the only ones in the room.

"You're beautiful as always."

Jessie blushed. Leo's silky black hair had grown to the middle of his neck, and he had more facial hair.

"Thanks," Leo blushed. "You just . . . what's the word?" Leo rubbed his chin.

"Metamorphed?"

"That's not a word," Leo stated.

"Yes, it is." Jessie argued.

"No." He shook his head.

"Yes."

"No, Jess. It's metamorphosed."

"No, Leo. It's metamorphed," Jessie sighed.

Here we go again . . . .

CHAPTER 2

Reinventing a Former Self

Jessie stood staring at her open closet. Black shirts filled seventy-five percent. I stood adjacent to her from behind. She didn't move for a moment.

"I need music."

Jessie walked over to her stereo and clicked the power button. It glowed a bright green letting her know that the stereo was ready for use. She clicked the button that read disk five and then turned the volume two notches before it read maximum. It was loud music as always. I stood and watched her as she waited for the CD to play. Her face grew with impatience, then the CD began to spew out music. Jessie's face lit with exhilaration. "Something Beautiful" by the Newsboys started to amplify through the speakers. Jessie closed her eyes and sighed. She walked back up to her closet and filtered through her clothes. I walked up next to her and leaned against the wall. She tossed out some of her old band t-shirts, Jack Daniels, Jim Beam, and Samuel Adams t-shirts, all her long-sleeved fish net shirts, and her trip pants. When she came to her Mudvayne shirt, though, she didn't touch it. She went to the next shirt. Some things were hard to let go of, and Jehovah understood that. Jessie would let go . . . in time.

"Oh, my gosh. I have five t-shirts left. Either I bring out my old stuff or maybe, just maybe, I can see if Dad or Bubby will lend me some cash," Jessie said aloud as she tapped her chin. "Next, I go through make-up."

Jessie sighed and then walked over to her vanity. She opened the middle drawer. It contained an assortment of make-up but mainly black eyeliner and chapstick. She did have her little compartment that held brown eye shadow, eyeliner, colorless lip gloss, and some light pink blush. Jessie stared. She looked at the different assortment of eyebrow rings. Karla had bought two for her and she had one for herself. Jessie thought for a moment. I remember when she had gotten her eyebrow pierced. She begged and begged her dad. He said no for a long while but suddenly one day he broke and said that he didn't care. I was taken back by this. It wasn't the fact that she was getting her eyebrow pierced but that her father broke down and let her get it done after he had told her no. Jessie's mom took her to get it done. The guy was really nice and talked to her the whole time. Before we knew it, a metal ring penetrated Jessie's eyebrow. I stood there and looked at my Jessie transform. I never thought she would have gotten her eyebrow pierced, but she did and she loved it. She would strut in front of all her friends and family. Her friends liked it but her family despised it. Jessie reached up and felt where her eyebrow ring once wa. She traced her finger over the bump that it had left.

"Those days are over."

Jessie grabbed the handful of rings and threw them into the trash. Then she smiled in triumph. Jessie took the black light posters and some of her band posters off of her wall, neatly rolled them up, and placed them in the back of her closet. I watched her as she did all of this, praying for more and more confidence. The process was interrupted when Jessie's phone rang. She walked over to the nightstand on which her phone resided.

"Karla," Jessie sighed and then answered the phone.

"Hello?" Jessie answered.

"Jess, what are you up to?" Karla asked.

Jessie pushed a button allowing Karla to be put on speaker phone. She placed the phone back on her nightstand.

"Going through some stuff."

"You want to talk about it?"

"Not emotionally, literally." Jessie chuckled.

"Like what?" Karla huffed.

"Oh, I took some posters down, got rid of some clothes and CDs . . ."

"Oh, if you don't want them, I will take them." Karla insisted.

"Okay," Jessie said as she shrugged her shoulders.

"I need to go shopping for some clothes like for real."

Jessie closed her closet door and picked up the trash bags full of clothes and threw them in the corner of her room.

"What all are you giving to me?"

"Um . . . Jack Daniels, Jim Beam, Samuel Adams, and some band t's that I know you like," Jessie smiled.

"Cool. I appreciate it."

"Well, I didn't want to throw them away, and I'm going to give you my posters."

"Wow, Jess. When you change, you really change."

"I'm a woman of my word."

"True. Can you pick me up for school tomorrow?"

"Absolutely," Jessie said as she straightened the stuffed animals on her bed.

"Well, the rest of the week my mom will give you gas money," Karla bribed.

"Okay."

"Well, I will see you tomorrow," Karla blared through the phone.

"See ya," Jessie said and then hung up. "Oh, my Lord!"

Jessie laid back on her bed and covered her face with her hands. Being a human seemed like hard work and a tough road.

The week was going by surprisingly fast. It was already Friday and Jessie and I were sitting in sixth period. One more period was left and we were home free for two days. Two days didn't seem like much time to have off, and sometimes it wasn't. Jessie slumped in her chair as Mr. Grouse went on about how balancing a checkbook was important. Jessie looked all around at her friends. Shelby was writing a letter to her boyfriend, Jared. Justin was pretending to slit his wrists. Danni kept nodding off. Good ole Eric was taking notes, and Carrie caught Jessie's eye and leaned forward to whisper something to her.

"What are you doing tomorrow?" Carrie kept her eyes on the teacher.

"Nothing." Jessie did the same.

"Want to go to a Christian festival with me?" Carried turned her attention to Jessie.

"Sure. Who all is going?"

"Me, Dannie, Shelby, Justin, Ellen, and hopefully you," Carrie answered. Jessie's face grew with irritation when Carrie mentioned Ellen.

"Ellen?" Jessie arched her brow.

"I know you don't care for her, but I want you to go," Carrie insisted.

"Keep Ellen at a safe distance from me and you got yourself a deal," Jessie smiled.

"Ha! Alright. I will call you tomorrow around 1 p.m.," Carrie said as she leaned back in her seat and focused on Mr. Grouse. Jessie smiled.

I sat in the empty seat next to Jessie. I would have to admit that life was going pretty well these days. No demons were attacking us. Karla wasn't overbearing. Jessie didn't seem so focused on boys, and her attitude was great. More people wanted to hang out with her and talk to her. The teachers loved her and asked her to help them with things. She got asked to be on the cheerleading squad. She turned them down because she said that she didn't want anything in the way of her grades since she had messed up the years before. In all reality, though, it was because she couldn't really afford to keep up with the latest trends a cheerleader had to keep up with. The salon-styled hair, the manicured nails, trips to the gym or a gym membership, the uniforms, money for away games . . . . She just couldn't afford all of that, and she was okay with it. She had her friends and went to the games to see her friends play and cheer. Sadly, the only downfall that others saw in her was her friend, Karla. Jessie didn't think it was right to just drop her best friend just to be popular or maybe not popular, but to have certain friends because they didn't like Karla. That was pretty admirable.

"In conclusion, class, never write a check in pencil," Mrs. Grouse announced and then sneezed into his silky white handkerchief. "You may socialize with each other for the rest of the period." Mr. Grouse sat his tall frame in his desk chair.

"Didn't we learn this in the fourth grade," Justin said to his friends.

Justin was a very different person. He was tall, very thin, very pale. He was extremely smart and excelled in all he did. He was funny in a sarcastic way. He wore band t-shirts, tight blue jeans, a studded belt, a sock cap, and black eyeliner. He had rubber bracelets up to his elbows, a chain around his neck, three eyebrow rings in one eyebrow, two in the other, and he painted his nails black.

"It's the first week of school and they have nothing planned because they were too lazy, even though they have all summer. But they expect us to be ready." Carrie rolled her eyes.

Ah . . . Carrie . . . the activist of the group. She was very stubborn and set in her ways. She was one of Jessie's very best friends. She was tall, short brown hair, dressed in a t-shirt and blue jeans. She is very artistic and an amazing photographer. She could take a picture of the most simple thing and somehow when it came out on film it was like it was transformed into a masterpiece. It made you appreciate the object she had taken a picture of. She dreamed of going to an art school in Chicago, one of the best in the United States.

"I think it's all stupid," Jessie spat out.

"I don't care for this class much," Shelby said barely above a whisper.

Shelby is a very petite person, always wearing her hair a different color every week or two. She, too, was smart. Shelby folded her letter to Jared and stuffed it in her back pocket.

"You going tomorrow?" Justin asked Jessie.

"Yup," Jessie smiled, "as long as Ellen stays a safe distance." Jessie narrowed her gaze at Justin.

"Oh, yeah. I will make her. I will tell her where all the hot guys are and, trust me, she will be gone all night." Justin traced the scar on his wrist with his finger.

"Justin!"

Carrie shot him a dirty look.

"I call it like I see it." Justin growled. "You know how Ellen is. We all do. But what's going on with you, Jessie?" Carrie said, causing the group of friends to look at her.

"Me?" Jessie pulled back.

"Yes. No dark make-up, no eyebrow ring, no dark clothes, no F word." Carrie looked intently at Jessie as well as the others.

"I figured it was time for a change and that look was getting old and didn't look good on me." Jessie smiled.

Jessie was at that point where she could openly say that she had gotten saved. She would get there. It just took time. All of this was new to her.

"I like it," Shelby smiled at Jessie.

"Yup. Me, too. I like the way you look real now and are not putting on a front. Very nice," Danni chimed in.

"Not sleepy anymore now that Mr. Grouse isn't teaching, hum?"

Justin looked over at Danni who was wide awake. Jessie's friends were different, but they were cool kids. I liked them a lot. I may not like some of the things they do or say but, all in all, I really liked them and am glad Jessie was being friends with them again.

"So." Danni stuck out her tongue.

"You thought I was putting on a front?" Jessie looked at her friends.

"To be friends with Karla," Justin hesitated.

"Are you kidding me?!" Jessie began to become irate.

"Jessie, it's okay. Some people get influenced and some people don't," Shelby shrugged.

"You have got to be kidding. I was never trying to be like her." Jessie crossed her arms.

"Jessie, you're different now. You dress different, act different, you're just different. You're nice now and not a bitch. I now Karla is your friend, but she's a bitch." Carried confessed.

"Done?" Jessie shot a dirty look at her group of friends.

"Jessie, don't get mad. We loved you then and we love you now. You're reinventing a former self, that's all." Eric chimed in.

Eric noticed Jessie was getting infuriated with her friends. He and Jessie were good friends. They really didn't know each other all that well, but I could always tell that Jessie had a special place in Eric's heart and vice versa. Eric was one of the friends who never really gave up on her even when she was going through her difficult stage. I noticed Jessie calm down and then she spoke.

"I have changed. That's what matters and that all of you are my friends and you love me no matter what."

"We love you," Eric smiled. The others nodded.

"So, are we all going to the concert tomorrow?" Shelby changed the subject.

"Yes ma'am," Danni smiled.

"Good. I am so excited to see Casting Crowns." Carrie's face lit up with excitement.

"Oh . . . who all is going to be there, and how much does it cost? I forgot to ask." Jessie shrugged.

"It's free. My mom got seven free tickets from work. I had to promise to take my sister. She has the seventh ticket." Carried rolled her eyes. "Let's see. Casting Crows, Jars of Clay, Newsboys, Jeremy Camp, Barlow Girl, and Super Chicks!"

Carrie raised her fist in the air. The group busted out in laughter. I was so excited for this concert. I could listen to worship music and worship alongside Jessie, if she would worship. She's new to this kind of thing.

CHAPTER 3

Friends in Different Places

Jessie and I sat on the couch waiting for Carrie and the rest to pick us up. Jessie played with the hole in her jeans. They should be here any minute. Jessie flipped her phone to check it and then it rang. She looked down at the caller ID. She hadn't been familiar with the number that flashed across the screen.

"Hello?" she answered.

"Jessie?" I heard the other person faintly say.

"Who is this?" Jessie sat on the edge of the couch.

"Leo Gutierrez," the deep voice confessed from the other end of the phone.

"Oh, hey. How did you get my number?"

"Jess, I've had it, and I asked Shelby in Spanish if you changed it."

"Wait, Leo. You took Spanish. You're from Mexico. That's cheating." Jessie smiled. She had a point.

"I do that every year. So, what are you up to?"

"Me and some of the others are going to a Christian festival. How about you?" Jessie stood up as Carrie's car came into view in the driveway.

"Not much. I will let you go. Call me tomorrow if you want," Leo insisted.

"Okie dokie. I will. Have a good one," Jessie said. She hung up the phone and then threw it in her purse.

"Wow! My heart is beating super fast." Jessie placed her hand on her chest. She stood in the living room for a moment trying to regroup before she headed to the car.

"Jessie!" Justin yelled from the car he was hanging out of the back window.

Jessie had no one to say goodbye to. Her mom and dad were at Uncle Larry's, and her brother was at Danny's. Jessie grabbed her house key and we headed to the car.

"'bout time," Justin said and scooted over.

"Leo called." Jessie cocked her head at Shelby. Shelby smiled.

"What did he want?" Carrie looked at Jessie through the rearview mirror.

"Just to see what I was up to," Jessie shrugged. "Where's Ellen and Danni?" Jessie looked at the empty seat beside Justin that I sat in.

"They bailed," Shelby shrugged. She then looked out the windshield.

"Well, good," Jessie smiled at Justin who smiled back.

"So, are you and Leo like talking?" Shelby turned to look at Jessie.

"Uh, no. I'm over that," Jessie lied.

Jessie was not over Leo. She may be trying to get over it, but she wasn't there yet. I sat next to Justin and looked at the scars that covered his arms. Why did he do that?!

"Right," Carried winked at Jessie through the rearview mirror.

"Where's your sister?" Jessie asked Carrie.

"She, too, bailed. She went to hang out with her friend, Grayson. I'm going to give the extra tickets to someone who doesn't have any," Carried shrugged.

"Invite Leo!" Shelby suggested.

"Stay in the front seat," Jessie shot.

"Hey, I'm just saying . . . ."

"He doesn't like this kind of stuff, and I don't want to."

"He would like it because you will be going," Shelby smiled back at Jessie.

"No thanks."

"You know you love him," Justin poked Jessie in the side.

"No," Jessie poked Justin back.

"Dang, you poke hard!" Justin rubbed his arm.

"Justin, you're just a sissy," Carrie teased.

"So," Justin crossed his arms. There was silence for a short moment until Shelby broke the silence.

"Do you think Leo wants another chance because he knows he messed up?" Shelby looked intently at Jessie.

"Heck, I don't know, and I don't care," Jessie said with emotion but controlled.

"Maybe things will finally work out for you guys," Shelby said as she texted.

"Who knows," Jessie sighed.

The Concert

We entered this huge dome full of people from the age of two to their middle fifties. Some were older than that, but most of them were in their teens or early twenties. I saw most of my fellow angels. They were sitting in the rafters, hanging out at the concession stands, by the ticket booths, at the doors, all over the place. Musicians were setting up amps and drums, and they were tuning their guitars and basses.

"Tristan, my boy!" I looked straight ahead and saw Victor with his arms open to me.

"Hey, Vic." I embraced him with a brotherly hug.

"Long time no see. How have you been?" Victor asked as he looked past me and to Jessie.

"Good." I looked back at Jessie who stood socializing with her friends.

"I heard in the heavens that she's very well lately. She's a special and valuable vessel," Victor smiled.

"Yes. I am very proud of her." I smiled back at Jessie.

"Tristan! Victor!" Manaline swooped over us and flew to her human who was sitting in the balcony seats. I raised my hand to her in a hello.

"The show's about to start." Victor rubbed his hands together in excitement. "Have fun," he said and then bolted to his human.

I looked back and made my way to Jessie and her friends. Jessie stood perplexed by the whole ordeal. She looked uncomfortable. I stood closer to her.

"Jess, you okay?" Justin leaned in and asked.

"Yeah. It's just that something is weird." Jessie tried to shake away the thoughts.

Jessie hadn't been to a Christian festival. Since she was new to this, I can see her being uncomfortable.

"What's weird?" Justin looked around at all the people starting to gather around the stage.

"You claustrophobic?" Justin's voice started to rise as the bands started playing riffs from each song to tune their instruments and get the flow going.

"No, Justin," Jessie said irritated.

"Here we go!" Carrie said as she and Shelby walked up to us.

"Yup. Let's rock the house!" Shelby started to fist pump, causing us all to laugh hysterically.

Casting Crowns started to play and everyone went into a supernatural trans. I enjoyed myself very much. The music, people, and atmosphere were great. People danced, sang, and praised God. It was all amazing and breathtaking. When Jessie caught herself getting too much into it, she would stop and lightly bob her head or sway to the music, not letting herself get too carried away. I, on the other hand, let it loose along with my other angel friends. We danced and sang and just praised Jehovah. I had a blast!

"Tristan!" Victor yelled at me from the balcony.

I looked at Victor and he pointed to the top of the clear dome that enclosed us. There were demons sprawled out all around it, clawing and beating the dome trying to get in. Finally, one of the bigger demons slammed his fist on the dome causing it to crack. The demon looked at his fist and then down at the crack in the dome. He just smiled.

"We can't let them in," Manaline yelled to us.

I kissed Jessie atop her head and flew to the dome with the others. We put our backs against the dome. We grabbed each other by the hands making a line. Victor, Manaline, Truce, and I pressed against it, making a half circle. Victor gripped the edge of the dome and Truce the other. I closed my eyes as I felt the demons bang against the dome, making a thud against our back.

"Hold!" Truce yelled. The demons were wearing themselves out.

"Truce, they're dying down!" Manaline yelled.

"Jehovah!" we yelled in unison.

One last thud from one of the bigger demons and then it ended. We looked at each other and then behind us at the dome. Cracks, smudge marks, teeth bites, and dents decorated the dome, but no demon was found. I looked down at all the people who were still worshipping, except one person. He was tall with jet black hair, a prominent nose, eyes that were dark brown but full of compassion and wonder. He stared up at the dome, eyes as wide as half dollars. The girl next to him whispered something. He pointed to us as she looked, and then she shook her head and whispered something else. Who was this guy? I wanted to know who he was. Truce noticed me looking at the distinguished young man

"He can see us. Do you see that seal of Jehovah, how it's gold and not silver?" Truce said as we ascended toward the floor.

"What's that got to do with anything?" I looked at him with confusion and then at the young man who was now back in worship.

"Gold means power," Truce nodded to Jessie.

"Hers is silver. She hasn't gotten all the power that is waiting for her to partake in. On the other hand, Dismal the boy has. He is very powerful. He takes his faith very seriously. It's all he has." Truce frowned.

"Who is the lady next to him?"

"That would be his wife, Alexis Tanner. She doesn't wear the seal as you can tell. She is having an affair with Dismal's cousin." Truce bluntly stated.

"Does Dismal know?" I looked at him curiously.

"Yes."

"And?"

"He put it in God's hands."

Truce shrugged and then made his way through the mammoth crowd. I looked for Jessie and spotted her sitting on the stairs toward the back door. I walked over to her and took a seat next to her. Her phone was out and a text from Karla displayed on the screen.

"You know that you are not having as much fun there as you did with me at the Mudvayne and Slipknot concert."

Jessie sighed and then closed her phone.

The concert went by extremely fast. Jessie caught up with Carrie and the others.

"I had a blast!" Carrie said as she threw her Casting Crowns t-shirt over her shoulder.

"Same," Shelby and Justin said in unison.

"Jess?" Carrie asked.

"Absolutely," Jessie plastered on a fake smile.

Jessie slid her cell phone into her front pocket and headed toward the door.

"I bet Karla texted you like fifty messages," Shelby laughed.

"Sure did," Jessie shook her head. "She said . . ." Jessie flipped open her phone and found the message that Karla had sent her.

"You know that you are not having as much fun there as you did with me at the Mudvayne and Slipknot concert." Jessie read aloud to her friends.

"It's time for you to find friends in different places," Shelby said as she threw her arm around Jessie.

"I suppose," Jessie shrugged.

Monday, Algebra 2

Jessie sat in her desk trying to listen to the teacher. Karla hadn't said a word to her all period. She would look at Jessie with a blank stare. Thirty minutes before the period ended, Karla broke the silence.

"So, how was the concert?' Karla sneered.

"I had a blast!" Jessie bit off. Karla ignored Jessie's attitude.

"Who all went?"

"Let's see," Jessie tapped her chin. "Carrie, Shelby, Justin, and me," Jessie looked intently at Karla.

"You're friends with Shelby again?" Karla hissed.

"Yes. She's a really cool person. They all are." Jessie's tone softened.

"Right . . . well . . . good luck with all that," Karla shrugged and then packed up her backpack.

"Why are you being a jerk about this?" Jessie bluntly asked.

Karla moved closer to Jessie in a threatening way. I, too, moved closer in defense.

"Because you changed. It's all stupid. Those people you call your *friends* are stupid." Karla said with a dark discord in her voice.

"I just think you need to chill. You're still my best friend. That doesn't mean I can't hang with other people." Jessie shoved her books in her backpack. "Why don't you hang with other people, too," Jessie suggested and her tone softening.

"Whatever," Karla said irritated. "You think you've changed. You're just like me, just like you used to be. You just want everyone to like you." Karla spat out with hatred.

The bell rang. Karla turned on her heels and headed out of the classroom leaving Jessie standing there. Jessie's anger grew intense. I could feel it radiate off of her body. She stormed out of the classroom and we headed to the next class.

English, Period 7

Jessie and I seemed to finally get through the day. We were on our last class. Karla hadn't talked or texted Jessie all day. Good. Jessie walked down the ever-crowded hallways. She waved to her friends, waved to people who were not her friends. They stared at her like she was just released from the asylum. Can no one just be nice these days? Demons walked among the students as well as angels. It was natural territory, I suppose. We didn't say much to them and they didn't say much to us. They knew their boundaries. They had their students and we had ours. I walked down the hall and noticed Jessie's peers, girls wearing shorts that revealed way too much of their backsides, and shirts that revealed too much of the upper part. Guys were in baggy pants, black eyeliner, trip pants, showing their boxers with large chains that hung to the middle of their torso. They were cussing each other out. Girls dressed like guys, exactly like guys, and trying to hit on girls. One boy stood by the girls' bathroom applying foundation. God loves each and every one of them. No matter how they dressed or acted, He loved them. He just didn't like the things they did. My Jessie was one of the lost. She wore baggy pants, vulgar t-shirt, eyebrow ring, black nails, and had a bad attitude. Clothes don't always mean what the person is, but I don't know one kid who doesn't dress in all black, with piercing and tattoos that has a great attitude and lifts people up. I don't know a girl who reveals everything she owns that hasn't slept with someone or someone's friend. I don't know a girl who looks, talks, and acts just like a guy that isn't into the same sex, and I don't know a guy who applies foundation on a daily basis that doesn't like the same sex. The way you dress most of the time does show who you really are or want to be.

Jessie and I made it to English where we took our seats in front of Eric and behind Leo. She slumped in her desk and sank her head down, resting her chin on her chest. She sighed deeply.

"Jess, you okay?" Eric poked her back.

"Yes, I guess."

"What's the matter?"

"Karla," Jessie turned in her seat to look at Eric.

"What is her problem now?" Eric tapped his pencil on the edge of the desk.

I sat in the empty seat next to Leo. He was writing the question of the day down in his notebook and already answering. Good ole Leo.

"She hates the fact that I'm hanging out with you guys." Jessie lifted her hand and then dropped it on her thigh in defeat.

"Not worth it, Jess," Eric rolled his eyes and shook his head.

"What do you mean?" Jessie leaned in.

"That Carrie, Justin, Shelby, Leo, and I are your friends. She just wants to bring you down because, face it, a lot of people like you. She wants that drunken, mean rebel she was once friends with." Eric set the record straight.

"Agree." Leo turned around abruptly, his hair swaying.

"You never liked her." Jessie smiled at Leo.

"It's legit," Leo smiled back.

Leo's black hair settled to the middle of his neck, his eyes twinkled with adoration for Jessie, and his features were soft and gentle. But is he good enough for Jessie? Time will tell.

"Ha, right, right. Hey, I meant to call you the other night, but I got in late, and I forgot the following day." Jessie's eyes grew tender.

"It's okay. Call me tonight, though," Leo smiled.

"I need a favor," Jessie smiled. It was that smile. The "I want something" smile. I shook my head and rolled my eyes.

"Anything," Leo looked intently at Jessie.

"I'm carrying *all* my books and my locker does not open. I noticed yours was by most of my classes. May I please share with you?" Jessie closed her eyes and then opened one looking at Leo innocently.

"Of course," Leo smiled. He took Jessie's arm and wrote down the combination. "Anything for my Jessie."

Leo smiled and then turned around, ready for the class to start. You mean "my Jessie". I narrowed my gazed at him. ***You mean "my Jessie",*** I heard a voice whisper. I looked to the heavens.

"Our Jessie," I smiled. I felt peace rush over me. Jehovah was with me.

CHAPTER 4

Reviving a Nightmare

Algebra 2

"Jessie, did you get your notes done from yesterday?" Carrie asked as she leaned over to Jessie.

"No." Jessie sighed.

"Me either and neither did Justin." Carrie confessed.

"Ask Shelby." I saw irritation flash in Jessie's eyes.

"She's absent."

"Ask Jeremy." Jessie nodded to where Jeremy was sitting.

Jeremy was a tall, shaggy blonde hair with hazel eyes. He ran track and played basketball and baseball. He was a very intelligent guy. He was going to Purdue University to become a sports journalist.

"Jeremy?" Carrie squinted at Jessie.

"Ugh. Fine I'll ask."

Jessie looked over to Jeremy who was jotting down notes.

"Jeremy?" Jessie whispered.

Jeremy shot his head forward and caught Jessie's eye.

"What?"

"May we see your notes from yesterday?" Jessie smiled.

Jeremy didn't say anything or even move. He looked at Jessie and then brushed his hair from his face.

"I suppose. For you, Jessie."

Jeremy reached for his backpack and pulled out his notes and handed them to Carrie.

"Thank you so much." Carrie sighed.

"You're welcome." Jeremy said, and then started jotting down more notes.

Carrie placed the notes on her desk and started to copy them down on her paper.

"You gonna let me see yours?" Justin leaned in.

"After Jessie. After all, she did snake Jeremy's." Carrie nodded.

"I didn't snake them." Jessie rebutted.

"Jessie, he clearly said. 'For you, Jessie.'" Carrie batted her eyes.

"Carrie, Jeremy just said that to be nice and probably because he didn't want to say what he had really felt."

Jessie's irritation grew into anger.

"Who freakin' cares! I need someone's." Justin blurted.

"Mr. Lukas, is there a problem?" Mr. Delarosa asked.

His black beady eyes looked over his thick, gray-rimmed glasses. His tall, slender frame was slightly hunched. His wobbly legs looked as if they had had enough and were about to give out on him at any minute.

"No." Justin crossed his arms.

"Don't pout." Jessie rolled her eyes.

"How is it every time we talk I'm the one that gets in trouble?"

"Because you're the only one who gets caught, I guess." Carrie shrugged.

"I hate this." Justin pouted.

"Mr. Lukas, this is your last warning. Next time is detention." Mr. Delarosa turned around.

"But . . . I . . . ." Justin glared at Jessie and Carrie.

Jessie and Carrie kept their eyes on Mr. Delarosa.

Period 5: Government

Two more classes left and we were home. But anything could happen with two classes to go.

Jessie sat there doodling on her notebook.

"Jessie, I am so bored." Justin leaned forward.

"You're not lying. We've got this class then two more and we're home free." Jessie reassured him.

"But that doesn't help now."

"But it gives you something to look forward to." Jessie bit off.

"You okay?" Justin asked.

"Yes." Jessie rolled her eyes.

"You're lying!" Justin blurted.

"Justin, I'm really just not in the mood." Jessie replied as she began to doodle.

I looked behind Jessie and saw Karla as she looked intently at Jessie and Justin argue.

"Jessie, cheer up." Karla said as she tapped Jessie's back.

"I will. I just don't want to be messed with right now." Jessie squirmed.

I smelled burned flesh and oppression engulf the room. The smell made my stomach knot up and jerk. I felt like I wanted to vomit. I felt my throat tighten and my lungs try to retain as much fresh air as they could possibly hold. I looked behind me and saw Maaz and Hagab standing behind me. Their tall frames stood still. Blood oozed from their cracked skin. Their long, black hair reached well past their knees. They wore their greasy hair in one, long braid. Gold pellets were displayed in different places throughout the braid. Their silk, black pants were trimmed in gold and their vests were dark green with gold rhinestones embroidering the edges. Their boots had blades sticking out from all round. Maaz held a Tommy gun with a belt of bullets around his waist. Hagab was dressed similarly but with silver embroidery instead of gold. I kept my eyes locked on them. Their faces didn't look as beat up as the rest of their bodies. Their vests were open and their scared, pock-marked chests were displayed.

"Well, hello, pretty boy." Hagab flashed an evil grin.

"What do you want?"

"Nothing." Maaz gripped his gun.

"Gonna shoot me?" I looked at his gun then to him.

"Nope."

Maaz pulled the gun up and aimed it at Jessie. I instantly moved in front of her. I stretched out my wings. The next thing I hear is the fire of his gun and the faint laughter of Hagab. The bullets ripped through my wings. My body jerked as I tried to maintain my balance. The pain was unbearable, and I clenched my teeth until I tasted blood. A bullet struck me in the back and I fell to the ground. I placed my hand where the bullet had exited through my stomach. Blackness started to spread up my hand, and I ripped my shirt where the bullet had exited. I looked at the bullet wound and it started turning black. The blackness spread up my side and around to my back. I began to grow weak. I heard Maaz and Hagab laughing at me. I then looked around and the floor was covered in blood. My head felt weak and everything went black.

"Tristan . . . Tristan . . . Tristan."

I felt someone shaking me. Her voice was soft and soothing. I slowly opened my eyes, which were fixed on the bright, silver eyes in front of me. She finally came into focus. It was Purity. She was beautiful, tall, and slender with pale skin, and she had long, blonde hair that landed past her waist. Her curls bounced as she tried to shake me awake.

"Purity."

My mind went to Jessie. Where was she and what happened?

"Jessie!"

I jumped up. I looked at Purity, who brought herself to her feet.

"She's fine. Jesaiah is with her." Purity said calmly.

"She's my human. Mine. I protect her."

I looked down and I had been healed. I looked around. We were standing in a pure, white room. No one but Purity and I were there.

"Tristan, relax. You've been hurt. Jessie is okay." Purity informed.

"No. I shouldn't have left her."

"Tristan, you didn't. I had to bring you here."

"Why?" I grew irritated. "I am not supposed to leave my human."

"We have someone with her and she's well-protected."

"Purity, take me back to Jessie," I said as I walked up to her. Her silver eyes were now green.

"Not yet."

"Why?"

"Because God doesn't want you back there yet."

"Why?"

"I don't know." Purity sighed. "I just don't know. We don't always know why God does the things He does."

"Purity! She needs me! Let me back down there!" I grew more infuriated. I needed to be with Jessie. She needed me.

"No." Purity stood firm.

"Is this a teaching of patience or something?" I turned my back to her.

"I don't know."

"Is this a test?" I turned around to look at her.

"I don't' know, Tristan." Purity smiled.

"This is crazy!" I yelled and, at that time, I was standing next to Jessie in front of her mirror. I didn't like what I saw. Black eyeliner caked her eyes, a black dog collar was wrapped around her neck, her jeans were baggy and tattered, and she wore her Mudvayne shirt. Her face had a dark shadow about it and her eyes looked more gray than blue. She was reverting back to what she had used to be.

Period 4: Accounting

Jessie sat slumped in her desk. No one said anything to her. I hope that she isn't going to be like this for long. Maybe she only did this when she was having bad days. I'd rather she not do it at all.

"Back to Mudvayne, I see." Allen hissed.

"So." Jessie spat.

"Yeah. I think she looks nice." Karla beamed.

"Probably because you're in love with her." Allen smarted.

"Shut the hell up, fat ass!" Karla raised her voice.

Allen was a rather large guy. He was six feet and two inches and at least three hundred and fifty pounds . . . and it wasn't muscle.

"Whore!" Allen stood up.

"Allen, Karla is there a problem?" Mr. Grouse said looking up from his desk.

"No," they said in unison, not taking their eyes off of each other.

"Then, Allen, take a seat." Mr. Grouse pointed to his desk.

"Surprised he can fit." Karla chuckled.

"Karla," Jessie sighed.

"What! He's making me mad!" Karla hissed.

"You don't have to say mean things like that."

"Jessie, look at you. You're no better than I am." Karla tapped her pencil on the edge of her desk.

"Karla," Jessie narrowed her eyes.

"What, Jessie! Getting' sick of being like all preppy and shit?"

"I wasn't preppy, and I don't know. I miss the old me." Jessie shrugged.

"Face it, Jessie. You're not meant for nice and polite. You're hard core and mean. Live with it!" Karla glared and then smiled.

Period 7: English

Jessie didn't say a word to Leo when he walked in. They usually greet each other with a hug. Leo was taken aback by the way Jessie looked. He looked over at Carrie, Justin, Allen, and James but they all shrugged. Leo lightly took his seat in front of Jessie.

"Hey, Jess."

Jessie didn't look up.

"Leo." Jessie said harshly.

"How are you?"

"I'm not three, Leo. You don't have to baby talk me. Just ask me what my problem is."

Jessie looked up at him. Leo shot a look back toward Carrie and the others and then back at Jessie.

"Did someone make you mad?" Leo asked concerned.

"No."

"Did a guy hurt you?"

"No."

"Jessie, you can tell me who it was and I swear I will take care of it."

"Leo, no one hurt me and no one made me mad. I just have a lot on my mind right now."

"Jessie, why are you dressed like that? To show people you're ticked off?"

"Leo, for the last time I'm not mad and I just wanted to dress like this."

"Did Karla get you, too? I really don't like her."

"Leo! It's clothes . . . just clothes and make up! What is the big deal?" Jessie yelled.

Carrie and the others looked over at them. Carrie shook her head to Leo as if to tell him to just lay low for a while and let Jessie do her own thing. If I had to let her do her own thing, so did Leo.

"Sorry, but I'm here if you need to talk." Leo turned back around.

Class was long and boring and Jessie didn't talk to anyone. On the way to the senior parking lot, she didn't say much to Karla.

"Jessie, you don't have to be like that with me. I'm your best friend. I understand you more than anyone. More than God really." Karla chuckled.

Jessie spun around to face Karla.

"Don't you ever bring God into this! He's done nothing to either of us. Just leave Him out of it. You don't even believe in Him, so do not bring Him up! Ever! You understand me?"

"Jess, I didn't mean to ffend you." Karla put her hands in front of her.

"Well, you did." Jessie replied angrily as she jerked open the door to her truck and climbed in. Karla got in the passenger's side.

"I'm really sorry. Wanna hang out?" Karla asked as she buckled her seatbelt.

"Yeah." Jessie sighed.

"You can just stay at my house until curfew." Karla suggested.

"Alright."

"Jessie, here." Karla passed Jessie the cigarette.

"Good." Jessie took a drag. "Oh, wow! That tastes good."

"Beer?"

Karla walked to the fridge. Her parents had gone to Indianapolis for a week to celebrate their anniversary. Her siblings were all with friends or a relative, and the house was empty.

"Yes, please." Jessie called from the couch.

Karla brought in two beers and a bag of Doritos. No, Jessie! No! I was so disappointed. Demons surrounded us. I looked at them and they at me but no one said anything. This was a watch and wait.

"So, what's up?" Karla asked as she took a sip from her beer.

"Life sucks. I hate school. My friends are getting boring. My grades suck. Did I mention I hate school?"

"Yeah, but this is our last year." Karla tucked her knees under her and leaned against the back of the couch.

"Yeah, I know."

"Look. We'll be out in no time and then it's off to Florida to bartending school." Karla tapped the neck of her beer bottle to Jessie's.

"Florida!" Jessie said, then took a swig.

Jessie wasn't in her right state of mind. She wasn't completely drunk but she had more than three beers. She wasn't supposed to be driving home. God keep us safe. We did get home safely and Jessie stumbled through the door. Her parents, brother, and cousin, Rodney, looked at her.

"Hey, family!" Jessie greeted loudly and then laughed.

"Jessica Jane, are you drunk?" Toni got off of the couch and walked over to her daughter.

"Ha, no." Jessie laughed.

I shook my head in disappointment. She was embarrassing me. I looked over at Mike. His eyes were full of hurt.

"Where were you?" Travis asked.

"Karla's." Jessie slummed over to the couch and slammed in the empty seat by Rodney.

"My baby cousin." Jessie greeted and kissed him on the lips.

"Jess." Rodney sighed, pushing her off of him.

"You are to come straight home after school from now on." Mike looked at Jessie.

"No can do, Pops. I'm eighteen and I will do whatever the hell I want." Jessie's eyes grew black and her face twisted demonically.

"Jess." Mike narrowed his gaze.

"Mike." Jessie dipped her head looking at Mike with demonic eyes.

"Jessica!" Toni yelled.

"Mom!" Jessie laughed.

"You drove home drunk, Jessica!" Mike got up from his chair.

"Dad, sit down. It's okay. I'm alive."

"Barely!"

"Don't yell." Jessie looked over to her brother.

"I love you, Bubby, and only you." Jessie smiled and then looked to her dad who was standing in front of her.

"Jessie, don't try to play favorites or get your brother on your side." Mike ordered.

"I'm not. It's the truth, and Travis is always on my side." Jessie crossed her arms.

"Jessie, you can't keep doing this." Toni chimed in.

"Mom, I don't care. I already told you that I didn't want to be a Christian. I said that before I got 'saved'. I don't want it."

Jessie stood up and faced Mike. I saw demons peeking through the windows. They weren't allowed in the house, although if Jessie invited them to her room, they were more than welcome.

"No more hanging with Karla." Toni shook her head in disappointment.

"News flash. I'm eighteen and you really can't tell me what to do anymore." Jessie glared at Toni.

"Get out of my sight!" Mike sat back in his chair.

"With pleasure." Jessie said as she grabbed her purse and headed toward her room.

"They're not back, are they?" Travis asked in concern.

"If she's not careful, they will be." Mike answered.

I entered Jessie's room. Anton was standing by Jessie's window looking out into the backyard and Achish was sitting on Jessie's bed.

"Well, Tristan, how are you?" Anton said without turning around.

"Get out of here."

I watched Jessie as she flopped on her bed next to Achish. My stomach turned in knots.

"No can do, pretty boy. I'm welcome here."

I saw Anton smile through the reflection of the window.

"What are we going to do about this? You know, if she lets us back, I have to go get seven more of my soldiers."

Anton turned to me. I looked at Achish, who smiled from ear to ear.

"She's not going to let you come back. She's just having a rough time."

"No, Tristan, she's not just having a rough time. She doesn't want to be a Christian. Just let her go." Anton nodded to Achish.

"He's right."

Achish placed his hand on the side of Jessie's face and moved his hand down her cheek to her neck and brushed her hair away.

"Don't touch her." I said through clenched teeth.

"Relax, angel. I'm not going to hurt her." Achish glared at me, still playing with Jessie's hair.

"Humans are marvelous yet despicable creatures." Anton shook his head and looked at Jessie.

"See, Tristan, this is why our Father, Lucifer, thinks God is ridiculous. Jessie, whom God made, has turned her back on Him . . . twice. What's the point in humans. No one really believes in God." Anton smiled maniacally at me.

"No, they're his companions."

"Tristan, look! You're an angel. You've seen heaven. You've lived there and now you're here. You were taken out of your element with God to . . . to protect . . . this!"

Anton pointed to Jessie. "Isn't that a little unfair?" Anton squinted at me.

"No. I love God and what He wants is for the best of all of us. I love Jessie. I am her servant and that is fine by me. I will protect her until she is taken away . . . in God's timing."

"You keep telling yourself that, Tristan."

"Leave, Anton! You're not welcome here. I'm praying against you and so is Jessie's family."

"Ha, you make me laugh." Anton started laughing causing Achish to begin to laugh.

"Listen to me. This is not over. Do you hear me? She will be ours again. I'm going to revive this nightmare. I will not give up, Tristan!"

Anton's eyes grew black. His pale nose stretched out and his fangs grew below his lips.

"I will have her soul."

He and Achish disappeared into thin air. They left behind a cloud of red smoke. I looked to Jessie who had fallen asleep. I noticed her Seal of Jehovah was fading. We had to come up with a plan and fast.

CHAPTER 5

Truth in Mirrors

Period 3: Business Foundations

It's been three weeks and Jessie hasn't changed back. The attacks from Anton and Achish are getting more intense. Instead of showing up at least twice a week, it was now becoming an every day thing. Jessie's friends haven't given up on her. Karla was loving every minute of it. She had her old friend back and the others were losing theirs. Jessie sat between Eric and Leo. Leo was still talking to her and helped her with her assignments, and he carried her books for her every so often. I could see that Leo hated the distance Jessie was putting between them, but he had to let her go and do what she wanted before she came back to him . . . or came back to us.

"Jessie, do you want to hang out tonight?" Shelby asked as the teacher closed on the lecture.

"Um . . . I don't know. Let me get back to you in English. That cool?" Jessie didn't look up at Shelby.

"Yeah. That's fine." Shelby said while trying to hide the rejection she felt. Leo overheard Jessie and Shelby talking.

"You should, Jess. Get away from . . ."

"Karla?" Jessie rolled her eyes at Leo's comment.

"Jessie. She's a bad friend. I don't like her."

"Leo, just because you don't like her doesn't mean I'm going to stop being her friend. My world doesn't revolve around you." Jessie argued.

"No, it revolves around me." Jeremy came up to Jessie and put his arm around her shoulder.

"Right." Jessie smiled. Shelby looked at Leo, and Leo rolled his eyes.

"Whatever the case may be, just be careful." Leo said with concern.

"I'll take care of her." Jeremy stated.

"Yeah, right." Leo rolled his eyes.

I don't know why they were talking about who was going to protect her because, in all reality, I am her protector, not these boys. I crossed my arms over my chest and listened to them argue over something that was clearly irrelevant.

"Look, Leo. We all know you're her best friend, but back off a bit. Hell, even I feel smothered." Jeremy laughed. Shelby and Jessie shot each other looks.

"I think that we're all Jessie's friend and we should all protect her." Shelby butted in trying to make the conversation lighter.

"I think this conversation is over." Jessie gave Shelby a thankful look.

"Whatever." Leo rolled his eyes.

"Jessie, we totally need to hang out. I could help you with your Algebra 2 homework." Jeremy smiled then looked at Leo.

"Really?" Jessie looked down at herself.

"Yeah. Your new look doesn't bother me. I actually think the dark mysterious thing is kind of hot."

Jeremy pulled Jessie closer. Alright. That was enough. We got his point. I moved closer to Jessie.

"Wow! Thank you. Um . . . yeah . . . I would love to have some help with my Algebra 2 homework." Jessie beamed then looked at Shelby. Shelby smiled.

"Great." Jeremy squeezed Jessie then headed back to his group of friends.

"Holy crap." Jessie said to Shelby and Leo.

"That's amazing, Jess. You've had a crush on Jeremy like forever!" Shelby said with excitement.

"He's a user." Leo rolled his eyes.

"I don't care. He's hot and I have a study date with him." Jessie took her dog collar off.

"Oh! So when Jeremy gives you a little bit of attention, you start to change." Leo said with irritation.

"Yeah . . . maybe because I like Jeremy. And don't even go there. Ellen said she liked a clean-shaven face and the next day you had no facial hair."

"Jessie, that was in the tenth grade."

"I don't care. You're just as guilty as I am." Jessie smarted and threw her dog collar in the trash can.

"Whatever." Leo said. The bell rang for us to get to our next class. Leo left without Jessie.

"Ew, he's mad." Shelby mentioned.

"I really don't care. Let's go" Jessie laughed.

Period 6: Orchestra

Jessie, Justin, and Carrie sat tuning their violins. Carrie tuned her viola.

"My A string is messed up." Jessie pulled the violin up to her ear and plucked the A string.

"My G is off." Justin did the same.

"Mine's good." Carrie smiled.

"We have a playing test today." Justin remembered.

"Yup. What section?"

"One through forty-six." Justin sighed and got his music out of his tote bag.

"Hey, guys, you ready for a playing test?" David Castleton came and sat next to us.

"Not really. I kind of practiced." Justin shrugged.

"I've totally got this." David squeaked. Justin shot a look at Jessie who shot a look at Carrie.

"Oh, yeah. I practiced for five hours last night." Carrie smiled in triumph.

"Honey, please." David rested his hand on Carrie's arm. "Well, I'm going back to my seat. See you in English." David said as he walked to his seat and picked up his cello.

"Technically, it doesn't count—him being better because he's a cello and we're violins." Justin looked at Jessie.

"True, and it doesn't matter with Carrie either because she's a viola. It just matters between you and me, hot stuff." Jessie lightly pushed Justin.

"Right. I totally got you smoked."

"Yeah, right." Jessie rolled her eyes.

"Can I ask you something?" Justin grew serious.

"Of course." Jessie laid her violin on her lap.

"You think that David is . . . gay?" Justin squinted at Jessie.

"Um, I don't know. I thought so, but I can't judge. It's crossed my mind."

"I think he is." Carrie entered the conversation.

"Well he may be." Jessie shrugged.

"Twenty bucks says he comes out before graduation." Justin held his hand out to Jessie.

"I will do you one better. Before this semester is over." Jessie shook Justin's hand.

"Ha! I got you."

"You guys are mean." Carrie laughed

"Duh." Jessie and Justin said in unison, and started laughing.

Period 7: English

We stopped at her and Leo's locker before heading to class. Carrie, Justin, and David tagged along.

"So, does Leo have a girlfriend?" David asked as we approached the locker.

"No. I'm going to be the closest thing he ever gets to one." Jessie laughed. "Why?" Jessie looked at David.

David was tall and semi-muscular. His brown skin looked as soft as chocolate and he had big brown eyes. He sagged but had a basketball jersey covering his boxers, and he always wore flashy shoes.

"I just asked."

David looked away from Jessie. Carrie and Justin looked at each other with knowing looks and then to Jessie.

"Ah!" Jessie jumped as Leo squeezed her hips. "You scare me every time!"

"Awe." Carrie and Justin said in unison.

"Stop!" Jessie glared.

"Ouch!" Leo said. "Bad mood?"

"No sir." Jessie switched books.

"Hello, Leo." David smiled.

"Hey, man. How are you?" Leo lightly slapped David's arm.

"Great." David beamed.

Jessie looked from Justin to Carrie to David to Leo. I knew what she was thinking and I think she was right. Not good. The group got all of their stuff together and headed toward English.

"Class, you need to make sure you get your fifteen-hundred word essays into me by the end of next week."

I heard Jessie let out a sigh.

"Is yours done?" Leo turned around to face Jessie.

"Almost. I got like two hundred words left. I feel like I keep babbling." Jessie admitted.

"Yeah. I understand."

"Ours are done." Carrie beamed as she flashed her and Justin's essays.

"Finish mine." Jessie laughed.

"Hey, Jess." Jeremy approached.

"Ugh." Leo groaned. Jeremy ignored Leo's comment.

"When do you want to work on Algebra?" Jeremy leaned against the desk.

"Whenever." Jessie shrugged.

"Um . . . I will text you later. Is that cool?" Jeremy asked.

"Of course." Jessie sighed. Jessie slipped into her desk and rested her head in her hands.

"See ya." Jeremy said. He then made his way to his friends.

"I'm telling you, Jessie, something's fishy."

Leo then sat down in his seat turning around to face Jessie.

"Leo, let the girl have fun." David blurted from the seat behind Jessie.

"But what if she gets hurt?" Leo looked passed Jessie and to David.

"Look at all of us she has—me, Carrie, Justin, Shelby, Erick, and you. I think she's well taken care of. You don't have to take full responsibility." David rested his hand on Leo's shoulder.

"Oh my gosh. I'm not an infant!" Jessie raised her head to look at Leo.

"We just care about you, Jessie."

"I'd rather you not." Jessie gave Leo a dirty look.

I finally saw why Jessie was starting to revert back to her old ways. I'm not justifying it. I mean, it's wrong but people needed to let her breathe. Jessie's phone buzzed. She pulled it out of her pocket and read the message to herself. I stood behind her and read it. It was my job to make sure she was safe. I wasn't invading her privacy.

"Omg, Jessie. My friend Charlie just texted me and said he bought 3 bottles of Jack Daniels, 2 Jim Beams, 2 tequilas and some frozen pizza. Let's go over there tonight around 7." Jessie sighed heavily and texted her back.

"Um . . . okie dokie. I will have to tell some bullshit story to my dad."

"Shelby, I'm going to have to take a rain check." Jessie smiled.

"Alright. Next weekend then." Shelby gave Jessie a fake smile.

"Why a rain check?" Leo asked. Jessie leaned forward. "Karla just texted me and said her friend, Charlie, got Jack, Jim Beam, and some tequila at his house and I'm going there."

"Jessie, that doesn't seem smart."

"Don't' care." Jessie pulled on the chain that hung from her pants.

"Jessie, please don't go."

"I will do what I want, Leo." Jessie glared.

Jessie's phone lit up with a text.

"Alright that's my Jessie; we r going to have a blaaaaaaast. See ya l8er."

Jessie shut her phone and shoved it into her pockets. She looked at the clock. Fifteen more minutes left.

"Now I just have to tell my dad some bullshit story." Jessie laughed.

"Let me know when you grow up." Leo smarted.

"Go to hell." Jessie condemned him.

Leo slammed his hands on Jessie's desk. The class looked.

"You are so lucky you're a girl."

"Oh is that the only thing stopping you!" Jessie yelled.

"Jessie and Leo, what is going on?" Mrs. Lazarus stood up from her desk.

"Nothing." Leo glared at Jessie.

"Then stop yelling!" she yelled. Jessie and Leo took their seats.

"You're so lucky I don't kill your ass." Jessie hissed.

I took in a deep breath. Leo didn't say anything to her. I looked around the room. Girls were whispering to each other. Jessie and Leo's friends sat, not saying a word. Jeremy looked shocked. Maybe he needed to see this so he wouldn't get too close to Jessie. Teens were complicated. They did things they knew would hurt them and others. If they wanted something, they went after it no matter what.

"Dad, I'm going to Leo's to study and then going to spend the night at Shelby's." Jessie said as she entered her dad's study office.

I saw a demon peeking through the window. He was going to attach himself as soon as we stepped out of the house.

"Leo's house?"

"Well, I'm going to pick him up and go to the library and then drop him back off and go to Shelby's." Jessie lied.

"Alright." Mike sighed. Be home tomorrow before four.

"Why?"

"Because we have stuff to do."

"Alright."

Jessie rushed out of the room and headed to her truck. I looked at Mike wondering why he wasn't going to stop her. I knew he knew she was lying.

Charlie's House

"Give me the damn bottle!" Jessie laughed trying to reach for the bottle of Jack Daniels.

Demons surrounded us. They sneered and barked at me like a pack of wild dogs. I shook my head in disappointment. I didn't want this to happen again. I saw Anton enter the room from the kitchen.

"See, Tristan, I told you."

He smiled and I grabbed the handle of my sword.

"No, we're not fighting. I clearly got what I want."

"No. We're going to fight. She's mine and you're trying to steal her."

"No! You idiot! She's always been mine."

"Jessie, you can't even stand. Go sit on the couch." Karla said laughing hysterically.

"I got this." Jessie said and then vomited all over the floor.

"You're cleaning that up," said Kirk, who was one of Charlie's good friends.

"Shut up! She will do what she wants." Karla growled.

I looked around. Empty bottles of beer, Jack Daniels, and Jim Beam were strung out all over the place. Jessie had vomited twice already. She couldn't stop laughing.

"I'm getting hot." Jessie said as she crawled to the back door.

I walked over to her and grabbed her arm to help her up. I felt a sharp pain hit the back of my neck. Anton had hit me with his staff causing me to fall to my knees.

"Don't touch her!"

Anton picked me up and threw me against the wall.

"Please, Jessie. Stop!" I pleaded. I picked myself up and looked at Anton. He threw Jessie out the back door and she landed on the lawn vomiting uncontrollably.

"She gonna be alright?" Charlie asked.

"Who knows." Karla shrugged and then started kissing Charlie. I was disgusted.

"See how low your human's gotten?" Anton pointed to Jessie.

Tears filled my eyes. She was jerking on the ground and vomiting. Her head rested in her own puke. She clutched at the ground. I ran over to her and knelt down.

"Oh, God!" Jessie cried as she grabbed at her stomach. "I'm going to die." Jessie cried out again. Karla came rushing to her.

"Jessie, get up! You're going to wake the neighbors."

"Karla . . ." Jessie said and then passed out.

Charlie came outside, picked Jessie up, and literally threw her on the couch.

"What happened to her? She used to be able to hold her liquor." Charlie pointed to Jessie with anger.

"She did have a lot, Charlie." Karla hissed. "I'm going to go lay down."

Karla rubbed her head and headed upstairs. Three other people laid on the floor passed out. They had brought their own drinks. I sat on the couch with Jessie's head resting on my lap. I stroked her hair. In the corner of my eye I saw Anton enter the room.

"You really make me sick." Anton crossed his arms over his broad chest. I ignored his comment.

"This human is worthless."

"Then why do you want her so bad?" I glared at him.

"Because I don't care about her. I care about her soul and, as long as it doesn't belong to God, I could care less."

Anton made his way to where we were.

"She is beautiful, though. I wonder what she's like in bed?" Anton laughed.

"Shut up, Anton!"

"Don't' act like you never thought about it!" Anton rolled his eyes.

"I haven't."

"I have." Anton licked his lips.

"Go to hell, Anton!" I told him. I kept stroking Jessie's hair and rubbing her side and back trying to soothe her.

"Um . . . If you haven't noticed, this is my territory. Hell's getting boring. I mean, the torture and the pain are outstanding, but I like it up here much, much better." Anton smiled.

We heard moans from the floor. The people were tossing and turning.

"Let the process begin!" Anton laughed.

"What?" I looked up at him.

"We're possessing them as we speak. If you would step aside we can Jessie."

"I'm not stepping aside." I clenched my teeth in anger.

"Tristan." Anton looked down at me. His long, black hair fell over his shoulders. His deep, green eyes glittered with hatred.

"You think I'm just going to step aside?" I didn't take my eyes off of his.

"You did last time." Anton got in my face.

His comment made my spirit angry. I got up and lightly placed Jessie's head on the couch. She was breathing heavy.

"She is not coming back to you. She's confused right now."

I got closer to his face. Anton pulled his arm back and threw a punch at me. I caught him by the wrist.

"Listen to me. Greater is He who is in me than he who is in the world." I spoke. Anton grew weaker. "God will not lose her again. It's not in His will."

Anton fell to the floor . . . wheezing. I let go of his wrist and looked over to the couch where Jessie was. Jessie's eyes were wide open. She slowly got up and headed to the restroom. I followed. She slammed the door and leaned against the sink.

"Oh, God, help me. Show me." Jessie pleaded.

Tears rushed from her eyes. Her face was stained with tears of a sinner.

"God, please."

I wrapped my arms around Jessie. We looked up into the mirror at the same time. A demon looked back at us rather than Jessie's human reflection. Jessie's face lit with terror. She started to shake violently. The demon's eyes were slit, his face contorted, his teeth were razor sharp, and his skin ash gray. He stared back at us, and she started clawing at her slipknot shirt. She violently rubbed the make-up from her eyes.

"No, God." Jessie fell to the bathroom floor.

You can always find the truth in mirrors.

CHAPTER 6

Jealousy

Period 3: Business Foundations

In the past couple of weeks, Jessie went back to light colored make-up, decent shirts, jeans that fit with no tatters or holes, and hair that was kept better. The light in her blues eyes was coming back. However, once again, we have run into a problem. She goes by the name of Ellen Gray. She was mentioned before, but she's a bigger deal than we let on. Ellen Gray is Leo's dream woman, if you will. He likes her a lot. She's petite with strawberry blonde hair, has straight white teeth and a curvy figure, and she gets good grades. She's your All-American beauty, thus causing Jessie to dislike her. Jessie, Leo, and I stood at the locker getting their books as usual.

"Library this week?"

"Leo, I'm so tired of school. Can you just give me a bre . . . ?"

Jessie was cut off. Leo had left Jessie to go talk to Ellen. Jessie slammed the locker shut, and she stomped into class.

"You okay?" Erick asked.

"She's a slut!" Jessie threw her backpack on the ground.

"Who?" Shelby asked.

"Ellen."

"Jessie!" Shelby gasped.

"I don't care if ya'll are friends with her. She irritates me to no end."

"Because Leo likes her?" Erick asked.

"No. I don't appreciate him just up and leaving our conversation to talk to her." Jessie's anger started to build up.

"Jessie, it's okay. He'll probably stop liking her soon." Erick tried to reassure her.

"I don't know. He was gaga over her freshman year. I thought he'd be over her by now." Jessie shrugged.

"There are some people that no one can ever get over." Erick took his seat.

"Sorry, Jess. I had to talk to Ellen." Leo said as he entered the room.

"Spare me!" Jessie rolled her eyes.

"Are you mad about that?"

"No, Leo. I am not, but I would like it if you didn't talk to me for right now."

"Jessie, this is ridiculous." Leo threw his hands in the air.

"I love you, Leo, but I don't like you right now." Jessie crossed her arms and looked away.

"You're being a baby."

"Nope." Jessie didn't look at him.

"Fine." Leo said as he took his seat.

Jessie and the rest took their seats as Mrs. Tully began the lesson.

"Hey." Jessie whispered to Leo.

"Not mad anymore?"

"Never was. I thought it was crap that you left me to go talk to Ellen." Jessie whispered keeping her eyes on the teacher.

"I had to. She's just so beautiful and perfect." Leo sighed.

"Don't make me see my breakfast again. It won't look good the second time."

"If I didn't know any better, I'd say you were jealous." Leo turned around to look at Jessie.

"Whatever." Jessie chuckled.

"I think you are."

"No I'm not." Jessie argued.

"Then why did you get mad?"

"Because you straight left me when I was talking to you. That was really mean." Jessie spat out.

"You did that to me with Jeremy."

"Leo Alexander Gutierrez, I did not!"

"Bull crap, Jessie! You are so obsessed with Jeremy that no one exists when he's around; not even me." Leo grew angry.

"Sounds like you're jealous." Jessie smiled.

"Uh . . . I . . . I am not!" Leo said a little louder than intended.

"Right." Jessie smiled.

"Look at me, Jessie. We may get jealous sometimes but it probably doesn't mean anything. I'm speaking for both of us."

"Oh . . . my . . . gosh, Leo, that made no sense. When you get jealous, it means something." Jessie rolled her eyes.

"I mean . . . it doesn't mean that we're jealous in a lover kind of way. Maybe in a 'you're taking my best friend' kind of way." Leo smiled.

"Whatever you say." Jessie looked down at her paper.

"Jessie, you don't even know Ellen."

"Apparently you don't either." Jessie replied as she gave him a look that told him to drop the subject.

"Jessie, please don't be mad." Leo pleaded.

"I'm not mad. When you get hurt, though, and I'm saying you will, don't come crying to me. When it comes to Ellen, it's inevitable."

"Maybe it will be different when she's with me."

"You won't get her. Leo, she's dating Blake."

"So."

"Oh my gosh." Jessie started rubbing her temples.

"Oh my gosh. This is stupid how you're letting this little insignificant thing get you so worked up and stressed out." Leo rolled his eyes.

"No! You're not hearing me out."

"Jessie, it doesn't matter."

"Hey, what's going on?" Jeremy sat in the seat next to Jessie.

"Nothing." Leo looked at Jeremy.

"Jessie . . . you and me . . . Wednesday . . . Algebra." Jeremy winked.

"Yes, sir." Jessie smiled. Leo glared at them.

"Good. Meet me at the library at five?" Jeremy asked.

"Yup."

"I see you've gotten rid of the black make up and other stuff." Jeremy smiled.

"Yeah. I got sick of it."

"It's cool. I prefer not to have a black blob at my side." Jeremy smiled. I think that was supposed to be a compliment.

"Blob?" Leo looked at Jeremy. "You're a real charmer." Leo scoffed.

"I know what you were meaning." Jessie touched Jeremy's arm.

Leo's face grew with anger. I think Jessie was right. They were both jealous of each other's other people.

"I didn't mean it in a mean way." Jeremy brushed his blonde hair away from his hazel eyes.

"No. You're fine . . . literally." Jessie laughed.

"Lame." Leo mumbled.

"You're lame." Jeremy shot back.

"Right. Well . . . you can continue using people. I'm gonna get my work done." Leo said as he turned back in his seat and started his worksheet.

"I don't use people. Is it a shock that someone besides you wants to spend time with Jessie?" Jeremy argued. Leo didn't answer.

"Just let it go." Jessie touched Jeremy's arm.

Period 5: Government

Jessie and Karla sat in government class doodling and texting. I wasn't interested in the topic either. If people only knew the truth. Schools only teach at least twenty-five percent of the truth. I was there when the world wars happened. I watched as the Jews were tormented by Hitler. I saw the Trojans snake their enemies. I was there for all of that. I know what happened and, believe you me, schools don't know the truth.

"Get me out of this hell hole!" Karla moaned.

"I hear ya." Jessie commented.

"So, I heard you and Leo got into a little argument today." Karla leaned forward and Jessie leaned back.

"Yeah, he straight walked off to meet with Ellen and I was still talking to him. So I got mad and he's like accusing me of being jealous. Then, when Jeremy comes to ask me to study, Leo gets all mad." Jessie shrugged.

"Wait. You're going to study with Jeremy McVayne?" Karla said in excitement.

"Yup. Sometime this week he's going to help me with Algebra." Jessie turned around and smiled.

"Wow, and I think Leo is jealous. Are you jealous of him and Ellen?"

"Oh, I don't know. Yeah, maybe a little, but it's not like really bad." Jessie admitted.

"I say 'go' for Jeremy. Leo isn't showing you any kind of signals to say that you should go after him."

"Yeah, I know, but what if I do go for Jeremy and really Leo likes me and he can't do anything because I'm with Jeremy?"

"So you do like Leo?"

"Well a little. I mean, he's sweet and funny and nice and really smart. What's not to like?"

"And he's hot!" Karla added.

"Yeah, and he's hot!" Jessie laughed.

"I don't know what to tell you, Jess." replied Karla. She flipped open her phone and smiled as she read the text.

"Who's that?"

"Gerard Garrett." Karla smiled and started texting.

"Are you guys like talking?"

"Kinda. Don't tell anyone." Karla put her phone up to her chest.

"Your secret's safe with me." Jessie smiled.

"Jessie." Ellen called out.

Jessie saw Ellen approach them. It was ten minutes before the class was over, so the teacher let the kids visit with each other.

"What." Jessie said coldly.

"It's about Leo." Ellen smiled raveling her perfect, white teeth. Karla rolled her eyes.

"What." Jessie looked back at Karla and then to Ellen.

"Do you think he could help me with my zoology homework?"

"Uh . . . news flash. He doesn't take zoology."

"Well, he could still help me." Ellen said with more of an attitude.

"Then why don't you take your perky little self and ask him?" jealousy pierced Jessie's tone.

"Why are you being mean?" Ellen's voice shrank to almost a whisper.

"Because, Ellen, I don't like you." Jessie blurted.

Karla laughed. I smelled lilac perfume engulf me. Cold chills ran up my arms. She was here. Jezebel. I turned around and saw a tall, curvy figure standing in the doorway of the classroom. She was wearing a long, black skirt with a dark blue tank top and black high heel shoes.

Her skin was creamy white, her long, auburn hair fell past her shoulders in perfect layers, her red pouty lips could seduce anyone, and her dark green eyes glittered with lust.

"Tristan, long time no see. You're still as attractive as ever. You know me and some of my friends. You know Indigo and Magus. Well, we were sitting around the table talking about you and Jesaiah and Truce and who was the most attractive. I vouched for you. Your long black hair, toned skin, deep compassionate eyes." Jezebel walked toward me. Her hips swayed. I prayed to myself to overcome her seductive ways.

"Your flattery will get you nowhere, Jezebel." I said firmly.

"Is it flattery when it's simply the truth?"

Jezebel touched my face with her slender hand. I grabbed her wrist and threw her hand off of me. She caught her balance and stood before Jessie, who was talking with Karla.

"Tristan, we've been through this before. The more aggressive you get, the more I'm attracted to you." She turned around and looked at me.

"Jezebel." I sighed and clenched my fists.

"I heard from Anton that you're attracted to Jessie." Jezebel hissed. "I'm so jealous."

Jezebel's eyes filled with hate and then turned to face Jessie. She stood before Jessie as if to study her. Her arms were crossed and her feet were planted firm.

"I am not! She is my human. That's all."

"I bet that if she saw you in the flesh she'd fall madly in love with you. Have you ever thought about being with Jessie? . . . Really being with Jessie?" Jezebel turned her head slightly to look at me. "I mean, you can't because you're an angel. But you love her very much; we all see it. Imagine it . . . just having her to see you and to talk to her. Wouldn't that be glorious?" Jezebel threw her head back in laughter. "You could touch her face, run your fingers through her hair, and kiss those innocent lips."

Jezebel ran her fingers over Jessie's pink lips. She walked over to stand behind Jessie and looked at me with a deep stare. A grin crept across her face.

"I know what you're trying to do. I rebuke those lustful thought and words you have spoken on me." I walked closer to her. I was inches away from her, waiting to strike.

"Oh, Tristan. Look at Jessie. She's beautiful. You never thought of being with her? A love between and man and a woman that . . . well, angel and human . . . that cannot be broken the way she will feel when you kiss her!" Jezebel laughed.

"Enough!" I grabbed Jezebel by the throat. "It isn't going to work! I rebuke you Jezebel!" She squirmed in my grip.

"I am her guardian. That is all. She will have true love some day without any of your help." I threw Jezebel to the ground, and she fell on her knees clutching her throat.

"Too late, Tristan. What do you think Ellen is here for? I'm going to make Jessie so miserable with jealousy that she will lose herself. It will consume her. Believe me, Tristan, I won't give up." With that, Jezebel disappeared.

Period 7: English

Jessie and I didn't stop at the locker. We just went straight to English class and took our seats. She didn't say a word to anyone. My encounter with Jezebel was still fresh in my mind. Jessie sat there stewing in her own jealousy. There really wasn't anything I could do. I looked up and saw Jezebel standing in the doorway. She smiled at me and then moved from the doorway. Leo was embracing Ellen. I looked down at Jessie, who looked up. Her eyebrows grew together with anger, her face turned red, and her nostrils flared. Ellen's head was rested on Leo's chest. His strong hand ran through her strawberry blonde hair. Ellen placed her hand on Leo's waist and looked up at him. Her hair fell down her back, gracefully lying in the middle of her back. He looked down at her and smiled.

"I swear to God . . . if he kisses her . . . !" Jessie gripped her pencil so tight that it broke. Jessie kept her eyes on the train wreck in the hallway. Ellen embraced him again and then left for class. Leo turned on his heels and entered the class. Jessie looked down and tried to put together her broken mechanical pencil.

"What happened?" Leo asked cheerfully.

"I stepped on it." Jessie said not looking up. She was hoping that he wasn't going to mention anything about Ellen.

"Today is such a beautiful day." Leo smiled then took his seat. Jessie rolled her eyes.

"It's okay." Jessie huffed.

"You alright?" Leo unzipped his backpack and got out his English homework.

"Yes." Jessie smarted.

"You seem mad."

"Nothing gets passed you, Leo."

"Ellen said the funniest thing." Leo ignored Jessie's comment.

"I doubt it." Jessie mumbled. Jessie looked back at her hands with a plea for help. Carrie just shrugged her shoulders. "Some friends." Jessie groaned.

"So, she's telling me how in Biology 12 they're dissecting this pig. Well . . . ."

"Leo, I don't care." Jessie raised her voice.

"It's a funny story."

"The only thing that I'm going to laugh about that relates to Ellen is when she finally gets pregnant or an STD. Until then, I don't care." Jessie slammed her hands on her desk.

"That was really mean."

"Leo, I don't care." Jessie lightly laughed. "She sleeps with everyone and I hope she gets what she has coming to her."

"I see. Well, you keep hating someone you don't know."

"Well, by as much as you talk about her, I feel like I've known her since birth." Jessie shot back.

"I will leave you alone." Leo turned around facing the front of the class.

"Good." Jessie scoffed.

I looked up and saw Jezebel standing in the doorway. Her auburn hair was done up in a loose braid. Her long black skirt had a slit that went all the way up to her hip. Her red tank top revealed her torso. She had a red sucker in her hand. She reached up to her lips, blew me a kiss, and then she walked away.

Jessie, Karla, Justin and I walked down the senior hallway to the parking lot. Kids were talking on their cell phones and making out with one another. You know . . . doing the things that teens did. I kept looking for Jezebel. I knew she was going to pop up out of nowhere.

"You've got to be kidding me." Karla said.

Jessie and Justin stopped talking and looked to where Karla was looking. Leo was standing up against the wall. Ellen had herself pressed against him with her head on his chest. He ran his fingers through her hair. Jealousy rushed over Jessie.

"I hate my life." Jessie growled.

Jessie heard Leo and Ellen laugh. She, Justin, and Karla stood there looking disgusted.

"She's such a slut." Karla shook her head. "What about Blake?"

Karla looked around to see if she could find him. Ellen reached up and ran her fingers through Leo's jet black hair.

"Wow! Talk about PDA." Justin rolled his eyes. Leo laughed every time Ellen said something. "I really just want to kick her in the face."

Jessie started walking toward the double doors. Karla and Justin followed.

"Hey, Jess." Leo called. Jessie didn't turned around, threw her hand in the air, and flipped him off.

Jessie sat in her room doing her homework. She would stop ever so often and sigh. She looked up at her and Leo in her "best friend" picture frame.

"I really hate Ellen." Jessie said aloud, inviting Jezebel in. Jezebel appeared in front of me.

"Tristan." she smiled. I rolled my eyes. "Don't get so mad. I'm not here to fight. We both know Jessie has feelings for Leo." Jezebel lit a cigarette and took a long drag.

"I don't like how she's getting so jealous and hateful."

"Look, my sister. Jealousy is still in the pit, so I have to deal with this Jealousy, Lust issue." Jezebel sneered.

"Leo is just as jealous of Jeremy and Jessie as Jessie is of him and Ellen." Jezebel laughed. "It's life, Tristan. People get jealous." Jezebel reared her ugly head at me.

"No, Jessie doesn't need to worry 'bout this."

"Well, too bad, Tristan. You can't stop this. She has feelings for this boy and I will use it against her. That's what I do."

"Jezebel, leave." I clutched my fists.

"In a minute."

Jezebel walked over to Jessie. She bent down and kissed her cheek. Jezebel's lipstick stained Jessie's cheek and seeped into her skin. I lifted my leg up and kicked Jezebel. She slammed against the computer desk.

"Too late, angel." Jezebel laughed.

I grabbed her auburn hair, wrapped it around my fist, and pulled her up to make eye contact with me. Her deep greens eyes turned black.

"Dispose of me, Tristan. I don't care. I got to Jessie. That's all I care about." Jezebel squealed in laughter.

I looked down at Jessie. Jezebel's poison had engulfed Jessie's cheek and was moving throughout the rest of her face. I couldn't stop it. Jessie was going to have to deal with this. I took my sword out of it sheath and stabbed Jezebel in the abdomen. I felt the pressure of her body on my sword. Blood squirted from the wound. She grabbed the sword. Her eyes rolled back and her body jerked. Blood expelled from her mouth, and she laid limp in my grasp. I looked at her. Her beautiful features had disappeared. Her once creamy skin was ash gray with blisters. Her deep greens eyes were black bottomless pits. Her long auburn hair was now singed and spotted about her head. Her nose was flat, almost pig-like. I dropped her to the ground, and she slowly disappeared. I took a silk cloth from my satchel, whipped her blood off of my sword, and put it back in its rightful place. I looked at Jessie. Her homework had been finished, and she looked up at the picture of her and Leo.

"He won't be with her. I won't let it happen." Jessie's eyes grew black. An evil grin crept across her face.

CHAPTER 7

The Tutor

"Jessie, you need to get someone to help you in Math." Mike held Jessie's Algebra paper at arm's length.

"Jeremy said he would help me."

"Jeremy?" Travis asked, shaking the box of cereal.

"McVayne." Jessie stated.

"No way." Travis scoffed.

"Yeah, really. He's going to help me."

"Wow. How did you snag that?" Travis laughed as he threw a handful of cereal in his mouth.

"Nothing, he is the one that suggested it." Jessie played with the loose thread on the couch pillow.

"Woe . . . Jeremy McVayne. He's pretty smart. If he crosses the line, I will kill him. You understand? You're to study Math; not get impregnated!" Travis slammed his hand on the arm of the chair.

"Bubby, stop! He's just helping me with Math, that's all. No one is impregnating anyone." Jessie rolled her eyes.

"I agree with your brother." Toni added.

"Oh, my gosh." Jessie started to rub her temples.

"Listen. If Jeremy doesn't get the ball rolling, you need to ask someone else." Mike looked over at Jessie.

"I will." Jessie sighed.

"What about Leo? He's super freakin' smart and would do anything for you." Travis butted.

"No. He's on my bad side right now."

"Uh oh." Travis groaned. "What happened?"

"He's so focused on Ellen that he doesn't have time for me." Jessie whined.

"Who's Ellen?"

"Some slut!"

"Jessica!" Toni shot Jessie a warning look.

"She is! All he cares about is her. And, the funny thing is, they're not even boyfriend and girlfriend. She's dating Blake." Jessie put the pillow over her face.

"Jess, he'll come to his senses. You just need to bring your Math grade up." Mike removed the pillow from Jessie's face.

"I know. I will get Jeremy to agree to a study date tomorrow." Jessie sighed deeply.

"You can't let Leo make you miserable again, Sis. It's really not worth it."

"Bubby, would you stop bringing up Leo? I'm fine." Jessie rested her head on the back of the couch.

"I don't care if you date Jeremy or Leo, or if Leo dates a sheep. Get this Math grade up." Mike commanded.

Mike tossed the Math test at Jessie and it landed in her lap. She picked it up and studied it. A big red "F" popped out of the paper.

"It's gonna be okay." Travis kissed Jessie on the forehead and exited the room.

Mike and Toni got on their coats.

"Do you need anything?" Toni asked as she shoved her hands into her coat pockets.

"No, I'm good." Jessie waved a hand in the air.

"Alright. We'll be back." Mike said.

Mike and Toni left for the store. Jessie and I sat there for a moment. She pulled her phone out of her pocket and dialed a number.

"Hello?" the male voice said.

"Hey, Jeremy, it's Jess."

"Jessie, babe, how are you?"

"Good." Jessie smiled at the fact that he called her babe. "Is there any way that we could study after school tomorrow?" Jessie winced at the question.

"Um . . . yeah, of course." Jeremy chuckled.

"Good, because my dad got my Math test and he isn't too happy. I wanted to ask you on the phone now so that I didn't spring it on you in school."

"Ha! No problem, Jess."

"Thank you."

"No problem."

"Well, I will let you go. Bye."

"Bye, Jess." Jeremy said.

Jessie closed her phone and nibbled on her lower lip. She flipped the phone back open and started texting. I turned my head to look. Once again, I was not invading her privacy. I was simply protecting her.

"Kar . . . Jeremy and I have a study date tomorrow. Omg." Jessie hit send. She opened her phone to read the reply.

Karla: *"Omg. I can't believe it. He's so into you. I mean tons of girls, including Ellen, have asked Jeremy for help and he said no."*

Jessie: *"I know. Right. I'm so excited. What if he likes me?"*

Karla: *"That will def. show Leo. lol"*

Jessie: *"I'm not doin' this just to show Leo. I mean, it's a perk tho. lol"*

Karla *"Ha! Right. I agree 100%. I think it's cool that you and Jeremy are talking. Omg. You, Jeremy, Gerard, and I should totally double."*

Jessie: *"Holy crap . . . yeeeeeeees! J"*

Karla: *"Yay! I love you, Jess! U r the best friend a girl could ever have."*

Jessie: *"Awe, I love you too . . . u r too."*

Karla: *"Well, my break is over. I will txt you l8er. Love you."*

Jessie sat on the couch for a while. I knew she was thinking about her study date with Jeremy McVayne. Since Jessie was in the fourth grade, that name has become a household name, and she was finally having one-on-one time with him. Let's hope all goes well.

Period 3: Business Foundations

Jessie and I sat at the desk going through notes. I tried to see if I could find the notes that she was looking for. Nada. Couldn't find them. I don't even think she took notes that day. Jessie shuffled through her stacks of papers three or four times. Nothing.

"I swear I had those notes." Jessie shuffled through more papers.

"You can copy mine." I heard the melancholy in Leo's voice.

Jessie and I looked up to see Leo looking down at her. His eyes were drooped, a smile didn't plaster his face, and there was no brightness about him that he usually had.

"Are you okay?" Jessie said concerned.

Leo took his seat beside her. We shifted our bodies to face Leo.

"No." Leo cocked his head.

"Wanna tell me?" Jessie squinted.

"You'll be happy."

"How can I be happy when my best friend is sad?"

"Here is why. Ellen just told me that she just saw me as a friend and that she didn't want to lose Blake." Leo sighed heavily and slumped back in his chair.

"Okay, not gonna lie. I'm not completely sad."

"Oh well! Thanks, best friend!" Leo said sarcastically.

"But!" Jessie held up her hand. "There is a "but". I don't like seeing you like this. No matter who makes you happy, even if I don't like them, at the end of the day I want to see you happy. I mean it."

Sincerity became Jessie's face. Her features softened and her eyes sparkled with compassion. Leo looked at her for a moment probably waiting for her to make a wise crack. Not to lie but I was waiting for it, too, but it never came.

"Oh, well. Thanks, Jessie. That means a lot." Leo smiled.

Leo's smile was sincere. I heard other footsteps get closer. A figure stood in front of Jessie.

"We going to study today?" Jeremy asked. A smile owned his face.

"Yes, I was hoping to." Jessie smiled back.

"Jessie, I could help you with her Math." Leo interrupted.

"She's got help, amigo." Jeremy smarted.

"Jeremy." Jessie cocked her head.

"Well, I will help you."

"Jessie, who would you want to help you? Me or him?" Leo asked.

Jessie looked from Leo to Jeremy then back to Leo.

"Don't do this to me." Jessie shoved her papers into her folder.

"Simple question, Jess." Jeremy shrugged adjusting the backpack that hung over his shoulder.

"Class, I need you to please be seated." said Mrs. Tully as she entered the room.

Mrs. Tully was short and stout with blonde fluffy hair. She wore high heel shoes that had to be at least one size too big. She always wore white panty hose, a light gray skirt, an off-white silk shirt that tucked in, and a bright red blazer over it. Her make-up was two shades darker than her skin tone. Her eyebrows looked like she had drawn them on with a Sharpie. The color of her green eyes was taken away by the immense purple and blue eye shadow that she wore. Her blush was a deep red and her lipstick matched. Mrs. Tully grabbed the dry erase marker from its holder and wrote a question on the board. I don't know how she grabbed anything with those long, bright red nails, which had to have been two inches long. After the class was settled, Mrs. Tully started her lecture. Although Mrs. Tully's clothes and personality were loud, she was a very intelligent woman. She was married to the same husband for thirty-nine years. They had four kids and two grandkids. Her husband was a district attorney and was very intelligent. Jessie had listened intently to what Mrs. Tully was saying. She would jot down a note or two.

"Jessie, I really can help you with Math." Leo leaned in.

"I appreciate that." Jessie flashed him a smile.

"Let me. Come on. You're used to me and we're best friends."

"Leo, Jeremy said he would help me." Jessie reassured him.

"You're only doing this because you like him." Jealousy flashed in Leo's eyes.

"Don't go there, Leo." Jessie warned.

"Jessie, I know guys like Jeremy. They're hit it and quit it kind of guys."

"Leo Alexander Gutierrez! If you think I'm just going to drop my pants for him, I'm really hurt." Jessie glared at him.

"I didn't mean it that way."

"Then what way did you mean, Leo?"

"It's him I don't trust."

"Oh my gosh. I see it." Jessie looked up as if a light bulb had turned on in her head. "You don't want me to be with anyone because you're not with anyone. You don't want to be left out. I'm shocked." Jessie put her hand to her throat.

"Jessica Jane, that is not it!" Leo raised his voice.

"Everything okay?" Mrs. Tully looked at Jessie and Leo.

"Fine," they said in unison.

Mrs. Tully turned her stout self around and began to teach where she had left off. Jeremy glared over at them. His eyes were filled with anger.

"Jessie, I see guys like Jeremy snake girls all the time."

"Leo, this conversation is over." Jessie bit off.

A part of me believed Leo was right and was trying to protect her, but another part of me knew he was jealous.

"Fine. But if you get hurt, don't come crying to me."

"Shove it, Leo!" Jessie rolled her eyes.

I sat there not really knowing what I thought about the whole scenario. Was he really that jealous? Was she trying to make him jealous? Did she really like Jeremy and not care what Leo thought? Would Leo try to move in and not let Jeremy have a shot? Teens.

Period 6: Orchestra

Jessie and Carrie had to sit out of today's performance because they had forgotten their instruments. Jessie looked bored as she and Carrie watched everyone play.

"I'm never forgetting my violin again." Jessie crossed her arms over her chest.

"Nor my viola." Carrie sighed.

Carrie and Jessie were sent to sit in the back of the class. Those who didn't have their instruments were made to sit in the back so they didn't get in anyone's way.

"So, Shelby told me you and Leo got in a little argument during third period."

"I swear to God, why does my business travel so fast?" Jessie played with the hole in her jeans.

"What's going on?

"Well, Jeremy is going to help me study for Math. Well, Leo found out and got all pissed off at me because I asked for Jeremy's help and not his. In all reality, Leo is jealous. I know that, he knows that, you know that, and God knows that."

"Right." Carrie nodded to Jessie to go on.

"Shhhh."

One of the violin players turned around. Her short brown hair bounced as she did. Grace Foray was tall, very thin, no curvature to her body, and a very perfectionistic kind of person. Jessie and the others didn't like her, but she was an exceptional violin player.

"Screw you." Jessie said and then continued. "Well, now I don't know who I want to tutor me." Jessie sighed.

"You like Jeremy, though."

"Right, and, like all girls, we want to be tutored by the guys we like."

"Unless you're a lesbian." Carrie added.

"What the hell does being a lesbian have to do with anything?" Jessie looked at Carrie confused.

"I was just saying that girls want to be tutored by the guy they like unless you're a lesbian."

"Carrie, that comment wasn't even relevant." Jessie still had a puzzled look on her face.

"It wasn't' supposed to be. It's just a fact."

"Oooookay." Jessie's eyes widened. "I'll pick who I want to be my tutor and it will be the guy I like." Jessie smiled.

"Jessie, what's going on for tonight?" Karla caught up with Jessie by the library.

"Nothing; 'bout to get tutored then off to home. You?"

"I was wondering if you wanted to go see this band called Death Boot." Karla arched her eyebrow.

"They sound lame." Jessie shifted her backpack.

"I know, but I heard they were good." Karla brushed her red bangs out of her face.

"Um . . . I think I'm going to have to pass." Jessie laughed.

"Alright. Maybe next time." Karla touched Jessie's arm. "Good luck with the tutoring." Karla smiled.

"He's probably already in there." Jessie peeked through the slit in the door.

"Going to make your move?"

"Ha." Jessie laughed. "I'm taking my time with this one."

Jessie hugged Karla and they went their separate ways. Jessie grabbed the straps of her backpack, turned on her heels, and faced the doors to the library.

"The guy I like is sitting in there and is about to tutor me in Math. I know this means he cares about me. I hope something comes of this. Here goes nothing."

Jessie walked into the library and saw her tutor sitting at the table going through notes. Her breath was shaky, and she was really nervous. He looked up and smiled at her as she approached.

"Thanks for tutoring me, Leo."

CHAPTER 8

Walking Away

Jessie and Leo had been working on her Math for weeks and it had definitely improved—from an F to a high B to almost an A. We're hoping it gets that high. Jessie and Leo have been getting along extremely well. There was no talk of Jeremy or Ellen. She and Leo met at the library every Wednesday and Friday. It was supposed to be every Monday and Wednesday, but Jessie put up a fight about Monday. 'Leo, it's bad enough I gotta get up on Monday after a great weekend. I don't need to study on Monday. It's Monday. No one studies on Monday.' That was Jessie's excuse. Leo let it go. He was just happy that she was trying to improve her grade. Every Wednesday and Friday we met at the library. Jessie had sacrificed many times to hang with Karla to get her Math grade up, and I knew that she didn't mind because she was spending time with Leo.

Period 2: Geometry

"So my Math grade went from an F to a C to a high B and is on the verge of an A. I would definitely be lost without Leo." Jessie put her hand to her chest.

"Are you doing the work or is he?" Danni looked over at Jessie.

"I am." Jessie scoffed.

"Jessie." Erick lowered his gaze.

"I am hurt to think that you don't think I'm doing my own work." Jessie took a deep breath.

"Jessie, we love you but we also know how you have Leo wrapped around that pretty little Caucasian finger." Erick laughed.

"Why you gotta bring color into this? Jessie threw her hand in the air.

"Because I can."

"Why, because you're black?" Jessie bit off.

"Uh." Carrie looked from Erick to Jessie then back at Erick.

"Well, I'm just glad your Math grade is up so you can graduate on time with us." Shelby said as she changed the subject. Erick and Jessie glared at each other.

"Me, too." Jessie smiled at Shelby.

Awkward. I felt awkward. Jessie glared again at Erick then turned around in her seat and started her Geometry work.

"Class, may I have your attention please?" Mr. Greere asked.

Mr. Greere stood up from his desk. His bald head reflected the fluorescent light that was above him. His grayish black mustache frizzed out as if he had put his finger in a light socket. He wore khakis with a navy blue polo shirt. His brown loafers were so worn out that they looked almost yellow.

"You need to study for the exam, so I have made a practice packet."

Mr. Greere put his hands together and smiled at the class.

"Noooooooo!" the class moaned.

"You should thank me because it will help your grade a lot if you just attempt it, and a lot of your guy's grades suck." Mr. Greere walked over to the thick stack of packets.

"Holy crap! Those have to be forty pages long!" Jessie yelled.

"No, Miss Craig, fifty." Mr. Greere smiled, reveling his crooked white teeth.

"I can't handle this." Jessie rubbed her temples.

"We'll help each other," Danni said as she put her hand on Jessie's shoulder.

"Someone in your row, please come get some for your row." Mr. Greere tapped the packets a couple of times with his middle and index finger.

"Allow me." Carrie held up her hands.

"Don't play the martyr." Erick sighed.

"I'm not!" Carrie shot back as she walked to get the packets.

Carrie counted the packets she needed and headed back to her seat. She handed them to her friends. They grabbed one and started flipping through it.

"I'm not going to college." Jessie grew angry.

"Yes, you are. We're going to get through this." Danni sighed.

"I don't know. I don't think I'm going to college." Jessie glanced up from her packet to see all her friends were staring at her.

"Jessie, you have to go to college." Erick closed his packet and flipped the corner of it several times.

"I don't want to. It's not worth it. You can be successful without going to college." Jessie defended her decision.

"Says who?" Erick crossed her arms.

"God." Jessie looked intently at Erick. No one said anything.

Period 5: Government

"Jessie, I would appreciate if you wouldn't do your Geometry in this class." Mrs. Debla sat on the corner of her desk.

"If I wasn't so bored in this class I wouldn't be doing other work."

Jessie didn't look up from her packet. I heard Karla snicker. There goes Jessie and her attitude and Karla to keep the flame ablaze.

"Miss Harris, is Jessie's rebellion funny to you." Mrs. Debla turned her attention to Karla.

"Ma'am, I would have to agree with Jessie. Why would I want to learn about something that I hate?" Karla tapped her pencil on her desk.

"Agreed." Jessie chimed in, still not taking her eyes off of her Geometry.

"You hate the government? Without the government you couldn't function." Mrs. Debla crossed her arms over her chest.

"Other way around." Jessie finally looked up.

"How so?"

"Without us." Jessie looked around the room at her peers. "Who would the government have to steal from and survive off of?" Jessie replied.

"Go on." Mrs. Debla nodded.

"Face it. The government, excuse my language, is a bunch of back-biting bitches out for themselves. They don't care about America." Jessie shook her head.

This might be a long conversation. The two things that make people argue the most are politics and religion. I stood behind Jessie and adjacent to Karla.

"Yes, and we wouldn't be in wars we shouldn't. The students in this school have family members, loved ones, and friends in the service for what? To save another country that really isn't fond of us?" Karla leaned forward. "We're killing our own to save others." Karla added.

"Right." Jessie put her hand in the air.

"So you hate the government? Would you call yourself anarchists?" Mrs. Debla asked.

"Yes." Jessie and Karla said in unison.

"I see. So, if a soldier came in, you would tell him what?" Mrs. Debla smiled. It wasn't a cocky smile; it was more of an intrigued smile.

"I would tell him that he should have thought twice and to make sure he was fighting for America and not a country that hates us." Karla blurted.

The class didn't say a word, not even Taylor Clemons and she always had an opinion.

"Yeah, but they blew into our twin towers. We have to find Osama." Mrs. Debla rebutted.

"Then protect our airports and each other better. But, no! We have to go to the extreme and go fight for something that really isn't worth fighting for. If someone from Chicago kills someone from Indianapolis, do we have a war between Illinois and Indiana?" Jessie looked at Mrs. Debla.

"Well, no, they're just states."

"And Iraq is just a country," Jessie said. The class and Mrs. Debla were silent.

"A country is bigger than a state." Mrs. Debla had her second wind

"Then murder is just murder." Karla entered.

"We have to fight for our country." Mrs. Debla drew in a deep breath.

"To prove what? That we're big and bad?" Karla asked.

"To show we won't let people hurt us."

"Then focus on making America better with the people she contains. Americans helping Americans is what we need. I want the soldiers to come back for God's sake. It isn't worth it. We need to get them back. They deserve to be home. It's like we're buying time. Let's bring them home," Jessie closed. The argument was over.

"You two are interesting." Mrs. Debla looked at Karla and Jessie.

"Anarchists." Jessie teased.

"Fair enough." Mrs. Debla held her hands up.

Period 7: English 12

Jessie, Justin, Carrie, and David all headed to Jessie's locker. I was still thinking about Government class. I was really proud of Jessie for standing up for what she believes in. She had done it with a better attitude than I had thought she would. She didn't blow up, throw a desk, or break a pencil like she would have before.

"Where's Leo?" David asked as we approached the locker.

"Probably already in class. He doesn't always wait on me. Sometimes he likes to get some other homework done before class begins." Jessie put in the combination.

"Wished he'd tutor me." David sighed. We all turned our heads quickly to look at David.

"Well . . . I mean . . . he's so smart that I could get a good grade." David covered.

Carrie, Justin, and Jessie looked at each other. Jessie closed her eyes for a second and then turned to her locker and opened it.

"O-m-g, you guys." David grew angry.

"Hey, if that's what you're into."

Justin put his arm around David and then finally registered what he had done and quickly removed his arm.

"Ugh, I'm not like that. I'm just saying that Leo brought Jessie's F in Math almost up to an A." David crossed his arms over his broad chest.

"Right." Jessie grabbed her English book.

"Oh, I am running late." Leo threw his Anatomy book into the locker and grabbed his English book.

"Leo." David straightened his poster.

I rolled my eyes and shook my head. I hope this wasn't what we thought it was.

"David." Leo nodded to greet him.

"Leo, sweetheart. We've got three minutes to get to class and our English class is right around the corner." Jessie laughed.

"Oh, Jessie, I know but I didn't get my homework quite finished." Leo squinted at Jessie.

"You sinner!" Jessie teased.

"Jess." Leo sighed.

"Leo, it's going to be fine." Jessie smiled.

"I'm going to be late for my class if I don't hurry." David stated. "Bye guys. Good luck Leo."

David smiled and then headed to his class. Jessie looked at Leo and gave him a wicked smile. Leo glared at Jessie.

"Shut up!" Leo said. It was too late, though.

"He totally likes you." Jessie burst out in laughter.

"We're out. Good luck, Leo." Carrie patted Leo on the shoulder.

"Smooches!" Justin teased.

"I hate my life." Leo hung his head.

"Oh, I love ya." Jessie closed the locker and put her arms around Leo's shoulder.

"No you don't." Leo glared at Jessie.

"Yes. So a guy has a crush on you. Big deal. We all know you're straight . . . or are you?" Jessie teased.

"Get off of me." Leo slapped Jessie's arm off.

"Calm down." Jessie and Leo walked to their seats.

"You guys seem to be in good spirits," Jeremy said as Jessie sat in her seat.

"We are." Jessie smiled.

"I gotta get the rest of this work done." Leo sat down and started getting busy on his homework.

"How's your Math grade?" Jeremy said grudgingly.

"Almost an A." Jessie chirped.

"Well, good." Jeremy glared at Leo.

"Jeremy." Jessie caught him.

"It's whatever." Jeremy shrugged.

"It's okay. I do most of the work. He's basically just been a guide." Jessie assured Jeremy.

I noticed Leo stop writing. He was listening. I closed my eyes and took a deep breath.

"Really?" Jeremy asked intrigued.

"Oh, yeah, I do all the problems myself and he just kind of looks over it. That's it." Jessie smiled.

I can't believe she was doing this. She was giving Leo no credit for doing any of the work he did. I was upset with her. Leo didn't have to take time out of his day on Wednesday and Friday to help her. He did his work. He was a good student.

"Oh, I see. Well, that's good. So you didn't really need him?" Jeremy asked.

"Eh, not really." Jessie shrugged.

I cannot believe this. I looked over at Leo. His knuckles were white from gripping his pencil. Lord God, please calm him down.

"I will talk to you after class." Jeremy touched Jessie's cheek.

Jeremy sat with his friends and Jessie just sat there and smiled like she was on cloud nine. Leo turned around.

"We need to talk. After school by your truck." Leo glared at Jessie. Anger flashed in his eyes.

"What?" Jessie smarted.

"You heard me." Leo glared at Jessie then turned back around.

Jessie and Karla stood by Jessie's truck.

"Did he seem really mad?" Karla asked. Other students revved their engines and bolted out of the parking lot.

"Yeah, there was like a hate in his eyes. I don't know what I did. Probably breathed wrong." Jessie sighed.

Jessie leaned against her truck as Karla sat in the passenger's seat with the door open. Her body was shifted in the seat to where she was facing the outside.

"Jess, this boy seems like a handful." Karla lit a cigarette and took a drag.

"No kidding." Jessie said as she reached for the cigarette from Karla.

Why couldn't I just smack that out of her hand. Jessie took a drag. I saw a demon's face in the smoke. They were here. A battle was about to begin.

"Now you're smoking." Leo said as he approached us. Jessie turned around and Karla looked up.

"Chill." Jessie handed the cigarette to Karla.

"I wanted to talk alone." Leo looked at Karla and then to Jessie.

"Too bad, hot stuff. She's my ride." Karla jumped out of the passenger's side.

"Well, we can talk another time."

"No! Tell me what you have to tell me. Get it over with." Jessie slipped her hands into her hooded sweatshirt pockets.

"Look, Leo. Whatever it is, I'm sure it's not a big deal."

Karla flipped the hood of her sweatshirt over her bright red hair. Her freckles were darker now that it was turning winter.

"This doesn't concern you." Leo brought his body closer together to fight the cold.

"Alright. Gee." Karla rolled her eyes.

"What, Leo?" Jessie cocked her head and sighed.

"Why did you tell Jeremy all those lies about Math grade."

Leo crossed his arms over his chest. I smelled them. Burnt flesh and sulfur danced in the brisk cold air. I looked behind Jessie and saw Maaz, Gareb, and Hagab standing in the distance. They thought they were so big and bad. They just *had* to make a dramatic entrance. Like I care how they get here. I just wanted to get rid of them. They walked closer. Their tall, muscular, scarred-up bodies finally came into focus. I didn't say anything. They'll soon get over here.

"So, Tristan, how's it going?" Maaz boomed, with her dark, red hair blowing in the winter wind. I looked away from them and to Karla, Jessie, and Leo.

"Leo, would you chill? You have to know that I didn't mean that."

"No, Jessie. You never do. Even when you compliment someone, you don't mean it. All you do is freaking use people." Leo threw his hands in the air.

"Really, Leo? You want to go there!? Jessie moved forward with her face contorted into hatred.

"Jessie, I didn't have to help you. I helped you because I care about you. You don't even deserve help. You don't do any of your work, you skip class, you smoke, and you run around with this banshee." Leo pointed at Karla.

"Shut up, douche bag! I don't make Jessie do anything she doesn't want to do." Karla yelled.

Maaz walked up to Karla and whispered in her ear. I stood watching. I never really said much. Words were pointless. Like the old saying goes, 'Actions speak louder than words'.

"Plus, if it wasn't for Jessie, you wouldn't even have friends. People only like you because you do their homework." Karla blurted. Hagab laughed, and I looked at Leo. The comment had pierced his heart.

"Jessie, are you going to let her talk to me like that?" Leo looked at Jessie.

Jessie's eyes filled with sorrow. I looked to the teen, then to the demons, and then rested my hand on my sword.

"Tough angel wants to fight." Gareb licked his lips.

"Do something, Leo." Karla held her arms out. They were ganging up on him.

"Karla." Jessie shot Karla a look and walked over to Leo.

"Leo, I told you." Jessie glared at Leo and hate coated her eyes.

Maaz walked over to Jessie. Before she could get to her, though, I stabbed her in the side. Her body pressed against the blade and her labored breathing vibrated my sword. I grabbed my sword with both hands slowly ripping it from her side. She fell to the floor screaming. Blood flowed into the gravel of the parking lot, and it puddled under Jessie and Leo's feet. I felt my head jerk back. Gareb's hand clutched my hair in a death grip. Bending my body backward, he repeatedly started to punch my face. My teeth cracked together, and I felt my face immediately start to swell. My sword fell from my grip. I grabbed Gareb's fleshy forearm and pulled down as hard as I could. Maaz laid on the ground grabbing her wound. Hagab walked over to me and kicked my knees. I dropped to the ground with Gareb. I struggled to breathe.

"No, Jessie! I can't believe you would do something so mean just because you like Jeremy." Leo shouted.

"Oh, shut the hell up! You're making this too big of a deal." Jessie spat out.

"You shut up, you conniving bitch!" Leo lunged his body forward. Jessie balled her hand into a fist.

"Get out of my sight, you worthless Mexican, you moocher of the American people."

Jessie threw her fist at Leo. I saw Karla climb into the passenger side of the truck. Leo grabbed Jessie's wrist. His eyes filled with sorrow, and his face fell with hurt. I could hear his heart breaking.

"I am done with you." shouted Leo.

Leo threw her back against the truck. Jessie slammed against it. Rain filled the cold hair, slapping their faces with the harsh reality of their words.

Water drenched us as we wrestled trying to get up. I finally stood to my feet and ran to get my sword. I crashed to the ground and the gravel pierced my face. I felt it make itself a part of me. I groaned with pain. Hagab tripped me before I could reach my sword. He pulled me toward him and my face scraped against the gravel. *"Lord, send me help."* Hagab grabbed my hair that was matted with blood, water, and sweat. I gritted my teeth together. *"Lord, where is my help?"* Hagab pulled me up to his eye level, and I looked into his black, soulless eyes. A dagger penetrated his eye through the back of his head. It was not even an inch away from my face.

"Ah!" Hagab fell to the floor, dropping us. It was Truce. His tall frame was a shadow in the rain. Hagab grabbed at his eye. I looked over to Maaz. Her breathing was labored, and she didn't have long. Gareb mustered up the courage and shot a poisonous arrow at Truce. Truce grabbed its stem before it hit him. He broke it in half and threw it to the ground. Not saying anything, he walked to Gareb who shivered in fear. Truce grabbed Gareb by the throat and pulled him up to his eye level. Truce didn't say anything. The rain was beating down on us.

"Tristan, take Jessie home." Truce called to me, not taking his eyes off of Gareb.

The rain was pouring down, but I stood to my feet. My face was bleeding with gravel stuck in my skin. I limped to Jessie.

"Good! I hate you!" Jessie yelled as Leo walked away from her. *"God, keep him safe."*

Leo kept walking until the rain engulfed him and we could see him no more.

"Truce, I will help you." I called.

"Go!" Truce yelled.

Jessie stood in the rain. It hit so hard that I couldn't tell if she was crying or not. Karla sat in the passenger's seat with her eyes widened and transfixed on Jessie. Jessie stood there watching him walk away.

"What have I done?" Jessie whispered to herself. "What have I done?"

I heard Gareb scream in pain. I heard his bones popping, his guts squishing. Truce had taken care of him.

"Oh God! What I did I do!"

Jessie fell to the ground crying. I knelt down beside her and put my wings over her.

"I lost my best friend." Jessie said as she pounded her fist on the ground.

The gravel ripped her skin. Blood and rain mixed on the gravel and flowed across the parking lot. Karla jumped out of the truck.

"Come on, Jess. Your gonna get sick."

Karla lifted Jessie up and hoisted her in the truck. Karla made her way to the other side and climbed in, and I made my way to the half cab.

"Karla, he's done with me." Jessie cried.

"No, honey. This will all blow over. You just got in a fight." Karla put her arm around Jessie's shoulder.

"Karla, I said some really mean things."

I saw Truce standing in front of the truck. The heads of Gareb, Maaz, and Hagab were in his hand. He lifted them up and smiled. The rain pelted down on the windshield, distorting his image.

"Karla, what am I going to do?" Jessie sniffled.

"Get over it. He's not worth it."

"Really?" Jessie breathed unsteadily.

"Jessie, he walked away. It's his loss. He walked way."

CHAPTER 9

Fighting for a Loss of Words

Life had drastically changed for this season. Leo and Jessie didn't say anything to each other. Although they still shared a locker, they didn't talk. They barely even looked at each other. In class, Jessie sat on the other side. She told her teachers that it would be best if she didn't sit next to Leo. She needed to learn to be independent and do her own work. The teachers had no problem with that and let her move seats. Mrs. Lazarus, on the other hand, had known something was wrong. You never saw Leo without Jessie or Jessie without Leo, and now they were sitting a room apart. Leo would walk into the room about three minutes before Jessie. They didn't work in a group together and didn't partner up on projects. Jessie isn't the person to deal with conflict, especially if the conflict is with someone she really loves and cares about. So, she would make mean comments when Leo would speak up in class or when his partner and he would present their project. Leo ignored the comments. He, on the other hand, never said anything to or about Jessie. When she spoke up, he listened. When she and her partner presented their project, he sat there and looked to the floor. He would look up occasionally and catch Jessie's eyes. When he looked down again, Jessie looked away. It was ripping them apart, but both Leo and Jessie were stubborn and prideful. Someone was going to have to swallow that pride or they would never be friends again.

Period 1: Algebra 2

Jessie vigorously erased the wrong answer off of her paper. Carrie and Justin looked at each other with worried expressions.

"I freakin' hate this class." Jessie slapped the eraser marks off of her paper.

"Jessie, is everything alright?" Shelby tapped Jessie's back.

"Yes." Jessie bit off.

"Jessie, you can't let this Leo thing drag you down." Justin chimed. Everyone knew that that was Jessie's problem.

"Justin, this has nothing to do with Leo." Jessie's eyes narrowed and her voice grew raspy with irritation. "I simply don't like Math or English or Government. I hate school." Jessie lightly laughed.

"Oh, well. We have the rest of this semester and one more left. You're going to get through this." Carrie leaned in and whispered.

"Why do I hear talking?" Mr. Delarosa looked up from his desk at Jessie and her friends.

"Because you're not deaf?" Jessie looked up.

"I don't need your sass, Miss. Craig." Mr. Delarosa looked at Jessie from the top of his thick, black glasses.

"Well, you asked a question and I figured I'd answer." Jessie shrugged.

"Miss Craig, why this attitude?"

"Because I have to come to this hell hole every day, and if it wasn't for me promising my grandfather before he died that I would graduate, my happy ass wouldn't be here."

Jessie slammed her Algebra book shut. I took a deep breath and my stomach jerked with irritation. Jessie's fight with Leo was interfering in all aspects of her life. She was mean with her parents, brother, and cousins. She hated school even more now and was short with her friends.

"No one is making you be here. We're all better off when students like yourself don't attend. We don't have time for slackers." Mr. Delarosa crossed his arms over his scrawny chest.

"Really? I'm a slacker when my F went to an A? That's a slacker?" Jessie yelled.

"Jessie what's gotten into you." Shelby whispered.

"Nothing, but I'm not gonna have some lame teacher talk to me like I'm worthless."

Jessie pointed her hand to Mr. Delarosa who was leaning back in his chair listening to Jessie go on and on. The class sat in silence. Looking from Mr. Delarosa to Jessie, Jeremy sat in the back of the class shaking his head in disappointment. I don't even think, though, that would make Jessie shut up and stop arguing with her teacher.

"Are you done?" Mr. Delarosa closed his eyes for a moment.

"I'm never done bad-mouthing a teacher, but I will let you off the hook." Jessie clicked her tongue.

"I'm honored and also honored to give you three days worth of detention."

Mr. Delarosa reached his long, slender hand in the front drawer of his desk and pulled out a blue form. DETENTION. I wasn't surprised. Jessie and I spent a lot of time in detention since she even started high school. I stood there with my arms crossed, looking down at Jessie. I studied her. I didn't see as much anger as I did hurt. Her face was masked with hurt. Her eyes especially reflected hurt. The only way Jessie dealt with the hurt was to lash out at others. I didn't know which was better: being mean and hateful to others or keeping it bottled inside. I just didn't know. Well, I never experienced Jessie ever bottling her feelings inside. She was always one to let them out.

Period 3: Business Foundations

Jessie, Shelby, and Erick sat in silence. Shelby tried talking to Jessie, but she would only get a shrug. All Erick got was a 'Shut up! You get on my nerves!'.

"Don't take it personally, Erick. She's mad at Leo." Shelby reassured Erick.

"Yeah, well, if he doesn't do something about it, I'm going to kick his ass." Erick grew angry.

Jessie could hear what they were saying, but she didn't care. She sat at her desk with her head rested in her hand. She was asleep, or pretended to be anyway. That was one way to shut people out—just fall asleep. Leo entered the room. He looked over at the sleeping Jessie and shook his head. Erick and Shelby smiled and waved. He gave them a weak smile and waved back.

"Jessie!" Jeremy boomed as he entered the room. Jessie jumped up startled.

"Holy crap." Jessie laughed. "You scared me to death." Jessie rested her hand over her heart.

"No sleeping. You're spending time with me." Jeremy ran his fingers through Jessie's long, blonde pony tail.

"Ha, I'm not in the mood for anything." Jessie sighed and went back to her sleeping position.

"Jessie, come on." Jeremy nudged her as he took his seat next to her.

"What?" Jessie moaned.

"Oh, cheer up. You still have me." Jeremy smiled.

A half smile crept across Jeremy's face. I didn't care much for Jeremy showing her all this attention, but at least he was making her smile. I stood behind Jessie and next to Jeremy. Hopefully, I could find an empty seat nearby, and I did. The kid that sat behind Jessie was absent. I hope they were alright. I looked over at Leo. He had his head slightly turned so he could hear Jessie and Jeremy's conversation.

"Well I hope you can get her in a good mood." Erick looked at Jeremy.

"I got this. Jessie's my girl." Jeremy rested his arm on Jessie's shoulder. "Right?" he looked down at her.

"Right." Jessie flashed a fake smile.

"No one can make her happy." Leo said as he turned to look at them.

I guess Leo had had enough of them. Shelby and Erick looked at Leo and then to Jeremy. Jessie opened her eyes and glared at Leo.

"No one asked you." Jessie said with a dark discord in her voice.

"Oh, please, Jessie. You mean to tell me that you're going to just pretend everything is okay because Jeremy said?" Leo rolled his eyes.

"Dude!" Jeremy butted. "When I say everything is okay, that means everything is okay." Jeremy said lightly.

"Right." Leo bit off and then turned back around.

I looked over to the door and, to no surprise, I see Hagab and Maaz. Lucifer must have let them out of the pit early. They were given a second chance to prove themselves, I'm guessing, since Truce had cut their heads off.

"Hello, pretty boy." Hagab hissed.

I said nothing. They entered the room with their tall frames squeezing through the door. Maaz, although a female, was rather large. She had dark blood red hair, jagged yellow teeth, stood six feet five, and her calves were enormous. Her biceps were the size of watermelons. This was a really big lady. Her enormous stature was topped off with a tiny scrunched up face. Hagab was just tall and ugly. He was huge but ugly. He had a black mohawk that rested atop his enormous pockmarked head. His biceps and thighs were much larger than those of Maaz. His razor sharp teeth clicked together when he walked. He was one ugly dude.

"Thought your other little angel friend got rid of us?" Maaz laughed. I still said nothing.

"Well, we were in the pit for a couple of days, and then father Lucifer summoned us." Hagab laughed. He crossed his arms over his enormous chest and looked intently at me. "Oh, and look at the scar your friend left." Maaz pointed to her swollen neck. A huge scar ran from one side to the other from where Truce had cut their heads off.

"Oh, wow!" I said sarcastically. Their faces grew angry. "It could be worse." I shrugged. I was still seated in my desk, and I wasn't getting up for these bozos.

"Is that a threat?" Maaz reached in her satchel and pulled out a knife. She licked the blade.

"Make it what you want." I rolled my eyes.

"Jealousy says hi and she will see you soon. She really misses you." Hagab boomed with laughter. I rolled my eyes.

"Your eyes are gonna get stuck like that, gorgeous."

Hagab grabbed his knife and stuck it to my throat. The tip of the blade barely pierced my skin but enough to draw blood. I didn't say anything. I looked Hagab in his dark, soulless eyes. I said to myself, *"Show no fear. Greater is he that is in me."*

"Hagab." I gave him a warning look.

"What! You gonna call on Truce again because you can't take care of your own human?"

Time stopped. I balled my hand into a fist and struck Hagab's face. The force of my punch sent him crashing to the ground. I stood up and looked at Maaz. She smiled at me, licking her lip. I jumped up and kicked her in the stomach. She flew back with so much force that, when she hit the wall, it cracked. She moaned, trying to come to her senses. Hagab wrapped his large arm around my neck, chocking me with his forearms. I grabbed his arms with my hands and pulled as hard as I could. Nothing. I reached for my sword and took it out of its sheath. I fumbled the handle for a minute trying to get a grip on it. Hagab was too focused on trying to kill me that he never noticed. Aha! I had a solid grip. I raised the sword over my head, stabbing Hagab through his chin. I pushed as hard as I could. The sword ripped through his chin and tongue and went out the top of his head. His tongue split. His grip began to loosen, and I kept my hand on the handle of the sword. I twisted my body to where I was facing him. His eyes bugged out and blood ran from them. I had to quickly dispose of him before Maaz came to. I twisted the sword. He didn't say a word. He just wheezed and squeaked as my blade shifted in his brain. I said nothing. His blood ran down my arms. I looked down at Jessie who was asleep. I tried not to get irritated. I looked back up at Hagab. His eyes popped out of his head and landed on the floor. I smiled at them and then stomped on them, squishing them. They lay on the floor like deflated basketballs. Hagab winced and made a sound of despair. I finally, with all my might, ripped the sword toward me, practically slicing his head in half. His brain starting squirting blood. It got all over my face, in my hair, and on my clothes. He fell to the ground with a boom. The ground slightly shook. The two pieces of his head folded inward while steam rose from the opening in his head. I took my sword, stabbed his chest, and spat on him. I heard footsteps from behind. I was not waiting. I turned around and, with lightning speed, penetrated Maaz with my sword. It entered through her stomach and out of the lower part of her back. She grabbed the blade in front of her. Her eyes were rolling back with death. "Now, this is the second time you have been destroyed." I said through clenched teeth. I moved the sword up and down like an old saw. She flinched with every movement. Her breathing was labored.

"Tristan!" she managed to yell. Her scream was drowned out by the gurgling of her own blood. I grabbed my sword and ripped it from her enormous body. She fell to the ground and steam came off of her wound. I raised my sword high above my head and stabbed her in the chest. I felt the beat of her heart vibrate my sword. Thud thud . . . . thud thud . . . . thud thud. Then nothing. I sighed deeply and then ripped my sword from her chest. I grabbed the anointed handkerchief from my satchel and wiped the blood off of my face. The anointing oil sucked up the blood like a sponge in water. I ran it over my hair. Same outcome.

I then went over my sword and clothes, but my wings would have to wait. For the most part, I was clean. I placed the handkerchief back into my satchel and my sword in its sheath. I looked at what I had done.

"I can't take care of my human alone?" I scoffed at them. I stepped over their lifeless bodies.

"Well done." I looked up and saw Truce smiling at me.

"I knew you could do it alone. Kind of hard without the prayers of humans." Truce had his hands together at his waist.

"Agreed.' I chuckled.

"This is my favorite part." Truce nodded to the bodies of Hagab and Maaz.

I walked over next to him. I looked down at the bodies. They started to twitch violently. "Uh, going to the pit?" I looked at Truce.

"First to their father, Lucifer." Truce smiled, not taking his eyes off of them.

Truce's burnt orange hair fell way past his waist. He had it pulled back in a braid with gold hair ties holding it together. His face was rugged, yet handsome. His tall frame was broad and full of anticipation to fight. I noticed his arms had several scars on them—from battle. He had burn marks on his neck and arms. His long, silk baggy pants covered his legs. His eyes were almost transparent but had a hint of blue in them. He was one to look up to. The bodies combusted, leaving a light red smoke behind.

"And that, my friend, is the power of the Living God—to defeat those who are out to destroy us, and the people who are a part of us." Truce put his hand on my shoulder and looked me in the eyes. His stare was intense, almost scary.

"Well done, brother. Well . . . until next time. God be with you." Truce said.

Truce then dissipated into thin air, probably back up to Heaven or to help another angel with battle. I wonder if Truce ever got tired of fighting. I wonder if he might want to be assigned to music, to a guardian, or to architecture in Heaven. Wouldn't hurt to ask, I guess.

Period 5: Government

Jessie and Karla looked so bored. This was their least favorite class. Mrs. Debla went on and on about the importance of law. Jessie doodled on the study guide Mrs. Debla passed out to them before she began her lecture.

"How are you and Leo?" Karla instigated.

"Same, although he did make a smart comment to Jeremy and me," Jessie scoffed.

"No talking, please." Mrs. Debla said not taking her eyes off the lesson on the chalkboard. Jessie and Karla sat silent for a moment.

"He's probably jealous." Karla whispered.

"Probably. Well, maybe Jeremy can be my new Leo." Jessie shrugged.

"Jessie, no one can be Leo. We both know that." Karla smarted. Her attitude was cocky, and she wasn't helping the situation.

"Well, I have to move on somehow." Jessie sighed.

"Uh, try to talk to Leo." Karla insisted.

"He won't listen."

"Then forget about him, Jessie." Karla rolled her eyes.

"I know you're trying to help, but you're doing a really suck ass job of it." Jessie turned to face Karla.

"Fine. I'll drop it." Karla held up her hand in front of her.

"Is there a problem?" Mrs. Debla slammed her yard stick on her desk.

Jessie and Karla didn't even flinch. Others in the class did. They casually looked up at their teacher.

"No." Jessie sighed.

"Good. Let me finish this lesson." Mrs. Debla glared and then went on teaching her lesson.

Jessie and Karla perked their ears to hear the nearby conversation between Ellen Gray and Nicole Holmes.

"Well, Leo said he wanted to hang out tonight, so I think I'm going to." Ellen smiled at her best friend Nicole.

"Oh you definitely should. He's a hottie." Nicole blushed.

"I know." Ellen sighed. "Blake and I are on the outs. Maybe I should give Leo a chance. He seems like a good guy." Ellen smiled.

Karla looked at Jessie who fumed with Anger and Jealousy. "This is too good."

I turned around and saw Jealousy standing in the doorway. She wore a skin tight red dress, a diamond heart necklace, red pumps, and bright red lipstick. Her curly hair fell down her back, and her bright green eyes stared at me.

"I don't have time for you." I turned back to face the teens.

"Well, Jessie's out of the way." Nicole said. It was funny how they didn't think we could hear them.

"It's funny how they think we can't hear them." Karla smarted.

She took the words right out of my mouth. I looked over to Jealousy who had made her way to Ellen. She bent over Ellen's desk and looked at me. Her elbows rested on the desk and her head in her hands.

"Hey, dumb ass, we can hear you!" Karla boomed. Ellen and Nicole flinched and looked toward them. "Are you freaking retarded?" Karla tapped on her head.

"I didn't know you could hear us." Ellen chocked out. I could tell Ellen was afraid of Karla.

"Miss Harris and Miss Craig!" Mrs. Debla yelled.

"Well, we can hear you. And news flash . . . Leo only wants to spend time with you because he and Jessie are on the outs. He's using you. I figured you would have noticed that instantly. You know it takes a user to know a user." Karla said to Ellen ignoring Mrs. Debla.

"Miss Harris!" Mrs. Debla grew fierce. Karla held up her hand to Mrs. Debla shushing her. The nerve of teens these day.

"Listen, Ellen 'I think I'm perfect' Gray. You ain't nothing but a two bit hussy. And it ain't gonna take no time before Leo and Jessie are on good terms again. You hurt my best friend. I will beat you so bad that you'll be eating your food through a straw. If you even do eat."

Karla looked Ellen up and down with a disgusted look on her face. Ellen's eyes glossed over with tears. Nicole said nothing to stand up for her friend.

"Oh my gosh." Justin whispered.

"You want some of this, too, Justin?" Karla lunged at him.

"Shut up, Karla! You aren't anyone to be afraid of." Justin scoffed at her statement.

"Right." Karla glared.

"Look, Karla, I know you're taking up for Jessie but you don't need to treat people like that." Justin stated.

"Well, I don't see you guys, her supposedly true friends, (Karla lifted her hand signing quotation marks.) taking up for her." Karla hissed. Laughter came from Jealousy.

"Class!" Mrs. Debla yelled.

"Shut the hell up, Karla." Justin warned, ignoring Mrs. Debla.

"What you gonna do, you little queer."

"Karla Harris!" Mrs. Debla got out a stack of papers and shifted through them. Jessie didn't say anything.

"Karla, shut up. You aren't helping, Jessie. You're making things worse. You always have to open your mouth." Carrie entered.

"Oh my gosh . . . battle of the losers." Taylor commented to her friend Alyssa.

"No kidding, but it's better than listening to Mrs. Debla's lesson." Alyssa flipped her long, brown hair over her shoulder.

"No doubt."

"Carrie, I like you. Don't make me fight with you, too." Karla stated.

"EVERYONE SHUT UP!" Jessie yelled. "Stop fighting! This is stupid!" Jessie hissed.

"This fight is between me and Leo, and if Leo wants to spend time with her, it's whatever."

Jessie had a change of heart. I could tell she was losing her will to care.

"Well, people need to . . . ."

"Harris and Craig, up here now." Mrs. Debla demanded.

"I love this so much." Jealousy smiled at me. "Well, I just wanted to check up on you guys."

Jealously laughed. I looked around the room. The classroom was now in an uproar. Kids were yelling things at Karla, other kids were comforting Justin and Carrie, and Ellen and Nicole just sat in silence. Jessie and Karla made their ways to Mrs. Debla's desk. She handed them slips. DETENTION for a week.

"I already have three days." Jessie informed.

"Well, now you have ten days." Mrs. Debla glared. "In the meantime, go gather your things and go to the office. Sit there for the remainder of the period. I can't have you disrupting my class." Mrs. Debla pointed to the door.

"This is bogus." Karla huffed as she gathered her things.

"You got us into this." Jessie hissed.

"Me?" Karla came up for air.

"You always have something to say. Just let things go."

Jessie threw her backpack over her shoulder. The class watched as they left. Jessie turned to Carrie and Justin and mouthed "I'm sorry". They nodded back, accepting her apology.

"Look, Jess, people have been treating you so horribly. You used to not stand up for that. You would tear those people down. Jessie, you're losing your power over these people." Karla said as soon as she got into the hallway.

"Look, some things are just better left alone to weigh itself out." Jessie sighed.

"I guess. I'm sorry for being a bitch to your other friends, but I was just so heated." Karla lightly laughed.

"I know your heart's in the right place, but where the hell is your brain?" Jessie laughed.

Karla put her arm around Jessie. "As long as you're my best friend, I won't let anyone hurt you." Karla smiled.

"Thanks. That means a lot, it really does."

"That's what friends do."

I looked behind me and saw Jealousy standing by Jessie and Leo's locker.

"I'm just gonna wait here, lover." She called to me.

I can't stand her.

Period 7: English 12

Jessie and I didn't stop at the locker. We went straight from the office to English. Jessie found her seat in the back left corner of the room. She opened her backpack and got her homework out. She ran through it and made sure she answered everything. Jessie tensed up. I looked to the door and saw Leo walk in. She didn't even have to look up. She felt his presence. Impressive. She flipped her homework around to check the back. Everything was filled in.

"Jessie, I heard what happened in Gov." Jeremy took his seat next to Jessie.

"Yeah, Karla went nuts." Jessie laughed.

"I heard she snapped on Ellen." Jeremy said. Leo looked over at Jessie and Jeremy. Jessie ignored his stare.

"Yeah, and me and Carrie." Justin entered the conversation.

"What happened?" Jeremy looked over to Justin.

"She said that people were treating Jessie bad. She was sick of it and snapped, and Mrs. Debla was, like, yelling at all of us to shut up."

"Karla's nuts." Jeremy shook his head. He straightened his shirt and brushed the hair away from his eyes.

"What did she say to Ellen?" Leo butted into the conversation.

"She basically called her a skinny hoe." Carrie cocked her head down.

"I really hate her." Leo shook his head.

"Likewise." Jessie smarted.

"Uh oh." Danni tapped Carrie on the shoulder.

"Jessie, say what you want. God, I'm so sick of you." Leo said in almost a whine.

"Leo, we need to talk. This crap has gone on long enough." Jessie stated. I heard Jeremy let out a growl.

"No, Jessie. I told you I was done with you. What you said was mean and hateful." Leo slammed his book on the desk.

"Class." Mrs. Lazarus sighed. "You know what? Get it out of your system." Mrs. Lazarus gave up.

"And what you said wasn't?" Jessie stood up. The class was looking at them.

"Jessie, just stay out of my life." Leo sighed. Sorrow filled his eyes.

"Leo, you don't mean that." Jessie laughed him off.

"Not here, Jessie. Not in class." Leo looked around at all the people that were staring at them.

"Fine. Karla is getting a ride with Gerard after school. Meet me by my truck. We need to talk." Jessie called the shots.

"Fine." Leo said then sat down in his seat. Jessie looked around the room. All eyes were on them.

"We're done." Jessie widened her eyes at them.

"Jessie, I won't let him hurt you." Jeremy clasped his hands together and rested them on the desk.

"I thank you for that."

Jessie bent down and hugged Jeremy. She breathed in his cologne. Jeremy placed his hand on the small of Jessie's back and pulled closer. Maybe Jeremy really did care about her and didn't want to see her hurt.

Jessie and I stood by her truck watching all the other students leave.

"Hope everything works out." Shelby said as she climbed into her car.

"Thanks." Jessie mumbled.

"Me, too." Carrie and Justin said in unison.

"Okay." Jessie nodded at them.

They got into Shelby's car and drove away. The sun was shining bright for a fall day. The wind was brutal. Jessie's hair whipped in the wind. She shivered as she waited for Leo. The parking lot was almost empty except for a baby blue mustang. The engine revved as it made its way to Jessie. Jeremy pulled the blue mustang up to Jessie.

"Want me to stay?"

"Ha! No thanks. I can handle Leo. We've been through a lot." Jessie bent to look at Jeremy through the window.

"Well, call me later."

"I will." Jessie nodded.

"Alright. Later." Jeremy raised his hand then took off. Jessie and I waited.

"Waiting for?" Anton came up beside me.

"Leo." I said irritated.

"That's why Jealousy sent me here. She's off on a mission with some girl in Kentucky named Sarah. She and Iscariot are trying to get Sarah to kill her ex-boyfriend's new girlfriend, Hannah. I guess Sarah got knocked up by him and he left her for Hannah. Whatever. I hope it all works out for the worse." Anton smiled a wicked smile. "There he is." Anton nodded toward Leo who was making his way to Jessie. Leo approached.

"Sorry was talking with Ellen." Leo already started the conversation on a bad note. Anton laughed. I sighed.

"Whatever." Jessie rolled her eyes.

"Well?" Leo looked at Jessie.

"Well what?" Jessie cocked her head.

"You going to apologize?"

"Are you kidding me?" Jessie squinted.

"No."

"You need to apologize, too." Jessie crossed her arms over her chest.

"I'm getting bored." Anton commented. I stood next to Jessie not saying anything.

"Leo." Jessie put her hands on her hips. "We don't have to be best friends, but I don't want hard feelings between us. If you want to date Ellen . . . whatever." Jessie threw her hand in the air. She dropped it to her side.

"Right. You don't want me dating anyone." Leo smarted.

"Holy crap, Leo. I just told you I don't care. I think you want me to not want you to be with anyone but me. News flash, hot stuff . . . As much as I may like you, I'm not going to let you run my life. Date Ellen. I don't care." Jessie held her arms out in front of her as she explained herself.

"Well, are you going to date Jeremy?" Leo asked.

"Oh . . . so you won't date if I won't date, but you'll date if I date. That's sick!" Jessie arched her brow.

"I never said that . . . God, you're so annoying." Leo laughed with irritation. He put his hand to his forehead.

"You're hateful."

"You broke my heart!" Leo blurted.

Jessie stopped. Anton and I stood there with our mouths gapped open. Anton and I exchanged looks. He admitted it. Jessie broke his heart.

"Oh." Jessie just stood there with the wind blowing her hair. She pulled herself closer trying to keep warm.

"I can't deal with this." Leo said. He looked at Jessie. Sorrow, compassion, hate, and love filled his eyes. He cared about Jessie more than he had let on, and I finally saw it today.

"Wow." Anton looked at me. I turned my head to look at him.

"Now, I have something to use against her." Anton smiled.

"Oh, shut up for once. You're so annoying."

"Oh, Tristan, you broke my heart." Anton mocked.

"Well, until next time, dear Tristan."

Anton stuck out his hand for a hand shake. I looked at his hand, not touching it. "Well then."

Anton flipped up his black collar, turned on his heels, and walked away from me. I watched as his figure became smaller and smaller until I could see him no more. I looked over to Jessie and Leo. They still stood there.

"I'm not ready to trust you again." Leo broke the silence.

"Fine." Jessie turned on her heels and walked to the driver's side of the truck. "Until you get over being hateful, I'm sharing Jeremy's locker and I don't want you to talk to me or even look at me. Stay with Ellen. I can't deal with this." Jessie started to cry.

I stood next to Jessie, putting my hands on her shoulders and resting my head on hers. *"Peace. I speak peace to this dear child."*

"Jessie." Leo said barely above a whisper.

Jessie climbed into the driver's seat, slammed the door, and started her truck. I made my way to the passenger's seat, looked out, and saw Leo still standing there. Jessie floored the gas and we sped out of the parking lot. I looked out of the side mirror. Leo's head hung, his body getting beat by the fall winds. He kicked the gravel and swung his hands in the air. I then saw Anton standing beside him. A wicked smiled plastered his face.

CHAPTER 10

In the Distance

Life was moving forward as it should. Jessie and Leo never talked. He did what she requested. He didn't even look at her—that she knew of anyway. Jessie shared a locker with Jeremy. They spent a majority of time together. They would go to lunch together, study together, go to the basketball games together. But they weren't dating. Ellen and Leo spent a great deal of time together studying, going on movie nights and to basketball games. It struck a nerve that all of this was going on yet no one was dating or had dated. It made no sense.

Jessie would see Leo and Ellen leaning up against the wall talking and laughing. Her high girly laugh made Jessie want to cringe. Jessie's friends actually started shunning Leo and Ellen for what they were doing to Jessie. They didn't care, though. Leo was seeking revenge and Ellen liked the attention. Leo would stare straight ahead when he saw Jessie giggling with Jeremy and running her fingers down his arms. This had to end. Jealousy had a bigger grip on these teens than I had thought. Truce and I had to come up with a battle plan and fast. I had a feeling there was a battle brewing.

One word . . . Brutal.

Period 3: Business Foundations

Jessie and Jeremy sat in class, going over notes and quizzing each other. Shelby and Erick did the same. Leo had paired off with a girl named Kristen Moon. Other kids had paired off together to help study for tomorrow's test.

"You think you're ready for the test?" Jessie leaned over and asked Shelby.

"I don't feel like I am, but more than likely I'll get an A or a B." Shelby sighed.

"Same here. I always feel like I'm bound to get an F or a D and always end up getting higher." Erick laughed.

"Not me. When I feel I'm going to get a bad grade, I usually do." Jessie sighed.

"You need to give yourself more credit. You're really smart, Jess." Jeremy said as he flipped to the next page of the study guide packet.

"Awe, thanks. You're the best friend a girl could have." Jessie smiled at Jeremy. Leo looked over at them.

"Um." Shelby gave Jessie a look then nodded her head over to Leo.

"His loss." Jeremy scooted his seat right in from of Jessie, obstructing her view of Leo.

"Jer." Jessie sighed.

"Jess." Jeremy sighed back.

"Come on; we have to be prepared." Jeremy smiled.

Jeremy asked Jessie a series of questions. Then, after she had answered as many as she could bear, she grabbed her packet from Jeremy and quizzed him. He had gotten more than half right. I think he only missed at least five. Probably not even that. Jeremy rested his head on his desk as Jessie flipped the packet back to the front page and placed it in her backpack.

"You did good, Jeremy." Jessie stroked his hair.

"Shew. I don't want to rush senior year, but I am so tired of school." Jeremy lifted his head to Jessie.

"I hear ya. Where are you going to college?" Jessie asked.

"Probably Purdue for Sports Journalism." Jeremy smiled.

"I see. You'll do great." Jessie said softly.

"Where are *you* going?" Jeremy tilted his head to the side. "I never hear you talk about college."

"I don't know if I'm going to go." Jessie admitted.

Jeremy's face fell. Leo looked over at her. "Jessie, why?"

"I don't know, Jer., I don't think school is my thing." Jessie sighed.

"Yeah, but college is different. High school sucks. College is more free, more independent." Jeremy persuaded.

"I know, but all that school work. I can barely get my high school work done, and I always need someone's help." Jessie said frustratingly.

"No, Jessie, please go to college. Tell me you're going to further your education and better yourself." Jeremy grabbed her hands in his.

"Okay." Jessie said defeated.

I took in a sigh and rested my hand on Jessie's shoulder. I looked over at Leo. His face showed that he was extremely angry, probably because he had tried to talk Jessie into going to college and she still stood on no. But, when Jeremy talked to her and tried to get her to go, she agreed.

"Great." Jeremy perked up.

Jessie and I both knew that, even though she told Jeremy okay, she wasn't going to go.

"So, you're going to go?" Shelby entered the conversation.

"Well, I think I'm going to apply to IPFW with you, if you wanna be roommates." Jessie squinted.

"Oh my gosh! Absolutely! You, me, and Carrie!" Shelby said with much excitement. "I am above happy. We gotta tell Carrie." Shelby hugged Jessie.

"Dang! I didn't think you would be this happy."

"Oh, I am. I love you, Jeremy!" Shelby hugged Jeremy tightly. "You're amazing! Probably the best person ever right now."

Shelby was so excited that she could barely stand it. Her best friends were going to be her roommates. Leo was now irritated to the max. He glared over at them. Would things ever go back to the way that they were? Jessie's friends were really starting to warm up to Jeremy. He wasn't just another jock anymore. He was becoming Jessie's best friend.

"I'm glad, too." Jeremy laughed. Jessie looked over to Leo. Their eyes locked. Anger reflected in his eyes. Jessie's eyes filled with sorrow as she looked away from him.

Period 4: Accounting

Jessie and Shelby sat in their desks talking about college. Who would share rooms? How would they decorate? Then there were movie nights and study time together. It was good to hear them talk about the future. Carrie and Justin approached them during their conversation.

"Carrie, I have good news. Jessie is going to apply to IPFW and be our third roomie!" Shelby exclaimed.

"Holy crap! That's the most awesome news I've had this week!" Carrie said with relief. "I am so excited. Us three. Sounds like a dream." Carrie stared off into space.

"I wish they would let guys room with ya'll." Justin said grudgingly.

Poor Justin. He didn't have many guy friends. He had some but not ones that he wanted to room with. I stood up against the wall and listened to them talk about college and the future.

"What are you guys doing this evening?" David approached us.

"Nothing." they all said in unison.

"Can you all meet me at Schnapps at seven-thirty?" David seemed depressed.

"Yeah. Why? What's up?" Justin asked.

"Just need to talk to you guys." David said.

David then turned to take his seat next to Miles Kale. Miles was David's gay friend. Miles didn't care who knew, and he wore it proudly that he was gay. *God, save us.*

"I bet . . ."

"Justin!" Carrie shot him a look, cutting him off.

"Whaaaaaat?" Justin bobbed his head. "We all know what it's about but no one wants to say it!" Justin blurted.

"Would you sit down?" Danni grabbed Justin by the shoulder and slammed him in his seat.

"Ouch!" Justin rubbed his shoulder.

The group had always thought that Danni and Justin had had a thing for each other, but no one said anything. The bell rang to start the class. Mr. Grouse barreled his way into the classroom. He looked ticked off. The students stared at him.

"I have gotten some extremely devastating news. Mr. Cook from PE will be taking over my class. Until then . . . study, talk, draw, text, sleep. Hell, I don't care." Mr. Grouse pulled at his yellow polo shirt. Word was that Mr. Grouse was due in court to end his thirty-seven year marriage to his wife, Ginger. She had fallen for another teacher in this school and planned on marrying him after divorcing Mr. Grouse. *God, give him strength and clarity of mind.* Mr. Grouse gathered his things and left the room in a hurry.

"Wow! Something bad went down." Jessie sighed.

"Divorce." Carrie informed. I shot my head toward Carrie. She knew?

"Yeah. I overheard Mr. Bile and Mrs. Kenkirk talking about how Mr. Grouse's wife was having an affair with someone else in this school." Carrie nodded.

"A student?" Danni's eyes widened.

"No, you twit! Another teacher." Justin rolled his eyes.

"Well, you never know."

"That's so sad." Jessie put her hand over her heart.

"So." Carrie said with no compassion.

"Just saying it's really sad." Jessie shook her head.

"Whatever." Justin sighed. "I really think David is going to come out to us." Justin said nervously changing the subject.

"Homophobe?" Carrie attacked.

"No. I have a gay cousin. I mean, I never talk to him but I still have one. If I did talk to him, I would talk to him like he's normal." Justin shot back.

"So being gay isn't normal?" Danni arched her brow.

"Ewwwww." Jessie grinned at Justin.

"Here we go." Carrie sighed and then rested her head in her hand.

"Well, if it was normal, would people make that big of a deal about it?" Justin defended.

"Well, being gay doesn't mean you're not normal." Danni argued.

"If you like to have sex with a person that has the *same* parts as you, you're demented." Justin threw his hands in the air.

"But God loves them!" Shelby added.

"I didn't say God didn't. I'm saying that I don't. I don't think I can be friends with David if he admits he's gay."

Justin looked over at David who was cutting up with his friend, Miles. He would lightly touch Miles' shoulder. Justin shivered.

"Justin, you're going to have to get over that." Jessie informed.

"Hey, I don't have to be friends with a gay if I don't want to." Justin was getting annoyed.

"You're friends with him now and you don't care." Danni noted. "Because once he admits he's gay, he's gay and it's out there and it's true."

"Justin, now you're being ridiculous." Shelby shook her head.

"Carrie, a little help." Justin looked over at Carrie.

"You're on your own, love." Carrie shrugged.

"Danni." Justin lowered his gaze. "You wouldn't even be sticking up for gays if your brother wasn't, so don't go there."

Justin's word split the room into. Silence fell on the group. I looked around and Mr. Cook had never shown up and the class period was almost over.

"Don't talk to me." Danni turned around.

"Danni." Justin sighed. He placed his scarred up hand on Danni's shoulder.

"Justin." Danni warned and smacked his hand off.

"Ugh. Women." Justin glared at his friends.

Period 5: Government

Jessie sat in front of Karla and rolled her eyes every time Karla giggled at a text message from Gerard. Ellen wasn't in class. Nicole sat alone with her head down. Something wasn't right. I felt the spirit of shame washing over Nicole. I wanted to reach out to her. Something was wrong. Karla kept giggling.

"He's that funny?" Jessie turned around.

"He's talking dirty." Karla bounced her eyebrows.

"Ha! Wow, that's funny." Jessie couldn't help but laugh.

"You and Jeremy do that?"

"Um . . . I don't think so." Jessie blushed.

"You should." Karla smiled. Uh . . . no . . . she should not!

"That's not my thing."

"Suit yourself." Karla shrugged replying to a text. "Here. Read this." Karla showed Jessie one of the messages he had sent her.

*"We def need to hang out more. I know we've been hangin almost every day this week but, man, when I look at you I just wanna *   *   *."*
Not reveling what the rest says but you get the picture.

"O-m-g, Karla." Jessie choked out. "Are you guys gonna . . . ?"

"Oh, probably not. I'm a tease." Karla smiled. "Are you and Leo talking yet?" Karla changed the subject.

"Nope." Jessie said popping the p.

"Ahhh." Karla said and then kept texting Gerard.

Karla and Jessie didn't talk all period. Karla texted Gerard and Jessie doodled. Jessie and Karla hadn't been hanging out much now that Karla had Gerard and Jessie and Jeremy and her other friends.

Period 7: English

Jessie and Jeremy walked together to English class. They talked about the day and about the new English assignment. Jessie and Jeremy passed Ellen and Leo talking.

"Can you believe Nicole would do that?" Ellen started to cry.

"What happened?" Jeremy whispered to Jessie.

"I don't know. Act like we're getting a drink of water." Jessie bent down to the smaller drinking fountain. Jeremy took the taller one.

"What?" Leo tucked Ellen's hair behind her ear.

"She got pregnant by Blake." Ellen fell into Leo.

"What the . . . ." Jessie spat out her water. Leo looked up at her.

"Wow!" Jeremy looked at Ellen. "Sucks to be you." Jeremy laughed. Leo glared at Jeremy.

"It's true. My best friend, well . . . ex—best friend . . . got pregnant by my ex-boyfriend." Ellen cried to Leo. People in the hall stared as they passed them.

"Ha! That's kinda funny." Jeremy adjusted his backpack.

"Jeremy, shut up." Leo glared.

"Or what?" Jeremy lunged forward in an attempt to scare Leo. Leo just looked at him.

"Jessie, get your friend." Leo glared at Jessie.

"I don't think he's doing anything wrong." Jessie shrugged.

"Come on, Ellen, let's get you to class." Leo wrapped his arm around her shoulder and walked her to class.

"Well, he can always knock Ellen up. Nicole always liked Leo." Jeremy noted. "Even the score." Jeremy laughed. Jessie hit Jeremy in the stomach.

"Don't talk like that." Jessie warned.

Jeremy gave Jessie a confused look. Jessie and Jeremy headed into the classroom and took their seats.

"Carrie, it doesn't matter. Jared's my boyfriend and I don't care what you think." Shelby argued.

"Oh, so you want a guy that stays in jail all the time." Carrie's eyebrows grew together and her cheeks turned red.

"It's none of your business." Shelby said almost crying.

"He's not good for you, Shelby!" Carrie argued.

"Shut up, Carrie. You're on my nerves."

"What's going on?" Jessie whispered to Justin.

"Well, Jared got locked up again and Carrie is pissed that Shelby is still with him. So now they're fighting." Justin informed.

"You've got to be kidding me." Jessie rolled her eyes.

"Oh, and Danni isn't talking to me." Justin glared over at Danni.

"James, just shut up." Allen said as he entered the classroom.

"No, Allen, I won't shut up. You took my car again without asking and I'm going to kick your ass." James lightly pushed Allen.

"Don't touch me." Allen warned. Allen and James were rather big guys. Allen was six foot three and James just as big. Each weighed three hundred and something pounds. So, if they got into a fight, it was going to be a very big and brutal one.

"Well, don't go stealin' people's stuff."

James sat at the table at the side of the room. The desks were too small for him and Allen.

"What happened?" Jeremy asked.

"This apple head took my car without asking to take some bimbo out." James gave Allen a dirty look.

"What's with them?" Allen ignored James's comment and nodded toward Justin and the others. Jeremy walked over to them.

"Well, Justin and Danni are mad at each other. I guess Danni was taking up for gays and Justin wasn't and Justin said the only reason she was is because her brother was gay. So that made Danni mad and now she's not talking to Justin. Carrie is arguing with Shelby because Shelby's boyfriend got locked up and she's still dating him, and Carrie doesn't think he's good enough. Erick is always mad for no reason, and now you guys are fighting." Jeremy unloaded information.

"Well, I'm not talking with Allen till I can gain his trust again." James turned his head away.

"You're such a baby."

Allen rolled his eyes and took his seat next to James at that table. The class was silent all period. I don't think Mrs. Lazarus knew what to do with a quiet class. She sounded nervous. Usually, when she was teaching, someone was talking. No one said a word.

Jessie climbed out of her truck and headed toward the house. Travis and her cousins, Ben and Rodney, were sitting and watching TV.

"Jess!" Rodney held up his Pepsi can.

"Rodney!" Jessie held up her car keys.

"How was school?" Ben asked.

"Not good. Everyone is fighting. I mean everyone." Jessie slammed down on the couch between Rodney and Ben.

"Who's everyone?" Travis looked over at Jessie from where he was sitting in the recliner.

"Me and Leo, Allen and James, Shelby and Carrie, Justin and Danni, and Ellen and Nicole. Ellen and Nicole I don't care about too much."

"Why are they fighting?" Rodney nibbed.

"Well, Danni and Justin got in a fight about gays. Shelby and Carrie got in a fight about Jared being locked up, and Carrie thinks he's not good enough for Shelby."

"Why did he get locked up?" Travis asked.

"Weed." Jessie widened her eyes. "Allen and James are fighting because Allen took James's car without asking. And Leo and I are still butting heads." Jessie sighed and rested her head on Rodney's shoulder.

"Wow. Why are Ellen and her friend fighting?" Ben asked.

"Nicole," Jessie took in a big sigh, "got knocked up by Ellen's ex-boyfriend, Blake." Jessie exhaled.

"Drama, drama, drama!" Travis laughed. "There wasn't that much drama when I went to high school." Travis shook his head.

"Me either." Ben agreed.

"Oh, there was that much drama. Ya'll just wasn't a part of it." Jessie patted Ben's knee and used it to lift herself off of the couch.

"That, and David wants all of us to meet at Schnapps at seven-thirty. He has to talk to us." Jessie rolled her eyes. "Justin thinks he's going to come out of the closet." Jessie shrugged.

"Oh." Travis looked at Ben and Rodney.

"Yeah. That's why Danni and Justin got into a fight. That's what started the whole gay thing." Jessie walked into the kitchen. "I'm going to grab a snack and do my homework." Jessie called.

"Alright." Travis called back.

Schnapps

Jessie, Justin, Danni, Carrie, and Shelby all sat at a rounded booth. I stood near Jessie who was seated at the end. No one said anything to anyone.

"I'm just here for David." Danni broke the awkward silence.

"Congratulations." Justin smarted.

"Screw you." Danni shot back.

"Guys!" Carrie yelled, shutting everyone up. There we sat in silence. Thirty minutes later, David and Miles entered the restaurant. David waved at us and started walking toward us.

"Here we go." Justin mumbled.

"Hey, peeps!" David chirped and hugged his friends one at a time. Justin lightly tapped David's back.

"Hello, David." Shelby smiled.

"Ya'll still fighting?" David grew sad.

"No, we're fine." Jessie faked.

"Hi everyone." Miles said as he grabbed two vacant chairs from a nearby table and gave one to David and one for him.

"Miles." Justin cleared his throat.

Everyone was uncomfortable. They knew what this meeting was about. They stared at each other and at David.

"Oh, child. Baby, you got to get happy." David laughed. It was a feminine laugh. I think he was trying to break the ice. "Everybody order?" David looked around the table.

"We have a boat load of cheese sticks and breadsticks and just these drinks. We all chipped in." Jessie smiled.

"Okay. Good . . . good." David placed his hand behind his neck and rested his arm on the table.

"David." Miles nodded to him.

"Okay." David hesitated. His voice was shaky. "You guys are my closest friends. I love you and I'm tired of lying." David's eyes filled with tears. Jessie looked at her friend who kept their eyes on David, everyone but Justin.

"We love you." Carrie spoke for all of them.

I stood back and listened. A part of me was nervous for him and a part of me was terrified for him and his chosen lifestyle.

"I . . ." David started to cry.

"It's okay." Miles rubbed his back.

Miles was very tall and skinny, pale skin, dark blue eyes, and light brown hair. He wore really tight jeans, a V-neck t-shirt, and a scarf. He almost always wore the pink one.

"I'm gay." David blurted. A sense of relief fell over him. He exhaled and smiled over at Miles.

"We know." They said in unison, and smiled . . . everyone but Justin.

"Oh my gaw. I feel so much better. My family knows and now my best friends." David exclaimed. He hugged Miles for a really long time. I hung my head and looked at Jessie. Justin was raging mad.

"Let me out." Justin stood up.

Jessie got out of the booth. Danni didn't move.

"Justin, you okay?" David asked.

"Shut up." Justin glared at David.

"Justin." Carrie glared.

I looked at David. His eyes glossed over with tears. Miles looked around at David's group of friends.

"Move, Danni, or I will move you." Justin threatened.

Jessie stood next to me. I could smell the ocean breeze scent of her hair. Danni didn't move. She kept sipping on her drink. Justin then pushed her and she fell to the floor.

"Justin, what the hell . . . ." Carrie yelled. Carrie and Shelby slipped out of the booth to Danni.

"I'm leaving." Justin grabbed his coat, looked down at Danni, and then exited the restaurant.

"What's wrong with him?" David asked as he got up to help with Danni.

"He doesn't like the fact that you're gay. He feels like he lost his only true guy friend." Jessie blurted. She sat down after Danni had gotten up and taken her seat.

"I'm still a guy," David argued, "that likes guys." Carrie said almost in Justin's defense. "I'm still the same person."

"Not to him." Carrie sipped her coke after they all had gotten resettled. Danni rubbed her elbow where she had fallen on it.

"He'll come around." Jessie bit into a cheese stick.

"I hope." David sighed.

The week went by slowly. Everyone was still mad at each other. Jessie and Karla had gotten into it about being distant. Jessie and her friends started getting distant. Justin refused to talk to Danni or David. Jessie and Leo were still not talking. Carrie and Shelby talked every so often, and Allen and James were still not on good terms. Everyone was fighting, and this is just what Hagab and his friends wanted—to turn everyone against each other.

Period 7: English 12

Jessie and her friends sat, not saying a word, not even looking at each other. Jessie had no one to talk to because Jeremy was absent. He and his family took a trip to Purdue University for a college day. The class was silent. No one talked, not even the students that got along. Jessie walked over to the pencil sharpener, passing Leo's desk. On the way back, he stopped her.

"Everyone's in a fight, huh?" Leo had his hand around Jessie's wrist. Jessie tossed her blonde hair over her shoulder with her free hand.

"Yes. It's sad, but we'll all come to our senses . . . all of us." Jessie looked down at him. He looked at her for a moment and then let her go.

Jessie sat in her room and stared at the floor. She had no one to call because everyone was in a fight and, if she called someone, they would bad mouth the other one and Jessie didn't want to get caught in the middle. Jessie missed Leo. She had Jeremy, but I know she missed Leo. Karla and Jessie had grown distant because of Gerard. Maybe these fights were for the best so they can see how much everyone's friendship meant to one another.

I smelled them. My skin crawled. Anton and Jealousy casually walked into Jessie's room.

"Well, our plan is working." Anton smiled at Jealousy. "Teens are so easy to manipulate. Oh, by the way, Iscariot and I got Sarah to kill Hannah. Now her baby has nowhere to go. I am amazing at what I do." Jealousy said to me as if trying to impress me.

"Leave us." I said through clenched teeth.

"Oh, I don't think so. We hold these worthless teens in the palm of our hands." Jealousy laughed, followed by Anton.

"I won't warn you again."

"Tristan. Lover. I am not going anywhere. These teens are trapped." Jealousy walked seductively toward me. I stood still with my fist clenched. Anton grabbed a dagger and threw it at me. I put my hand up to protect my face and the dagger penetrated my hand. The pain shot up my arm and to my brain. I grabbed the dagger with my other hand, ripped it out, and threw it to the ground. There was a nickel-sized hole in my hand.

"Ha, now you look like your precious Christ."

Jealousy hissed her forked tongue, slithering in and out of her mouth. I grabbed my sword and drew it to Jealousy's throat.

"Gonna do away with me?" Jealousy held up her hands. I said nothing.

"Give it up." Anton rolled his eyes.

The hole in my hand started to heal already. I took my sword and pushed it through Jealousy's throat with one thrust. She yelped and then fell to the ground. The thin handle of the sword hit the ground not letting Jealousy fall completely to the ground. It held her up. Anton came at me with his fists, punching me several times. Blackness covered my vision. I grabbed his ears and yanked down as hard as I could, ripping his ears off.

"Ah!" He let go of me and placed his hands where his ears had once been. Jealousy couldn't move. The sword had her propped up. She squirmed like a worm on a hook. Anton jumped forward and landed on me. My head cracked against Jessie's computer desk. His blood flowed from the open gashes at the sides of his head. He clawed at my face and his long fingernails dug into my skin. I grabbed his hand, took his fingers, and bent them back. I heard them snap as the bones broke. He yelled in pain, fell back, and rested against the computer desk. I looked at Jealousy still struggling. She was now her demonic self. Her beauty had left her. I walked over to where she was and kicked the sword down. She dropped and the sword went all the way through. I looked at Anton. He couldn't move. I then looked at Jessie, who was now asleep. I rolled Jealousy over with my foot, grabbed the handle of my sword, and ripped it out of her throat. Blood and steam left her body. I looked at my sword—the sword I've had for eighteen years. It was made by Truce to protect Jessie and it has been through a lot. I walked over to Anton. He looked up at me. He tried to show despair in his eyes, probably trying to get me to spare him. I don't think so. I looked down at him, and my eyebrows grew together with anger. I lifted up my foot and kicked him repeatedly in the face. I ripped his nose off, and his jaw cracked under the pressure of my kick. He started to jerk, and he was choking on his own teeth. I kept kicking. I just couldn't stop. I had kicked him so badly that his face was so distorted. I couldn't even recognize him. I finally stopped and looked down at him. He laid limp. I was tired of them. I was tired of them ruining people's lives. I looked around Jessie's room and blood had painted the walls. We needed a clean-up in here. Jealousy and Anton's bodies did the normal thing after they had gotten defeated—violently twitched and then combusted. Green smoke filled the room, followed by a white fog which engulfed the smoke. I covered my face with my arm. After several minutes, I opened my eyes. The room was blood free and the fog was gone. They cleaned up for me. *Thanks*. I looked to the heaven. Another battle fought. Another battle won. Another battle yet to come.

CHAPTER 11

Leo and Jessie

Period 2: Geometry

Jessie and her friends still weren't getting along with one another. When one said something, another would smart off causing the other one to get mad and lash out. Nothing was going right. I figured it would all blow over by now, but it was almost Christmas vacation and then the semester would change two weeks after we got back from Christmas break. The classrooms were decorated with bright colors of green, red, blue, and silver. I was definitely into the Christmas spirit. It was only two weeks away. When it got around Christmas time, the teachers tended to be more lenient on their students. I guess the happy, joyful, and loving spirit just took over them.

"I can't believe it's almost Christmas." Jessie whispered to Shelby.

"I know. I am beyond excited." Shelby beamed.

"Is Jared going to be out for Christmas?" Jessie leaned closer to Shelby so Carrie wouldn't hear.

"Yes. He said he's got a surprise for me." Shelby giggled.

"Oh. Are you getting him anything?"

"Yeah. I got him a really nice watch, an Indianapolis Colts jersey, and a gas card." Shelby informed. She looked over at Carrie, who sat with her head in her hand working on her packet.

"That's a lot." Jessie squinted.

"I know, but I love him." Shelby sighed.

"Ha! It's all good." Jessie tapped her pencil on her desk.

"You getting Jeremy anything?"

"No." Jessie laughed.

"Why?"

"I don't want to do that, and I really don't have the money. Plus, I don't think he's getting me anything." Jessie shrugged.

"I'm sorry, Jess."

"Psh. I don't care." Jessie shrugged at Shelby's apology.

"Have you talked to Leo at all?" Shelby drew in a sigh.

"Nope." Jessie clicked her tongue.

"Wow, Jessie, it's been like a month."

"I know. It's all good." Jessie shrugged.

"Jess." Shelby narrowed her gaze.

"Okay, okay. I miss him a lot, and I hate that he's all close to Ellen." Jessie started to rub her temples. "But what am I going to do? He doesn't want to listen to what I have to say." Jessie looked over at Shelby.

"Could you guys shut up? Some of us are trying to do our work." Erick smarted.

"We're not even being that loud, so shut up!" Shelby bit off.

"I'm with Erick." Carrie batted her eyes mocking Shelby.

"You would be." Shelby scoffed.

"Come on, Shelby, it's not worth it. Just let it go." Jessie caught Shelby's attention.

"You're right." Shelby turned around and started working on her packet again.

Jessie and her friends sat in silence the whole period. A couple of dirty looks were thrown here and there, but nothing was said. Anton and Jealousy had their grip on these teens. They did have them right where they wanted them. Well, God was going to turn this around for the better. I was praying for reconciliation. This is their senior year and there shouldn't be all these fights. They should be cherishing these moments, because I know that after graduation they will more than likely never speak again or speak very seldom. *God, bring peace and love to these teens. Show them how much friendship means and how much they need each other. Squash their pride and cause them to reconcile.*

Period 3: Business Foundations

A big Christmas tree sat in the corner of the room. There were fake presents beneath it. It had blue bulbs and silver garland (school colors).

The bulbs ranged from big, medium, and small. The lights were blue, and there was popcorn garland tangled around the silver. There was also a beautiful angel that sat on top of the tree. She really reminded me of Purity—long, blonde curly hair and eye.s that penetrated your soul. Just beautiful.

"Woo! Christmas!" Jeremy pumped his fist as soon as he saw the Christmas tree. The kids who were in class erupted with laughter. Jessie smiled and rolled her eyes.

"I am so ready for Christmas. Florida, here I come." Jeremy looked down at Jessie.

"No. Christmas isn't Christmas without snow." Jessie cocked her head at him.

They walked over to their seats. Jessie plopped down in her seat and rested her head on her desk.

"What's the matter?" Jeremy asked as he took his seat next to Jessie.

"I really need to make things right with Leo." Jessie sighed and looked over to Jeremy.

"But everything is going great. You're not stressed and your grades are still up." Jeremy explained.

"I know, but he's my best friend. He always has been and always will be." Jessie shrugged and then rested her head on her desk.

"Jessie. I would let it go." Jeremy said.

Jeremy looked over to where Leo was seated. Hate and jealousy overcame him. Jessie popped her head up and looked over at Jeremy.

"Do you not want me to be friends with him again?" Jessie squinted. Busted!

"I don't care." Jeremy shrugged and his face was starting to turn red. Guilty as charged!

"Jeremy." Jessie lowered her gaze. "We'll still be friends, but I miss him."

Jessie looked over at Leo. He sat doing his work assignment that were on the board. Jessie sighed and smiled. Leo's hair had grown quite a bit since the beginning of the year. It was now down to his shoulder. His facial hair was neatly trimmed. He had been working on his body appearance. I noticed his arms were bigger and his stomach was more lean. Jessie saw it, too, and liked it. Leo looked behind him and caught Jessie's eye. She smiled. He stared for a moment and then smiled back. Baby steps. Jeremy looked from Jessie to Leo, and a growl surfaced in his throat.

"Jeremy." Jessie sighed.

"If you want to be miserable, fine." Jeremy bit off.

Jeremy turned his attention to his work assignment. He didn't say anything to Jessie for most of the period. She sat there taking the cap of her pen on and off, on and off, on and off. The period was almost over and I could tell Jessie was getting irritated with how slow the time was going. Even though she knew she had absolutely no control over it, I think that made her irritated more than anything.

"I'm so over this class." Jessie moaned.

"Jessie, it's going to be okay. Thirty minutes left is all." Shelby rested her hand on Jessie's shoulder.

"These thirty minutes seem like ten year. I could have gotten married and popped out a couple kids." Jessie laughed.

"Same here." Shelby joined in laughing.

"I have a while before that happens, though." Jessie sighed.

"Me, too. Heck I might have to get married in a prison." Shelby teased.

"Awe, don't think that." Jessie sympathized.

"Jessie will have to get married over the border." Jeremy blurted.

Jeremy glared at Jessie. Leo turned around. The comment had traveled. Jessie looked at Leo, and her eyes filled with regret.

"Jeremy, that was really uncalled for." Jessie lowered her head.

"He didn't hear me." Jeremy shrugged.

"Um, yes he did." Shelby pointed. Jeremy turned around to find Leo glaring at him.

'Face it. You have one of those voices that carries." Jessie smarted.

"My bad, bro." Jeremy pushed his head up at Leo.

"That apology was weak." Jessie scoffed.

"Well, that's all he's getting."

Period 6: Orchestra

Violins screeched, cellos rumbled, violas grumbled, and basses moaned. The students were tuning their instruments. Jessie had had hers tuned, so she started practicing the latest song "Never an Absolution" from the movie "The Titanic". Jessie was the first person in the second row of violins, which means that she sat next to Carrie in the viola section. Justin sat next to Jessie on her other side, and David was clear across the room with his cello. He was a mean cello player. He was first cello and the best high school cellist I had ever seen. The music vibrated from the strings and filled the room with blissful music. Jessie squirmed in her seat for a while before attempting to talk to Carrie or Justin.

"I hate that everyone is fighting. It's our senior year." Jessie blurted.

"Jessie." Justin grew irritated.

"You started yours." Jessie looked over at him. Justin shrugged in attempt to not care.

"Well, I can't help how I feel."

"Come on. I'm about to swallow my pride and talk with Leo." Jessie looked to Carrie.

Carrie flinched at Jessie's remark causing her to hit a dirty note on her viola. Mrs. LeBell looked up from her piano.

"Sorry." Carrie blushed.

"Watch your fingering." Mrs. LeBell cast a glare upon Carrie.

"We're not even playing yet. She's tuning a violin. Carrie, it's all good." Jessie reassured.

"Look, Jess. I love Shelby. She's one of my best friends, but she's making a really bad choice."

"Carrie, then let her make it. If you've tried talking to her and she doesn't want to listen, just let it go." Jessie said with certainty.

"I don't want her with him. He's worthless."

"Then you need to tell her that in a nicer way. I know that's not your thing, but come on. This group is being ripped apart."

"It's all your fault." Justin blamed. Jessie turned around shocked.

"My fault?" Jessie put her hand to her chest.

"Yeah! If you wouldn't have been so mean to Leo, none of this would have happened. Have you noticed that you broke the group first?"

Justin glared at Jessie. He rested his violin between his shoulder and cheek. His scruffy brown hair peeked out from beneath his black and gray striped beanie.

"I said I was going to talk to Leo. It's been a month and I'm going to try to get my best friend back. If he doesn't hear me out, then that's not my fault. But I know you guys all care about each other and never once have I seen you fight. Get over it." Jessie looked from Carrie to Justin. Not one said a word.

Period 7: English 12

Jessie had made it to the last class of the day. Today went by rather smoothly. There were some pumps along the way but not major. Jessie walked in and found Shelby and Carrie laughing and talking. Relief overcame both of us. *Thank you, Jesus.* "Thank you, Jesus." Jessie repeated. Jessie saw Justin talking to Danni. His face was serious and he was using a lot of hand movement. Then they would start laughing. Seems like everyone was reconciling. Jessie took her seat and smiled at her friend.

"You were right, Jess. It's our senior year and it's time to have fun." Shelby smiled.

"Right. I gotta talk to Leo, at least attempt to anyway." Jessie sighed.

"He'll listen." Carrie reassured.

Justin and Danni were laughing hard now. Their faces were red, and their eyes were watering. They grabbed their stomachs from the cramping because they were laughing too hard. Jessie smiled as she looked at her friends. Love and understanding washed over her. Her next step was Leo. Fear came over her as she contemplated on what to say to him. The minute bell rang to start class. Jeremy ran in at lightning speed before the tardy bell rang. He fell on his desk.

"Woo. Thought I was going to be late." Jeremy straightened his posture.

"You made it." Jessie beamed.

"Class. Listen up. I've made a fun little Christmas packet for you. It's for extra credit, and some of you need it." Mrs. Lazarus laid the stack of packets at the corner of her desk. "Now, I have written on the board which pages to read and assessment questions to answer when you're done reading. We're going to have a down day. I have a lot of grading to do and a lot of preparing to do for the final exam." Mrs. Lazarus sighed.

"Holy crap, Mrs. L., that's a lot of stuff." Jessie pointed to the board with her pencil. The chalkboard was completely covered with reading assignments.

"I know it will keep you busy." Mrs. Lazarus smiled.

"So, we have to do all of it?" Jeremy asked.

"Yes." Mrs. Lazarus smiled again.

"I'm . . . going . . . to . . . die." Jessie said slowly. She rested her head on her desk.

"Oh, Craig, you're going to be fine." Mrs. Lazarus assured.

"No, I'm not!" Jessie argued.

"Oh, stop whining. Jeremy will help you." Mrs. Lazarus nodded over to Jeremy.

"Good point." Jessie smiled. Jessie opened her English book to page 452 and started reading. The story was called "Too Late to Call". It was about a man and a woman who had been in love but let others get in the way of that love. They eventually broke the bond between them. The woman went off to Africa on mission trips and he studied medicine at Harvard University. Years and years had gone by. They finally met each other one day in South Florida for a medical retreat. They rekindled their love, but the lady was dying of AIDS that she contracted in Africa. She was a nurse and one of the kids who was born with AIDS had had a cut. The woman fixed the child up. Sweat had poured off of the lady's face because the heat in Africa was so intense. She wiped her forehead and eyes not realizing she contracted the AIDS virus. She and her old love couldn't be together because of her having AIDS, but he stayed with her until she had died. Sad story. I noticed periodically Jessie would glance over at Leo and he would glance over at Jessie. *Come on, Lord, if it's your will.* The bell rang to release the students for the day.

"Turn in what you have, please." Mrs. Lazarus shouted over the hustle and bustle of the students packing up and heading home.

Jessie and Leo approached the desk at the same time. They looked at each other but said nothing. Jessie placed her papers on the pile of work at the corner of Mrs. Lazarus's desk. "Thank you, Miss Jessie."

Jessie and I headed to her locker. Jeremy didn't stop at the locker at the end of the day. He went straight to the senior parking lot to talk with friends. Jessie and I stood at the locker, and I watched her as she exchanged books.

"See ya tomorrow, Jessie." Carrie said as she walked passed.

"Bye." Jessie smiled sweetly at her friend.

Jessie's long, blonde hair swung back and forth as she reached for her Geometry book on the top shelf. All of Jeremy's books fell out.

"Ugh. I told him to stop that." Jessie scoffed to herself. Jessie bent down and started picking up Jeremy's books.

"Jessie."

Jessie turned around and saw Leo standing in front of her at a distance. Jessie had all of Jeremy's books gathered in her arms. She looked at Leo and blew her stray bangs away from her face.

"Leo, how are you?" Jessie asked like nothing had ever gone wrong. It was like she was saying hi to a long lost friend.

"Good. Um, I . . . uh . . . I really miss hanging out with you." Leo blurted.

Jessie turned around and placed Jeremy's books back on the shelf. She didn't turn around for a moment. She took in a deep breath. *Lord, give her strength.* I leaned my back against the locker and folded my arms over my chest.

"I really miss hanging out with you, too."

Jessie grabbed her Accounting book out of the locker. Leo walked closer. He was at her side now. I leaned forward.

"Can we put this all behind us?" Leo asked while shifting his back pack to his other shoulder.

Jessie looked into the locker not saying anything. Finally, she looked to Leo.

"You have to promise that you will never throw this fight in my face, and I promise I will never throw this fight in your face."

Leo smiled. "I promise."

"Alright. The past is the past." Jessie stated. "I missed you." Jessie lunged forward hugging Leo. His laughter filled the vacant hallway. They hugged for a long time.

"I feel so much better." Jessie said almost crying.

"I know. It's senior year, and we cannot waste it with being mad at each other." Leo said with a half smile.

"I agree." Jessie nodded her head and smiled.

"Jeremy's gonna be pissed."

"Oh, he'll get over it." Jessie laughed. "What about Ellen?"

"Oh, we weren't as close as I led on. She liked to hang out with a lot of guys all the time and I couldn't handle being with someone like that . . . kinda not even as just a friend." Leo's face fell with defeat.

"Awe." Jessie hugged Leo again. They laughed and talked about life all the way down the hall and out of the school.

Jessie and I got to her house. She practically flew out of her truck and into her house.

"Mama!" Jessie ran into the house. "Mama!"

Jessie walked into the kitchen. No mom. She walked into the laundry room. No mom. She finally walked into her mom and dad's bedroom. There she was. Jessie smiled at her mom as she folded towels on the bed.

"Daughter." Toni looked up.

"Leo and I are friends again!" Jessie squealed.

"Really?!" Toni grew excited.

"Yup." Jessie walked over and hugged her mom.

"That's great, sweetie. He's a good kid."

"I know. I'm so happy we're friends again." Jessie grabbed a towel and started helping Toni fold.

"So, how are all your other friends?" Toni asked.

"It had to be a miracle from God, because we all like reconciled in the same day. It was really cool." Jessie finished folding her towel and put it on the pile of other ones that Toni had already folded.

"Tell me what happened with you and Leo" Toni smiled.

"Oh . . . well . . . I'm at me and Jeremy's locker. I reach for my Geometry book and all of Jeremy's books fall out. They're all on the floor." Jessie grabbed another towel from the heap of unfolded towels. "Then I gather them all up and I hear this deep voice say 'Jessie'. I turn around and see Leo standing there looking as cute as can be. All I said was 'How are you doing?' like nothing had ever gone wrong. Well, he said 'Good. Um . . . I . . . uh . . . I really miss hanging out with you', and that floored me. Leo doesn't say stuff like that." Jessie shook her head.

"Hardly any man does." Toni interrupted.

"True. Well, then we started talking about how we shouldn't fight and everyone else was getting along now. Well, we hugged and stuff. Then we walked to the senior parking lot and then went our separate ways." Jessie finished folding the towel and placed it on the pile.

"I'm so happy for you, honey. I really am. You were different when you guys weren't friends. It's like there's no Leo without Jessie and no Jessie without Leo." Toni grabbed a pile of freshly folded towels and headed to the bathroom. Jessie followed.

"Yeah, that's what a lot of people told me. It's always Jessie and Leo." Jessie leaned against the doorframe of the bathroom.

"True. You guys have been through a lot." Toni turned and smiled at Jessie. "I knew it was all going to work out. You just have to do your own thing for a while." Toni shrugged. She placed the towels in the cabinet then faced Jessie. "Well, now you guys have a fresh start, and now it can be Leo and Jessie again."

CHAPTER 12

New Semester

Christmas break went really well. Jessie had fun with her family and some friends. She decided to give school life and teen drama a break and just hang out with her family for two weeks. Jessie got clothes, stuff for her truck, gift cards, and tons of books for Christmas. She was happy with all she got. Leo had gotten Jessie two Spongebob DVDs and a pair of Spongebob pajama bottoms. Jessie loved Spongebob. She watched him every day since she was in the sixth grade. Jessie had gotten Leo a really nice jacket. It was black with red, white, and green stripes going down the sleeves. It said "MEXICO" across his chest in green letters when you zipped it up. At the corner of the jacket was a Mexico flag with the soccer symbol underneath. He loved the jacket. He thanked Jessie several times. He told her 'It's the best gift I've ever gotten' and then would hug her for the tenth time. Karla got Jessie a teddy bear and some body spray, lotion, and body wash. Jessie got Karla a friendship bracelet, a stuffed animal that was a penguin, and vanilla body spray.

The new semester was coming around the corner. When we went back to school on Monday, we would have exactly two weeks till the next semester started. Time was going fast. Before we know it, Jessie's going to be a high school graduate. Then she was going to be thrust out into the real world and that meant I was working double time. High school life is hard, but nothing is harder than the real world—leaving your parents' protection, striving to become who you want to be, and people shooting you down along the way. Jessie is my human and I'm in for the long haul.

"I don't want to go back to school." Jessie leaned her head on Mike's shoulder.

"You have one semester left." Mike patted her head.

"Yeah, but do you know how long those semesters last?"

"Awhile." Mike chuckled.

"Three, six-week periods. That's eighteen weeks!" Jessie exclaimed.

"I know." Mike said stirring the chili.

"Where's Mom?" Jessie threw some onions into the chili pot.

"With your aunt Indy." Mike sighed.

"Gag me." Jessie rolled her eyes.

Jessie and her dad didn't get along with Jessie's aunt Indy. Aunt Indy was a very conniving person. She lied about anything and everything. She tried to cause other family members to turn against each other but glorify herself when she brought them together. She was very strange.

"I know, I know, but it's your mother's sister."

"Who's a back biting . . . ."

"Don't finish that sentence." Mike pointed the spoon at Jessie.

"Okay, okay." Jessie held up her hands in front of her. "I'm just saying, Dad."

"And I agree." Mike said with a grin, causing him and Jessie to burst out in laughter.

Jessie and her dad cooked supper for the rest of the family. I sat at the kitchen table as Jessie told her dad about life, and he helped as much as he could. I heard the front door open, and a cold breeze rushed through the house.

"They're here." Jessie's eyes widened.

"Hide the weapons." Mike teased.

"Mike, honey, I'm home. It smells good in here. Indy is staying for dinner. Is that okay?" Toni called from the living room.

"Fine." Mike said dryly.

"Smells good, Michael." Indy called.

"Smells good, Michael." Jessie and Mike mocked in unison with their faces scrunched up and their voices high.

"Thanks." Mike grew serious.

Jessie tried not to laugh. I couldn't help but let a smile creep across my face.

"Mike, I have a question about my car if you don't mind answering."

Indy walked into the kitchen. I looked up at her. Her face was drawn and her skinny body was haggard. She reeked of cigarette smoke. Her oversized coat draped over her body and her jeans were soaked at the end from the snow.

"Um . . . sure. We can talk after dinner." Mike said, not taking his eyes off of stirring the chili.

"Thanks." Indy said coldly. She then turned on her heels and headed to the living room with Toni.

"No one told me the witch was here." Travis said as he barged through the kitchen from the back door.

Travis lowered his head and tried not to see aunt Indy because she would always ask him to draw her up something or try to get him to date her best friend's daughter Maria. Also, Travis, like Mike and Jessie, didn't care for Aunt Indy.

"You can't avoid her all night." Mike arched his brow.

"Yes. I'm just here to pee. I'm leaving with Danny and Matt. They're in the ally. I saw Indy's car and was like 'Go the back way. Go the back way!' Travis exclaimed. "Can I use your bathroom?" Travis lowered his voice barely above a whisper.

"I don't care." Jessie said and gave him a look that said 'Why would you ask me that?'.

Travis bolted to Jessie's room. He jumped into the kitchen, kissed Jessie on her head, and darted out the back door. I walked over and stood next to Jessie. She and I looked out the window and watched Travis scurry across the back yard jumping over piles of snow and mud puddles. Danny and Matt were hanging out the window cheering him on. It was a funny sight to see. Travis dove into the car, slammed the door shut, and Danny sped away.

"Boys." Jessie laughed.

"Supper's done." Mike called. We heard Toni and Indy get up and head toward the kitchen.

"I'm so hungry." Toni grabbed her stomach.

"Me, too." Jessie added.

Jessie greeted her mom with a kiss on the cheek. She caught Indy's eye. Indy just glared at her. She had five boys and no girls and was always jealous of the relationship Jessie had with Toni.

First Day Back from Break

Jessie laid in bed until thirty minutes before having to leave for school. She groaned and grunted as the minutes passed her by. Finally,

Jessie turned on her bedside lamp and stumbled out of bed. She grabbed her clothes and headed to her bathroom. She quickly got dressed and brushed her teeth and hair.

"I don't want to go back." She sighed as she slipped on her Adidas shoes. She grabbed her backpack and headed to her truck.

"You get your new schedule today." Toni kissed Jessie's cheek.

"Yeah . . . not too excited. What if I don't have any of my friends in my class?" Jessie feared.

"You will. You have a lot of friends. It would be hard for you not to." Toni reassured.

"I guess, Mama." Jessie said.

We headed out the door. Jessie looked at her cell phone. School started in fifteen minutes and it would take her ten minutes to get there. She had Algebra first period and it would take her five minutes from the back of the parking lot. Hopefully, traffic wouldn't keep us. We made our way into the senior parking lot. Jessie found a vacant spot between Gerard and Carrie's car. She and I jumped out of the truck and dashed to the double door. Jessie pulled on the large silver handle. They were locked. The hallways were vacant.

"Piss!" Jessie yelled. "I'm not going to freakin' walk around if I can't get in. My happy ass is going home." Jessie kicked the door in anger. *Lord, let us in* I prayed. About five seconds later, Leo was walking down the hallway. He saw Jessie at the door and jogged over to her. He opened the door.

"Apparently, my watch is off." Jessie said as he opened the door.

"It's fine. I'm late, too. All seniors are supposed to be in the auditorium for schedules." Leo led Jessie by the arm.

"Leo, I know the way there." Jessie released from his grip.

"Sorry, but I don't like being late and there's going to be a huge line for schedules." Leo hurried Jessie.

"Oh my gosh." Jessie and Leo finally made it to the auditorium which was packed with their peers.

People studied their schedules, compared with their friends, and complained about what teachers they had. The line wasn't very long, so Jessie and Leo got in the back. We waited, and they finally got to their counselor.

"Leo and Jessie. Together again." Mrs. Finley smiled.

"Like mac and cheese." Jessie teased.

"Here's yours, Jessie." Mrs. Finley said as she handed Jessie her schedule. Jessie moved out of the line and looked over her schedule.

Art/ Jewelry with Ms. James
Algebra 2 with Mr. Delarosa
Business Foundations with Mrs. Tully
Accounting with Mr. Grouse
Sociology with Mr. Neal
Orchestra with Mrs. LeBell
English 12 with Mrs. Lazarus

Her schedule was basically the same, only two classes had changed.

"Jessie, let me see." Carrie said as she walked up to us.

Shelby, Justin, David, Danni, and Erick followed. Jessie handed her schedule to Carrie. All of them huddled around their schedules.

"Two classes with me." Shelby ran her finger down the line of classes.

"Five with me. Gee, Jess, we practically have all day together." Justin said shocked.

"Four" David said.

"Three." Carrie followed.

"One" Danni sighed.

"Let me see." Karla demanded as she barreled through and ripped the paper from Carrie's grasp.

Karla scanned her eyes over the schedule. Gerard stood behind her, not saying anything to any of them.

"We only have two classes together." Karla whined.

Karla handed the schedule back to Jessie. Carrie and the rest stood glaring at Karla. Karla paid no mind. Leo made his way toward Jessie and the others. Karla jerked his schedule from him and scanned over it. Leo grew angry.

"Thank you!" Leo snatched his schedule back.

"It's cool we have no classes together." Karla shrugged and then put her sucker in her mouth.

"Good." Leo said and then looked over at Jessie. "May I?" he asked for her schedule.

"Oh, yeah." Jessie handed it to him. Leo scanned it with a smile on his face.

"Three classes together. That's awesome." Leo beamed.

"I know. I was so afraid I wasn't going to have any friends in my classes." Jessie sighed.

I saw Jeremy walking over to us.

"Jessie" he nodded. "Jessie's friends" as he greeted the rest.

"Hey, Jer. You like your schedule?" Jessie played with the straps on her backpack.

"Depends." Jeremy looked at Jessie.

"On?"

"If I have classes with you." Jeremy smiled.

"Awe." Jessie put her hand to her chest. Her friends smiled at her.

"Please." Leo scoffed and looked away.

"Let's see." Jessie stood next to Jeremy and pulled her schedule up next to his.

"We have three together!" Jessie exclaimed.

"Now I'm happy with my schedule." Jeremy smiled and brushed his hair out of his eyes.

I stood and looked at Jessie and her friends, who were talking amongst each other.

"Hey, Leo, you have one of those classes with me and Jeremy." Jessie turned and got Leo's attention.

"Oh, great." Leo said sarcastically. Jeremy and Leo shot each other a dirty look.

A part of me was dreading this new semester, but I had to be strong. Jehovah knew what he was doing. I just had to keep my faith in Him.

Jessie and I drove home from school. On the way home we listened to Drake Bell. Jessie got a call from Karla.

"Hello?" Jessie answered.

"So I thought it was really rude for you to ignore Gerard the way you did." Karla lashed out.

"What?"

"When we got our schedules." Karla hissed.

"No joke. I really didn't see him. I was busy with other friends." Jessie rebutted.

"Right, because those wannabes are like your new best friends." Karla boomed through the phone.

"Karla, are you being for real?" Jessie sighed.

"Yes, I am. We better not grow distant. You do not want me against you." Karla threatened and then hung up. Jessie looked at her phone and then to the road.

"What the hell was that?"

Jessie put her phone on her seat next to her. She shook her head in annoyance and kept driving. I sat in the passenger's seat. Out of nowhere, Hagab's large frame was standing in the middle of the road. We were gonna hit him. We drove right through him. As Jessie's truck was only a foot away from him, he jumped into the bed of the truck. I climbed through the half cab and out the window. I faced Hagab. His large frame made the truck look like a hot wheel car. The cold wind slapped against us. My hair danced with the wind. Hagab said nothing. He grabbed me under my arms, flipped me on the roof of the truck, and pinned me down. His face was an inch away from mine. His eyes stared into mine, and I saw demons dance in his eyes. His razor sharp teeth pierced his gums, and his tongue was covered in boils.

"You got me sent to the pit again, pretty boy."

He hissed at me. I lifted my leg and kicked his stomach. He flew backward and crashed against the tailgate.

"You just won't stop, will you?"

I jumped up and stood in the bed of the truck. His massive body caused the tailgate to fly open. His head fell back. He grabbed onto the metal levers that helped the tailgate open and close.

"I don't think so."

I jumped on him, grabbed his head, and, with all my might, pushed his head to the road. It slammed against the road. It jerked up and bounced. Hagab screamed in pain. His head ripped open from the pavement. I gritted my teeth trying to keep his head down. His arms flew in the air, and his body was about to fly off of the bed of the truck and onto the road. He grabbed my hair in a death grip and we both flew out of the back of the truck.

"Jesaiah!" I managed to yell.

I knew I couldn't leave Jessie unattended for even a minute. The enemy would be all over her and would destroy her. Jesaiah bolted down to earth and was on his way to Jessie. Hagab and I rolled down the street. Gravel sliced our bodies and our skin burned from the friction of the pavement. Hagab let go of my hair. We finally came to a stop. I got up and looked down at him. He grabbed his head, which was gushing with blood, and screamed in pain.

"Don't' start stuff you can't finish."

I kicked him. I clenched my teeth in pain as the wind struck against the rips and burns on my flesh. He turned over with a smile—a wicked smile.

"Happy New Semester." He boomed with laughter. "Be prepared for a fight, Tristan." he yelled at me. He pulled his body forward and gnashed his teeth at me.

"I'm prepared and I'm bringing heaven with me!"

I kicked his face and he fell back. I turned around and, in front of me, stood more than ten thousand demons. Some were on four legs, some six, some eight. Some had a head full of eyes. Some had their mouths sown shut. They all twitched their heads at me. I looked at them showing them that I wasn't afraid. They licked their lips and snarled at me. Jealousy and Anton stood in the front with Jezebel next to her and then Jealousy, whom I haven't seen in a very long time. No one said a word. Peace came over me. Then, for some reason, I took a step forward. I looked behind me and saw more than fifteen thousand angels standing behind me. Truce, Purity, and Victor stood in front and Michael stood in front of them. His cape was blowing in the wind and his gold breastplate shining in the sun. I smiled at them and then turned to the demons and smiled. Let the battle begin.

CHAPTER 13

Ready for Battle

There was something eerie about this night. The air felt warm and it was in the middle of winter. It was midnight and the sky was a mixture of orange and black color. The moon looked darker in color. Something was wrong. I closed the drapes and looked toward Jessie as she slept. She seemed at peace. Then I pulled the drape slightly back. This night did not feel right. My spirit said so. It was like the demons were out there and more fierce than ever before. I looked back over at Jessie. Her breathing turned heavy. I walked over to her and, when I went to touch her cheek, a scaly black hand grabbed my wrist. I looked up and saw a demon glaring at me. Its head twitched from side to side, as if trying to study me. I pulled my hand away.

"Tristan." Its voice was scratchy and demonic. It was a lady. She walked closer to me. Her face was scaly, and she had a black cloak that hung over her shoulders. Her eyes were dark blue, almost like indigo. She didn't attack me, and I stood there looking at her.

"Tristan" she choked out. "I'm not here to fight."

"Your kind is always here to fight."

"My name is Tallulah. I'm here to tell you about the great war." her voice trailed. I stood a distance from her.

"You're not welcome here." I clenched my teeth.

"Shhhh." I saw her forked tongue slither out. "Dear angel, Lucifer is calling a great war against you and your kind."

She raised her hands in the air. The hood of her cloak dropped back reveling an enormous brain that was not covered by a skull. The sight made me want to throw up. I put my forearm over my mouth.

"Listen, Tristan. Lucifer has sent me."

"And I suggest you leave. I don't want to hear anything you have to say, Tallulah!" I yelled at her.

"Yes, you do."

"No. The only information I need is from God."

"Tristan, listen." Truce now stood beside me.

"Listen to your angel friend." Tallulah hissed. Her brain pulsated while information spewed from her mouth.

"Prepare for a great war, one like you have never fought before, Tristan. Prepare to be slain." she said with a laugh.

"Woman!" Truce drew his sword and placed it on her throat, drawing blood.

"Listen, you stupid twit." She swallowed.

"What war?" Truce asked as his eyes flashed with anger.

"A war for Jessie's soul. It has begun." Tallulah laughed.

"It's been this way since she was born." I crossed my arms over my chest and stared at Tallulah.

"No, stupid." She turned her attention to me. "She's powerful spiritually. I know you know that, and Lucifer knows that."

Tallulah looked up to the heaven and pointed her scaly finger up to God. Her yellow, cracked fingernails reached toward the sky. "He knows that," she growled. "We can't let her be on His side. We need her with us!" Tallulah yelled.

"Shut up!" Truce pushed the tip of his sword harder against her neck. She struggled to breathe. The more she inhaled, the more the sword cut her.

"Be prepared, angels. Be prepared."

She laughed and then disappeared. Her laugh still echoed in Jessie's room. I looked around the room. Jessie had calmed her breathing and was now sleeping peacefully. I looked to Truce and he had put his sword back in its place.

"Truce." I looked at him.

"You stay here and keep protecting Jessie. That's your job. I will get the others ready. We'll lay out a plan and attack."

"What if they attack first?" I asked.

"They won't. We're attacking on their way to her." Truce smiled at me. "Trust me, dear brother." He put his hand on my shoulder.

"I do." I nodded to him.

"I thank God every day that I'm not a human." Truce looked over at Jessie sleeping and shook his head.

"Why?"

"They have it too hard." Truce boomed with laughter. I didn't see what was funny, but he did.

"What?" I wasn't grasping what he was saying.

"Tristan, think about it. They have to choose Lucifer or God. We are already with God. They have to choose whether they want to be tormented in hell or live an everlasting life in heaven. They're tempted every day. Bad things happen to them every day. They stress and they struggle. That, my brother, is not the life I would want to live." Truce explained.

Now was the best time to ask.

"You ever get tired of being a warrior?" I looked into his rugged face.

"I wasn't always a warrior, you know." Truce looked at me from the corner of his eye.

"What?" I said in disbelief.

"Really. Before you became Jessie's angel, you were an angel just walking around oblivious to all that was around. You were happy and you spent a lot of time with Jesus and Gabriel." Truce smiled at me.

"I was on earth guarding my human." Truce revealed.

"Wait. You were a guardian angel?" I said shocked.

"Ha! You say that like it would be impossible, Tristan." Truce laughed. "He was a doctor. He had just lost his wife to breast cancer. His sixteen-year-old daughter was pregnant, his twenty-year-old son just told him he was gay, his little eight-year-old daughter told him she hated him, and he killed their mom."

Truce looked at me with tears filling his eyes. I've never seen Truce show this much emotion.

"Life was too hard, so Iscariot got to him. See these scars?" Truce pointed to the scars on his arms.

"Yes." I said to him.

"That's when God let me reveal myself. Those are the scars I got from trying to pull the gun away from my human." Truce let a tear slip from the corner of his eye.

"What was his name" I asked barely above a whisper.

"Gregory Frank. I loved him. He was my best friend." Truce looked away. "It was too much for him. He didn't think that he could go on and he killed himself."

"Truce, I had no idea." I pressed my fingers to my lips.

"I then asked God if I may become a warrior. I will fight the enemy until this earth is put to rest. I vowed to kill any who came between a human and his angel, a human and God." He turned to look at me. The moonlight exposed his hurt features.

"Truce, I'm sorry."

"It was his choice. I just didn't protect him well enough." Truce bowed his head.

"But it was his choice. Iscariot and depression got the best of him."

"Well, I am a warrior now and, to answer your question, I am never sick of being a warrior." Truce smiled.

"Did Gregory have a second chance right before he died?" I asked.

"Yes. He saw me and I told him that Christ loved him. He said that there is no Christ." Truce cleared his throat . . . "His wife is in heaven."

"That should have motivated him to stay alive." I noted.

"You would think so, but he didn't believe in God anymore. He refused. My title of guardian was stripped from me. Several demons came." Truce choked up. He could barely speak. "They dragged his soul away to hell." Truce choked back the emotion he felt.

"Don't ever regret your position." Truce grew more serious and looked over at Jessie. "That girl needs you and you need her." He pointed to Jessie.

"I . . ."

"You're a guardian. Be proud, Tristan." Truce grabbed my shoulders, pulled me toward him, and embrace me.

"Until next time, dear brother, God be with you." Truce nodded then disappeared into heaven.

I stood there looking at Jessie, thinking about what Truce had been through. I didn't know that he was once a guardian. No one had ever told me that. Emotion rose in my throat as the story rang in my ears. I laid next to Jessie on her bed and put my arms around her and cried. I couldn't handle thinking of Jessie ever doing that—just throwing her life away. I wonder what happened to his family. What happened to his sixteen-year-old daughter and her baby, his gay son, his eight-year-old daughter who blamed her father for her mother's death. What had happened to all of them? My mind was spinning. Truce's story really shook me up. I can't imagine Gregory looking and seeing Truce, his guardian angel, trying to get him to live and telling him that Jesus loved him. I would love to show myself to Jessie for her to see me and know that I exist and that someone is always watching out for her. I would rather she never see me than be put in a situation like that of Truce and Gregory.

Period 1: Art/Jewelry

The new semester was somewhat of a change. Jessie even went to her first period Algebra 2 class a couple of times until she realized it was second semester. We were starting to get into the groove that Art class was first. I could tell Jessie regretted her decision to take Art the first period of the day. This art class was jewelry-making class. Torches were going, machines to cut metal were grinding, and it all got on Jessie's nerves. Leo sat at the table across from her designing his charm for a necklace he was making. Jessie sat slumped in her seat watching him.

"You know that you have to do this, too." Leo informed without looking up at Jessie.

"Yeah, I know." Jessie sighed. "I think I'm going to get my schedule changed and bail on this class." Jessie tugged at her sleeves, pulling them slightly over her hands.

"You can't do that." Leo looked up at Jessie.

"But I can." Jessie smiled.

"Don't leave us." David butted in.

"What he said." Leo nodded his head toward David. David just smiled.

"But I don't feel like making art this early in the morning." Jessie rested her head on the table and looked over to David.

"I love you, baby girl." David put his arm around Jessie and leaned his head on her back.

"Awe, I love you, too." Jessie smiled.

"Miss Jessie, that project isn't going to do itself." Ms. James sang.

Ms. James was tall with short, gray hair and big hips, and she dressed like a gypsy. She was high in spirit, always upbeat, and never missed a day of school unless she had to.

"I know, Ms. James, I know." Jessie moaned.

"You have to do this project. No one is going to do it for you." Ms. James smiled.

"If God loved me he would." Jessie griped as she took some supplies from the middle of the table.

"God doesn't love any of us right now." Shelby said grudgingly.

"Uh oh." Jessie looked at Shelby. "What happened?"

Shelby looked at Jessie and then to David and Leo.

"Well, apparently Jared had someone sneak weed into his cell and now he won't be coming home for a while. I don't understand why he does that. He didn't come home for Christmas like he was supposed to. I'm really getting tired of him doing stuff that makes him stay longer. I love him to death, I really do. We've been together since sophomore year." Shelby jerked a piece of loose metal off of her charm. "But my gosh. I don't want to be in college and my boyfriend in jail. Maybe Carrie is right. Oh, Lord, don't let her know that I said that." Shelby laughed.

"What is said at this table stays at this table." David placed his enormous black hand over Shelby's tiny, pale hand.

"Thanks." Shelby blushed.

"You're welcome."

"Yeah, I think that should be a rule. We're all really good friends. I say what happens and is said at the table stays at the table, Leo." Jessie pushed her head forward. Leo was in his own little world working on his charm.

"I hear you, Jessie."

"Well?"

"Well, I'm down with it if they are." Leo said not looking up.

"I'm in." David said. "So, whatever happens really doesn't leave this table?" David looked over at Jessie.

"Right!" Jessie exclaimed.

"Well then. Leo, I think you look very handsome today." David winked at Jessie. Leo knew that David was gay. David was playing a little joke on Leo. Leo looked up with a frown on his face. Jessie, Shelby, and David burst out in laughter.

"Not funny." Leo gave them a dirty look.

"A little?" Jessie squinted.

"No. That's just mean." Leo shot. David was still laughing.

"I mean, you definitely aren't ugly." David popped his lips. Jessie looked at Shelby.

"Ha! Jessie, start your project already." Shelby laughed.

"I'm going." Jessie groaned.

"What are you going to make?"

"The outline of an elephant—for my mom." Jessie smiled.

"That's really sweet." Leo placed his hand over his chest.

"Bite me." Jessie glared.

Period 2: Algebra 2

News for today. Danni McCord has a boyfriend—her very first one—and Justin was not at all happy about it. Danni was dating Shane Griffin, who was tall and gothic. That explained Shane, who was just tall and gothic. He was monotone when he talked, if he talked. His skin was pale, he wore black make-up and nail polish, he wore trip pants with spikes and chains (which was a dress code violation), he wore older band t-shirts, and he had a bright red mohawk. Why Danni was dating him? I have no clue. Danni is tall, thin, curvy, short brown hair that flipped under, and blue eyes. She wore brighter colors but opposites attract, I guess. All of her friends were thrilled for her—all of them except Justin.

"Why does she have to date Shane Griffin of all people?" Justin doodled on the edge of his math paper.

"I don't know, Justin, maybe because they like each other?" Jessie cocked her head to Justin.

"He's simply not good enough." Justin scoffed.

"Dude, do you like Danni?" Karla blurted from behind them.

"No, she's like my sister and I just want to protect her." Justin lied.

"Right." Karla rolled her eyes.

"I don't care what you think." Justin turned around to face Karla.

"I don't care that you don't care." Karla hissed. "I always thought you were a queer anyway."

Karla!" Jessie shot Karla a dirty look.

"Is there a problem, Miss Jessie?" Mr. Delarosa looked up from his desk.

"No, sir." Jessie said and then pretended to work on her math.

"Oh my gosh, Jessie. Stop trying to be a peacemaker." Karla rolled her eyes.

"What's been your problem, Karla?" Jessie said glaringly at her.

"Well, that fact that you don't even care about me anymore." Karla grew angry.

"Uh, news flash. You were spending all your time with Gerard, so I let you do your own thing. It's not like I cared!" Jessie rolled her eyes. "Instead of being mad at me, you should thank me."

"Don't be ridiculous." Karla scoffed.

"You spent all your time with him and I spent all mine with friends. You just up and left me high and dry for some boy. So it's your fault we're distant." Jessie shot back.

"Jessie, you've let them get to your head. Are they trying to turn you against me?"

"Oh my gosh." Jessie grabbed her head. "No one is turning me against you. That's your own paranoia."

"No, I don't think so." Karla hissed.

"I do. Now, I'm going to finish my math before both of us get into trouble." Jessie stated.

Jessie turned around in her seat and began her work. Karla was mumbling in the background. Jessie rolled her eyes and ignored her.

"She's uptight." Jeremy leaned and whispered to Jessie.

"I know. She's getting on my nerves. She's been so hateful." Jessie answered.

"I can tell." Jeremy tucked Jessie's hair behind her ear. "Can I tell you something that I had heard from Jenna Girth?" Jeremy rested against Jessie's desk.

"Oh Lord, what?" Jessie looked at him out of the corner of her eye. Jenna Girth was the queen of gossip.

"Gerard is dating someone." Jeremy looked up at Jessie. Jessie looked back at Karla who was doing her work.

"Oh no." Jessie sighed.

"Yes, and you're going to be even more ticked when you hear who it is." Jeremy squinted.

"Just tell me." Jessie grabbed her desk preparing herself for the worst.

"Tiffany Zane." Jeremy whispered.

"Holy crap! Karla hates her."

"I know, but Gerard asked her out like a week ago."

"Jeremy, Karla, and he hang out all the time."

"Either she's lying or he's playing them." Jeremy shrugged and then rested himself back in his desk.

"This is not good." Jessie shook her head.

Jessie knew what would happen if Karla found out about Tiffany and Gerard. It would not be pretty. Jessie decided that she wasn't going to tell Karla. She would just let Karla find out on her own. Jessie could understand why he would choose Tiffany over Karla. Karla was pretty but only certain guys dated red heads with freckles. Why it was like that, I don't know. Tiffany is tall, with slender legs and long, thick brown hair. She had her nails professionally done, her clothes were always in style, and she had a beautiful face with not one blemish or freckle. Compared to Karla, some boys (as sad as it was) would pick Tiffany. Not that Karla wasn't pretty. She was. But I think it was her attitude that made her not very appealing to people.

School went by rather fast. Jessie just kind of coasted through the day. We headed toward her truck. She was arm in arm with Justin, and Carrie was on her other side. The rest followed. Jessie saw Karla getting into Gerard's car. Jessie stared at them for a moment. Jessie and I saw Karla lean over and kiss Gerard. Jessie stopped walking, jerking Justin and Carrie back.

"Jessie?" Carrie looked down.

"So you know how Jeremy knows everything about everyone because he's friends with Jenna. Well, he told me and Justin that Gerard was dating Tiffany Zane. I just saw Karla get into his car. They kissed." Jessie looked at her friends who were standing in front of her.

"She really irritates me." Justin scowled.

"I know. She's starting to irritate me, too." Jessie rolled her eyes, turned around, and grabbed the handle of her truck door.

"Yeah, well, I mean you don't *have* to be friends with her." Shelby smiled.

"I know. I know." Jessie climbed into her truck. "See ya'll tomorrow." Jessie smiled.

Jessie slammed the door to her truck. I climbed into the passenger's side. As I was sitting next to Jessie, I had a vision. God showed me Karla and Gerard sitting in his car talking.

"Jessie thinks she's so perfect with all her little friends and her newfound faith. And, oh, we can't forget about Mr. Perfect Leo." Karla took a swig of Jack Daniels.

"So what are you going to do? Stop being friends with her?" Gerard asked as he turned on Kem Road.

"Never! She's my best friend and always will be." Karla sat the bottle on the floor. "I think it's a phase," she shrugged.

"Maybe it's not." Gerard raked his hand through his black hair.

"If it isn't, I will get her back. I have a huge influence on her. Let's see if her God is more important. I told her she does not want me against her." Karla glared and looked forward out the windshield.

"Why don't you let it go?"

"Because she's supposed to be on our side." Karla leaned and looked at Gerard.

"Our side?"

"You wouldn't understand." Karla folded her arms over her chest and leaned back in the seat. "I'm not done with her."

I came back to reality. We were already home. I looked at Jessie who gathered her backpack and headed toward her house. I went to get up but was forced back down in my seat. I grabbed the rearview mirror and turned it to where I could see who was behind me. I was relieved to see that it was Truce. His face was stern and angry.

"Tristan, watch out!" he warned me.

"I know." I hung my head.

"I can't keep you long. Just be careful."

Truce released his grip and then vanished. I hurried out of the truck and into the house. Jessie was seated on the couch between her brother's two best friends—Matt and Danny.

"So, wait a minute. You're going to Detroit for a Flogging Molly concert next weekend?" Jessie looked at Travis who was looking at tickets online.

"That's the plan." Travis laughed.

"Not fair." Jessie crossed her arms over her chest.

"Don't pout."

Matt threw his arm over Jessie's shoulder and pulled her close. Matt and Jessie had known each other since Jessie was in the third grade and he was in the fifth. Jessie had known Danny since she was in the eighth grade and he was in the tenth. They're all pretty much childhood friends and they've all watched each other grow up.

"Well, I never get to do anything fun." Jessie pouted.

"Yes, you do. You're hanging out with us now, and what's more fun than that?" Danny punched her very lightly on the arm.

"Sis, ask Dad if you can go. If he says 'yes', we'll take you." Travis shrugged.

"Yeah." Matt looked at Jessie.

I felt my skin tighten and my spirit jerk. Sulfur filled the room. I was sitting in a chair across from Danny, Jessie, and Matt. I looked over to the hallway that led to Jessie's parents' room, the bathroom in the middle, and Travis' room on the other side. There stood a demon who was five feet tall, but nothing but a black shadow. Jessie laughed with Matt and Danny. She turned her head to face Matt but looked passed him. She turned white and all the color had drained from her face. Her eyes widened. She could see him. She stared at him for a minute, which seemed like hours.

"Jessie, are you okay?" Matt looked at Jessie with concern. Jessie said nothing. She just kept staring at the demon. I leaned forward in my chair. *She needs to see this,* I heard a soft voice say to me. I still sat on the edge of my seat, making sure this thing wasn't going to attack.

"Jess, you're freaking me out." Matt looked behind him to see what she was looking at. He couldn't see it. Jessie's expression changed from scared to curious.

"Jess?" Travis hollered at her. Jessie jerked and then looked over at Travis.

"What's the matter?" he asked her. Jessie looked back and the demon was gone.

"Uh, nothing. I got home work to do."

Jessie sprang off the couch, grabbed her backpack, and headed for her room. Travis turned his attention to the computer.

"She freaked me out." Matt choked out. "It was like she had seen a ghost or demon."

When Matt said that, Travis took his attention away from finding tickets.

"Demon?" Travis grew angry.

"That or a ghost, bro." Matt shook his head.

"I hope it wasn't a demon." Travis sighed. He pinched the bridge of his nose with his index finger and thumb.

"Why, what's up?" Danny shifted his body to face Travis.

"Long story. I'm going to go check on her."

Travis made his way to Jessie's room. He knocked on the door but didn't wait for an answer.

"Jessie, what happened." Travis shut the door behind him and sat on Jessie's bed next to her.

"I saw one." Jessie looked up at Travis.

"What?" Travis asked as if he didn't already know.

"A demon."

Jessie looked at him with eyes full of fear. My spirit grew angry. How dare they show themselves. Then that voice came to me again— *She needs to see this.* Then I felt a reassuring peace come over me. He knew what he was doing.

"Jessie, you don't think they're coming back, do you?" Travis whispered.

"I haven't done anything I shouldn't." Jessie's eyes filled with tears.

"Oh, Sis. Maybe it will just be one of those things." Travis put his arm around Jessie's shoulder and pulled her to him.

"Maybe you were blessed to see demons and angels. Maybe God just blessed you with that." Travis tried to calm Jessie down.

"I don't want to."

"But, Sis, you can use that against them."

"I could?"

"Absolutely. A lot of people get attacked by these demons because they don't know that they're there." Travis hugged his sister tighter.

"Yeah, I guess you're right, but how do I go about that?" Jessie looked up at Travis as tears stained her face.

"Get closer to God."

Jessie was asleep in her bed. Her breathing was steady, and the moonlight laid upon her golden hair making it shine. I sat at the end of the bed watching her sleep like I used to when she was a little girl. I miss those days. Time was going by at super speed. I miss Jessie being little. She had a dependent faith that was out of this world. Now her concerns were high school, boys, friends, her future career. I sighed to myself.

"Tristan." I heard someone hiss. "Triiiiiistan," they sang to me. I looked around the room but no one was there. I walked over to Jessie, pulled the covers up to her chin, and bent down to kiss her forehead. A sharp pain rang through my head. I fell at Jessie's bedside and managed to turn around. No one was there. I slowly got up and checked on Jessie. There lying in the bed next to her was Jezebel. Jessie was lying on her stomach as Jezebel ran her fingers through Jessie's long, blonde hair.

"Get out!" I reached over and grabbed Jezebel by the arm and threw her off of the bed.

"I just want to have some quality time with Jessie. I have missed her." Jezebel caught her balance and looked passed me to where Jessie was.

"I was sent here by a certain someone anyway." Jezebel pulled a cigarette out from behind her ear and lit it with a match she pulled out of her cleavage.

"Jezebel, who sent you?"

"Karla, duh. Well, she didn't say 'Hey, Jez, go attack Jessie.' No. But her negativity and gossip sent me here." Jezebel took a drag. "You know, Tristan . . . Father Lucifer is getting really tired of you and your "gang" of worthless angels. Why are you fighting for someone who is just going to die and go to hell?" Jezebel flicked her ashes on the ground.

I grabbed Jezebel by the throat. "I rebuke those words of death!" I glared at her. Her eyes widened and she squirmed in my grasp.

"Tristan, you fool!" she choked out. "Do you have any idea how much stronger Karla is than Jessie? She's influenced her before. She can do it again!"

Jezebel brought her hands up to my face and dug her claws into my flesh. She turned her hands inward, hooking herself to my face. I tightened my grip around her throat but she pulled her fingers more inward while blood trickled down my face. I threw Jezebel to the ground. She rubbed her throat and rested on her knees. She then leaned forward, gasping for breath, and turned and looked at me.

"That's no way to treat a woman," she rubbed her throat with her long, slender hand. "You beat Jessie when she does something wrong?" Jezebel hissed.

"Nope." I lifted my foot and kicked Jezebel in the face. Her body flew back.

"My nose."

Jezebel cupped her hand over her face. I was showing no mercy. I walked over to her, grabbed her long, raven hair, and pulled her to her feet.

"Don't kill me. Lucifer will be mad." Jezebel wiped the blood from her nose.

"And I care because?" I crossed my arms over my chest and stared at her.

"He will send me to the pit again. Please, Tristan, have mercy on me. You're a lover not a fighter," she said as she held her hands out to me. I backed away from her. "Tristan you don't understand! If I don't accomplish what I'm here for . . . I will be in serious trouble."

She tried to play the pity card. I watched her as she unloaded the drama on me.

"Have you ever seen Lucifer mad at one of us?"

"No." I shook my head at her. "And, quite frankly, I don't care." I cocked my head at her. Her eyebrows came together in anger, her lips pierced together making a thin red line, and her nostrils flared.

"He makes everyone in hell watch as we get beaten and then thrown in the pit." Jezebel pinched her nose trying to put it back the way it once was.

"Uh huh." I looked at her with sarcasm.

"Humans get treated even worse than usual. You don't want to be the cause of their inflictions, do you?"

Jezebel, I will admit, was good with the theatrics.

"If I succeed, he will stop torturing them so we can celebrate my victory. They stop being tortured, Tristan.

"Wow. I think it's time to tell you something." I dropped my arms and leaned down toward her.

"What?" she sniffled.

"I really . . . don't care." I clicked my tongue.

Jezebel became furious. She lifted her hand up to strike me and I grabbed her by her tiny wrist.

"Bad choice." I gripped her wrist and then, with one thrust, broke it. She fell to the ground, and I looked over at Jessie who was still fast asleep.

"And you lie." I looked down at her. She fell to her knees grabbing her wrist.

"Hell never stops torturing the humans. He has no compassion for them, no love, nothing, and I doubt your victory would stop the madness." I kicked her down.

"Tristan, no!"

I grabbed her by the hair and raised her up higher on her knees. I then grabbed my sword. She took her claws and dug them into my calves. I winced with pain but I was sending her back to the pit where she belonged. Her claws dug in so deep that they hit bone. I lifted my sword high in the air and then she growled and snarled at me.

"I rebuke you, Jezebel, in the Name of God the Father who art in heaven!" I yelled into the air. She started twitching as soon as I spoke of the Heavenly Father. "I destroy you in His Name."

"Noooooooo. Noooooooo. Noooooooo!" she screamed as her demonic voice echoed in the room. She squirmed in my gripped. With one swipe I cut her head off. I let go of my grip and her head fell beside her twitching body.

"I will no longer stand by. Whenever you come to me, I will destroy you in the name of Jehovah God!" I shouted. I wanted to make sure they all heard me. My body jerked and flew forward and I landed on Jessie's bed. I then fell to the ground and a burning sensation coursed through my body. I didn't know what was going on. I wasn't getting attacked by the demonic forces. No . . . this was something different, something that I couldn't explain. My body twitched as I laid on the floor of Jessie's room. The carpet scratched at my skin. My arms began to go weak along with my legs and the rest of my body. What was happening? I was pinned to the ground and the room was spinning. A light filled the room. I felt a sharp pain on my hand and looked down. My hand started to swell and turn red. My breathing labored. I tried to look up to see if Jessie was all right, but my head was forced to the ground. I looked down at my hand and something was being inscribed on me like a tattoo. I watched as the lines swirled and etched. I tried to jerk my arm up, but it wouldn't move. This unbelievable force had me pinned. I couldn't move, not even an inch. The engraving on my hand stopped. I looked sown. It was a shield, a silver shield with what looked like vines wrapping around it. It was a warrior shield. I was now a warrior and a guardian. My head was spinning, and I couldn't grasp what had happened. The room went back to being dark, and I heard Jessie breathing. My body regained its strength as I slowly stood to my feet and raised my hand to the moonlight. There engraved on my hand was the symbol of a warrior. I didn't think I had done much to deserve this. I had just slain Jezebel; that was all. I raised my other hand to the moonlight. The engraved symbol of a golden eye glistened in the moonlight. The golden eye meant 'guardian', so I was now a guardian and a warrior. I dropped my hands to my side. The Silver glistened in the moonlight. I became proud of this symbol, but what could I have possibly done? Jezebel is no one to be afraid of in the first place. I looked to my right and saw Truce and Jesaiah facing me.

"Why?" I asked Truce.

"Because we need you. And you've earned it. No questions. Just thank Jehovah." Jesaiah smiled at me.

"You've been Jessie's guardian for going on nineteen years, and you've fought for nineteen years. I say you're due to be a warrior. Don't you think, Jesaiah?" Truce turned and smiled at Jesaiah who was at his left.

"I think." Jesaiah smiled.

"We're proud of you, Tristan." Truce nodded at me. "You're doing great and becoming stronger." Truce walked over and kissed me upon my cheek. Jesaiah stood where he was.

"Be prepared. Now they know you are a warrior for Jehovah and they will come at you stronger than ever." Truce informed. "They don't understand the consequences for messing with us."

I noticed an orange and pink light hit Truce's face. I looked behind me at the window. It was already morning. It was a Saturday and I knew Jessie would be sleeping in.

"Remember, Tristan, be prepared. Until next time . . . God be with you," Truce said and then vanished.

I looked at my hand again. The warrior symbol looked back at me. A warrior; I was a warrior. My spirit jumped with excitement. I looked over at Jessie who was fast asleep. I was a warrior but, above, all I was a guardian and I was ready for battle.

CHAPTER 14

Mission of Love

The night was cold and the coolness bit at our skin. The wind beat against our faces. The moonlight shone down upon us and had a warmth to it. The trees bowed to the wind submitting its branches to its fierce commands. The grass was no longer light and carefree. It stood hunched over as frost started to take over. A nearby bush shook in the night. Truce, Victor, Jesaiah, Purity, and I were all standing in a straight line waiting for them to come. We heard them in the distance as horse hooves beat against the ground. Whistles, whoops, and hollers came calling after us. The smell of death and oppression filled the night air. Truce kept his straight posture. He didn't say anything and didn't look at anyone. He was ready for battle. His tall frame didn't even flinch. I looked over at Victor and Jesaiah. They were hunched over with swords drawn. Their armor was silver with hunter green designs painted on it. Hunter green jewels were seared into the edges of the armor. They looked tough. I then looked over at Purity. Her long, blonde hair was pulled high up into a braid. Her armor was white gold with baby blue designs painted on them. Baby blue jewels were seared into the edge of the armor, which looked just like that of Jesaiah and Victor. Mine was almost the same, but I didn't have rubies or jewels. Mine was silver with red stones and red designs painted on it. Purity was a woman, but she could fight. She was sweet and gentle until the enemy messed with her or someone she loved. She then became a warrior. Purity saw me staring at her from the corner of her eyes. She turned her head to me and smiled. She was caught back into the moment when the hooves grew louder and the shouts were more intense. I looked up and saw Anton, Gallio, Letushion, Maaz, Rokbah, and Getti coming at us on black steeds. Their steeds had long, black wings that expanded a mile across, and they had dark, red eyes and razor sharp teeth.

"Ready!?" Truce shouted over the noise.

"Ready!" we said in unison. I felt a rush of wind close behind me. I looked back and saw ten thousand angels behind me ready to fight. They were in attack position. I then heard a roar and looked down. My faithful tiger, Skoto, was at my side. Demons from all over came rushing at us alongside Anton and the others. They came from the neighbor's yards, out of their houses, and off of their roofs. They jumped out of trees, slammed to the ground, and barreled after us.

"Ready!" Truce yelled. We lifted our swords to fighting position. They got closer and closer. My heart was beating fast, and all I could hear was my pulse in my ears. My skin turned clammy and I gripped my sword. Skoto roared and growled. Saber tooth tigers, three-headed lions and tigers came running after our lions and tigers. They roared for battle. As they grew closer, the earth shook and then we engulfed each other. Demons jumped on us, grabbing our hair and clothes. Skoto was fighting off two black panthers, and I felt a demon pull my head back. I thrust my sword upward and stabbed his face. He fell to the ground and started twitching. I shrugged my shoulders. That wasn't too hard.

"Don't get so cocky." Purity hollered to me as she repeatedly stabbed a demon in the chest while ripping others off of her.

Demons were everywhere, clawing and spitting at us. I couldn't find Truce anywhere. Forty or more demons had Jesaiah on the ground and were kicking and punching him repeatedly. As I ran toward him, a demon jumped on my back and I fell to my knees. He choked me with his forearms. He breathed down my neck making disgusting breathing noises, and his chest sounded like it popped every time he took a breath. He squeaked in my ear. He was really getting on my nerves. Then I grabbed the top of his head and pulled him over my shoulder. His back slammed against the ground. I wasted no time and kicked him in the face repeatedly.

"Tristan!" Purity yelled. I looked to my right from where I heard her call. More than fifty demons came charging after me. Many other angels stopped them in their tracks by stabbing them before they reached me. I was attacked by a massive lion, and I fell to the ground. His mouth opened and, as it started down at my face, I put my hands up. Nothing happened! I looked up and Skoto came from the right and attacked the lion, causing him to fly off of me. They tumbled to the ground and Skoto grabbed the lion's massive neck. The lion clawed at Skoto. It ripped his face and sides open, with blood flowing from his wounds. Skoto bit down on the lion's face. Its snout cracked under the pressure. I got up, looked around, and then grabbed my sword. I started stabbing demons. At one point in time, I started to get fed up with everything. I closed my eyes, ran toward a mass huddled of demons, and started swinging my sword. I felt the pressure of their bodies beat against my sword. They actually weighed a lot and pulled my sword down as they fell to the ground. When I opened my eyes, the spot where I was fighting was cleared, except for the fifty demons that lay on the ground. I looked to my right and saw that a demon had taken a good, solid bite out of Truce's forearm, which left a wide-open gash. His flesh left with the demon, but it didn't seem to phase Truce. I then saw a demon jump onto the roof of Jessie's house. He stood there surveying the area. I went after him and jumped up onto the roof. We stood face to face with one another. His eyes narrowed. He lunged at me with his sword and I backed away. The blade was only an inch away from me. I lunged my sword forward only to miss him. He ran down the roof, and I followed. I bent down and, at the right moment, grabbed his leg causing him to fall on his face. He quickly turned away to face me. His eyes widened.

"You're the one they call, Tristan."

"Yes," I answered.

I took my sword and stabbed him right between the eyes. I ripped my sword out of his now lifeless body and kicked him off of the roof. I looked out onto Jessie's backyard. Demons and angels were everywhere. Demons shrieked, while angels yelled in victory. Blood puddled itself in the grass as the demons lay limp and dead. Anton and Truce were battling. I jumped off of the roof and headed toward the others. I grabbed a demon that was on Purity's back and stabbed his chest with my sword. Purity pulled an arrow out of her leg.

"Ah!" she yelled in pain.

Purity pulled out the arrow and stabbed a demon in the eye that was running toward her. She pushed him backward and the arrow pierced the ground, pinning him down. He wasn't dead but he struggled to break free, ripping the arrow further and further down his face. Purity kicked the end of the arrow driving it further into the ground. Now he was never getting up. I looked behind me and saw three demons attacking Jesaiah. I grabbed two of them and slammed them together. I grabbed a nearby arrow penetrating one and then the other. They hung on the arrow together, one at each end. I took each end of the arrow, bent it upward, and lifted them over my head. I twirled them around in the air and threw them into the demons that were around Victor. They fell to the ground with a great thud, shaking the earth below us. The night was getting colder and I could see my own breath as I fought the hoards of demons. The clouds rolled by our heads with not a star in sight, and the moon grew darker in color. The ground cracked beneath us, and I saw red light showing through the cracks. I looked down and then looked over at Truce. His eyes were growing wide. Purity, Jesaiah, and Victor looked at one another and then to me and Truce. I looked to the ground. The red light was getting brighter and the cracks bigger. Was that . . . ? No! It couldn't be hell! The ground gave way beneath us and my body fell at great speed. I tossed and turned in the air and then slammed against the cold, wet ground. I heard the rest fall beside me but one actually fell on me. I pushed him off because his massive frame was cutting off my air. I heard Truce cough. I couldn't see anything. It was damp and I smelled mold and sulfur. All of a sudden the ground grew hotter, and I heard the others jump up as I did.

"Truce?" Purity's voice echoed. We backed away as the ground glowed red with heat. We all backed against the wall.

"Truce?!" Purity grew more anxious. I looked over at Truce. His eyes widened.

"Okay guys and Purity. That wall is about to open up. When you see what is before you, I want you to keep your heads on straight. You cannot lose focus of God. You understand me?" Truce hollered over the rumbling of the rock starting to split open. An intense heat rushed at us.

"What about Jessie?" I yelled. "She's not protected." I looked around in panic.

"How dare you!" Truce yelled at me. "Adoram is with her. She is well protected," he yelled at me.

I didn't like being away from Jessie. I was her guardian angel. It was my job to stay there.

"Truce, it's my job to stay with her." The heat grew intense and then I felt Purity grab my hand.

"What you're about to see is what you are going to keep Jessie from. You had to be here, Tristan," Jesaiah yelled. I felt like everyone knew what was going on but me. "After this, you probably won't leave Jessie's side."

Jesaiah choked on the smoke. We heard screaming and wailing. The sound made my heart beat hard against my chest. I couldn't breathe. The sounds struck fear into my very soul. We heard rushing sounds like a blow torch. I looked around. *Oh no! I'm in hell!* The rock split open. I closed my eyes at the sight. Purity started crying and Jesaiah put his hand over his mouth. Victor actually threw up. Hell has three stories. The higher, the more less intense the punishment was. The heat was intense. Truce put on his game face. I looked out. Fire blazed everywhere. People were being burned alive. Their skin hung off of their skeletons, and their eyes bugged out. I couldn't handle it. I wanted to go be with Jessie. People were being dragged by chains, the cuffs ripping their wrists. I saw a woman wrapped in chains. She stood on a vent, and a rush of fire consumed her. She screamed in pain.

"Keep your eyes on God!" Truce yelled to us.

I heard Purity praying under her breath. I looked at the woman consumed by fire. The chains that wrapped around her now burnt body just melted into her flesh. She gnashed her teeth at the demons, and blood trickled from her mouth from clenching her teeth so hard. She screamed in pain along with many others. A demon grabbed the chain and jerked her away. Her body split in half but was held together by the chains. People cried out to God for help and said that they loved Him. Could God hear them? The sight brought tears to my eyes. This is what would happen to Jessie if we lost her.

"This is just a part of it." Truce choked out.

"Why are we here?" Victor grew irritated.

I looked out into hell and saw a girl who was five feet tall. She had singed hair wrapped in enormous chains. Her mouth was sown shut with barbed wire, and she looked over at me. I fell to my knees because she looked exactly like Jessie. A sharp pain took over my chest and I grasped at my heart. I felt like I was going to die. I looked back out and her eyes were filled with tears. I reached my hand out, and Truce grabbed my hand and pulled me to my feet.

"That's not Jessie!" Truce shook me.

"I have to save her!" I tried to move forward as tears ran from my eyes.

"That's not Jessie, Tristan!" Jesaiah cried to me.

"Save these people!" I yelled. "They need help!" I beat my fist against the rock wall. "Why, God, why am I here?!" I cried. "Let me go back to Jessie!" I screamed at the top of my lungs. Hell stopped for no one.

"You needed to see all aspects of this life. All you know is being a guardian. Here! This is what happens." Truce pointed his finger out to hell.

"I know about hell, Truce!" I screamed. I was growing furious with him.

"No! You have no idea, Tristan. This is why we fight so hard for man's soul!" Truce grabbed me in a bear hug. "This is why," he whispered in my ear. "God doesn't' want this for them. They choose it. We fight for them so we can make sure this never happens." Truce held me.

I couldn't help but cry. We stood in the cave for what seemed like forever. The screams and wailing of people rang in my ears. I couldn't take this. It was just all too much. I just wanted to be with Jessie.

"If Jessie isn't careful, this could happen to her." Truce warned me. "Tristan, you're here to see. God isn't tormenting you." Truce reassured me.

"I want to go back with Jessie." I clenched my teeth. The ground shook. The people in hell screamed for water, screamed for peace, screamed out for God's mercy, but it was all too late. The rock started to close again and the light became smaller. The people were out of view. The rock covered the opening and the red light slowly started to dim. The heat became less intense and then we were standing in total darkness.

"How do we get out?" Victor broke the silence.

The sounds of hell rang in my ears, and the sight burned into my corneas. My heart was still pounding and the smell lingered beneath my nose. I grew angry with the enemy. I heard Truce groping around in the dark searching for a way out.

"Aha!" Truce said. He pushed a huge rock, which scraped against the other rocks. He pulled on the rock and it hit the floor with a loud thud.

"It's a tunnel." Truce said to us. I heard him pick something up. He tossed it down the tunnel, and we heard it finally hit the ground.

"Let's go." Truce grabbed Jesaiah, Victor, Purity, and then myself.

"Are we just going to leave them?" I asked Truce.

"Tristan . . . brother . . . that's their life now. There's nothing we can do. Not even God tampers with it."

Truce practically threw me into the dark tunnel. He followed behind me, and we crawled for miles and miles. My arms started getting tired. The thought of people burning in hell who were just below us haunted me. I don't think I should have seen that. I tried to focus on other things.

"Ouch!" Jesaiah came to a halt, causing us to run into each other.

"We're at a dead end." Jesaiah called to Truce.

"Push the wall!" Truce yelled back.

Jesaiah did as he was told. Light peaked through, and he fell out of the tunnel. We heard a thud.

"Well, he made it to the other side," Truce laughed. I couldn't see how he could laugh when people were burning in hell.

"You're just going to have to deal with it, Tristan. They chose that life. Now it's your job to protect Jessie from it." Truce said practically reading my mind.

"Fall out, Purity," Jesaiah called.

Purity scooted to the edge of the tunnel and dropped off. Victor, Truce, and I followed. We were in a large hole.

"Alright. We'll throw Purity up first and then the rest will follow."

Truce knit his fingers together, making a bowl for Purity to put her foot in. When she did, he hoisted to the top and she jumped to the side. He did the same with Jesaiah, Victor, and me. Truce always put others before himself. We looked down at him. I looked around and we were by an old, white shed. I walked around the shed, opened the door, and peeked inside. I found a rope, made a loop at the end, and took it to Truce.

"Here, I handed an end to Purity and Jesaiah. They tossed down the rope with the loop at the end to Truce.

"Who's idea?" he called to us.

"Tristan's." Purity called. She looked over at me and winked.

"Better than my idea."

Truce put the loop around his waist and tugged on the rope. We all started pulling and Truce helped us out. He used his massive legs to climb himself up. The hole was deep. Since Truce was strong, he could throw a whole building a mile away, but the poor guy couldn't jump. You would think just because we're angels we could have flown out. We don't use our wings as much as people think we do, at least not for situations like this. We finally got Truce up and on the ground. He rolled over on his back and looked up at the bright, blue sky.

"Good to be back!" Truce laughed.

I looked around and we were in the neighbor's yard. Jessie's house was right behind this shed.

"We gotta put the rope back."

Truce started wrapping it around his arm to put it back in original form. He walked over to the shed and placed it back on the giant nail that stuck out of the wall. He made his way back to us.

"I'm spent," he laughed.

Jesaiah looked as if he were going to pass out. Victor turned and hugged Purity. We all turned toward Jessie's house. I looked back and saw that the hole had disappeared. I don't know what God had planned that day or why He made us sit through that and watch as His humans were being beaten and burned. All I knew is that I was now prepared more than ever to protect Jessie from what I had seen. No one said anything about the former events that took place. It was a part of life and there was nothing more to talk about.

We departed from each other and I made my way into Jessie's house. It was ten o'clock a.m. when I entered Jessie's room. Adoram was sitting on her bed watching her sleep.

"She slept great. Are you okay?" Adoram looked at me with his big, brown eyes.

"Yes." I nodded to him. I really hoped Adoram wouldn't want to talk about what happened.

"Alright. Till next time. God send peace," he said and then vanished.

I walked over to Jessie's computer desk and sat in her chair. I watched her sleep. I rubbed my hands over my face and ran my fingers through my hair. My mind was still on the humans in hell. I had to get over this, but it had such a big impact on me as it would anyone. I don't see how Jesaiah, Victor, and Purity weren't affected by it as much as I was. Maybe they were. If so, they covered it up really well. All I knew now is that I wanted to protect Jessie with the best of my abilities. I would always be fighting for her. She needed me. I walked over to Jessie's bedside and looked down at her. The vision of the girl that I saw flashed in my mind. I grew angry. *I command those thoughts to leave now!* I bent down and kissed Jessie's cheek. She moaned and moved a little bit. Did she feel me here? Now? I really hope so. I want her to see me soon. What I am doing is no longer a job to me. Now it was more of a mission of love.

CHAPTER 15

Closest Deceit

Karla and Jessie sat in the cold for a while not saying much of anything. Jessie pulled her arms together trying to find warmth. She tugged her beanie, pulling the sides over her ears. She shivered and then looked over at Karla. Karla was writing stuff in the dirt with a large stick. Her red hair was pulled back into a long, pony tail. She wore more make up to hide her freckles, and her eyes were fixed on the ground.

"I'm freezing! Can we go in?" Jessie asked. She stretched her legs out resting her feet on the step below her.

"Not till Mom says. She and Dad got into a big fight, and she asked me to go sit on the porch. So, I've been here before you got here." Karla sighed.

"Okay, I got some cash. You wanna go somewhere and get something to eat?" Jessie offered.

"No." Karla said coldly.

"Are you mad at me?" Jessie shivered.

"I don't know."

"Karla, we're eighteen. Let's not be stupid." Jessie rolled her eyes. "The drama is for the underclassman."

"I feel like I'm losing my best friend." Karla stopped writing in the dirt and looked up at Jessie.

"You're not. It's senior year. We'll drift for a while, but it happens to everyone."

"Do you want to drift?"

"Karla, you don't like my friends and they don't like you. What do you want me to do?" Jessie threw her hands in the air.

"Stop being friends with them." Karla stated.

"Can't do that." Jessie laughed lightly.

"I heard people talking. I do have your friends in my classes." Karla informed. "Said you were applying to IPFW and going to room with Shelby and Carrie." Karla huffed.

"It was an option. No one knows the future." Jessie rolled her eyes. "Why don't you try to go to college?" Jessie asked.

"Because college is for conformists."

"A true conformist would say that." Jessie scoffed.

"Give me a break." Karla hissed.

"Face it, Karla, we have no money saved. We're not going to Florida, and our plans aren't going to work." Jessie blurted.

"You don't want to go." Karla crossed her arms over her chest.

"No, I don't. I don't want to be a bartender. I don't want to help people get drunk." Jessie explained.

"Get off your high horse." Karla stood up. Jessie sat on the step looking up at her. "Jessie, I know you will change your mind before graduation." Karla looked down at her.

"Look, I really doubt it. I don't know what God wants for me." Jessie stood next to her. "I better go before this friendship does end." Jessie started walking to her truck. Karla called to us as we got in.

"They're not your true friends, Jessie. I'll show you." Jessie ignored Karla and sped off toward home. When we got to the stoplight, Jessie called Leo.

"Hello?"

"Leo!" Jessie exclaimed.

"Jessie!" he mocked.

"So I just got back from Karla's."

"And?"

"She's sooooo mad."

"Why?"

"Because she wanted me to stop being friends with my friends and I told her no, and then I told her I didn't want to move to Florida and be a bartender. She got really mad and told me to get off my high horse."

"Jessie, don't listen to her. She's just jealous because you want to do something with your life and it's possible. It's not for her because she isn't even trying. I'm proud of you, Jess. I really am." Leo unloaded.

"Awe, thanks." I noticed Jessie blush.

"Welcome. Is that why you called?"

"Yes. I had to vent, and I don't have anyone in the truck to talk to." Jessie sighed.

"Well, you know I'm here whenever you need me."

"Thanks, Leo. Well, I know you have to babysit your sisters."

"Yeah. Great way to spend a Saturday." Leo grew irritated.

"But it's cool. You're there for your parents and sister."

"Mom and step-dad." Leo corrected.

"Whatever." Jessie laughed.

"Alright, Jess. I will talk to you later."

"Ha! Alrighty. Bye." Jessie said, and then closed her phone.

Period 1: Art

"I hate Mondays!" Jessie slammed her backpack on the art table, causing Shelby, David, and Leo to jump. Jessie snickered.

"I hate it when you do that." David rolled his head to look at Jessie.

"Sorry." Jessie smiled.

"Forgiven." Leo's deep voice rumbled.

"So, Leo," Jessie cocked her head, "are you coming to my orchestra concert tonight?"

"I am." Leo looked up and smiled. I'm going to sit in the middle section, if there's room."

"You can sit with my family." Jessie insisted.

"Alright." Leo shrugged. "Are you nervous?"

"No, I've been doing this for like seven years." Jessie sat down in her seat and grabbed some supplies from the middle of the table.

"True. Do you have a solo?" David asked.

"Not alone, but the first violins have their own part."

Jessie placed her supplies in front of her. She got up and headed to her small locker that contained her elephant charm and some saw blades.

"I'm kind of excited to see it." Leo looked up at Jessie. "I've never seen the orchestra perform."

"We're good. Oh, and Carrie has a viola solo. She is so amazingly good." Jessie sighed.

"She is." Shelby agreed. "I've heard her; she's really good." Shelby looked over at Leo.

"Are you?" Leo asked Jessie.

"I guess. I'm a first violin in advanced orchestra." Jessie shrugged.

"I'd say that meant you were really good." David said as he sawed off the last piece of his charm. "Aha!" David held up his charm.

The charm was the symbol for males, the circle with the arrow coming out of the side. I couldn't help but roll my eyes. Leo looked at David with confusion, and David looked at Leo.

"I like boys." David blurted. Leo turned red.

"Are you blushing?" Jessie teased.

"Uh, no. He just said it so bluntly," Leo shivered.

"Awe." Shelby teased.

"Hey, I'm proud of who I am." David defended himself.

"That's fine." Leo shrugged. Leo started sawing off the last metal piece that hung off of his charm.

"Aren't you proud you're Mexican?" David placed his charm on the table. Jessie and Shelby looked at each other.

"It's not the same." Leo shook his head at David.

"Really?"

"Really. I was born Mexican."

"And I wasn't born gay?" David crossed his arms and rested them on the table.

"No . . . look . . . everyone likes to kiss gay people's butts. News Flash: You're not born that way. You got some kind of chemical imbalance." Leo blurted.

Jessie and Shelby's eyes widened. I agreed with Leo but not about the chemical imbalance. David was not born gay. David's mouth gaped open.

"I'm sorry. It's how I feel. It's like it's a competition with straight people of who has the most gay friends. And, quite frankly, I don't care if I don't have any."

Leo jerked the saw down, cutting the last piece loose and breaking his blade. He grabbed his charm and blew the dust off. No one said anything. I think Leo had that built up inside ever since David came out to them. David's eyes started to water.

"Don't you dare cry." Leo looked up at David with anger. Uh oh.

"Leo." Jessie ducked her head low.

"What, Jessie?" Leo boomed.

"Nothing," Jessie said as she sat back in her chair.

Jessie had never seen Leo act like that. Shelby was in shock and David's feelings were hurt. Jessie didn't know that Leo was so uncomfortable around gay men. I mean, most straight guys were but she didn't even think twice to ask Leo how he felt about it.

Period 2: Algebra

Jessie sat doodling on her notebook (typical day). Mr. Delarosa wrote the lecture on the board. Jessie felt a tap on her shoulder. She turned around to see Karla holding out a folded piece of paper. Jessie kept her eyes on Mr. Delarosa and slowly unfolded the paper. She placed it on her desk and read it.

Hey. Sorry about Saturday. Wanna go to lunch and talk?
Jessie wrote back. This went on for most of the class period.
I can't. I promised Shelby and Leo I would go with them.
This is more important!
How, Karla?
I'm your best friend.
So are they, and they asked first.
Whatever. Backstabber
Karla! Grow up!
Me grow up!? Ur ditching me for ppl that don't even care about you.
Omg. I'm not going through this again, Karla. We can have lunch tomorrow.
No! Have lunch with your new best friends all year.
I will!
Good!

Jessie tossed the paper over her shoulder. No response. Jessie huffed and rubbed her temples. Jeremy looked over at her.

"You okay?"

"No." Jessie looked at him.

"Can I help?"

"Not with this." Jessie shook her head.

"Alright. You let me know if there is anything that I can do." Jeremy rubbed Jessie's shoulder.

"Thanks," Jessie said. The folded piece of paper came from over her shoulder. Jessie opened it.

Look Jessie, I'm really sorry. You're my best friend and I don't want to fight. We can have lunch tomorrow. I just miss hanging out with my best friend. And, well, if I wanted to bad enough, I could try to be friends with Shelby and them. I'm sorry. Best Friends?

Jessie wrote back a short reply.

Best Friends J Jessie tossed the paper over her shoulder. She heard Karla catch it.

"Yay!" Karla said happily. Jessie laughed.

Period 6: Sociology

Jessie and I stood at her and Leo's locker exchanging books. Jessie grabbed her Sociology book and placed her accounting book where her Sociology book was.

"Jessie, I'm sorry about David." Leo said as he approached the locker. He unzipped his backpack and exchanged his books.

"Don't tell me sorry. You didn't hurt my feelings."

"Jessie, he makes me so uncomfortable. If he wasn't so 'I like boys' all the time, it wouldn't bother me, but he talks about boys all the time." Leo rested his forehead on the closed locker next to theirs.

"Look, Leo. He's gay and he's happy he's out of the closet. All we have to do is let him get it out of his system and he'll die down with it. I promise." Jessie hugged her textbook.

"Alright. Sorry. I didn't say it at lunch, but I just wanted to talk to you one on one."

Leo placed his hand on the small of Jessie's back, closed the locker, and walked her to class. Leo hugged Jessie as he dropped her off at her class. Jessie took her seat beside Karla and James. Jeremy and Shelby were cat-a-corner behind her and Justin was right behind her.

"Hey, Jessie, how was lunch?" Karla glared at Shelby.

"Great! Had fun. You should come next time." Jessie took her seat. I looked over to Shelby and her face was glowing with anger.

"No. We can't be doing that. Shelby doesn't like me." Karla cocked her head and looked at Shelby.

"You don't like her either," Jessie stated.

"Ew, I wanna hit her so bad." Justin shook his fist at Karla. Allen and the rest laughed.

"What's so funny?" Jessie turned around.

"We'll tell you in English," Allen said.

Allen flashed a wicked grin at Karla. She stared at him for a minute and then flipped him off. Everyone looked at her.

"I hate her." Jeremy whispered to Shelby.

"Me, too." Shelby rolled her eyes.

"Why does Jessie stay friends with her?" Jeremy nudged Shelby's arm.

"Have no clue." Shelby shook her head. "Have no clue."

The class period seemed to go on forever. Sociology was taught by Mr. Neal. Everyone loved him because he didn't make anybody do anything. He told them to read a chapter, do the assessment assignment at the end, and the rest of the time the students talked, texted, and slept. So, they all grew to love Mr. Neal and his Sociology class.

Period 7: English 12

Jessie didn't wait for Leo at the locker. She grabbed her books and headed to class. She had forgotten to the read the poem on page 546 and answer the ten questions about it. 'How can there be ten questions on a poem that's only five lines long!?' Jessie asked Leo the day the assignment was given. Jessie slammed in her seat and started reading the poem. She wrote down the questions and answers rather quickly.

"Dang, Jessie." Jeremy laughed as he took his seat beside her.

"I know. I know." Jessie said still writing.

"I know . . . how can there be ten questions about a five-line poem?" Jeremy asked Jessie.

"Yes," Jessie looked up at Jeremy, "my point exactly! Finally someone gets it!" Jessie said and then started writing down her answers as quickly as possible.

"I hate poetry anyway." Jeremy mentioned.

"Me, too" Jessie agreed. Leo took his seat in front of Jessie.

"Didn't do your homework last night?" Leo asked as he unzipped his backpack.

"Nothing gets passed you." Jeremy smarted. Leo didn't pay any mind to Jeremy's comment. Jessie scribbled down her last answer right before the bell rang.

"Saved by the bell," Jeremy and Leo said in unison. Jeremy gave Leo a glare, and Leo returned it.

"I'm so ready for your orchestra concert." Leo said as he sat in his seat and then turned to face Jessie.

"Really?" Jessie squinted.

"Really."

"Cool. One of the songs we're doing I am personally in my heart dedicating it to you," Jessie smiled.

"Awe. I feel honored, Jessie. I really do." Leo tossed her a smile. I looked at Jeremy. His eyes narrowed and his face was full of jealousy.

"Good." Jessie rubbed Leo's shoulder.

The class began. Mrs. Lazarus taught on the five-lined poem and then gave the assignment—an assignment I know Jessie would hate.

"I want you guys to write your own poems." Mrs. Lazarus clasped her chubby hands and dropped them in front of her.

"No!" Jessie yelled.

"Yes! Miss Craig, I know you can do it." Mrs. Lazarus said as she grabbed a tin can. "I will pass this around and you have to draw a piece of paper. Whatever it says is what you have to write about."

Mrs. Lazarus started walking around the room and people drew from the tin can.

"No!" Jessie yelled again.

"Yes!" Mrs. Lazarus yelled back.

I heard kids moan and groan. Some were happy about what they got; most were not. Mrs. Lazarus came to Leo. He drew a piece of paper, read it, and sighed.

"I hate this." Jessie looked up at her teacher.

"I know."

Mrs. Lazarus shook the tin can. Jessie reached in and grabbed a piece of paper. She opened it and didn't say anything.

"Good and Evil?" Jessie looked up at her teacher.

"That will be interesting for you, Jessie." Mrs. Lazarus smiled.

"Better than what I got." Leo huffed as he turned to face Jessie.

"What?"

"Love." Leo sighed.

"Ha! Just write about me. Hahaha!" Jessie slapped her hand on the desk laughing.

"Funny," Leo said sarcastically.

"I got sports!" Jeremy fist-pumped.

Jessie looked back at her friends. Shelby got the future, Carrie got cats, Justin got music, Allen got school, and David got the meaning of life.

"I'm content actually." Jessie shrugged to Leo.

"I guess I am, too." Leo shrugged back.

"These are due in a week." Mrs. Lazarus took her seat at her desk. "You may talk till the end of class," she informed.

The students sat talking about the subjects they got for their poems. I was excited to see what Jessie was going to come up with.

"This sucks," Jessie griped.

"I thought you were content?" Jeremy asked.

"I thought I was, too." Jessie sighed.

"I agree," Carrie chimed.

"I have the meaning of life," David said as he rested his head on Carrie's shoulder.

"Awe."

"Hey, Jessie, you want to . . ."

"Jessie, wanna work on it together?" Leo butted in cutting Jeremy off.

Jeremy shot Leo a dirty look. If looks could kill, Leo would have been dead.

"Sure," Jessie shrugged. "What were you going to ask?" Jessie turned to Jeremy.

"Nothing," Jeremy glared at Leo, who stood there grinning in triumph.

Orchestra Concert

Jessie, Carrie, and Justin stood together behind the curtain waiting to assemble into their seats on stage. Jessie looked nervous, probably because Leo was supposed to be there.

"You okay, Jessie?" Carrie leaned to look at Jessie.

"Yes." Jessie said nervously.

Mrs. LeBell motioned them to enter the stage. The students walked on stage taking their seat. Jessie peered out into the crowd. Her mom, dad, cousins, and brother were in the center section, and next to her brother was Leo. He beamed from ear to ear. Jessie smiled to herself.

"He's here." Carrie leaned.

Mrs. LeBell cleared her throat and gave Carrie a death glare. Mrs. LeBell tapped her "wand" on the music stand. She lifted her hands above her head and then dropped them. As soon as she did, the students started to play. Beautiful music filled the air. I was standing behind the curtain watching Jessie play. My arms were crossed over my chest. I watched as she moved her finger on the neck of the violin and, at the same time, she moved her other arm up and down strumming the strings with the bow. The song went from cheery to sad. They moved peacefully in unison. Carrie's solo was coming up. She adjusted her bow as the first violins finished their segment. She lifted her bow and started playing. The first violins' last note lingered in the room as Carrie played her solo. She was graceful; absolutely amazing. I saw Jessie beaming from ear to ear as her best friend played her heart out on her viola. The concert went by surprisingly fast. The students filed off of stage and headed back to the orchestra room.

"Carrie, you did beautifully!" Jessie ran up to her friend and hugged her.

"I was so nervous." Carrie admitted.

"But you were amazing. I think I choked up." David said as he lightly laid his cello on its side.

David grabbed his case, picked up his cello, and hoisted it in. He closed the case and then leaned it against the wall.

"Awe, thanks."

"It was really pretty." Justin placed his hand on Carrie's shoulder.

"Leo is here." Jessie smiled.

"Oh, that's who you were looking at?" Carrie placed her viola in its case and loosened her bow strings.

"Yeah! Who else?" Jessie did the same with her violin.

"Jeremy is here, also." Carrie looked at Jessie.

"Oh."

"Oh, wow, two hotties after you. Go girl." David placed his hand on Jessie's arm and laughed.

"No, this isn't good." Dread washed over Jessie.

"Why?" Justin asked.

"I just have a bad feeling about Leo and Jeremy, that's all."

Jessie tugged at her red dress. In this orchestra, the girls wore long, red dresses and the boys wore tuxedos. Very professional.

"Jessie, you were so good." Leo approached them.

"I'm glad you came." Jessie hugged Leo.

"I told you I was going to." Leo smiled.

"Get it girl." David winked.

Leo looked at David. He went to say something but stopped himself. I think he was going to apologize.

"I have to get out of here, though. Got homework." Leo hugged Jessie. "You were great," Leo said and then turned on his heels and walked out. Jessie sighed as she watched him walk away.

"Girl, you're in love." David broke Jessie's train of thought.

"I am not!" Jessie argued.

"Uh huh." David cocked his head upward.

"He didn't even comment my solo." Carrie frowned.

"When Jessie's in the room, no one else exists." Justin blurted.

"Not true." Jessie argued.

"Very true." Justin placed his violin in his orchestra locker.

"Maybe so." Jessie smiled to herself.

After every orchestra concert, Jessie and her family go out to eat. Jessie changes back into her street clothes and they all head to Applebee's to top off the night. It was like this every time Jessie had a concert. Her family was proud of her for sticking with it for so long and being really good at it and practicing her songs all the time. She practiced at least three hours every day or every other day. Jessie took her violin very seriously. I am very proud of her.

Period 2: Algebra 2

Jessie and Karla seemed to be getting along. Karla didn't say anything that made Jessie mad and Jessie kept her cool when she talked to Karla. Even if the conversation wasn't going wrong, Jessie had this agitation that she started to develop toward Karla.

"I have to tell you something, Jessie. I wasn't going to because I didn't want to hurt your feelings." Karla dropped her head down.

"What?" Jessie grew worried.

"I was walking to this class and I always see Leo talking with Allen and James. Well, they asked him if he went to your concert."

"Yeah." Jessie started getting angry.

"Well, he said he did but he would never go to another one because it was really boring and he noticed you you kept messing up." Karla lied.

I was mad. Karla just clearly lied to Jessie. I know that Leo did not say that.

"You're lying." Jessie came forward.

"I wouldn't lie about that, Jessie. You're my best friend. I have your back."

"He really said that?"

"Yes, he did. He said that you kept messing up really bad but tried to play it off. Jessie, I didn't want to tell you but, as your best friend, I had to." Karla tried to play innocent.

"Wow, I can't believe this!" Jessie slammed her hands on the desk.

Everyone looked at Jessie. I was getting angry with Karla. She was trying to rip Jessie and Leo apart and she knew how because she knew Jessie took her music and her violin extremely serious.

"I am so mad!" Jessie exclaimed almost crying.

"Don't tell him I told you," Karla hissed.

Jessie should have known right then that she was lying. Someone that lied always says that.

"Wow. Thank you for telling me. He seemed so excited and happy at the concert and when we were here in class and talked about him going."

Jessie sighed in defeat. *Don't believe her, Jessie!* I wanted to scream at her.

"Jessie, well, he . . ." Karla tried to make up a lie. "He probably did that to make you think he cares." Karla made her voice go soft. She was milking this for everything she had.

"My violin is very important to me. I'm done with him lying to me and patronizing me."

Jessie fumed with anger. I couldn't say anything and don't believe her but she couldn't hear me. Jessie turned back around in her seat. Karla had a perfect opportunity because Justin and Jeremy were both absent and Justin would have told Karla she was a liar. Jeremy, on the other hand, might have tried to help Karla pull it off.

Period 3: Business Foundations

Jessie bolted to her business class. She knew that Leo would already be there taking notes from the board. She was fuming mad. I walked beside her. *Lord, please don't let her believe this. Please.* Too late. Jessie barged into the classroom.

"I can't believe you said that!" Jessie yelled.

"Hello to you, too." Leo looked up at Jessie.

"Did you tell Allen and James that my concert was boring and that I kept messing up?"

Jessie's eyebrows grew together in anger, her lips pierced into a flat line, and her nostrils flared. Leo looked around him.

"Jessie, what are you talking about?" Leo said softly.

"Don't play dumb." Jessie scoffed. She was still standing up.

"Jessie, I really don't . . ." Leo said.

The poor guy was being attacked for no reason and it was all Karla's fault.

"Karla told me that you . . ."

"Okay, stop right there." Leo held his hand up. "Whatever Karla says is a lie." Leo grew angry.

"No, she told me that you said that my concert was boring and that I kept messing up."

The class looked at them. The teacher wasn't in yet and the bell wouldn't ring for another five minutes.

"Jessie, I never said that. I loved your concert." Leo stood up.

"Then why did you tell James what you did?"

"I never talked to James about it." Leo defended himself.

"Allen?"

"No." Leo shook his head. He was actually keeping his cool and not getting mad.

"I don't believe you. You've lied to me before and you'll lie to me again!" Jessie slammed her hand on his desk.

"Jessie, Karla's deceiving you." Leo pleaded.

"I care about you and what you think about the things I do and how I am. And when you bash one of my passions, something I truly love and live for, I can't believe you."

Jessie turned on her heels and walked out of class. Karla waited for Jessie at the door. She gave Leo a wicked smile. I stood there for a moment. Leo didn't blink; he didn't move at all.

The day was almost over. Jessie didn't go to lunch with Leo. she didn't talk to him at the locker. She was very cold to him. She shut the locker when she saw him approach and pushed his desk away from hers.

"You're being childish," Leo blurted when he saw Jessie kick his desk away from her.

"You started all of this."

"No, your bitch of a friend did." Leo shot back.

Jessie's friends heard what had happened. They were all mad at Karla. Jessie had yelled at all of them to leave her alone and all of them were just out to hurt her and didn't really care about her. Karla had told Jessie at lunch how her friends didn't seem like they cared much. It was the perfect time to tell her because Jessie was already mad about the "Leo Lie". I was getting irritated and wanted to shake Jessie as hard as I could and tell her to snap out of this trance. Jessie glared at Leo and said nothing. The class went by quickly. Jessie didn't talk to anyone. She just sat and texted Karla. My heart was breaking. A little insignificant lie from one deceiving person could break up a lifelong group of friends. I didn't even think it was that big of a deal, but Jessie took her music very, very, very seriously. The class ended and Jessie headed to the locker. Leo followed her. He saw Karla standing at the locker. Leo stopped in his tracks, took a deep breath, and approached.

"You lie like a snake, Karla!" Leo yelled.

"What?" Karla played dumb.

"You know what I'm talking about!" Leo threw his hands in the air. Students stared at them as they passed.

"No, I don't." Karla acted shocked.

"You told Jessie a lie."

"Leo!" Jessie tried to cut him off.

"No, Jessie!" Leo's voice grew louder. "You told Jessie that I said her concert was boring and she kept messing up. I never said that!" Leo slammed his hand on the closed locker in front of him.

"Don't yell at her!" Jessie came to Karla's defense.

"You did. You told Allen and James." Karla cocked her head to the side.

Jessie looked at Leo. I looked at Karla and she wickedly grinned at Leo. Jessie turned to face Karla. She instantly put a frown on. Leo was extremely mad and his hands shook with anger.

"You can ask them, Jessie. I never said that." Leo pleaded. "Karla's a liar." Leo accused.

"Oh, yeah. Well, who didn't tell Jessie that he went to Mexico but then came back junior year?" Karla dug up the past.

"That's the damn past."

"Stop!" Jessie put her hands against her ears. "I'm leaving."

Jessie grabbed her backpack, faced Leo, and smiled. Leo caught the smile. He looked at Jessie with confusion. Oh, my gosh. She knew Karla was lying and was playing this. I couldn't believe this! Jessie was smart. It was kind of deceitful, but it was smart nonetheless.

"Listen to me." Jessie looked at Leo. "I left a note in your notebook when you weren't looking in English." Jessie whispered in his ear. She pushed him back to make it look like she threatened him.

"I told my other friends, too. They know." Jessie faked. I was shocked. I thought Jessie believed Karla. Note to self: Never underestimate the human. Jessie looked over at Karla.

"Let's go." Jessie turned on her heels and started walking. I stood there just shocked. Karla walked up to Leo.

"I told you not to take my best friend from me. Now I have turned her against you. She doesn't love you." Karla laughed. "Say goodbye to your precious Jessie."

Karla stuck out her lower lip. A wicked grin crept across her face. Leo stood trying not to laugh, because Karla didn't know what Jessie was doing. Karla ran and caught up with Jessie. Leo pulled his notebook out and looked for Jessie's note.

Hey, babe. Sorry about third period. I was trying to act mad because Karla was there. She doesn't know that I know that you don't see James and Allen before first period. And I know you wouldn't say that about me. I then prayed to God and something in my spirit told me that she was lying. Hope you can forgive me. I'm about done with her. The others know what I'm doing. It may seem mean, but I'm protecting myself. God wants me to move on. Sorry about earlier. I'm not mad at you. I had no way of telling you what I was doing till now. Best Friends? Love you. Jessie.

Leo smiled and then headed home.

CHAPTER 16

The Chief

Jessie and Karla were spending more time together. I hope Jessie knew that she was doing. Karla would bad mouth Jessie's friends and Jessie would laugh along like nothing was going on. It was deceitful but all at the same time it was really smart. Jessie and Karla were sitting on her front porch listening to music.

"I'm so glad you're done with those losers." Karla laughed as she turned to face Jessie.

Karla's red hair bounced on her shoulders. She had gotten it cut earlier and was really into her new hairstyle. She had cut it above her shoulders and had layers. It was a really pretty cut.

"I really like your haircut." Jessie changed the subject feeling guilty about deceiving Karla, but Jessie didn't know of any other way to get rid of her.

"Oh, thanks. I thought I needed one," Karla smiled. "Gerard likes it." She beamed and I rolled my eyes.

"Can I tell you something?" Jessie winced.

"Of course." Karla sat on the step next to Jessie.

"Gerard has a girlfriend." Jessie blurted.

"Oh, I know." Karla smiled.

"And you're still wanting to date him or fool around with him?" Jessie sounded shocked. It was Karla I wouldn't put it past her.

"Yeah. I like him and I'm not going to let some hoe take him from me."

"Karla, he's not yours," Jessie laughed.

"I know that, but if I want something I go after it till someone gives up." Karla bounced her eyebrows.

"And this doesn't bother you?" Jessie lifted her shoulders.

"Nope."

"Do you know who the other girl is?

"No, he didn't tell me."

"I do." Jessie admitted.

"How do you know?"

"Jeremy told me and you know Jeremy hangs out with all the girls who know everything about everybody." Jessie noted.

"True. So, who is it?" Karla ran her fingers through what was left of her once long hair.

"Don't get mad." Jessie said.

"I won't." Karla rolled her eyes.

"Tiffany Zane." Jessie said. The name lingered in the air and Karla's face turned red making her freckles pop out and look 3D.

"Karla." Jessie titled her head.

"I can't believe this. She always gets in the way." Karla punched her thighs repeatedly.

"Karla, it's okay. If your content with sharing him, then share him."

"That's the thing, Jessie. I was okay with it till you told me it was Tiffany Zane. Now I got to make sure I get him away from her." Karla put her hands over her face. "How long have they been dating?" Karla said in her hands.

"Since like November, I guess."

'They're never in the halls together. I never see them together."

"Well, Leo and I have seen them making out in the parking lot. He like grabs her butt and pulls her up against him. They go at it all the time." Jessie blurted.

I knew Jessie was telling Karla this on purpose. She wants to make her as miserable as possible, and it was working. I sat on the swing shaking my head at this ridiculous conversation.

"Ugh. He does that same thing to me!" Karla stood up. "They're dead." Karla's eyes filled with hatred.

"Thanks for telling me." Karla hissed.

"Are you going to confront them?" Jessie looked out into the road.

"No, I'm going to get him caught." Karla smiled.

"Right on!" Jessie agreed.

"Yeah. He needs to decide—me or her." Karla scoffed. "Let's go get some food."

Karla shut the stereo on the porch off, grabbed her purse, and we headed to her car. Jessie jumped into the passenger's seat. Karla turned on the ignition and Mudvayne blared through the speakers. Jessie tensed up.

"Jessie, it's okay. They're not going to jump out of the speakers and attack you." Karla laughed as she turned on the ignition.

"I know that." Jessie rolled her eyes.

"It's just music, Jessie. I don't see what the big deal is." Karla put the car in drive.

"I wouldn't expect you to understand." Jessie rested her head against the head rest.

"Well, I know that you're a Christian, but don't you think you're taking it a bit far?"

Karla looked over at Jessie. The car slowly came to a stop. Karla looked both ways and then we headed forward.

"Look, Karla, I will explain to you sometime. I just don't want to talk about it right now." Jessie sighed.

"Okay, I'm sorry. You be you and I'll be me." Karla turned onto the bypass.

"Sounds good to me." Jessie agreed.

"So how is it going with Leo and them?" Karla said with slight irritation in her voice. I sat in the back seat and looked at Karla through the rearview mirror.

"Oh, they hate us for sure," Jessie smiled uneasily.

"I'm glad you believed me." Karla put on a front.

"Yeah, you're my best friend. I know that you wouldn't lie." Jessie said trying to make Karla feel guilty.

"Oh, I got your back for sure. They talk about you all the time." Karla looked over at Jessie. My spirit was officially mad!

"Yeah, well at least I have you," Jessie faked.

"You know it!" Karla laughed.

"I'm really sorry all this happened," Jessie apologized.

"Hey, let's just forget about problems. There's a band playing at the 309 down from Charlie's. We can get some Jack and Jim and just rock out all night." Karla pulled the car into Wendy's parking lot.

"You know I don't do that anymore." Jessie sighed.

For old time sake?" Karla smiled.

"No thanks." Jessie hesitated.

I could tell that she wanted to. I saw a black shadow come up to my door. I looked to my right and saw Achish standing outside looking down at me. He smiled. I looked at Karla and Jessie, waiting for them to get out.

"Jessie, one time is not going to hurt you?" Karla pleaded.

"Karla, I said no." Jessie stood firm. Anger flashed in Karla's eyes and her gaze narrowed.

"This Christian thing is really getting on my nerves, Jess."

Karla's voice had a dark discord. Achish pulled the handle of my door and just stood there.

"You not accepting and getting over it is on my nerves." Jessie argued.

"Whatever."

Karla grabbed her purse and jumped out of the car. Jessie took in a deep sigh and followed. I grabbed the door handle as quickly as I could and flung the door open. It slammed into Achish causing him to fall to the ground. He moaned and then looked up at me. I watched Jessie as she entered the restaurant. I looked down at Achish.

"You're not welcome near us." I informed.

"Yes, I am." Achish jumped to his feet.

"Well, you just heard Jessie reject Karla's offer." I walked toward him.

"I heard but, as long as Karla is around, I'm allowed to be. This isn't over, Tristan. Karla has just begun her manipulation."

Achish's dirty, blonde hair blew in the breeze. The smell of alcohol radiated off of his body and filled the air. His tall stature blocked the sun and I could see his features better. He was drunk. The wind almost knocked him down. I rolled my eyes at him but he didn't seem to notice. He just stood there.

"I'm sure Jessie will be strong enough to ward off whatever Karla and you guys throw at her." I kept my eyes on him.

"I don't think so," Achish said as he wobbled and tried to walk to me. I kept my eyes on him.

"Jessie loves to drink, Tristan. It's in her blood, handed down from generation to generation. Her great grandfather was a drinker, her grandfather was, her dad was, and now she is." Achish laughed at his comments. "She's not that strong, Tristan." Achish grunted.

"I've had about enough." I balled my hand into a fist and then blasted Achish in the face. He flew back against Karla's car, slid down, and sat on the ground not knowing what had hit him.

"Big mistake, angel dust."

Achish looked up at me. He grabbed a bottle of Jack Daniels out of his packet and threw it at me. I dodged it and it fell to the ground breaking open and all the contents leaving. The liquid flowed down the parking lot.

"Oh no."

Achish got up and ran to the broken bottle. He picked up the bottle, trying to saver what was left. I looked beside me and saw the neck of the bottle beside my foot. I looked over at Achish who was too busy trying to save his precious whiskey. I picked up the broken neck and slowly walked up behind him. I gripped it with my hand leaving the point poking out of my palm. Achish grunted and sighed in ecstasy as the whiskey touched his tongue. I raised the broken glass above my head and then thrust my hand forward stabbing Achish in the neck. He dropped the part of the bottle he was holding and grabbed his neck. He wheezed and spat out blood. I let go of the piece of glass and watched Achish fall to the ground. The piece of glass stuck out of his neck. Blood was squirting all over the place—the ground, nearby cars, and me. He tried to choke out a sentence but he couldn't. His eyes grew wider. A high-pitched noise filled the air. I put my hands over my ears and looked around. The trees were bent over. The birds in the sky lost formation and scattered trying to find shelter. I looked down at Achish. The sound still resonated in the air. Finally, Achish's head exploded. I covered myself with my wing and felt chunks of flesh and shards of glass hit against my wing. I heard parts hit the ground. When all was silent, I looked around me. Pieces of Achish's head laid strewn all over the place. I looked at the outside of my wing. I pulled a hunk of flesh with hair attached off of my wing and flicked it to the ground. *That's disgusting,"* I said aloud. At that time, Jessie and Karla exited the restaurant and got into the car.

Period 1: Art

Jessie sat working hard on her elephant charm for her mom. She didn't say much to the others at the table. Leo looked up at her for a moment but, when she didn't look up or say anything to him, he went about his business.

"So, you're going to catch Karla being . . . well . . . herself?" Shelby broke the silence.

"I don't know," Jessie said annoyed.

"You mad?" Leo asked.

"No. I just want to get this project done." Jessie growled.

"Sorry," Shelby apologized. Jessie didn't reply.

"I think it's smart." Leo stated.

"Me, too. I think that she deserves to be caught and for people to see her for who she really is." Shelby added.

I could tell Jessie was getting annoyed. She slammed her saw on the table and looked at Leo and Shelby.

"You know what I think?" Jessie looked from Leo to Shelby. Their faces grew almost fearful. "I think we should shut up about it. It's manipulative and deceiving. It would make me no better than her." Jessie clenched her teeth.

"Jessie, it's not mean. You have to do something." Leo stated.

"I will. I will pray and put her in God's hands. Now drop the subject."

Jessie went back to her elephant charm. Leo and Shelby exchanged looks. I could tell Jessie didn't want to do that to Karla. She didn't even want to see the friendship take that dark turn. Jessie knew that she and Karla wouldn't stay friends forever or for very long.

Period 4: Accounting

Jessie and I walked down the hall toward Accounting class. Her friends waved as they passed, and she waved back. She wouldn't see Karla again till sixth period. I knew it was hurting Jessie to see her best friend being deceitful, manipulative, mean, and untrustworthy. Jessie didn't want to see her friend go down that road and she certainly didn't want to end being friends. Jessie and Karla weren't the same anymore and they hardly got along. Even though that was going on, Jessie still cared about her and still considered Karla her best friend. She probably always would. The hall started to become vacant as the students found their classrooms. Jessie moped into Accounting class. All the seats were taken except for the one by Tiffany Zane and Carrie. Jessie saw the brown beauty sitting quietly at her desk. She walked over and took her seat. Tiffany kept her eye on Jessie.

"Why are you sitting here? Your friend hates me." Tiffany arched her brow.

"She hates you. I don't." Jessie shoved her backpack under her seat.

"Oh. Why not?"

"Well, Tiffany," Jessie clasped her hands together and rested them on her desk. "I don't know you enough to form an opinion. Karla's opinion isn't mine."

Jessie looked over to Tiffany. Tiffany smiled. Her long, brown hair was pulled back into a long pony tail.

"Wow, I wasn't expecting that," Tiffany admitted. Neither was I.

"Jessie, did you get your work done?" Carrie leaned in.

"Yes."

"Good. 'bout time." Carrie chuckled.

"Right." Jessie nodded.

"Doesn't Karla hate Tiffany?" Carrie whispered.

"Yeah. So?" Jessie shrugged her shoulders.

"When she hears you talked to her and was nice about it, she's gonna be pissed." Carrie laughed.

"I don't care. She's not my mom. Tiffany doesn't seem so bad." Jessie shrugged.

"Cool." Carrie patted Jessie on the back and turned around to Erick and Danni.

"I know she's the other girl seeing Gerard." Tiffany blurted to Jessie.

"I was afraid of that." Jessie sighed.

"I don't understand why she hates me." Tiffany shook her head.

"Karla hates everyone and, if she can make someone miserable, she will." Jessie informed.

"I don't like her either. So, I guess I shouldn't complain about her hating me." Tiffany shrugged. She grabbed a piece of her pony tail and started to twirl it.

"Look, Karla is a can of worms. She really is. She is never happy, so she thinks she has to make people feel the same way. I don't mean to defend her behavior with Gerard, but she really does like him. I just think that she didn't care because it's you he's cheating on, and that was just a perk in the relationship." Jessie added.

"Should I break up with him?" Tiffany looked over to Jessie.

"And let Karla win?" Jessie grinned. "I don't think so."

Period 6: Sociology

Karla wasted no time to grill Jessie about talking to Tiffany.

"I can't believe you would stab my back like that." Karla huffed.

"Karla, get over it. I don't have to hate people because you do. Tiffany is not a bad person."

Jessie sat in her seat. Shelby and the others watched Jessie and Karla argue.

"She stole my boyfriend." Karla crossed her arms over her chest.

"News Flash!" Jessie yelled. "He's not your boyfriend. She's the one that owns that label of being his girlfriend. He's actually dating her. You're off to the side, so that's got to make you think of what he really thinks about you!" Jessie exclaimed.

"Ewwwww!" Carrie instigated. Jessie and Karla ignored her comment.

"Oh wow, Jessie," was all Karla came up with.

"Well, it's true, Karla. Stop being mad because I'm friends with people. Get over it." Jessie turned forward in her seat.

"You know I already told you, you don't want me against you."

"I'm so sick of you thinking you're some kind of bad ass." Jessie argued. The class was looking at them. Carrie and Jeremy exchanged looks.

"This may get ugly." Jeremy whispered to Justin.

"I really hope Jessie knocks her the hell out." Justin grunted.

"Us, too," Danni spoke up.

"I'm not afraid of you. If you think you're so tough and I should be scared of you going against me . . . well, Karla . . ." Jessie stood up, walked over to where Karla was seated, and got in her face. " . . . bring it!"

Jessie's spirit defended her. Her spirit and Karla's clashed. I could see that their friendship was now . . . over.

Jessie and Karla didn't speak or text for the rest of the day. I could tell Jessie was fed up. I could also feel the evil that was after us. More than before. They were coming at us with vengeance. They were after blood. From here on out, it would be nothing but war.

That Night

Jessie and I came home from hanging out with her friends. It was a fun time. We went out to eat and then bowling. No one fought and everyone seemed to enjoy everyone's company. Jessie slugged to her room. I think the excitement of the night got to her.

"Jessie, are you okay?" Toni asked as Jessie flopped on her bed.

I stood next to Toni looking at Jessie. Her face was pale and she looked clammy. I looked out the window and saw Letushion standing outside her window. He was making Jessie sick.

"I just need to sleep. Mom, my head hurts and I just need to lie in darkness."

Jessie got up and practically forced her mom out of her bedroom, closed the door, and shut off the light. I heard the box springs of Jessie's bed squeak and pop. It was very dark in Jessie's room, so dark that I waved my hand in front of my face and couldn't see it. The room grew cold and damp, and a musty smell arose in the room. I covered my mouth with my forearms. I heard laughing and moaning and I couldn't see anything. I turned my body around trying to hear where the voices were coming from.

"Over here, Tristan." I heard a voice giggle.

"No, Tristan, over here." I heard the demonic voice call above me. I looked up and still couldn't see anything.

"Tristan,"

"Tristan."

"Tristan."

"Tristan," they called to me from all over the room.

I heard pattering on the ceiling and the walls. They called for me but I couldn't see them. I could feel and hear them but couldn't see them.

"She's pretty; she sleeps so soundly." I heard one hiss. "Karla was right when she said Jessie didn't want her against her," another demon laughed.

I was getting mad because I couldn't see them. I could just hear them. A cloud moved and the moonlight shone through Jessie's drapes. It lit up the room, and my eyes widened as the moonlight exposed them. Demons hung on the walls, hung from the ceiling, and rested on the floor. They turned their attention to me. Their ugly heads tilted back and forth as they studied me. They clicked and chomped their teeth, and they growled and gnashed at me. One hung upside down from the ceiling facing me. His face was an inch away, and he smiled at me. I just looked at him.

"Jessie," he whispered.

"Jessie," another one whispered. They started crawling down the walls and toward me. They blocked me from Jessie.

"Jessie," another called.

"Jessie."

"Jessie."

"Jessie," they all called in unison.

The demon that had been in front of me dropped to the ground, landing on all fours. The others hushed. The leader started to bubble up and transform. His skin broke at the shoulders and the others stayed quiet. Jessie tossed and turned in her bed. I looked from Jessie to the leader of these demons and then back to Jessie. The silver symbol on my hand grew brighter. I started to lose my fear. The demon grew extremely tall. His skin ripped, exposing another being. He busted through the skin. It was him! Beelzebub! I hadn't seen him since Jessie's deliverance. He stood naked before me. His horns protruded out of his skull. Beelzebub was chief of the demons and he was the only demon with horns. His army of demons stood behind him. I felt the room expand and Jessie had moved further away. She was out of reach. His long, strong legs bent at the knees as he held his large form up. He was at least three feet taller than I. He pointed his long, boney finger at me. The nail was yellow and cracked. His eyes were black, his teeth were yellow and razor sharp, and his nose protruded and twisted wickedly from his mangled face. He lifted his arms up and the demons didn't make a sound. I just stood staring at him. I looked around to see if Truce or the others would show up. I guess I was on my own. *God is with me. Greater is He who is in me than he who is in the world,* I said to myself. I grabbed my sword. Beelzebub looked at me, to my sword, and then licked his lips.

"Ha! You make me laugh, angel."

He barreled toward me with his knees still bent. I didn't move. He growled at me and stopped an inch away from me. I looked up at him and his tongue was pierced three times. I noticed that he wasn't much for talking. He took his scaly hand, wrapped it around my throat, and pulled me up. I dropped my sword, my feet dangled beneath me, and I felt helpless. I pulled at his massive hand.

"We're coming after her, Tristan. She doesn't stand a chance." He growled at me and his hot breath swept over my face.

"You will not have her. My God won't allow it." I choked out.

"Your God?" Beelzebub tightened his grip around my throat. "Your God doesn't care about her. We had her once, Tristan. We can have her again."

His growl grew deeper. I couldn't breathe, and I thought I was going to black out.

"Beelzebub!"

We heard a deep voice boom from behind him. Beelzebub and I looked behind him.

"Michael!" he clicked his tongue and growled.

Michael stood looking at us. The demons around were pushed down into submission. Beelzebub walked over to Michael. His knees stayed bent causing his body to bounce a little as he walked. Michael's long, reddish brown hair draped over his shoulders and rested on his chest. The rest fell in the back stopping below his waist. His dark armor shone in the moonlight. The moonlight showed his warrior features. His sword hung at his side. I stared at Michael, who was one of the most beautiful beings I had ever seen. He was fearless.

"What," Beelzebub cocked his head to Michael, "are you doing here?"

"I'm warning you, Beelzebub, of your demise." Michael warned.

Beelzebub stood there for a moment. All I could see was his back side. Michael's face grew serious and angry. I looked around. The demons were still in submission to Michael. Beelzebub lifted his head.

"I won't lose this time, Michael," Beelzebub growled.

Michael pulled out his sword and pushed the sword against Beelzebub's throat. I want to be fearless like Michael. He was up against the chief demon that's only one down from Lucifer himself.

"Your father would punish you if I had slain you again."

Michael pushed Beelzebub against the wall, with the sword at his throat. Beelzebub grabbed Michael's blade, and I stared into Michael's eyes.

"We're told to be here," he growled.

"I command you to leave in the name of Jehovah God!" Michael yelled. Beelzebub growled and twitched as Michael mentioned God the Father.

"You hear me? I don't care what Karla says about Jessie. You are not welcome here!" Michael yelled.

I couldn't help but just stand there watching. Michael removed his sword from Beelzebub. He lifted his foot and kicked him out the window, which shattered into a thousand pieces. Beelzebub crashed to the ground. Michael stepped out of the broken window and into the backyard with his enemy. Beelzebub jumped to his feet, opened his wings, and hovered. He had black wings that were twenty feet wide, and they had protruding veins with claws at the end of each wing. Michael whistled and his white stallion came at his side. His stallion opened its wings that expanded fifty feet. *We're always one up on the enemy.* I smiled to myself and stood looking out the window.

"You don't belong here!" Michael yelled.

The earth shook, the sky went black, and the moonlight lit up the battle ground. The demons in Jessie's room had disappeared. I looked over to Jessie who was sound asleep.

Michael was now at the same height as Beelzebub. His white stallion huffed at the enemy. Smoke expelled from his nostrils and fire followed, catching Beelzebub's wing on fire. Beelzebub fell to the ground and his right wing was now burnt and gone. The ashes blew in the wind and Beelzebub screamed in pain and anger. He reached up and grabbed the stallion by the leg and yanked it down. Michael rolled off as the stallion crashed to the ground and jumped to his feet. He pulled out his sword, stabbing Beelzebub in the other wing pinning him down. Beelzebub jerked his wing back, ripping the thin flesh and setting himself free. I was transfixed on this battle—a true battle between good and evil. Michael didn't need anyone to assist him. He was that powerful and that fearless, although I felt like I had to do something. But what? Michael and Beelzebub battled all over the backyard. Michael threw his sword in the air, striking Beelzebub in the head. He fell to the ground, taking Michael with him. Beelzebub grew fearful. The ground started to shake violently. I looked over at Jessie and she was still sound asleep. I looked back out of the hole where the window had been. Michael grabbed his sword and jumped to his feet. I looked closely. The ground cracked like it did with Truce, me, and the others. Beelzebub's eyes grew wide with fear. He knew that he was losing to Michael, and he was in trouble by his father. I had never seen the Chief demon look so terrified. I never had a close encounter with Lucifer. I had run into him on my way to Earth when he was on his way to council to talk to the heavenly hosts, but I had never seen him. He was just a black mass with a voice. I've heard stories of Christ Jesus and Lucifer fighting and of Lucifer and God the Father arguing, but I've never seen him. A part of me wanted to and a part of me didn't. Michael has seen him numerous times, before and after Lucifer had turned his back on God.

The ground was cracked even more. Michael stood back. Beelzebub couldn't move. His face was mortified. Red light filtered through the cracks. I was seeing it all over again—the time I had encountered Hell. As quickly as a blink of an eye, a hand thrust through the cracks and grabbed Beelzebub by the waist and pulled him. Beelzebub clawed at the ground, making a whining noise like a dog that was hurt or in trouble. Heat filled the atmosphere and thunder clapped as the heat and cold of the January night competed for ownership of the night sky. Michael shielded his face from the heat. Beelzebub was then dragged into Hell. The ground closed up and smoke lingered. Michael stood there for a moment and looked where Beelzebub once lay. Lucifer had seen him being defeated by

Michael; therefore, he snatched him and took him back to Hell where he would be punished. That was Lucifer's hand. I was kind of intrigued and wanted to see more. Michael glared up at me as if he had read my mind. I didn't say anything. If I thought Beelzebub was the most evil being to ever be created, I had no idea what Lucifer would bring to the table. Michael had told me about a time when Lucifer resided in Heaven and was like God's best friend. They talked all the time together, but Lucifer couldn't deal with the betrayal of God making man. The story is sad. Lucifer had lost everything and now lives to torture and make sure men burn in Hell for eternity. Michael stood in the backyard, not moving an inch. His stallion regained strength and nudged his shoulder. He looked behind him, grabbed the stallion's snout, and petted him lightly. He kissed his stallion and walked around it to make sure it was okay. He then tossed his leg over the giant stallion and looked to me. He smiled and then nodded. He kicked the sides of the horse ever so lightly, then the stallion expanded its wings and took off. I watched as they flew into the night sky and got closer to Heaven, leaving Earth with such a force that it left a bright star in the sky.

I stood at the window looking at the sky and the stars, which I could now see since the smoke had cleared. The cold breeze crept across my skin. I thought of Lucifer for a moment and how he had given all that up to hurt man. It wasn't worth it. Leaving the comfort and riches of God and Heaven was not worth it to me. Man wasn't that bad. Yes, humanity had some serious problems but there were also good men and woman who loved God and others. I wondered if I would ever encounter Lucifer. I wonder if he misses God. Maybe he missed God so much that it made him even more hateful because he knew that he could never go back to the way that it used to be. I wondered if under all that sin and dementedness there lingering inside—deep, deep, deep, deep beneath the core—if he still had a love for God. I wondered if God still had a love for Lucifer, if he missed his company. All of this was running through my head. I don't get how Lucifer could give it all up just to prove one lousy insignificant point. I walked away from the window and headed toward Jessie. I pulled the covers to her chin, bent down, and kissed her cheek. Her skin was no longer clammy and her color had come back. I would have to get used to this. They were going to fight me for her for the rest of her life.

I thought of Jessie being a woman, old and gray, and my heart sank. Jessie was going to get old and there was nothing I could do about it. Her life was going to be full of so many trials and battles. I couldn't wait to see Jessie in Heaven where she and I could be together with God and be free and happy with no battles. I didn't want her to die. She still had work to do here on Earth, and my time for protecting her wasn't going to end anytime soon. But thinking of us in Heaven made me smile. I knew she was going to make it there. It was going to be hard and she may lose her direction here and there, but she would always come back to us. Jessie let out a sigh and then fell back into a deep sleep. I wonder what she was dreaming about. There was a peace that finally filled the room. I looked down at Jessie and the moonlight lit up her face that had such beautiful features. Someday she's going to find true love. My thoughts went to Jessie finding that one guy whom God had picked out especially for her. I was nervous for her. She was going to get married and have children, and that thought made me smile. I knew the guy God had picked out for her was going to treat her great. That I trusted; however, was I ready to share Jessie with anyone but God? She would always be my human, my best friend, and I knew deep inside that she was going to start making a life of her own. It really felt bittersweet.

I looked down at the symbol of a warrior on my hand and smiled to myself. I was proud of it and ready to live up to the title. I then shifted my attention to the golden eye on my other hand—the Guardian. I was more proud of that symbol than anything. I was a guardian, and I was blessed with watching over an amazing, talented, smart and dynamic person who was now a God-fearing human being. I think it would be different watching over a guy than a girl. I would probably be more over-protective of Jessie than I would be if I were protecting a guy. Maybe that was just my crazy thinking, but I know that I couldn't think of life without Jessie. I thought about how long I've known her, what we've been through, and how she was changing into what God wanted for her. An overwhelming love surfaced in my throat and a tear slipped from the corner of my eye. I loved this human, and I loved God. I can't explain how I feel, but the love I have for God and Jessie overwhelms me. I am forever at their service.

CHAPTER 17

Fighting the Truth

Jessie was almost like a zombie, in a trance. Something wasn't right. I knew she was torn between Karla and her other friends. She knew that her other friends would benefit her more, but Karla was her best friend and they've been through a lot together. It had to be hard letting go of someone you were close to. I stayed by Jessie's side as she slugged through most of the day.

Period 5: Orchestra

"Hey Justin, do you ever feel like something is hovering over you?"

"What do you mean?" Justin asked as he tuned his A string on his violin.

"Like someone's always watching you?" Jessie looked around the room.

"Like a fleshy human or an airy ghost?" Justin looked over at Jessie.

"Like a . . . I don't know." Jessie shrugged. "A lot of times I feel like all eyes are on me," Jessie said as she pulled her violin up to her and rested it between her cheek and shoulder.

"You look like you've broken your neck." David approached us. "I've got amazing news."

David sat next to Justin and Justin pulled away. He still wasn't used to knowing for a fact that David is gay.

"What's that?" Jessie looked over at Justin giving him a dirty look.

"I, David Lee Castleton, have a . . . boyfriend!" David exclaimed.

Justin, Jessie, and I flinched at the news. That is not something we were expecting to hear. Jessie and Justin exchanged looks.

"Um . . . who is it?" Jessie asked, acting like she was happy about it.

"He goes to the high school in Muncie and is a junior. His name is Trevor Niles. He's so dreamy, tall, athletic . . . ."

"We get it," Justin cut him off. David glared at Justin.

Well, we all knew that he was gay, but I don't think any of us expected him to have a boyfriend.

"Well, I'm happy for you." Jessie blurted.

"Thanks, baby girl." David bent down at hugged Jessie. Jessie embraced him returning the hug.

"Well, gotta tune the cello." David blew them a kiss and headed to where his cello was.

"Out of all the days, Carrie's absent." Justin shook his head in disappointment.

"Omg! I gotta tell Leo!" Jessie exclaimed.

"Leo is going to be pissed. He feels about David like I do." Justin grinned.

"I don't care. I want to tell him before David shocks him and Leo gets all weird and doesn't talk at the art table." Jessie looked around the room. "He's gonna be so uncomfortable and that's going to make me uncomfortable." Jessie moaned.

"I'm on Leo's side." Justin smirked.

"You guys get on my nerves." Jessie gave Justin a dirty look.

"Oh well." Justin shrugged and then finished tuning his violin.

Period 7: English 12

Jessie ran to the locker so she could catch Leo before he headed to English. She caught him right as he was exchanging books.

"He's so hot!" Jessie said aloud to herself. I rolled my eyes.

"Leo!" Jessie stood beside him.

"Jessie!" Leo exchanged the greeting.

"I have got to talk to you like ASAP." Jessie threw her Sociology book in the locker and jerked her English book from the shelf.

"What is it?" Leo looked at Jessie like she was a mad woman.

"I am breaking this to you."

"Jessie, you're scaring me." Leo cocked his head to the side. "Why?"

"Are you dating Jeremy?"

"What? No!"

"Oh, okay." Leo said relieved. Uh huh.

"Okay." Jessie didn't catch the hint. "Anyway, remember that God loves everyone and we should, too, no matter what." Jessie placed her hands on Leo's shoulders.

"Jessie, get on with it. I hate when you prolong bad news." Leo sighed.

"David's got a boyfriend." Jessie closed one eye, keeping the other one open to see Leo's reaction. Leo stood there . . . face blank.

"Man, that means he's going to go on and on about how hot his boyfriend is and all that kissing." Leo sighed in dread. "This sucks. I don't want to sit with him if all he's going to talk about is him and his boyfriend. Straight guys don't like that." Leo rested his hands on Jessie's forearms. Her hands were still on his shoulders.

"Look, babe, I know, but he's our friend." Jessie sighed.

"What if he talks about like sexual experiences. Oh, my gosh. I'm going to puke."

"Ha!" Jessie laughed. Leo looked at her like how could she see humor in this.

"You're so cute. He won't. If he does, I will tell him I don't like to hear that. I know that Shelby won't want to either. I just wanted to break the news to you because, if he dropped the bomb on you, you'd get pissed. We know that when you get pissed you take it out on me." Jessie sighed.

"I do not." Leo rebutted.

"Leo, you do, too. I do the same with you. When we're uncomfortable or mad, we take it out on each other. That's what we do. We've done it since ninth grade." Jessie smiled.

Leo pulled Jessie close in a hug. I lifted myself off of the locker and stood closer to Jessie.

"Get a damn room." Karla scoffed as she and Gerard passed.

Leo and Jessie looked up at her. He and Karla exchanged glares. Let the battle begin.

"Gerard, Tiffany is looking for you." Jessie called out.

"Ouch!" Leo laughed. Karla turned around and flipped Jessie the middle finger.

"Love you, too, bestie." Jessie called back.

"Let's go." Leo shut the locker and wrapped his arm around Jessie's shoulder.

"I thought you were going to like play mind games with her."

"I can't. She drives me crazy. I don't like her anymore. She's mean and disgusting. We're gonna probably battle the rest of the year. We might act like we get along and hang sometimes, but deep inside we don't like each other." Jessie took her seat and Leo followed suit.

"I'm sorry, Jessie. You got me." Leo smiled.

"So, Leo, did you hear?" David approached. Leo looked at Jessie and he braced himself.

"What's that?" Leo plastered a fake smile on his face.

"Jessie, didn't tell you?" David pointed to Jessie.

Leo shook his head. "I don't think so."

"What's up bro?" Leo lifted his head in attention and Jessie smiled.

"I have a boyfriend and I'm so excited."

"Oh, wow. Well, that's great. I'm happy for you."

Leo flashed a smile at Jessie. If I say so myself, I think Jessie blushed a little. David and Leo talked for a while and then David headed to his seat. Leo eased himself, dropping his shoulders and letting out a sigh.

"Awe. I'm so proud of you." Jessie smiled.

"Man, I thought I was about to lose my seriousness." Leo laughed.

Leo looked over at Jessie. I noticed something different in his eyes. He had always cared about Jessie, but there was adoration and love in his eyes when he looked at her. *Uh oh.*

"I think I just fell in love with you." Jessie laughed.

I closed my eyes for a moment. Why did she say that!? Leo didn't say anything. He tucked his long, black hair behind his ear. They kept each other's gaze. *Lord, guide this for Your purpose.* They were caught off guard by the teacher.

"I hope your poems are done. I gave you an extra two days and they're due Monday for sure." Mrs. Lazarus said as she sat her chubby frame behind her desk.

"Omg. I haven't' even written it." Justin gasped. Danni and the others laughed.

"I'm almost done." Jessie turned around.

"Me, too." Shelby, Danni, and Erick said in unison.

"David?" Erick asked.

"I'm writing about my first, real boyfriend," David sighed.

Leo growled. Jessie looked over at Leo and he gave her a pleading look. Jessie just smiled at him. Her eyes filled with love for him. *Please, Lord, help this situation.* The students were allowed to work on their poems for the remainder of the class period. Jessie leaned over to look at Leo's. He hovered over it and covered it up with his forearm.

"I don't want you to read it. I just want you to hear it." Leo narrowed his gaze.

"Well, sorry. You got the poem on love, didn't you?" Jessie bounced her eyebrows.

"Yes, I did, Miss Craig." Leo sighed.

"Ha! Better you than me."

"So what if you got the poem of love?"

"I wouldn't write it."

"Why?"

"Because, Leo, how can you write about something you have no experience with?" Jessie cocked her head.

"I . . ."

"How do you have experience? Oh, please don't tell me you're writing it based off of Ellen?" Jessie rolled her eyes.

"No, I'm not, thank you very much." Leo smarted.

"I'm just saying." Jessie shook her head at him.

"Just chill. I'm pretty much over Ellen." Leo stated. I felt excitement rush over Jessie. *Don't jump the gun, Jessie.*

"Oh. Well, my poem's alright. I got 'Good and Evil'—the sory of my life." Jessie laughed.

"Huh?" Leo quickly turned his head.

"Never mind." Jessie laughed.

"No, Jess. What did you mean by that?"

"Nothing. It's nothing. I was just making a joke." Jessie brushed it off.

"Jessica Jane, I can tell when you're lying to me." Leo tilted his head down.

"Leo, I'm not lying." Jessie tucked her blonde hair behind her ear and focused on her half-written poem.

"Jessie, you're hiding something." Leo pried.

"Leo, babe, please just drop it."

"If you're not hiding something then you can tell me what you meant by that comment. What did you mean when you said that good and evil was the story of your life?"

"Leo it's everyone's story. Everyone has to choose good or evil."

"No one takes it seriously, Jessie."

"They should."

"You're not hiding anything, right?" Leo reassured.

"Right," Jessie smiled a nervous smile, lying to Leo's face.

Jessie lay on her bed tossing a football into the air. She did that when she had a lot on her mind. I sat at the end of her bed watching and praying. Her phone vibrated with a text message. She retrieved it from her night stand and opened it. It was Karla.

"I am so sorry 'bout flippin' ya off. L" Jessie rolled her eyes but texted back.

"That's fine. I shouldn't have said what I did 'bout Tiff and Gerard."

"Yeah, well, I shouldn't have paraded around like he was mine."

"Yeah, but u really like him. It's understandable. J"

"Thanks, Jess. We cool?"

"Yeah."

"Best friends?"

"Friends," Jessie sighed and then closed her phone. Her phone vibrated again. It was another text message.

"Best Friends?" Karla had replied again asking.

"Friends," Jessie typed back. She didn't get a reply for about ten minutes. Jessie then said aloud, "Great. She's going off on me. God, would you just take her out of my life?" Jessie got another message.

"God! I am so sick of you. Do you not want to be best friends? Well, that's fine with me. I am so sick of you being so wishy washy. It's annoying. I never did anything to you to make you mad at me and not want to be my friend."

Jessie grew angry. She pushed the buttons furiously. *"Kar, this is so stupid. Leo is my best friend. He doesn't start trouble between me and my other friends. I want to be your friend, but I'm dun with best friends."*

Jessie powered her phone down, fell back on her bed, and started to cry. I lay next to her. I pulled her hair out of her face and tried to wipe the tears from her beautiful blue eyes. She sobbed into my arms and I held her close.

Today is Saturday. Jessie's parents were with Uncle Rocco and his girlfriend Missa. They were all going out to eat, so Rocco and Missa could double with someone and Mike and Toni could see how Missa was with Rocco. Rocco is Mike's younger brother and is Rodney's father. His real name is also Rodney but he got the nickname Rocco because he loved rock music. He also said "yo" a lot. So, they took the "y" off of "yo", respelled "rock" to "rocc", and came up with Rocco (originally Rocko). Travis was with Matt and Danny again and Jessie was home alone for a while. She thought about asking Karla to hang out but quickly decided not to. She sat on the edge of her bed still in her pajamas and her hair unbrushed. She didn't want to hang with Shelby because she only talked about Jared. Carrie was at a wedding, Justin was grounded, and Erick was of no interest to Jessie. She didn't have Tiffany's number and wasn't in the mood for Jeremy. So, she walked over to her bookshelf, grabbed her Bible, and walked back over to her bed. Sitting Indian style with the sacred book in her lap, she flipped to the New Testament and started reading the book of James. Jessie turned her radio over to the Christian station. She prayed and read her Bible the majority of the day. When she did that, I felt myself get stronger. Her praise and worship were making me stronger. I was so proud that she spent her whole Saturday with God. She did the same thing all day Sunday, too. I am one proud Guardian Angel.

The weekend went by really fast. It was already Monday and Jessie's poem was due today. I wanted to see what she had written, and I was also anticipating Leo's. I really wanted to hear what he had to say about love. Next week started the first week of February. Time was going by really fast.

Period 1: Art

Jessie worked hard on polishing her elephant charm for her mom. It looked really good. Even Leo was impressed.

"I am so ready to read my poem." David placed his hand on his chest.

"You still write about your boyfriend?" Shelby asked.

"Omg, yes! And yesterday we shared our first kiss!" David exclaimed.

"Wow," Leo chimed. Jessie just laughed.

"What?" David said with an attitude.

"Nothing," Leo said blowing the dust off of his charm.

"Well, what about you guys?" David looked at his friends around the table.

"Mine's done," Shelby shrugged.

"Me, too." Leo smiled at Jessie.

"Yup. I finished this weekend." Jessie smiled as she finished polishing her charm and held it up.

"Wow, Jessie, that's really good." Leo said shocked.

The elephant was gold. It was just an outline, but you could tell it was an elephant. Jessie had pulled a tiny, fake diamond out of one of her old torn up necklaces and used it as an eye for the elephant.

"Miss Jessie, that is simply gorgeous. It's got to go into the art show." Mrs. James placed her hand over her chest.

"Thanks and okay," Jessie smiled.

Jessie pulled a gold chain out of her pocket and slipped it through the loop at the top on the elephant's back. It was a really great project and I was proud of her.

"I want it." David gasped.

"This is for Mama," Jessie smiled.

"It's really nice, Jess," Leo noted.

Period 4: Accounting

Jessie and I walked to Accounting. I had a feeling this was also one of Jessie's least favorite subjects. She took forever getting to that class. She walked in and the only empty seat was the one between Carrie and Tiffany. Jessie smiled at Tiffany and took her seat beside her. Tiffany had highlighted her hair with blonde streaks.

"Your hair looks nice."

"Thanks," Tiffany smiled sheepishly.

"How are things going?"

"Really good. I'm surprised you haven't heard." Tiffany sighed.

"What's that?" Jessie looked over at Tiffany.

"Gerard and I broke up because he's moving back to Utah with his aunt, and I don't want to do a long distance relationship." Tiffany smiled.

"I didn't know that. Karla and I don't talk much." Jessie shrugged.

"Well, here's my number." Tiffany wrote her number down on the corner of a piece of paper ripped it off and handed it to Jessie. "I could always use a best friend," Tiffany smiled.

"Okay, sounds good. You okay with the break up?"

"Oh, yeah. He's going to Utah, so Karla won't see him either. So, I guess that's a perk." Tiffany laughed.

"Right." Jessie wrinkled her nose.

"May I ask what's up with you and Leo?"

"Nothing," Jessie stated.

"I don't know, Jessie. You guys seem like you're dating." Tiffany ran her fingers through her hair.

"Oh, I know, but we're not. I wish, but we're not." Jessie's face turned into a frown.

"I'm sorry. Maybe it will happen." Tiffany tried to reassure Jessie.

"I doubt it. We've been like this since freshman year." Jessie looked over at Tiffany.

"You love him?" she bluntly asked.

"Um . . . yeah I do." Jessie admitted. She looked around the room and her other friends were busy with their work.

"I thought so. I would tell him before it's too late." Tiffany suggested.

"Yeah, I know I should, but I'm scared. What if he doesn't feel that same?"

"You'll never know if you don't talk about it with him. I honestly think he loves you back. I see you guys in the hall and at lunch. I really think he feels the same." Tiffany admitted.

"Thanks." Jessie gave a half smile.

"I'm serious." Tiffany placed her hand on Jessie's arm.

Period 7: English 12

Jessie and I stood at the locker exchanging her books. Leo came up to us.

"I am so sick of Karla. She keeps mean mugging me and calling me a faggot." Leo blurted.

"What!?" Jessie turned to face him. "I will beat the hell out of her if she doesn't leave you alone. I'm not playing around. She's not going to be mean to you." Jessie grew angry.

"Jessie, it's okay I will handle it."

"You can't hit her, but I can." Jessie was extremely mad.

"Jessie, listen to me. The school year is almost over. Do not ruin anything. It's not worth it." Leo pulled Jessie into a hug.

"If you say so." Jessie released herself from his embrace. "Done?" Jessie grabbed the locker door.

"Done. Let's go read our poems."

Leo wrapped his arm around Jessie's shoulder and walked her to class. They took their seats. Everyone had their poems on their desks and they were nervous about reading them. Mrs. Lazarus entered the class, took attendance, and then stood up to announce the reading of the poems.

"Any volunteers so they can get it done and over with?" Mrs. Lazarus looked around the room. No one volunteered.

"Alright. Well, I will call someone and, when they're done, they will call someone." Mrs. Lazarus flashed a smile.

Mrs. Lazarus grabbed her grade book and opened it. She closed her eyes and ran her finger up and down the list of names. She stopped her finger. "My first victim is Jeremy McVayne." Mrs. Lazarus smiled.

"Damn it!" Jeremy scoffed.

"Language, Mr. McVayne." Mrs. Lazarus warned. "Tell us what your poem is about."

"My poem is about sports. Here I go.

'I love sports. They're so fun.
I love to play in the summer sun.
I like to shoot hoops and hit a baseball.
I like to watch sports in the fall.
I am in sports at my school.
All the girls think I'm really cool.
I'd rather play sports than write this lame poem.
But I have to graduate so I can play pro someday.
And I love sports all the way.
By Jeremy. Thank you.'"

Jeremy bowed. the class was quiet for a moment and then erupted in laughter.

"Class. Jeremy worked hard." Mrs. Lazarus spoke up.

"It's cool, Mrs. L. I wanted it to be funny." Jeremy shrugged and then headed to his seat.

"Pick someone." Mrs. Lazarus reminded Jeremy.

"Um . . . Jessie." Jeremy smiled.

"Miss Craig." Mrs. Lazarus smiled.

Jessie walked up to the front of the class. I was nervous for her and prayed for her the entire time.

"My poem is about good and evil.

'Good and Evil—Which should I choose?
Do I pick Evil and be destined to lose?
Do I pick Good and be shunned by the world?
Do I pick Evil and, in the end, in Hell I'll be hurled?
Demons come at me.
Angels protect me.
But will that suffice me?
So many questions about good and evil.

Is there a God? Is there a Devil?
I do choose God no matter what.
I have chosen Evil and was stuck in a rut.
The road of Good is never easy.
The road to Evil is oh so deceiving.
Good or Evil—What would you choose?
Evil, and be destined to lose?
Good or Evil?'"

Jessie finished up her poem. The class was silent and Leo looked deeply at Jessie studying her. I was proud. The poem was really good and Jessie hated poetry. Jessie made her way to her seat.

"Jessie, that was really good. You can pick someone." Mrs. L. reminded.

"Carrie." Jessie looked back and smiled.

Carrie's poem was cute, Justin's was a little off, and David's was unexplainable. He finished and headed to his seat.

"Leo." David called. I looked over at Leo. He grabbed his poem and headed to the front. He raked his fingers through his hair.

"Um . . . I had Love. Here goes nothing," Leo said as he nervously shoved one hand into his front pocket and held the poem with another.

"Her eyes are blue, reminding me of the sky God shelters me with.
I feel protected.
Her advice reminds me of the book of Proverbs.
I feel truth.
Her laugh is like the sun.
I feel warm.
Her complexion reminds me of the first winter snow.
I feel alive.
Her hair reminds me of the fields of Gold.
I feel peace.
Her friendship reminds me of children.
I feel my childlike faith.
Is this love?
Infatuation?
Life's lesson?
I don't know, but I am in love with the feeling."

Leo finished. I looked over at Jessie and her eyes were tearing up. Everyone looked from Leo to Jessie. Carrie and the others exchanged glances between each other. Leo took his seat next to Jessie, not looking at her. She didn't look at him either. I felt extremely awkward and I know that they did, also. If Jessie didn't get the hint, she was completely blind.

English was finally over and Jessie, Leo, and I headed out of the class to the locker. We walked side by side in silence. Leo sighed once in a while and Jessie didn't make a peep.

"You like the poem?" Leo broke the silence. I took a deep breath and leaned against the vacant lockers.

"I did. It had a lot of meaning." Jessie said as she placed her Accounting book in her backpack.

"Yeah, it does because . . . well . . . that's how I feel. I mean, I never really have fallen in love but I bet that's what loves going to make me feel like." Leo mentioned.

"So the poem was about a future love or a now love?" Jessie zipped up her backpack.

"I guess a little bit of both." Leo tucked his hair behind his ear. "I feel like I put myself out there, though." Leo looked over at Jessie.

"I understand. It's all going to be okay and come together." Jessie gave him a reassuring smile.

"I hope. What part did you like the most?" Leo asked.

"Um . . . 'Her eyes are blue reminding me of the sky God shelters me with. I feel protected'. I really liked that." Jessie sighed. "That was really sweet."

Jessie rested her hand on Leo's shoulder. There it was—the stare, the epic stare I've seen in all of Jessie's chick flick movies. It's the time where they look into each other's eyes and realize they love each other. There it is! I hate basing stuff off pointless movies, but when it's there it's there. I've never seen two people fall in love. I've been with Jessie for almost nineteen years and this was new to all of us. My spirit kind of jumped with excitement.

"Yeah, I think I'm going to give the poem to Ellen when I get it back." Leo shrugged.

Jessie's hand fell to her side. Rejection washed over her. It washed over me, too. *NO! Why did he say that?!* Tears filled Jessie's eyes.

"Glad this day is over," Jessie let out a fake laugh. "Gotta run."

Jessie gave Leo a light hug and bolted down the hall. I stood there with Leo for a minute. I wanted to have a serious talk with this boy. His eyes filled with regret and he sighed deeply to himself. Fear radiated from him. He was scared. He didn't say that to Jessie to make her mad. He was just scared. He loved her and it scared him. My heart sank for him. He couldn't get close to anyone.

Jessie ran to her room as soon as she got home, fell on the bed, and cried. I didn't know what to do. I sat next to her, stroked her hair, and rubbed her back. This was too much, and I couldn't tell her what I saw when I stood there for a moment with Leo watching her walk away. *This girl needs to be able to see and hear me.*

"Sis, it's me." Travis rapped on the door.

"I don't wanna talk to anyone." Jessie sniffled.

"It's me, your big brother, your best friend." Travis said through the door.

"Come in."

Jessie sat up on her bed, wiped the tears from her face, and fluffed her hair. Travis knew she was crying. He entered the room, closing the door behind him. Travis wrapped his arm around Jessie's shoulder.

"Let me guess. Leo problems." Travis looked at his sister.

"Yes." Jessie sighed. "I can't believe he rejected me like that." Jessie sniffled.

"You asked him out?"

"Well, no." Jessie sighed.

"Tell Bubby what happened." Travis pulled her close. Jessie took in a deep breath and explained to her brother what had happened between her and Leo.

"He's scared, sis." Travis shrugged. "He doesn't want to get hurt either."

"Bubby, he knows that I like him." Jessie looked at her brother.

"I know, but guys are different. I don't know why, but we just are." Travis stood up and faced Jessie.

"Jessie, you have got to keep it together. Stay close to God and family and you're going to make it. I can't have you falling apart on me like last time. I love having my sister back. Please focus on the future, a future I know that you want."

Travis kissed Jessie on the forehead and took his leave. He was right. Man, was he right.

Jessie and Leo had had a study date the next day after school. Jessie didn't really say much in school nor do much. Her mind was another place, and I got that. Her and Karla's friendship was basically over Leo and Ellen. Jeremy was still trying to get with her, and her grades were slipping. That's only her natural problems. Spiritually, she was in trouble. They knew she was getting weak. The less she prayed and read her Bible, the weaker I was getting also. Jessie and Leo met in the parking lot by Jessie's truck. The wind was blowing hard against us and the sky was a pretty blue.

"Wow, look at that pretty sky." Leo looked up to the sky and then over at Jessie.

"Ellen must be proud." Jessie smarted.

Here comes the lashing out. Leo didn't say anything. He just got into Jessie's truck. Jessie got into the driver's side and slammed the door. She rested her head on the steering wheel for a while and then looked at Leo who was already looking at her.

"Let's get this over with."

"Jessie, you don't have to study with me."

"No. I need a good grade." Jessie turned on the ignition.

"So, you're just studying with me to get a good grade?"

"Um . . . yes. Why else would I be studying?"

"You don't want to spend time with me?"

"Um . . . yeah, in the process of getting a good grade." Jessie rolled her eyes.

"Right. You've been acting different." Leo shoved his backpack in front of him.

"Well, I'm sorry if I'm not perky and happy all the time. I'm human."

Jessie turned on her CD player and music filled the car. She turned the volume almost all the way to max. I knew that when she did that, she didn't' feel like talking to the other person who was in her truck. Leo rested his head on the head rest and took in a deep breath. I was sitting in the half cab. I reached my hand out and placed it on Leo's shoulder. I felt badly for him. I looked out of the side window and saw Achish and Jezebel standing on the side of the road. They were following us.

Jessie, Leo, and I got to the library and headed to the second floor. We found a vacant table. Jessie took a seat at the end of the table and Leo took the other end.

"Gives us more space," Leo said to Jessie.

Jessie just shrugged. The library smelled of musty, old books and rain. Jessie took her assignments out and started working on them. Leo looked up at Jessie every now and then but said nothing.

"I'm falling apart, Leo." Jessie said not looking up.

"What do you mean?" Leo stopped working on his homework.

"What am I supposed to do? I don't want to go to college. My friendship with Karla is like over. I don't know where my future is going."

Jessie stopped herself and choked back tears. She needed to get this off of her chest.

"Jessie." Leo walked over to the empty seat beside her.

"And then there's you."

Jessie looked up from her paper. Tears filled her eyes. My spirit sank, and my heart raced.

"Me?" Leo asked. "Jessie, I'm your best friend. I'm always here for you." Leo pulled her to him and embraced her.

"Then, who was your poem really for?" Jessie asked.

Leo held Jessie out at arm's length. He looked into her eyes and didn't say anything for a long time. I looked past them and saw Jezebel walking up the steps. Her hips were swaying, her long raven hair tied was back into a long braid, and her bright, red lipstick revealed a wicked smile. I looked from her and then to Jessie and Leo.

"Jessie, it was just a poem." Leo sighed.

Leo felt defeated. Jessie looked into his countenance as if trying to read what he really meant.

"The golden hair, the God, and the sky. You just wrote all that from the top of your head?" Jessie sniffled.

"Yeah." Leo lied.

"Yeah, I don't think so. For one, you had to write a poem on love and you told me that you have never experienced love. It that was the case then your poem would have sucked." Jessie grew angry.

"No, Jessie. People fake all the time." Leo argued.

"So the way you feel about me is fake." Jessie stood up.

"Jessie, sit down please." Leo pleaded.

"No." Jessie started to cry.

"How is the way that I feel about you fake?"

"I know you love me, Leo. I'm not stupid. Ellen is a really good cover-up. Would you stop fighting the truth." Jessie laughed in disbelief as she placed her books in her backpack.

"Jessie." Leo pinched the bridge of his nose with his thumb and index finger. He closed his eyes and sighed.

"I can't believe you're not man enough to admit it. I'm going to wait Leo, but I will not wait forever." Jessie pointed her finger at him.

"Jess, are you leaving?"

"Yes."

Jessie grabbed her purse and started down the stairs. I followed, and Jezebel followed me. I didn't just want to leave Leo there, but he only lived a block from the library anyway. I felt Jezebel right behind me.

"What!" I swung around and looked at her.

"Tristan." She jumped back shocked. I grabbed her by the wrist, bending it back. She started to crumble beneath my grip.

"Leave Jessie alone." I said through clenched teeth.

"Too late, Tristan." Jezebel sneered at me.

I looked around, Jessie was already to her truck.

"I mean it, Jezebel. I will kill you if you make this matter worse. You understand me?" I got in her face.

"Tristan, that warrior symbol on your hand means nothing to me." Jezebel spat out.

"Well, it means a lot to me."

I threw her on the ground and she landed on her knees. I bolted to Jessie's truck and looked up at the library. My spirit didn't feel right. When I looked up in the window, I saw Leo standing there looking down at us and Achish standing next to him.

CHAPTER 18

This Is War

Period 1: Art

Leo was in his seat going through notes from another class. Jessie stood a little ways away and just stared at him. She smiled to herself. I looked down at her and then over to him. Man, she was really falling for this guy. He raked his fingers through his shiny, black hair. He looked up at Jessie and smiled. Jessie walked over and sat next to him, which was originally Shelby's seat but she would understand if she sat there this one time. Jessie wrapped her arm around Leo's and laid her head on his shoulder. Leo looked down at Jessie but didn't say anything.

"I'm sorry for being rude to you." Jessie looked up at him. Leo didn't look at her.

"It's fine, Jessie." Leo then broke out into a smile.

"There's that beautiful smile." Jessie lightly shook his arm.

"What can I say? You make me smile even when I don't want to." Leo admitted.

"Same here. So it works both ways."

Jessie sat up in her seat. Shelby walked in the room. Her face was down and her walk was slow.

"Uh oh. This may be an ice cream night with the girls." Jessie told Leo as Shelby took the seat where Jessie normally sat.

"Oh, baby, what's the matter?" David looked over at Shelby.

"Jared. He got another six months." Shelby sniffled.

"What the hell!" David exclaimed. "Girl, you are too good for that!" David smacked his lips.

"Agreed," Jessie and Leo said in unison.

"I know, but I love him."

"Shelby, sometimes when you love someone in that way, it isn't always best to be together. You will probably always love that person. It may be hard once you lose them and you feel you love them even more because they're not around anymore. But if he's not good for you, you need to break if off." Jessie put her hand on Shelby's.

"I know, Jessie. It's just so hard. You're so smart for guarding your heart the way you do," Shelby shook her head, "not letting anyone in. I remember you told me in tenth grade how you can keep people at bay but look like you're close all at the same time. You're not attached to anyone. I want that, Jessie." Shelby sniffled.

Leo's jaw tightened. David glanced at Shelby and lightly shook his head no. Jessie rubbed her forehead with the palm of her hand. Shelby caught David's signal and shut up.

"Please don't tell me you're going to be mad at me," Jessie looked at Leo.

"Please don't talk to me right now."

"Leo, come on. I was in the tenth grade."

"But you still feel that way." Leo noted.

"You don't know that." Jessie crossed her arms over her chest. *Oh, this is bad.*

"Yes, I do. Trust me, I know."

"Leo, do you ever think there are things in my life that you just wouldn't understand, stuff that keeps me from getting as close to you as I would like to?"

"I doubt it."

"Hey, instead of jumping the gun, why don't you try to know what's going on. I'm not normal, Leo!" Jessie exclaimed.

I knew she was talking about her spiritual life and "exorcism", also known as deliverance.

"You're going to open up to me?" Leo grew soft.

"If you'll let me." Jessie said with nervousness in her voice. Leo smiled at her.

"I want you to."

Leo looked into her eyes. He reached over and tucked her hair behind her ear. I looked at Shelby and David to see if they saw what I saw. Was he inching his face closer?

"Jessie, I need an ice-cream night." Shelby blurted. Jessie took her eyes off of Leo and looked over at Shelby.

"Alrighty. Tonight. You, me, and the girls."

"Uh." David scoffed.

"You, me, the girls, and David, but you can't bring Trevor. This is a no boyfriend zone." Jessie mentioned.

"Deal. Do I bring anything?"

"Ice cream, cookies, candy, pop, anything sweet." Jessie added.

"My house at seven." Shelby chimed.

Shelby already seemed to be in a good mood. I looked over at Leo and Jessie. I did not trust this. Did not!

Period 6: Sociology

Jessie left Leo's side and we walked into Sociology. Irritation fumed off of her as soon as she saw Karla. Jessie cracked her neck and headed to her seat.

"Jessie, girls night tonight?" Carrie called.

"You know it!" Jessie laughed and sat in her desk.

"I'm bringing brownies and Moose tracks," Carrie told Jessie.

"Alrighty. I guess I'll bring the cookies and chocolate milk." Jessie shrugged.

"I got the pop and chips." Shelby said excited.

"What do I bring?" Danni chimed.

"Twizzlers," Carrie, Jessie, and Carrie said in unison.

"Wow." Danni laughed.

"Oh, yeah. Girls night isn't girls night without Twizzlers."

Jessie took her seat and Karla didn't say anything for a while.

"Can I come?" Jeremy asked. Jessie turned around.

"Ha! No. The only boy that gets to come is David." Jessie laughed.

"Why?" Jeremy arched his brow.

"Uh, because he's gay." Carrie slapped Jeremy in the back of the head.

"Oh. Forget that then." Jeremy rubbed the back of his head.

"I'm going to puke." Justin blurted.

"Whatever." Danni rolled her eyes.

"You guys gonna talk about us all night?" Jeremy smiled at Jessie.

"Well, Shelby will be talking about Jared, David will talk about Trevor, and I think Jessie will talk about Leo." Carrie batted her eyes.

"Not true."

"Can I come?" Karla looked over at Jessie.

"I don't care, but it's at Shelby's place. You might want to ask her." Jessie looked at Shelby.

"No." Shelby blurted. Karla glared at Shelby.

"Wow. Well, I see how it is." Karla turned her attention over to Jessie.

"Don't get mad at Jessie. It's not her house." Justin yelled to Karla.

"Shut up, queer bait." Karla sneered.

"Well, isn't Tiffany Zane coming?" Shelby asked.

"Yeah, I asked her fourth period." Jessie shrugged. She didn't look over at Karla. She could feel Karla's stare burning into her face.

"You're going to regret this, Jessie." Karla whispered.

"I'm going to hang out with Leo before I come over." Jessie ignored Karla's comment. Jessie was used to Karla's childish antics.

"You irritate me." Karla said to Jessie.

"Hey, did you know that Gerard and Tiffany broke up?" Jessie turned her attention to Karla. The whole group was looking at them.

"No! That's great." Karla grew excited.

"Yeah. She didn't want a long distance relationship." Jessie blurted.

"What?" Karla's face grew red with anger.

"Yeah. Gerard's moving back to Utah with his aunt." Jessie cocked her head.

Karla's eyes filled with tears. She grabbed her belongings and ran out of the room.

"It's better this way." Jessie glared.

Period 7: English 12

Jessie and I were at her locker exchanging books. She threw her Sociology book to the bottom of the locker. She looked down at the bottom half of the locker, and it was a mess. She saw a pile of papers and then looked up at Leo's part of the locker. It was nice and neat.

That was Leo. His books were stacked in the order that his classes were in. Jessie shook her head and smiled.

"Yeah. I should make you pay rent." Leo laughed. Jessie turned around to face him.

"I will definitely clean that after English. I didn't realize I was that messy. Why didn't you say something?" Jessie put her English book in her backpack.

"I never really let it bother me. Everyone knows you're the messy one out of the two of us." Leo teased.

"Ha! I forgot about how funny you're not." Jessie teased.

"Oh, Jessie's got jokes. Save them for happy hour, babe." Leo laughed.

"You're goofy today."

"Hey, are we still chillin' till you go to Shelby's for a girly ice cream night?" Leo looked at Jessie then shut the locker.

"Yes, sir." Jessie said as they headed around the corner. As we turned the corner, Karla and Gerard were kissing heavily in the hallway.

"Poor guy." Leo shook his head.

"I can't believe someone isn't saying anything. Well, besides, the kid's making rude comments."

"Jessie, she is so nasty."

Leo put his hand on the small of Jessie's back and led her into the classroom. Jessie got one last look at her former best friend and Gerard kissing. She shuddered.

"I mean, yeah, kissing is fun but not in front of a bunch of people." Jessie scoffed.

"Awe, do you not like PDA?" Leo laughed as he took his seat.

"No. Holding hands and hugging I have no problem doing in front of people, but not the kissing thing." Jessie shook her head.

"Awe." Leo teased.

"Leave me alone." Jessie blushed.

"You're blushing." Leo laughed.

"Ugh." Jessie turned her head facing the other way.

"I'm sorry. I will drop the subject. You excited about girls night?" Leo asked.

"Yeah. I'm always excited to hang with my girls and David."

"No, you were right. Your girls." David chirped.

"Oh, so you're the woman in the relationship?" Justin busted David out.

"Um . . . duh."

David ran his fingers over his hair. He popped his hip out. Leo and Justin exchanged glances. Jessie, on the other hand, laughed. The class period went by rather fast. Toward the end, Jessie got a text form Karla.

"Yeah. I'd like to see Leo and u kissing in the hallway like that. Oh, that's right. He doesn't want u."

Jessie had a shocked look on her face. She tapped Leo on the shoulder and let him read the text. Leo's face grew angry.

"Let me text her." Leo grabbed the phone from Jessie.

"That's not the case and u know it. We just respect each other, unlike you and Gerard. The way he treats u like a piece of meat, that should tell u something, dumb ass." Leo pushed send.

"She's really irritating me. I would never make out with you in front of people. That's so disrespectful to you. What we do is our business, not everyone else's." Leo rolled his eyes.

Leo opened the phone and he and Jessie read it together.

"Step into reality, Jessie. Leo doesn't feel the same way u do."

Jessie grabbed the phone from Leo and slammed it shut. She shoved it in her pocket. Leo stared at his hand that was now phoneless. I looked around the room, and no one seemed to notice what was going on. Leo looked to Jessie.

"Jessie?"

"I don't know what she was talking about. She tends to pop off at the mouth." Jessie sunk down in her seat.

"Jessie, she didn't know I was reading the text, so it's not like she was saying that because . . ."

"Leo, drop it." Jessie squirmed.

"Jessie."

"Leo, please drop it now." Jessie grew very serious, very fast.

"We can't just drop something like this."

"Leo, if you don't drop this, I'm going to get super mean, super fast." Jessie warned.

"Alright, Jess." Leo sighed.

Leo opened his English book and started reading the poem on page 474. Jessie stared at him for a while and sank back into her seat.

Jessie and I sat in the truck while Leo was in his house telling his mom he was hanging out with Jessie for a couple of hours. Jessie kept her eyes on Leo who was half out of the door and saying something to his mom. She couldn't understand it because it was all in Spanish. He closed the door behind him and headed to the truck. He shoved his hands in his pocket and pulled his body together, blocking the bitter wind. He then opened the passenger's side door and climbed into the truck. Jessie kept her eyes on him. He let out a sigh and ran his fingers through his long, black hair.

"Ma wants me to get a haircut." Leo let out a laugh.

"Is that what the conversation was about?" Jessie put the truck into drive and slowly started to drive around the cul-de-sac.

"Ha, yeah. She said, 'While you're out, cut your hair.'" Leo rubbed his hands on his thigh.

"Well, do you want to stop and get a haircut and forget studying?" Jessie pulled up to the four-way stop.

"Um . . . I don't think so. I like my hair and it's taken me forever to get it to my shoulders. I started growing it out when I went to Mexico during my sophomore year." Leo looked over at Jessie. Tension filled the truck.

"Yeah it's really pretty." Jessie agreed. The tension ceased.

"I really don't wanna study." Leo admitted.

"Omg. I never thought I'd hear you say that." Jessie pulled onto the bypass.

"We could do something else." Leo pulled out the money from his pocket. "How about that new restaurant? I didn't eat lunch." Leo looked over at Jessie. She didn't take her eyes off of the road.

"I don't have any of that." Jessie nodded her head toward the money.

"Jessie Craig, when have you and I been together and you have had to pay for something? That's not your job. I'm the guy. I pay." Leo rebutted.

"Well, maybe I'm tired of mooching."

"Jess," Leo let out a sigh, "you're not mooching. I don't like to make a woman pay, especially if it was my idea." Leo shoved the money back into his pockets.

"Yeah, but tonight's girls night and, if I eat now, I will never eat there." Jessie turned into the new restaurant.

"Jessie, it's at seven something. That gives you four hours kinda, and no one said you had to eat as soon as you get there. I won't eat in front of you." Leo looked into the little restaurants windows.

"I guess." Jessie pulled into a vacant parking spot and shut the truck off. We sat in the truck for a while.

"Jessie, we need to talk about that text Karla sent you today." Leo broke the silence. I looked over to Jessie. Her eyes narrowed.

"No, we don't." Jessie opened the driver's side door and jumped out.

"Jessie." Leo followed. "Jessie," he repeated as we walked into the diner. We were greeted by a tall, thin woman with long, reddish brown hair.

"Hi! How many?" She looked at Jessie and then to Leo.

"Two, please." Jessie plastered a fake smile.

"Booth or table?"

"Booth." Leo blurted. The young woman checked her chart and grabbed two menus.

"Right this way." She smiled at us and led us to our seats.

On the way to our seats, we saw Karla and Allen sitting at a table. Jessie and Leo stopped in their tracks. Allen looked up and caught their eyes. Karla turned around. A wicked grin spread across her face. Jessie looked from Allen to Karla.

"Hey, guys, didn't expect to see you here." Allen stood up to greet them. Jessie adjusted her purse.

"Same here." Leo raked his hand through his hair, shoving the other one in his pocket.

"Not studying?" Karla kept her eyes on Leo.

"No. I got hungry ergo, that's why I'm here." Leo scoffed. Jessie turned around giving Leo a dirty look.

"Is this a date?" Jessie looked at Karla.

"Ha, it is what it is." Karla grabbed her glass of pop and took a big gulp. Leo rolled his eyes.

"So, it is?" Jessie looked at Allen who shrugged his shoulders.

"Is yours?" Karla looked at Leo. Leo's face flushed with anger. His lips formed a straight line and his eyes narrowed.

"No." Jessie spoke up.

"Too bad." Karla laughed.

"Well, I'm starving." Leo looked over at the hostess who was still standing by their booth.

"Well." Karla ran her hand through the ends of her red hair. She wore more make-up than usual to hide her freckles. She must have gotten new contacts because her eyes were blue.

"Have fun." Karla hissed and then turned her attention to Allen. Allen nodded to Jessie and Leo. Leo, Jessie, and I took our leave and headed toward the table.

"Can you believe that?" Jessie sat down in her booth.

"Never thought I'd see that." Leo grabbed the menu and scanned it.

"Hi. I'm Drew, and I'll be your waiter. Can I start you off with something to drink?" Drew was tall, well built, brown hair and hazel eyes, and straight, white teeth.

"Cherry Coke." Leo said not looking up.

"I . . . uh . . . same." Jessie blushed.

I could tell Jessie thought this guy was a true looker. I sat next to her in the booth. I rested my arms on the table and scanned through the menu with Jessie. Leo looked up at Drew who was still smiling at Jessie.

"I'm thirsty." Leo caught Drew's attention.

"Right. Be right back." He tapped his pen on the tablet and headed to the back.

"Like him?" Leo asked not looking at Jessie.

"Oh, he's hot." Jessie chuckled.

"God, Jessie."

"Don't take the Lord's name in vain." Jessie sighed.

"Sorry." Leo closed the menu and sat it to the side.

"What are you getting?"

"Steak." Leo smiled.

"You can't afford that."

"Yeah, I can, and you get whatever you want." Leo looked back over at Allen and Karla. They were laughing and feeding each other.

"I think I'm going to throw up." Leo crossed his arms and rested them on the table.

"Why?" Jessie looked up.

"Look." Leo cocked his head toward Allen and Karla.

"Maybe they do like each other." Jessie shrugged.

"Or maybe she's trying to turn him against us." Leo said. Drew came back with their drinks.

"You ready to order?" Drew looked at Jessie.

Jessie and Leo placed their orders and then sat in silence. Jessie's phone vibrated. She knew it was Karla.

"Well you got him to take you to dinner. Gonna go have sex next? Make him leave a twenty on the table before he leaves."

Jessie's face grew with anger.

"Read this." Jessie shoved the phone in Leo's face. He pulled his head back and tried to adjust his eyes to the bright letters that popped out at him.

"She's such a bitch." Leo scoffed. He shook his head and then rested it on his arms that were folded on the table.

"Right. I'm not gonna reply." Jessie put her phone beside her. Another message.

"Not going 2 answer me? Fine. But I'll tell you this. It's me against u now. Good luck." Jessie slammed her phone shut.

"She's no one to be afraid of." Jessie grew angry. Leo looked up at her.

"Forget her. We need to talk about us." Leo stated.

"There's nothing to talk about." Jessie looked out the window.

"Jessie, maybe there is something to talk about." Leo sighed.

"Well, then, talk I guess. I don't have anything to say because, knowing you, you pretty much got everything in your head."

"What?"

"You've convinced yourself of certain things. I know you, Leo. I know how your mind works."

"And I know you, Jessie. You will keep everything bottled inside till you explode and do something stupid." Leo stated. I felt the tension again.

"Oh, whatever." Jessie said. Karla walked over to the table.

"Nice seeing you guys together. Jessie, may we talk in the parking lot for a minute?" Karla looked at Jessie and then at Leo.

"Sure." Jessie slid out of the booth.

Leo nodded to them. Jessie, Karla, and I headed to the far east corner of the parking lot. The wind had a bite to it. The clouds were gray and not a blue piece of sky was to be seen.

"You did this to yourself." Karla stopped crossing her arms over her chest.

"What?" Jessie put her hands in the pockets of her hoodie.

"You turned me against you." Karla declared.

"Karla, grow up." Jessie rolled her eyes.

I looked into the restaurant window and Leo was looking at them with his fist clenched on the table. Allen was in his car. Jessie's food had arrived and she looked in Leo's direction. She knew he was mad.

"No, Jessie. You throw away our friendship for those losers." Karla spat.

Jessie wiped the stray hairs from her face. They were here. I felt them—Anton, Jezebel, and Hagab. I saw them walking toward us from the other side of the parking lot. I said nothing and moved closer to Jessie. Karla was going on and on about how Jessie was a back stabber.

"Well, hello, pretty boy." Hagab stuttered. His speech had been impaired after our last encounter with each other.

"This is gonna be good." Jezebel chuckled.

She was wearing tight leather pants, a dark blue v-neck with a leather trench coat over it. Her long auburn hair was pulled back into a pony tail. Her eyes were darker green with blue make-up to accentuate them. Her lips were a maroon color. Anton wore black, baggy silk pants, and his black hair was tucked behind his ears. He wore a long-sleeved black shirt with a leather trench coat over it.

"Leave." I demanded.

"Nice try." Jezebel cocked her head.

"Those friends, the ones I have now, are true friends. They don't pressure me to go and be who I used to be." Jessie raised her voice.

"You've got to be kidding me." Karla took a step forward.

"No, I'm not. They accept that I'm a Christian. They love that I don't do what I used to." Jessie stated.

Anton rolled his eyes. Jezebel walked over to stand next to me.

"Let's see who's going to win."

She leaned up and whispered in my ear. Her tongue was grazing my earlobe. I shrugged her off, and I felt power surround us. I looked behind me and, standing there, was Truce and Victor.

"Oh, great." Hagab hissed.

Truce narrowed his eyes. He grabbed his sword and charged at Hagab. Hagab grabbed Truce by the throat, stopping him in his tracks. Truce grabbed Hagab's forearms and pulled down, ripping them out of their sockets. Hagab released his grip and fell to the ground. Anton stood petrified. I looked over at Him. He looked at me and then bolted. I ran after him and finally caught up to him, tackling him to the ground. He tried crawling away from me, but I grabbed his ankle and dragged him to me. I stood up, bringing him with me. He reached his hands up, clawing at my face. I then wrapped my forearms around his neck and applied pressure. He squirmed in my grasp. Nothing was said from either of us. His breathing got heavy. He started to wheeze and make popping noises from his chest. I gripped tighter and wrapped my leg around his, pinning him down. He struggled for a little while longer and then his body became lifeless in my grip. I dropped him to the ground and kicked him. His body broke down into little bugs that ran down the water drain. I could still hear Karla and Jessie yelling at each other. I ran to be next to Jessie. Jezebel snatched me up by my hair and pulled me toward her, my body twisted to face her. I fell into her causing us to crash to the ground. I laid on top of her for a moment and then raised to my feet. She smiled up at me. I backed away from her and she got up and walked toward me. My back hit the wall of the restaurant, and she pressed her body against mine. Heat radiated from her. She ran her hand through my hair. I clenched my fist and penetrated her face. She fell to the ground and looked up at me, her nose bleeding. I looked at her and then at Truce who had Hagab pinned down, and I started walking toward them and stepped over Jezebel. Victor grabbed Truce's sword that was over by the dumpster. He ran back with it and handed it to Truce. Truce grabbed it and struck Hagab in the head. Blood squirted from the wound, and Hagab hissed and gnashed. His body jerked violently as he let out a scream. Jezebel grabbed me by the waist from behind and planted her lips on my neck. I grabbed her by her hair and tossed her over my shoulder. She crashed to the ground, and I looked toward Jessie and Karla. The argument had calmed down, but they were still in a disagreement. Jezebel stood up and straightened her clothes.

"I want you, Tristan. I need you. Please become one flesh with me." Jezebel's voice had a dark discord to it. She growled as she walked toward me. I grew angry and grabbed my sword.

"Put that away! Love me, Tristan. All I want is to be loved. Father Lucifer shows me no love. A woman needs . . . ."

An arrow ripped through Jezebel's forehead. Her eyes grew wide as she looked at me and her arms stretched out to her sides. She stumbled to her knees and then fell against the cold ground. I looked behind where Jezebel had been standing. Purity had her bow up to her face. She smiled at me and lowered her bow. Purity's curly hair was pulled back into a pony tail, and she wore white silk pants with a white silk shirt.

"She just can't take no for an answer." Purity walked toward me. "No one tempts my brother."

Purity smiled at me. Truce and Victor came toward us. We looked down at the lifeless bodies that we had killed for at least the seventh time. They just didn't stop. We looked over at Jessie and Karla. I thanked the others for their help and support and headed toward Jessie. I stood beside her as the bitter wind brought rain with it. I looked back and my fellow angels were gone.

"Look, if we aren't going to be friends, say so now," Jessie insisted.

"Fine. You and I are done. Forever!" Karla spat.

"Ew, big loss for me." Sarcasm filled Jessie's tone.

"You'll think that." Karla. said.

"Karla, news flash! You're no one to be afraid of." Jessie called to her.

"All I can say is that you and Leo need to watch your backs."

Karla got into Allen's car and they sped off leaving Jessie alone in the parking lot. Jessie looked back into the restaurant's window. Leo hadn't touched his food. His eyes were locked on Jessie. She sighed and gave him a crooked smile. Jessie's phone vibrated in her pocket. It was Karla.

"This is war, bitch."

Jessie closed her eyes and sighed. She gathered herself and we headed back to the restaurant.

CHAPTER 19

Secrets Revealed

Girls Night

Jessie sat on the couch between Shelby and Carrie. Danni and David were on the floor sitting Indian style with a gallon of ice cream in their laps. Jessie had a bag of Famous Amos cookies tucked under her arm and a jumbo glass of chocolate milk in her lap. Carrie munched on Twizzlers and Shelby hogged a bag of Reese's pieces. They sat watching "Must Love Dogs". They've seen it a hundred times but it never gets old. Their attention was turned to the doorbell.

"Must be Tiffany."

Shelby got up and headed toward the door. She traipsed back into the living room followed by Tiffany.

"Hey!" Jessie lifted her jumbo glass to Tiffany.

"Hey, guys."

Tiffany dropped her bags by the others and headed toward the coffee table that was stacked full of junk food and movies that haven't been watched yet. Tiffany grabbed three brownies and a bottle of chocolate milk from the iced-down cooler that was sitting near the coffee table.

"Ya'll thought of everything." Tiffany laughed.

"Yup. When we say 'Girls Night', we mean girls night minus David." Jessie laughed.

"I'm every bit of girl as you are." David turned to look at Jessie.

Tiffany pushed the coffee table out a ways and sat in front of Jessie, resting her back on Jessie's legs. Shelby looked over at Jessie. Jessie just shrugged. The movie was almost over when Shelby grabbed two more from the table.

"Alright, what's next. Accepted. Or what the hell? Who brought 'Let's Drag'"? Shelby looked over at David.

"What! It's a really interesting documentary on Drag Queens of the now."

"Could you be any more gay?" Danni lightly pushed him.

"Ya'll will like it." David smiled.

"I say there's another movie on the table that you didn't pick up." Carrie nodded to the video.

"Cruel Intentions." Shelby arched her brow at Carrie.

"Sorry. I really like that movie." Carrie laughed nervously.

"You dirty girl!" Jessie teased.

"I have one more." David got up and walked toward his backpack. "I wasn't going to say anything but I didn't want to watch it alone and Trevor won't watch it with me." David pulled out the movie.

"Broke Back Mountain!" Jessie threw her back against the sofa and laughed hysterically. David glared at the group of girls. Everyone started laughing.

"Oh my gosh, 'Broke Back Mountain'". Jessie grabbed her stomach from laughing so hard. "Ha!" Jessie couldn't stop laughing. Everyone else including David started laughing.

"Alright, let's watch it."

Shelby got up and grabbed the movie from David. I wasn't about to watch this. I hoped that they would change their minds and watch "Accepted". I've seen that before. That I could handle.

"This better not show nothing gross." Carrie glared at David.

"Oh, hush." David laughed.

The movie started and all the girls looked intently at the screen. I closed my eyes and took myself to another world, blocking out all sin. I went back to the time when Jessie was about five years old and she watched her first horror movie with her older cousin, Gill. Gill was eighteen and was babysitting Jessie and her brother. Jessie walked in on Gill watching "Child's Play". It was a movie about a possessed doll. I liked to never get Jessie back to sleep that night. She was so scared. I killed off dozens of demons that night. She told her parents that she had seen a scary movie. It wasn't Gill's fault because Jessie was supposed to be in bed and she had gotten up and watched the t.v. from her bedroom door. Jessie still didn't do well with horror flicks and it wasn't good for people to watch them. Now Jessie watched "Broke Back Mountain", a movie about homosexual cowboys. Oh how times have changed.

I must have been in prayer for a while because, when my thoughts were broken by Jessie's laughter, I opened my eyes and they were now watching "Accepted". Tiffany and Jessie laid on their stomachs facing the t.v. and David was lying across Carrie and Shelby on the sofa. Danni was in the recliner with junk food spread out around her. The pizza was all gone but two pieces. I looked over and Carrie was rubbing her stomach, while Shelby started to doze off. I sat in the chair close to where Jessie was lying.

"Jessie, can I tell you something?" Tiffany looked over at Jessie.

"Yes." Jessie didn't take her eyes off of the movie.

"Jessie." Tiffany nudged her.

"What?" Jessie ripped her eyes from the screen.

"I'm pregnant." Tiffany blurted. Jessie's face grew serious and Tiffany's eyes started to fill with water.

"I don't want them to know yet, but I had to tell someone." Tiffany leaned in and whispered.

"No secrets." David called from the sofa.

"We're not!" Jessie called. She then turned her attention back to Tiffany. "Who's the father?"

"This is going to come as a shock." Tiffany's face grew with regret.

"Remember when we all went to Trevor's basketball game and then to a party at his uncle's farm?" Tiffany whispered to Jessie.

"You had sex with one of the guys there?"

"Not just one of the guys."

"Oh my gosh! Who?" I could tell Jessie was growing nervous because Jeremy was at the party with them.

"You can't tell anyone." Tiffany said barely above a whisper.

"Oh, Lord." Jessie shook her head.

"Let's just say that Trevor isn't as gay as he says he is." Tiffany smiled.

"Holy shit!" Jessie yelled pulling herself up from the floor. I flinched as I heard those words expel from Jessie's lips. She knew better.

"Shhhh." Tiffany grabbed Jessie's arms and pulled her down.

"What's going on?" Shelby and Carrie asked. Danni was asleep in the chair.

"You going to tell them?" Jessie sighed.

"I will tell them that I'm pregnant, but please keep between us forever that it's Trevor's. Please, Jessie." Tiffany begged.

"Alright, I will." Jessie studied Tiffany's face.

"Um . . . I have news." Tiffany rolled over to face them.

"What?" David asked.

"Oh, goodness." Tiffany grew nervous.

"What?" Carrie arched her brow.

"Um . . . I'm pregnant." Tiffany blurted. Shelby grabbed the remote and put the movie on pause. Everyone looked at her.

"Don't just stare at me. I don't have a disease." Tiffany laughed.

"Who's the father?" Carrie asked.

"Jessie." Tiffany teased. Bad joke. The others laughed.

"No, the father is Andy T. We hooked up at a basketball game." Tiffany shrugged. Shelby and the others started talking about it. "I did hook up with him but it wasn't at the game. So it can be his, but I think it's Trevor's." Tiffany whispered. She was digging her own grave.

"So much for not telling them." Tiffany glared.

"You could have made up a lie. I would have gone with it." Jessie shrugged.

The others turned their attention to Tiffany and started talking about her pregnancy. That was what I liked about Jessie and their friends. No matter what, in the end, they're still your friends and they've got your back.

"I did. I said it was Andy's."

"No, I mean you could have made up a story instead of telling them you're pregnant." Jessie looked toward the t.v.

"Yeah. They were going to know one way or another."

"What about Andy?"

"What do you mean?"

"Well, he's going to know it's his baby or think it's his."

"No, he won't. I got this all under control."

"Does Trevor know?"

"No, and he won't. We just need to go with it that it's Andy's."

"Why?"

"Because I know Andy is in love with me, so he won't mind if I'm pregnant with his baby. He'll probably be happy." Tiffany laughed. I couldn't understand how she could take this so lightly.

"If you say so, Tiff. Just be careful." Jessie reached over and hugged Tiffany.

Jessie's eyes fluttered open. She looked around the room and saw her friends sound asleep, all but David. He sat up from the spot where he was lying and he was texting. We could see tears streaming down his face. Jessie kept her eyes on him. He looked up and saw Jessie looking at him. Jessie sat up from where he was lying. Her ponytail had moved to the side in the middle of the night. She rubbed her eyes.

"He broke up with me!" David wailed, causing Shelby to jump up out of sleep. Shelby looked around the room and at David who was gasping for breath as he rocked back and forth crying.

"What?" Jessie scooted over to David.

"Trevor broke up with me." David cried.

Shelby shook Carrie awake. Carrie finally came to and looked over to where Jessie and David were sitting.

"He broke up with you over a text?" Shelby huffed.

"What's going on?" Tiffany woke up.

"Well . . ." David sniffled, "he likes someone else, and it's a girl!" David sobbed.

Jessie looked at Tiffany and wrapped her arms around David, embracing him in a hug.

"He's bi?" Shelby arched her brow.

"Well, here. I'll read the text. *David, I really need to talk to you.* Then I replied, *Alright, baby, what's up?* He said, *Please don't call me baby.* I said, *Why?* He said, *Because I'm not your baby. I want to break up. I met someone else. She makes me really happy and I really like her. I know that I was your first real boyfriend and I like hanging with you, but I really think that I'm not gay. I really wasn't comfortable kissing you. I couldn't find a girl, so I decided to try guys.* I can't believe this! I'm so mad. I loved him!" David cried into Jessie's shoulder.

"What did you reply?" Shelby asked. David pulled from Jessie's embrace, grabbed his phone, and read the texts.

"Oh, girl," I said. "How can you say that what happened between us and how you felt and sounded was not at all fake. You are gay but maybe you don't want to be with me," David said as he scrolled down the text, his head bobbing from side to side.

"Who's the girl?" Tiffany asked, knowing it was her.

"He said that I don't know her." David swiveled his head back and forth.

"What did he say to that text?" Shelby blurted. I looked over and Danni was still fast asleep. She must not be feeling well.

He said, "Yeah, well, guys can fake it like girls can. Please don't try to keep in touch. I'm done. I want to be with her now. Have a nice life." David slammed his phone shut and fell to the floor.

"Well, another girls night?" Shelby looked at Carrie.

"Agreed. Let's all get washed up and stuff and tonight we meet at my house." Carrie suggested.

"I can't live without him." David beat his hand against the floor.

"Someone needs to wake Danni up." Tiffany noted.

"I will." Carrie walked over to Danni, waking her.

"David, it's going to be okay."

"I won't find another person like him." David sobbed.

"David, look how hard it would have been for ya'll. You're a gay, biracial couple." Jessie tried to help.

"Ah! I lost my white boy." David squirmed.

"Oh, wow! I'm going home. See ya'll at six."

Jessie got up and we headed toward the door. She and I got into her truck and headed home. On the way home, she got a text from Tiffany. Jessie read it as we stopped at a red light.

"Jessie, what am I going 2 do? That girl he's talking about has to be me!"

Jessie couldn't help but laugh. She started to reply, looking from her phone to the red light.

"Hun, you're going 2 have 2 tell him. L"

Jessie closed her phone and tucked it under her leg. The ring tone she set to Leo's number went off. It was the song "One Week" by the Bare Naked Ladies. Jessie smiled and then answered.

"Hey."

"Hey, what are you doing tonight?" Leo asked.

"Hanging with the girls for girls night."

"I thought you did that last night?"

"We did, but there came another crisis and we are having it at Carrie's."

"What happened?"

"Well, Trevor broke up with David for a girl, and he told David that he was never gay. He couldn't find a woman, so he decided to try guys . . . something like that."

"Jessie, that's retarded."

"It's not my relationship, and you wanna know what?"

"What?"

"The girl that he's breaking up with David for is Tiffany Zane. She met him at the party we went to after one of the basketball games, and she had sex with him. Now she's, in fact, pregnant by Trevor . . . David's Trevor."

"Oh my gosh, Jessie. Are you serious? This is all so lame." Leo let out a sigh.

"Leo, this is real life, and these are my friends." Jessie gripped the wheel.

"Jessie, please hang with me tonight."

"I have an idea. You can come over for girls night at Carrie's and I will take you home around curfew." Jessie suggested.

"No, I'm good. Well, good luck with the David thing, and the Tiffany thing is messed up."

"Ha! I know!" Jessie laughed.

"Well, babe, I will let you go." Leo sighed.

"Alright, I'll call you later." Jessie informed.

"Alright, talk to you later."

"Bye." Jessie said and then closed her phone.

"This is too good." Jessie laughed as she pulled into the driveway of her house. We entered the house and heard Travis and Mike arguing.

"Dad, I like this girl. I don't care if she has a kid." Jessie looked at her mom.

"What's going on?"

"Travis likes a girl with a baby. He met her at work." Toni rubbed her temples.

"Dad's against it, I take it?"

"Very much." Toni sighed.

"Oh, it's not that bad." Jessie flopped on the couch next to Toni. "I wanna snuggle." Jessie leaned against her mom.

"The baby's mixed." Toni blurted.

"Like black and white, or Mexican and white, or native American and white?"

"Black and white." Toni sighed.

"Dad, it's not that bad. I didn't say I was going to marry her." Travis argued. Jessie couldn't see them, but just hear them as they were arguing from the kitchen.

"He'll marry her." Toni sighed. "I can just feel it."

"How does it make you feel?"

"As long as he's happy. You?" Toni looked to Jessie.

"I guess I'd like to have a niece or nephew." Jessie smiled.

"Niece."

"Awe, a girl!" Jessie clasped her hands together.

"I've seen them both." Toni stated.

"And . . . the girl's name is Adrianne and her baby is Arianna. They're both very beautiful." Toni nodded her head.

"Oh, well. I mean, Bubby likes her. Of course she's beautiful." Jessie laughed.

"I can date whoever I please!" Travis stomped into the living room.

"Hey sis. So you know?"

"I do." Jessie looked at Travis.

"And?"

"Whatever makes you happy." Jessie stood up and hugged her brother.

"Really?"

"Yup."

"Dad's being difficult."

"Dad's being Dad." Jessie laughed. "I have to get washed up and head back to Carrie's for another girls night." Jessie sighed.

"What happened now?" Toni asked. Jessie flopped back on the couch next to Toni and explained the David situation with her mother and brother.

"Wow, that's a pickle. At least I'm not gay!" Travis called toward the kitchen where his dad stayed.

"Good thing." Mike called.

"I'm off to Danny's. See ya." Travis bolted out the door and jumped into his car.

"Well, I don't know about the situation. Man, you young people are full of drama." Toni informed. Jessie laughed. "That we are."

Jessie's phone vibrated. She opened it. It was a text from Karla.

"u r really going 2 let this friendship go."

"Look." Jessie showed Toni the text message. "She irritates me."

Jessie replied with a simple "Yup" and shut her phone. She was surprised that she didn't get a text back, but she got a call from Leo.

"Hey." Jessie answered. She winked at her mom and her mom smiled.

"What the hell, Jessie?"

"What?" Jessie grew irritated.

"I got on to check my grade for Trig and Karla popped up on my messenger. Did you give her my address?"

"Um, no."

"Well, who did then? The only ones who have it is you, James, and . . . ."

"Allen." Jessie finished his sentence.

"What's she saying?" Jessie asked.

"All this crap about you being in love with me and stuff. When I'm done talking with her, I'm going to print the convo's out and let you read them Monday." Leo drew in a breath. "She's making me mad." Leo warned.

"I know. Me, too." Jessie sighed. "She just texted me and said, 'You're really going to let this friendship go.' So she's on my case, too. We gotta stick together, Leo. Don't let her come between us."

Jessie looked over at her mom. Toni wore a worried expression on her face.

"Yeah, and I'm going to kick Allen's ass for going against us." Leo stated.

"Just chill. Hey, I gotta jump in the shower and stuff. Call me if you need me." Jessie said.

"Oh, I will." Leo said and then hung up.

"Well?" Toni asked as Jessie laid her phone on the table.

"Karla got Leo's email address from Allen and now Leo's pissed. She's telling Leo all this stuff that I'm in love with him." Jessie sighed and leaned against Toni.

"Well, aren't you?"

"In love with him?" Jessie looked up at her mom.

"Yes, Jess." Toni sighed. She smiled at her daughter and ran her fingers through Jessie's long blonde hair.

"I think so." Jessie hugged Toni tighter.

Girls Night . . . .Again

Jessie, Carrie, Danni, Shelby, and David all piled into Carrie's living room.

"Where's Tiffany?" Shelby asked.

"Not feeling well." Jessie lied.

"Baby?" David asked.

"Prolly." Jessie shrugged.

"Well, what's with Trevor?" Carrie blurted.

"Oh, he texted me earlier and was like 'I really didn't mean to hurt you, but I have a friend named Wesley that's gay and he's white.'" David crossed his arms and rolled his eyes.

"Well, all I can say is that I was Trevor's first of anything," David laughed, "if you know what I mean."

"I don't think that counts." Shelby blurted.

"What?" David cocked his head.

"I don't think if the same sex has sex it's really sex. I think it's mere foreplay." Shelby shrugged.

"I kind of agree." Carrie chimed.

"No! Sex is sex." David started tearing up.

"No, don't cry." Carrie reached and hugged him.

"End of convo." Jessie blurted.

"Agreed." Danni entered the conversation.

"Ugh. That better not be Karla." Jessie looked at her phone. Leo's name lit up the screen. Jessie smiled and then answered it.

"Hello?"

"We need to talk." I heard Leo faintly say.

Jessie removed the phone from her ear and pushed the speaker button. She held it out for her friends to hear and put her finger over her lips to hush them. They sat quietly.

"What about?" Jessie sighed.

"Karla, she's telling me all this stuff about how you want me to be your first." Everyone looked at Jessie.

"That's not true. I want my husband to be my first." Jessie rebutted. Carrie and Shelby tried not to laugh.

"Well, whatever. She told me that I shouldn't mess with you . . . ."

"Leo, just don't listen to her."

"Jessie, she's irritating the piss outta me." Leo exhaled.

The group leaned in closer as Leo started to talk. Jessie held the phone out to the middle of the group.

"If you say so. So, is Tiffany gonna tell David about Trevor?" Leo expelled some very important information. Jessie closed the phone as quickly as she could and threw it on the couch.

"Wait! What?" David bobbed his head. "What's Tiffany got to do with Trevor?"

"Oh, Leo has such a big mouth." Jessie closed her eyes and sighed.

"You're the one that put him on speaker." Danni stated.

"I know that, but usually he doesn't take an interest in anything like that." Jessie crossed her legs into an Indian-style position and sat her pillow in her lap.

"I can't say anything. I told Tiff I wouldn't. Call her or text her. Leo's the one with the big mouth, so this will all fall on him." Jessie shrugged.

"No, no, no, Jessie. You put him on speaker so we could all hear, and you told him what happened." Carrie argued.

"I tell him everything." Jessie exclaimed.

David got out his phone and called Tiffany. They talked for a while. David grew mad and then became almost sympathetic. Teenagers. You never know what they're going to do next. David closed the phone.

"Going to her house to talk." David grabbed his keys and then bolted out of the house.

"And then there were four." Shelby looked over at Jessie.

"I don't feel bad." Jessie crossed her arms over her chest.

"They'll tell us all about it on Monday." Danni grabbed a DVD from the coffee table, got up, and popped it the player.

"Man, Karla is really after me. I need you guys to make sure she doesn't try to turn you against me. She's already started with Leo."

"We won't." Carrie confirmed.

"Nope. We're here till the end," Shelby stated, "and Leo won't turn either. He loves you too much."

Period 1: Art

Jessie, Shelby, and David slugged into art class. They had had a long weekend and now they faced another long week of school. Jessie fell into her seat. Leo had started working on his project. Shelby sat next to him and propped her legs on the table. David buried his head in his arms and rested them on the table.

"Long weekend, I take it?" Leo laughed.

"Hectic weekend, and we need to talk." Jessie looked up at him.

"Is this about Karla?"

"No." Jessie said intently.

"Then what?"

"You have a big mouth." Jessie sat up. David looked at Jessie and then glared at Leo.

"What?" Leo stopped what he was doing."

"You told David about Tiffany and now there's going to be a huge feud." Jessie stated.

"Whoa, hold the phone. I didn't tell anyone anything. You told me."

Leo grew angry. I knew that Jessie was going to try to blame all of this on Leo. I shook my head in disappointment.

"No, I had you on speaker phone and you blurted." Jessie glared.

"Wait, Jessie. None of this is my fault. It's yours, and what the hell were you putting me on speaker phone for?" Leo mocked Jessie's posture.

"Because I can."

"Well, I didn't know I was on speaker, and what I say to you and you say to me stays between us. So don't try to blame this on me!" Leo exclaimed. The class looked over at them.

"Look. What is done is done." Shelby reached over and put her hand on David's.

"No. Jessie needs to start taking the blame for stuff she does." Leo threw his hands in the air. "Now Tiffany and David are in a fight, and now you and I are in a fight." Leo turned his attention to Jessie.

"We're not in a fight." Jessie closed her eyes and sighed.

"Oh, yes we are." Leo bit off.

Jessie knew that she had made Leo extremely angry and it was going to take her all day to get him to calm down. When something was Jessie's fault, she tried with all her power to blame someone else. It was a human thing, but she was really bad at it. The one person who would never give into believing it was there fault and not Jessie's was Leo. He was tough with her, stern, and didn't cut her any slack. But, all at the same time, he was good for her. He lifted her up when she was down, he helped her get through most classes, and helped her with her grades. He was a good friend—stern, but loving.

Period 4: Accounting

Jessie and Carrie hesitated going to Accounting class because Tiffany was in that class. Jessie had avoided her all day. They usually met in the parking lot in the morning and would walk to school together, but Jessie went the other way to avoid conflict. She knew that she and Tiffany wouldn't fist fight or anything, but Jessie just didn't want to admit to her mistake. I put my hand on the small of her back and gave her a little push. We entered the classroom. Tiffany looked up and saw Jessie. She just smiled. Not what we were expecting. We made our way to our seat. Carrie was next to Jessie while Tiffany was on the other side. I sat in the empty seat behind Jessie.

"I'm really sorry I told Leo." Jessie blurted.

"Jessie, it's okay. Me and David talked." Tiffany smiled. She flipped her hair over her shoulder.

"I know, but you told me not to tell anyone." Jessie sighed.

"I know, Jessie, but you told Leo and I had a hunch that you would have." Tiffany laughed. "I actually should thank you. We got it all out in the open and I didn't have to lie. Trevor and I are a couple." Tiffany grew happy.

"You still don't think he's gay?"

"No just bi." Tiffany shrugged.

"You're going to date a bi guy?" Jessie asked.

"Yeah, and he's the father of my child."

"What if he leaves you for a dude?"

"He won't."

"He might."

"He won't, Jessie." Tiffany grew irritated.

"Fair enough." Jessie widened her eyes and then turned her attention to the teacher who finally entered the room.

Period 6: Sociology

It was so awkward, even for me, that Jessie had classes with Karla. They didn't talk anymore, but you could really feel the tension. Jessie and I walked into the class and took our seats. I stood against the back wall close to Jessie's desk. She took her seat next to Karla, not saying anything. Karla was dressed in all black, and her red hair was pulled back into a braid. She sat texting, ignoring Jessie's presence. Jessie sat in her seat and started going through her notes for English. They had a pop quiz today. Jessie's thoughts were interrupted by Karla.

"I talked to Leo on messenger." Karla hissed.

"I know. He told me." Jessie said without looking up.

"I told him how you feel."

"I know. You could have just let me do it."

"I hope I made you mad." Karla growled.

"You did." Jessie flipped through her notes.

"Good. You don't deserve to be happy."

"But," Jessie grabbed the stack of papers and tapped them on the desk, forcing them into a neat stack. She looked up at Karla and said, "I forgive you." Jessie smiled. I wasn't expecting that and, by the look on Karla's face, neither was she.

"But I don't want your forgiveness. I want you to hate me like I hate you."

"Well, too bad. And I don't hate you. I'm not going to waste my time and life hating someone that I will probably never see after graduation." Jessie shoved her notes into her folder.

"You irritate me, Christian." Karla growled, her face twisted demonically.

Jessie and I sat in the truck for a while before leaving for home. She turned up the radio and exhaled deeply. I knew the wheels in her mind were turning. She rested her head on the steering wheel and played with the hole in her jeans.

"Oh, Jesus, hurry up and bring graduation. I don't want to be here anymore."

I saw a tear fall from Jessie's cheek onto her pants. I reached over, put my arm around her, and held her as she cried.

"I can't do this. I lost my best friend, I'm in love with Leo, and I don't know if I want to go to college. Everything is a mess." Jessie cried. I kissed her head and stroked her long blonde hair.

"Ugh, I better get home."

Jessie looked up. Her face turned white and her eyes grew wide. I took my attention off of Jessie and looked where she was looking. There stood a demon. I didn't know his name, but he was there. His fangs were showing, and he didn't have many features. He was more of just a black cloud but with dark red eyes. He twisted his head as he studied Jessie. She didn't take her eyes off of him. I looked from Jessie to the demon, and the demon slowly turned to the side and walked over to Jessie's door. She frantically locked the door and tried to say something, but she couldn't. The sky grew dark gray and the wind picked up. It was rather warm for a March morning in Indiana. The wind blew hard enough to shake the truck. Jessie let out a scream. The demon's face wasn't even an inch away from the window. The sky turned black, the sun was gone, the wind was picking up, and Jessie tried to start her truck. It wouldn't start.

"Come on . . . come on!" Jessie turned the key. Nothing. The demon placed his hand on the door handle.

"Oh, my gosh." Jessie started to cry.

I stared at the demon. I knew he wasn't going to come in because, if he was, he would have already done it by now. Jessie needed to see the power that she had locked inside of her. I sat there and prayed for strength, for Jessie.

"What is this?!" Jessie cried. She looked up at the demon and fear had fled from her. She looked in its eyes. The demon grew angry and jerked on the door handle. Jessie grabbed the key that was in the ignition.

"Start in the Name of Jehovah!" Jessie yelled. The truck started. "Oh, my gosh! It worked!" Jessie exclaimed.

Jessie put the truck into reverse. The demon leaped onto the hood of the truck and stared at us. Jessie slammed on the breaks and stared the demon in the face. I sat in the passenger's side still praying. I looked from the demon to Jessie and then back to the demon. The demon looked at me and then to Jessie. Jessie gripped the steering wheel.

"I don't think so, Demon!" she yelled. The demon cocked his head from side to side.

"Yeah, I know who you are and I'm not afraid!"

Jessie slammed on the gas. The demon flew over us and landed in the bed of Jessie's truck. She looked back then kept her eyes on the road. She couldn't see him anymore and she defeated him. A smile broke across Jessie's face. She knew that she had defeated him. She had to keep it close to her heart, however, that she had to have Jehovah help her and that she couldn't do it herself. I looked out the back window and the demon wasn't there anymore. It was a test and Jessie passed it. I knew that, from now on, she would be seeing more of demons in time. She's seen them before and has been physically attacked, but this was different now. She was seeing and dealing with them in a whole new light.

Jessie didn't tell her family what she had seen and done. She kept it to herself. I don't know why, but she did. I had a feeling that Jessie was going to be one of those people who didn't share unless she absolutely had to.

That Night

Jessie walked over to her bookshelf and grabbed her Bible and a pen. She tucked herself into bed and turned to the book of Hebrews. She read a majority of it, underlining things that stuck out to her and making little side notes. She looked at her clock radio and turned it to the Christian station. Casting Crows faintly came from the little radio. She put her pen in her Bible and laid it on her night stand. She pulled her hair over her shoulder and snuggled into bed.

"I forgot the light." Jessie grunted.

Jessie reached up and turned the lamp off. I felt an immense amount of pressure in the room. I heard hissing and squealing. I drew in a breath. I couldn't see them. The light had just turned off and my eyes hadn't adjusted, but they were in the room with us. All of a sudden, the light turned on. Jessie breathed hard and looked around the room. We saw nothing. Jessie prayed, turned the light on, and snuggled back into her covers.

There it was again—the hissing and light laughter. My eyes started to adjust to the darkness. I saw the whites of Jessie's eyes. The moonlight revealed to me that she was awake and she was scared. There was a demon standing against the wall to my right. I looked at him as he walked over to Jessie. Her eyes grew wide and the demon towered over her. Her covers started to shake. The demon cocked its head back and forth. He breathed heavily on her. I took a step forward but stopped in my tracks. Jessie's eyes filled with tears. She squeezed her eyes tightly shut and shook her head no. The demon walked toward the end of her bed and then back to where Jessie was. He paid no mind to me. Could he even see me? Jessie shook in fear. Her eyes wouldn't open. The demon climbed onto Jessie's bed and laid on top of her. *I don't' think so!* Jessie struggled to breathe as his large frame was crushing her. She cried in her sleep. I grabbed the demon by the ankle and my hand went through. I looked at my hand and then at the demon. Jessie laid shivering beneath his frame. I grabbed my sword and lunged it in his side. Nothing happened. I was getting extremely upset and confused. Jessie struggled to break free, and I tried to break her free. I couldn't . . . she needed to do this herself. *Jehovah, help!* Finally, Jessie broke out in a sob and said, "God is with me!" The demon jumped off of Jessie and landed on the floor. His face grew angry. She looked up at him and took a deep breath.

"Get out of my room in the Name of . . ." The demon slapped his hand over Jessie's mouth. She struggled to speak. "Jehovah!" I heard her scream through his hand, which burst into flames. He fell back on the floor. "Jehovah!" Jessie closed her eyes and repeated.

The demon couldn't find a way out. I grabbed him by the hair (My hand didn't just go through. I could grab him now.) and I pulled him up and stabbed him with my sword. He twitched in my grasp. I didn't let go until his body was lifeless. Then I dropped him to the floor. He twitched and then combusted. He was going to the pit. I looked over at Jessie and her breathing was heavy. She was still crying. I walked over to her to soothe her. She did it! She made the demon leave! She was getting a little taste of the power she had. I couldn't help but laugh to myself. She did it. She was just simply amazing. She didn't need to take seeing demons lightly. No, this was her life. This is the road Jehovah had her on.

"Jehovah, keep them away all night." Jessie gasped for air. She started to sing with the worship song on the radio and finally fell asleep.

Period 1: Art

Even though Jessie had defeated the demon, she wasn't doing too well. I think she had finally realized her life was much more different from her peers. She wasn't depressed or angry but was confused and intrigued. She didn't say much for the majority of the period. She kept her mind on her project and her encounter with that demon.

"Jess, you alright?" David looked up from his project. Jessie worked vigorously on hers, not answering David. David looked at Leo and Shelby.

"Jess!" Leo boomed. Jessie jumped up and looked at Leo. Her eyebrows narrowed.

"What, Leo." Jessie huffed.

"What's the matter with you?"

"Nothing." Jessie said as she started working on her project.

"Don't believe you." Leo stated.

"Don't' care." Jessie shot back.

"Are you okay, hun?" David asked.

"Oh, yeah. I'm fine. Just got a lot on my mind." Jessie gave them a half smile.

"Karla?" Leo asked.

"No, something much more intense than that." Jessie laughed.

"What do you mean?" Shelby asked.

"Nothing. It's nothing." Jessie stared at the table. I saw the others glance at each other.

"Jessie, it's not just nothing." Leo said softly.

"I will tell you later. Until then, drop it." Jessie defended.

"Fine." Leo shook his head. Jessie started back on her project not saying a word to anyone.

Period 4: Accounting

Jessie walked in and sat in her seat next to Tiffany. She could see Tiffany getting a baby bump. It wasn't big, but it was the start of her baby starting to show. She looked cute. Tiffany was going through a magazine with prom dresses. Jessie glanced over.

"Going with Trevor?"

"No. Going with Blake."

"Ellen's Blake?" Jessie asked.

"Ex-Blake and, yes, him. Ellen's going with Tedder." Tiffany said as she flipped through the magazines. Tedder was the guy's last name. His first name was Blaine but everyone called him Tedder.

"Are you going?"

"Prolly not." Jessie shrugged. "Not my thing, and I don't think Leo wants to go. He hasn't mentioned it." Jessie sighed.

"He might."

"Doubt it." Jessie laughed. "I don't think I'm going to go." Jessie shook her head.

"You have to. It's senior year." Carrie butted in.

"I don't want to go." Jessie shrugged. "It's not my thing."

"What about Jeremy?" Carrie asked.

"He's taking Rachael Flannigan." Tiffany chimed.

"That's out." I could see Jessie grow a little jealous.

"Erick?"

"He's taking a girl from Madison-Grant. I think her name is Amber Chicker."

"Chicker?" Jessie rolled her eyes.

"Allen?" Tiffany asked.

"No." Jessie shook her head.

"Justin?" Carrie asked.

"Naw. He's going with Danni."

"I thought Danni had a boyfriend?" Tiffany asked.

"No, they broke up like two months ago." Jessie tapped her pencil on her desk.

"This sucks." Tiffany sighed and then closed the magazine.

"I really don't want to go." Jessie shook her head.

"If you say so." Tiffany shrugged.

"Ha, I say so."

Period 6: Sociology

Jessie and Karla sat in silence for a while till Karla broke the silence.

"Going to prom with Leo?" Karla hissed.

"No, we're not going." Jessie looked up from her phone.

"I'm going." Karla beamed.

"With?" Jessie asked not interested.

"Allen asked me." Karla laughed.

"Cool." Jessie looked back to her phone and rolled her eyes.

"Jealous?" Karla hissed.

"Of you? Naw." Jessie shook her head. The comment made Karla furious.

"Well, at least I have a date. You couldn't get your own best friend to take you. He must really like you."

"What is your obsession with me and Leo!?" Jessie slammed her hand on her desk. Her friends looked over at her.

"I don't have an obsession." Karla crossed her arms over her chest.

"Well, there's something because you cannot get over this." Jessie turned her body to face Karla.

"Is it because I'm friends with him and you hate the fact that I'm getting attention from a guy?"

"That's it!" Justin yelled from behind them. Karla glared. Jessie ignored his comment.

"No." Karla growled.

"What then, Karla? What do you have against me and Leo? I said I'd be friends with both of you and you didn't like that idea." Jessie threw the information in Karla's face.

"Fine. Maybe I have feelings for Leo!" Karla blurted. Jessie pulled herself back in shock. Her friends passed glances to one another. Jessie stared at Karla and Karla kept her eyes on Jessie.

"Screw you, Jessie. I hate you so damn much!"

Karla grabbed her backpack and bolted out of the classroom. The class watched her. The teacher called for her but she never came back. I stood there shocked. I can't believe after all this time and all this hate deep inside Karla had feelings for Leo. I just couldn't believe it and, looking at Jessie and her friends, they couldn't believe it either.

Jessie never told Leo that Karla had feelings for him. I guess after all she and Karla had been through, she could at least keep this to herself. She asked her friends to do the same. Her friends talked about how they would have never guessed that she liked him and that that's why she and Jessie weren't getting along. Jessie knew that that was one of the reasons, but the other reason was because they didn't match up spiritually, not even a little.

Leo and Jessie had walked to her truck.

"So, you going to tell me what's going on?" Leo stood in front of Jessie's truck.

"Oh, I changed my mind." Jessie shook her head. The sun was beating down. It was already April. Two more months and Jessie was graduating.

"I'm not going to prom." Leo blurted.

Jessie's face fell in defeat. I felt badly for her as rejection washed over her. My heart ached and my stomach twisted in knots.

"Oh, okay, yeah I didn't want to either." Jessie shrugged and laughed it off, pretending she was okay with it.

"Cool. I didn't think you'd mind." Leo shrugged.

"Well, I will see you tomorrow."

Jessie went to get into her truck. Leo walked over and slammed the door shut as Jessie tried to open it. Jessie looked up at Leo. He needed to calm down.

"I want to go home." Jessie looked down at the door handle.

"No, Jessie. You're going to tell me what's going on." Leo demanded.

"I don't have to tell you anything." Jessie said through clenched teeth.

"Too bad. I'm not going to let you leave until you tell me."

Leo slipped in front of Jessie, blocking her way into the door. Okay, this guy was irritating my spirit. I don't like how he was being with Jessie. I watched intently, waiting for his next move.

"Leo, I mean it. Stop."

Jessie took a few steps back. Leo grabbed her by the wrist and pulled her toward him. Their bodies pressed together. *Oh no! I don't think so!* I slowly started to walk closer to Jessie. She looked up at him and her eyes filled with tears. Leo looked down.

"Jessie, tell me. You can open up to me."

"No. I can't. You wouldn't understand." Jessie shook her head.

She released her wrist from his grip and walked back a few steps. He reached out and put his finger through the belt loop of her jeans and pulled her back in. *Too close for comfort!* I didn't like this! I looked up to Jehovah and uttered *May I please intercede?*

"Leo," Jessie whispered, "this moment made me feel really uneasy. You wouldn't understand." Jessie sighed.

Leo drew in a breath and dipped is head to look Jessie in the eyes.

"This is why I can't get close to you," he said softly. "You won't let me in."

Leo released her and started walking away. Jessie stood there with her back still to him.

"I can see demons!" Jessie yelled from where she was standing. Leo stopped in his tracks and then turned to face each other.

"What?" Leo walked closer to Jessie.

"I can see demons. They come to my room. I see them in school. I see them all time. That's why I stare out into space a lot or don't talk for the whole period. It's not because I'm mad." Jessie explained.

"Wait. You see demons, like demons from Hell?"

"Yes."

Jessie shook as she took in a breath. Leo stood there staring at her. I wonder if he grasped the concept.

"Jessie, I had no idea." Leo's voice grew soft and he embraced Jessie in a hug.

"You believe me?" Jessie looked up at Leo with tears staining her face.

"Yes. I mean, I don't know how I can help you, but I would like to learn more if you would share with me." Leo smiled down at her.

"Really?" Jessie smiled through her tears.

"Yes, Jessie. Anything that's going on with you in your life I wanna know about it."

Leo held her tighter. I personally was shocked by his response. I guess you should never underestimate people.

That Night

Jessie was all done with her homework and was cleaning her room. She slipped into bed, grabbed her Bible from the nightstand, and turned to the book of Luke. It was one of Jessie's favorites. She thought it gave more detail and life about Jesus than the other gospels. As she read, she wrote down a couple of notes. She clicked the pen closed and then put it in her Bible as a bookmark. She rested her Bible on her nightstand. Jessie looked at the time. "11:30!" Jessie sighed. She said her prayers and then turned off the light. The room grew silent and still. All I could hear is her breathing. I sat at the computer desk and looked out the window. That tree next to Jessie's room looked odd. I squinted to see if I could figure out what was going on. The branches bent low to the ground and the wind wasn't even blowing. What was going on? I walked over to the window and peered out. A large, black panther burst through the window and landed on me. I fell to the floor as its massive frame crushed me. I grabbed it by the throat. Its fangs weren't even an inch away from my own throat. He growled and pinned me down with his massive frame. I grabbed him from behind his pointy black ears and through him to the side. Still having a hold on him, I rolled over on top of him. I then felt a sharp pain penetrate my shoulder blades. I clenched my teeth in pain. I looked back and a huge, dark brown lion with a jet black main and dark blue eyes dug his claws into my back. I let go of the black panther and focused my attention on this gigantic lion. He took his paws and clawed down my back. I fell to the ground. The pressure of his claws left my back as I fell to the ground. I heard them growling and pacing the floor. I regained some strength and pulled myself to my feet. They stood side by side and slowly inched toward me. I started to back up until I was against the wall and had nowhere to turn. These cats were huge and fast. I grabbed my sword and, when I did, the lion jumped up, raised his claw back, and struck my face. I fell to the ground with blood seeping out of the wound. Pain stung my face as I went dizzy and then they both attacked me. Claws dug into my flesh and I did my best to fight them off, but I was growing weak. If only Jessie would wake up and pray so I could regain my strength. I heard a loud whistle and whip crack the air. I looked up and it was Anton. He had sent them. The lion and the panther quickly got off of me and stood by their master.

"Well, hello, Tristan," a wicked grin crept across his face. I laid there. My strength was gone and I could barely say anything let alone move. He walked over to me.

"This is it, Tristan." Anton squatted down to look in my face.

"You're not looking so good." Anton laughed. His black hair fell over his shoulders and I glared up at him.

"Trust me, it's going to get much worse than this." Anton grew serious. "You know what happens when worlds collide."

He looked back at his cats and whistled and then they were gone. I laid on the floor of Jessie's room and looked up at her. She had been sleeping peacefully. I looked by her bed and there stood my tiger Skoto. "You're a little late there," I said sarcastically. He walked over to me and ran his large tongue over my face. I gritted my teeth. His tongue was rough and scratchy, and he licked my face clean. My hair was still matted with blood, but I would take care of that. He grabbed my sleeve with his mouth and tugged on it. I then regained my strength and pulled myself to my feet. I looked down at Skoto and rubbed him behind his ears.

"This is it, Skoto. We're in for a huge battle of good versus evil." I looked over at Jessie while she slept. Skoto rubbed his head on my thigh.

"You staying here tonight?" I looked down at him.

Skoto jumped on Jessie's bed, circled a couple of times, and then finally laid down at the foot of her bed.

CHAPTER 20

When Worlds Collide

Jessie was fast asleep. The moon was barely making its appearance. I stood down looking at her. Something wasn't right. The atmosphere didn't feel normal tonight. I looked around the room and saw nothing. That doesn't mean I couldn't feel them. I started to get a tremendous headache, the ones that you get above the eyes. The pain is slight, but it's throbbing and just there. I felt my sight start to fade as the headache increased. I looked around the room. There was nobody there. It felt like someone put an enormous amount of pressure in the room. I grabbed my head and fell to the floor. What was this? My eyes started to water, and water came flowing out of them. It was unstoppable. I grabbed the comforter on Jessie's bed and tried to pull myself up. I tried wiping my eyes with the other hand and felt like my eardrums were going to explode. *Lord, what is going on?* I fell flat on my face. I reached my hand up to get a good grip on Jessie's bed. When I held my hand there, I felt a touch . . . a soft calming touch . . . and my eyes stopped watering. I slowly lifted my head and Jessie's hand had fallen on mine. She was still fast asleep. My energy started to come back, but I didn't understand what was going on. Her touch empowered me, and I felt this power hit my hand and course through my entire body. My headache started to go away and my vision started coming back. I was finally able to pull myself back on my feet. So, I looked around the room and then it dawned on me what this meant, what Jehovah was trying to tell me. Jessie had the power and the gift to heal others from sickness and disease, even down to a headache. I looked down at her as she slept peacefully.

Jessie woke up to the sound of her alarm. Today was prom. Jessie would be spending all day getting ready. She still fussed and complained that she was taking her cousin, but she didn't want to go stag. She had told her mom, "Well, at least I don't have to impress him." She was right. I think she was underestimating the amazing time that she was going to have. Jessie got out of bed and headed to her closet. She pulled out her Dinosaur shirt and a pair of light-colored blue jeans.

"Jessie, are you ready for prom!?" Toni exclaimed as Jessie exited the bathroom.

"No, Mama." Jessie sighed. She headed to the fridge.

"Oh, taking your cousin isn't that bad." Toni walked over to Jessie and hugged her.

"Mama, yes it is. It means I'm a freaking loser."

"No, you're not." Toni put her hands on her hips.

"Ma!" Jessie raised her voice.

"I am not happy with Leo right now. He is not on my good side."

"Let's not get into that, Ma." Jessie narrowed her gaze at Toni.

"Well, he's going to see the mistake he's making."

"Ma, I got to go get my nails done. You're taking me. I don't want to go with anyone." Jessie patted Toni on the shoulder.

"You want me to go?" Toni said shocked.

"Yes. I have an appointment in twenty minutes." Jessie said as she walked into the living room.

I looked over at Toni and her face lit up with excitement. Usually, Jessie went and did most of that stuff with her friends. I think it was cool that Jessie was going to take her mom. I walked in and found Jessie sitting on the couch watching t.v. She had to get her nails done in twenty minutes and then we had to go to her beautician, Sheryl, so she could get her hair done. We then had to go back to the house so she could do her make up and get her dress on. All of this in six hours! Her dad had to go pick up Rodney and he had to get his tux on and all his stuff done. Then they would be taking pictures. Allen and his date would be picking Jessie and Rodney up in a limo around six, then they would go out of town to Olive Garden where we would meet up with Tiffany and her date. You're probably wondering about Allen and Karla. Allen told Karla that he couldn't go to prom with her because it wouldn't be right. Karla, of course, got angry and her hate for Jessie and Leo grew. Allen is going to prom with Amanda Emison. Karla still hasn't spilled the beans about Jessie taking Rodney, but it was just a matter of time before she did. I hope Jessie would handle it in the right way if it comes down to that.

Jessie, Toni, and I bolted out of the nail salon and headed toward the beauty shop to get her hair done.

"Oh, my gosh. Prom is in four hours. How did it take two hours to get my nails done?" Jessie looked over at Toni.

"I have no clue, babe." Toni pulled onto the street that led to the beauty shop.

"I'm kind of nervous." Jessie grabbed her stomach.

"Why?"

"Karla might blurt that I'm taking Rodney." Jessie sighed.

"No, I really don't think she will."

Toni pulled into the parking lot of the beauty shop. She parked and then looked over at Jessie.

"How are you getting your hair done?"

"Curls." Jessie smiled.

"You're going to look so pretty." Toni smiled.

"Alright, we gotta get this done."

Jessie grabbed her purse and we exited the car. We entered the beauty shop and a petite woman with gray curly hair was getting her hair done.

"Hello, Jessie and Toni." Sheryl greeted them.

"Hello." Jessie smiled politely and took a seat in an empty chair.

"What are we going to do with you?" Sheryl asked as she sprayed the ladies hair with hairspray.

"I would just like curls." Jessie looked up from the magazine she was looking at.

"Oh, alrighty." Sheryl smiled.

"Thanks." Jessie smiled.

Jessie and I sat there for another thirty minutes. The old lady's hair was poofed to perfection. She climbed her petite frame out of the beauty chair and headed toward the coat rack. She grabbed her small purse and pulled out a twenty and gave it to Sheryl.

"Thank you, sweetie." Sheryl lightly took the money from the old lady's fragile hand.

"You did a wonderful job as usual."

The old lady hugged Sheryl, said goodbye to Jessie and her mother, and headed out of the beauty shop.

"She's a nice old lady," Sheryl said as she grabbed a broom and started sweeping up hair.

"Are you excited for prom?" she asked as she brushed the hair into a dustpan.

"I am. I hate that I'm taking my cousin." Jessie sighed.

"Oh, well. Don't feel bad. I took mine." Sheryl smiled up at Jessie.

"Really?"

"Yes. I had a really good time, too." Sheryl nodded her head in certainty. "Alright, Miss Jessie, in the chair." Sheryl pointed.

Jessie sat her magazine down and headed for the chair. She sat in it and stared into the mirror. By the look on her face, I knew that she didn't like what she saw.

"I am going to make your hair look amazing."

Sheryl got out her supplies and started working on Jessie's hair. I sat next to Toni as the ladies talked. Jessie's hair was being transformed and it was starting to look very pretty.

"There." Sheryl let the last curl fall and gracefully fall past Jessie's shoulder. Jessie looked in the mirror shocked.

"Wow!" Jessie exclaimed.

Jessie admired her curls, and I know she felt pretty. She instantly realized how she felt.

"They're decent." Jessie looked down.

"This is on the house," Sheryl whispered into Jessie's ear.

"You don't have to," Jessie whispered.

"No, it's fine." Sheryl spun Jessie around in the chair so Toni could see her.

"Jessie, you're breathtaking." Toni raised her hand to her throat.

"I look alright," Jessie smiled sheepishly.

"Don't be silly, Jessie. You look amazing." Sheryl spun Jessie back around.

"I really appreciate this."

Jessie hopped out of the beautician's chair and headed toward us. I couldn't take my eyes off of her. She looked amazing. Her hair held the curls perfectly. Emotion choked my throat. Jessie grabbed her purse, thanked Sheryl again with a kiss on the cheek, and we headed out of the beauty shop. It was already four o'clock. We had to get her in her dress and do her make-up before six when Allen and Amanda would pick us up.

"Omg, it's four!" Jessie said as she got into her mother's car.

"Oh, wow! We gotta get you home!"

Toni pulled out of the parking lot with so much speed that it jerked Jessie's head back and she slammed against the headrest.

"Dang, Mama! Break my freaking neck. I got this hair done for prom not my funeral." Jessie rubbed the back of her head.

"Sorry, sweetheart." Toni sped toward the house.

Jessie, Toni, and I bolted toward the house. Jessie barged through the door and headed straight to the bathroom. Danny and Travis sat on the couch staring at the door as Toni fell into the house. She caught herself on the coat rack by the door.

"Whoa, we got a lot to do yet."

Toni threw her purse on the couch between Danny and Travis and then headed toward the bathroom to help Jessie with her make-up.

"They running late?" Danny looked over at Travis.

"Yup. That's the Craigs for you."

Travis took a sip of his coke. I took a seat in the rocking chair cat-a-corner from Danny and Travis. Rodney and Grandmother Craig entered the house.

"Hello, guys." Grandmother smiled.

"Jess getting ready?" Rodney laid his tux over the computer chair.

"Yes. She's in the bathroom putting on her make-up." Travis pointed to the bathroom with his pinky.

"I'm getting dressed in your room." Rodney grabbed his tux and headed toward Travis' room.

"It really pisses me off that she's got to take her freaking cousin." Travis scoffed.

"Well, at least she's not going alone." Danny shrugged.

"Yeah, well, Leo's a douche bag and I wouldn't mind killing him." Travis narrowed his gaze. Grandmother headed toward the bathroom where Jessie and Toni were.

"I know, Trav, but if he didn't want to go, he didn't want to go." Danny shrugged. Travis turned his head to Danny.

"Why are you on his side?" Travis arched his brow.

"Ugh, alright, but you cannot be mad."

Danny looked over at Travis. I looked from Travis to Danny and then back to Travis. He didn't look happy.

"A month ago," Danny took a deep breath, "Jessie asked me to prom and I never gave her an answer because I was too scared to say no." Danny winced. Travis' face grew angry. He pierced his lips into a fine white line, and his eyebrows came together in anger.

"Dude, are you freaking kidding me?" Travis hissed.

"I didn't want to just say no."

"So, you make her wait it out. Dude, that was low."

"Trav, she had to end up taking her cousin anyway. I'm surprised she never told you this."

Danny looked confused. I was shocked at this, and I didn't even know that she had asked him. I felt sorry for Jessie. Two people had bailed on her and she had to take her cousin. It just wasn't right. Well, if I were able to show myself, I would have taken Jessie to prom. I wish I could have.

"No. She never told me, probably because she was feeling down because *you* rejected her." Travis shook his head.

"Is Dad out there. I'm ready." Jessie called from the bathroom.

"Dad!" Travis called for Mike.

"Coming." Mike came into the living room from the kitchen.

"I'm coming out," Jessie said.

I looked up toward the hallway that led to the bathroom. Jessie slowly appeared. She looked radiant. Her lilac-colored dress accented her bright blue eyes. Her blonde curls fell over her shoulders. She wore high heels that had straps that went over the top of her foot. They had an oval of diamonds in the middle, the heel was clear, she wore silver dangled earrings, and had glitter in her hair. She really looked beautiful. I stood up as she entered the living room. I looked over at Danny, whose mouth dropped. Travis' eyes grew wide and Jessie and her grandmother stood behind her with tears in their eyes. Rodney exited the bedroom and entered the living room. He looked up at Jessie shocked.

"Wow, Jessie, you look beautiful!"

"Yeah, me and Leo are pretty much dumb." I heard Danny mumble.

"Pictures." Toni started snapping the camera. Jessie and Rodney stood and posed as the family took pictures. Jessie's phone rang. She looked at the caller ID, and it was Allen.

"Yeah." Jessie answered.

"On our way. Be there in like ten."

"Alrighty. See ya." Jessie said and then hung up the phone.

Jessie tossed the phone into her purse. She walked back over to her family and they began to take pictures again—a couple with Mike, then Travis, then Danny, then Grandmother. I wish I could. Jessie and her family talked for a while and Rodney kept complimenting Jessie and telling her how dumb Leo was for skipping out on her.

"They're here!"

Jessie pointed out the window to the white stretch limo. Her whole family and Danny rushed to the window. I looked out the window on the other side of the wall.

"Let's go."

Jessie grabbed Rodney's arm and they stepped out onto the porch. A man in a tux walked around the front of the limo and opened the door. A rather heavy-set woman climbed out of the limo. She had a dark purple spaghetti strap dress on with black high heels. She had strawberry blonde hair that was wrapped up into a bun. Allen then stepped out. He and Rodney had the same tux on. They looked at each other and then to their dates.

"Wow! This is amazing!"

Jessie stood in front of the limo with Rodney and took pictures. I looked into the limo and then climbed in. It was black on the inside and had wine glasses with napkins in them that were the school colors. It was nice and smelled better than I thought it would. Finally, Jessie and the rest got in.

"You guys look nice." Amanda nodded.

"Thanks." Jessie smiled.

Jessie texted Tiffany to tell her they were on their way to the Olive Garden.

"You excited for prom?" Allen looked over to Rodney.

"Yes, I am. This is my first one."

"How's come I never met you?" Allen looked over to Jessie.

"He was a family friend and, whenever ya'll were around, he wasn't." Jessie lied.

"I see. Well, Jessie, you look beautiful. Leo is really stupid." Allen shook his head.

"Awe, thanks." Jessie laughed. Jessie fiddled with the gadgets in the limo.

"A radio!"

Jessie flipped on the radio to channel 104.1. It had been Jessie's favorite channel since the sixth grade, and she listened to it all the time. She turned up the volume on the song "Forever". Jessie loved it and would listen to it any chance she got, and the beat was catchy.

"I have been waiting for this day since school started." Jessie rubbed her hands together in excitement.

Jessie rested against the limo seat. She looked around in wonderment. It was the first time she had ever been in a limo. She didn't think that she would because only rich kids went to prom in limos. But Allen paid for the whole thing, and she thanked God for such a good friend.

Olive Garden

Jessie and the others exited the limo and we headed toward the entrance at the Olive Garden. We were greeted by a pretty young woman who was rather tall, curvy, and had short, blonde hair. She dressed in her professional black attire and took us toward the others who were already sipping on their drinks. Jessie sat toward the end of the table across from Tiffany, and Rodney sat at the end of the table. Tiffany looked more like she was ready for a wedding rather than a prom. I think the only thing she didn't have to make her look like a bride was a vale. Her date, Blake, wore a white tux with a baby blue tie and vest. Allen took the other end of the table and Amanda sat beside Jessie.

"You look really nice, Jessie." Tiffany smiled.

"Thank you. You do, too." Jessie smiled back.

"Tomboys can really dress up when they want to." Blake laughed.

"Yes, we can." Jessie sipped on her tea.

I looked around at the others in the restaurant smiling at the teens.

"Leo's stupid, Jessie." Tiffany shook her head.

"I keep hearing that," Jessie laughed.

"Don't you think so, Rodney?" Blake looked over to Rodney.

"Yes." Rodney nodded his head.

The group of friends ate and socialized with one another as they ate their meals. Jessie seemed to be having an extremely good time, and everyone got along.

"Oh, wow! We've got an hour to get to prom and it takes forty-five minutes just to get back to Marion and prom is being held all the way across town!" Blake checked his watch.

"Oh, wow! We better get going."

Tiffany laid her part of the tip on the table and got up to leave. Jessie and the rest followed. Jessie, Rodney, Allen, Amanda, and I got into the limo and got settled.

"To McFareway Drive." Allen ordered to the limo driver.

"Yes, sir."

"That's Leo's street." Jessie looked over at Allen. What did he have in mind?

"I know." Allen looked out the window.

"What are you up to?" Jessie arched her brow.

"I'm going to have him see you dressed like this so he can see what he missed out on." Allen looked at Jessie and I looked at Rodney. His eyes widened.

"Sounds like a good idea to me." Rodney laughed.

"Me, too." Allen said as he pulled out his cell phone. He dialed a number and waited for a moment.

"Leo, you home?"

"Yeah." Allen put Leo on speaker phone.

"Well, we're gonna stop by and see you before we head to prom." Allen insisted.

"Uh . . . you don't need to do that." Leo sighed.

"No, it's fine. We have time." Allen smiled at Jessie.

"Alright. See ya in a few." Leo said and then hung up.

"Ha! He's pissed." Rodney straightened the jacket of his tux.

"I don't care. What he did to Jessie made me mad."

Allen tucked his phone in his tux jacket pocket. I thought that he needed to see Jessie dressed up, also. No one said much on the way to

Leo's. I think everyone was playing the scenario in their heads. The limo pulled onto McFareway Drive.

"Third house on the right," Allen called.

The limo pulled up to Leo's house and Leo came out of the front door waiting.

"Jessie gets out last." Allen said.

He opened the limo door and climbed out, then Amanda, then Rodney, then Jessie. Well, Leo stood there talking with Allen as Amanda got out and greeted him. Leo's long hair was pulled back into a low set pony tail. He wore cut off sweat pants and a white wife beater. Rodney got out next and I got out with him. Leo's jaw tensed up and he shoved his hands in his pockets. Rodney returned the glare.

"You must be Rodney." Leo rocked back on his heels.

"Yes, and you're Leo. I've heard about you."

Rodney mocked Leo's posture. I stood beside Rodney and then Jessie exited the limo. She pulled up on her dress so she wouldn't drag it on the ground and then looked up at Leo. His mouth hung open.

"You keep your mouth hung open like that and you're gonna catch flies." Amanda said with her tiny southern accent.

"You . . . uh . . . you look really nice." Leo coughed out.

"Doesn't she, though?" Rodney said as if to rub it in Leo's face. Leo looked over to Rodney and then back at Jessie.

"The color of that dress makes your eyes really . . . uh . . . look bright." Leo said nervously.

"Thanks." Jessie blushed.

"Wow! You really look good, Jessie."

I looked at Leo's face. Regret filled his countenance, and Jessie kept her eyes on him.

"Thanks. I try." Jessie said barely above a whisper.

"Well, we need to go."

Allen clapped his enormous hands together, put his hand on the small of Amanda's back, and led her into the limo.

"Jessie," Leo called. He walked over and hugged her. "You really look beautiful," he whispered into her ear. Jessie closed her eyes and took a deep breath.

"Jessie."

Rodney slipped his arm in Jessie's and lightly pulled her away from Leo's embrace. Leo shot Rodney a dirty look.

"See you Monday."

Jessie called then she, Rodney, and I entered the limo. Allen waved to Leo, shut the door, and we left for prom. I sat there thinking about the look on Leo's face when he had seen Jessie. A part of me thought that he deserved it but another part of me felt really sorry for him.

Prom

The limo pulled up to a rather large building which was decorated somewhat on the outside. The limo slowly pulled up to the double doors and students looked around to see who was in the limo. The limo driver parked and then got out and walked around the limo. The door flung open and a cool breeze entered the limo. Allen and his date filed out and then Rodney and Jessie followed. Rodney held his arm out for Jessie to take. Everyone was looking at them. Some of the students' mouths gaped open as they watched Jessie walk into the building.

"Jessie, omg, you look beautiful!" David approached Jessie and Rodney. "And who is this stud?" David batted his eyes.

"This is my date, Rodney. He's from Madison-Grant." Jessie beamed.

"You guys look great. I'm going to go visit with Carrie and them."

David kissed Jessie on the cheek and headed toward the group. Jessie, Rodney, Allen, and Amanda took seats at a vacant table. Rodney pulled out Jessie's chair and she took her seat. I looked around at all the students. They really did look beautiful. You could always tell who had and who didn't. Krista Hanks wore this elegant dress, like she was going to a royal ball. Then I looked over at Emily Rant. She wore a simple red dress. Not much to it. All that aside, they looked beautiful.

"Jessie?" Jeremy walked up to the table.

"Jeremy." Jessie stood up at his presence.

You . . . look . . . wow!" Jeremy laughed nervously.

"You look good, too." Jessie smiled.

"Hey." Jeremy nodded to Rodney. Rodney nodded.

"You . . . uh . . . tomboys can really clean up." Jeremy laughed.

"Ha. We try." Jessie laughed.

"Leo is gonna kick himself when he sees the pics." Jeremy leaned against the table.

"He's already seen me. Allen decided to drop by his house before we came here." Jessie sighed.

"Well I bet he's kicking himself." Jeremy looked down at Jessie.

"Let's hope."

"Well, I agree with Allen that he did that. I gotta go talk to some more people. Save me a dance."

Jeremy brushed Jessie's arm and headed toward a group of friends. She sat back down next to Rodney.

"He likes you." Rodney said to Jessie.

"Naw. He's just being nice." Jessie straightened her dress.

"No, he likes you. He always has, Jess." Allen butted in.

"No." Jessie stated.

"Jeremy and Leo have been fighting for you since the beginning of the year." Allen rolled his eyes.

"Let's dance." Amanda looked at Jessie, who wore an uncomfortable expression.

"Okay." Allen got up along with Jessie and Rodney and headed toward the dance floor.

"Hey," Karla stopped Jessie.

"Hello." Jessie said.

"I ain't gonna tell them who Rodney is." Karla ran her hands over her red dress.

"I thank you for that." Jessie nodded.

"You look really nice, Jessie." Karla smiled. I stood next to Jessie.

"You do, too, Karla." Jessie smiled.

"Have fun tonight." Karla hugged Jessie.

"You, too, Kar." Jessie said as Karla released her.

"Leo really missed out." Karla said and then walked away.

Jessie and I stood there for a while and then headed to the dance floor with Rodney, Allen, and Amanda.

"What did she want?" Rodney placed his hands on Jessie's hips and they started swaying.

"She just told me that I looked nice, that she wouldn't tell people you're my cousin, and that Leo missed out."

"I see." Rodney looked around at all the students that he did not know.

"Yeah, she's being fake. Guarantee you when we get back to school, she will blab that you're my cousin and once again be out for blood." Jessie sighed.

"Just tell everyone she's jealous that she didn't have a date, so she's trying to make you look bad." Rodney suggested.

"That might not work." Jessie laughed.

The slow song had ended and an upbeat one began. Jessie didn't move at first till she realized that everyone else was and then she started moving to the beat. Jessie looked beautiful. I couldn't get over how amazing she looked. Apparently, everyone else felt the same way. People were always coming up to Jessie, telling her how amazing she looked. She hadn't really visited with her normal group of friends.

"I'm going to go sit down." Jessie called to Rodney.

Rodney stopped dancing and followed her out into the sitting area. Jessie fell into her seat. She reached for her foot and rubbed her heel.

"These freakin' heels are killing me." Jessie winced as she brushed her hand over a premature blister.

"Jessie!" Jessie turned around at a screeching voice.

Shelby and the rest of the groom approached us. She wore a bright orange, ball gown-type dress that was strapless. Carrie wore a deep green spaghetti strap dress with bright red lipstick. Danni wore a sleek little black dress (more for a funeral than a prom), but all people are different. Their dates' tux vests and ties matched their dates' dresses.

"Hey, you guys look amazing!" Jessie got up to hug them.

"Jessie, you . . . wow . . . you look beautiful!" Carrie smiled.

"Thanks. You look great!" Jessie hugged Carrie again.

"You having fun?" Shelby looked at Jessie and then to Rodney.

"Yeah, for the most part. I'm kind of hot, though." Jessie fanned herself.

"Jessie, you're amazing!" James came up to Jessie.

"Awe, thanks, and you look very handsome." Jessie hugged James.

"Leo's stupid." James grunted.

"You are like the tenth person to tell me that." Jessie laughed.

"Well, he is."

"He's already seen me." Jessie beamed.

"Really?"

"Yeah. Allen decided to stop at Leo's before we headed here."

"I don't blame him. What did Leo say?" Shelby leaned forward. Everyone looked over at Jessie.

"He was speechless at first but then told me I looked beautiful. Then, when he hugged me, he said he was sorry." Jessie sighed.

"Awe . . . well, I'm glad he's full of regret." Carrie's jaw tensed.

"Carrie." Jessie lowered her gaze

"Sorry, Jess, but he did you wrong." Carrie shook her head and then looked out into the crowd of students.

"Well, that's all over and I've gotten past it. Let's go dance and have fun!" Jessie high-fived her friends.

"You go ahead, Jess." Rodney nodded to dismiss her.

"Alrighty." Jessie smiled. Jessie and her friends headed back to the dance floor.

"Alright, students. If I can have your attention, we are going to announce prom King and Queen." Mr. Nelson announced. The whole place went silent.

"And the winner by seven votes for prom Queen . . . Krista Hanks!"

Mr. Nelson held the crown out to Krista. She ripped the crown out of Mr. Nelson's hand and paraded around the dance floor. Jessie and her friends crossed their arms and rolled their eyes. I couldn't blame them.

"Alright then." Mr. Nelson pulled at his tie. "And the King, winner by twenty-nine votes . . . Kyle Macarthur!"

"That's not fair! He's gay!" D.J. Ashla yelled out from the crowed. He was right. Kyle is gay but he won by the students' votes.

"Mr. Ashla, no comments."

Mr. Nelson handed Kyle his crown then he and Krista had the prom King and Queen dance.

"Well, I saw that coming." Carrie rolled her eyes. Jessie and her friends headed back to the seating area.

"I saw that coming." Karla approached them. I noticed the others getting tensed up.

"Well, you all look great." Karla flipped her red hair over her shoulder.

"Thanks," they all said coldly.

Prom was dying down and the students were starting to leave for after parties. Jessie had gotten invited to a couple of them but said no because she didn't want to put herself or Rodney in that situation. She grabbed her little jacket then she and Rodney headed out of the building. Students were out in the parking lot talking and smoking.

"Where did your dad leave the truck?" Rodney looked for Mike's truck.

"There." Jessie pointed.

Allen and Amanda followed. The wind started to pick up, unraveling Jessie's curls. She lifted herself into the truck and settled in.

"Well, prom was fun." Jessie laid her head on the headrest.

"I think so, too." Allen smiled. Jessie pulled out of the parking lot and onto the highway.

"Wow, prom's over with. The next big thing this year is graduation." Jessie sighed.

"True. That I'm excited for." Allen rubbed his hands together.

"Me, too," Jessie said. Leo's ring tone blared through the truck.

"Hello?" Jessie answered. The conversation went on for a while.

"No, Leo. Omg, I will see you Monday." Jessie hung up the phone.

"What's his problem?" Rodney looked over to Jessie.

"Nothing." Jessie sighed and gripped the wheel.

"You guys confuse me. I think you're good for each other, and then I think you guys are completely wrong for each other." Allen shook his head. I sat wedged between him and Amanda.

"We're wrong for each other." Jessie turned onto Allen's street.

"Are you staying the night?" Allen looked over at Amanda.

"Yeah, that's what I planned." Amanda smiled. Jessie and Rodney tossed each other a disgusted look.

"Good. My bed is . . . ."

"Allen!" Jessie yelled.

"What!"

"You're home." Jessie put the truck into park.

"Cool. See ya Monday, Jess." Allen patted Jessie's shoulder. He and Amanda climbed out of the truck.

"Well, that was eventful." Rodney chuckled.

"My feet hurt and I wanna take this make-up off." Jessie whined.

"The dress?"

"Oh, I don't know. It makes me feel pretty." Jessie laughed.

"I had fun, Jess. If someone busts you out that I'm your cousin, screw them because we had fun!" Rodney fist pumped.

I would have to admit that I had fun, too. Grant it, I didn't dance, or dress up fancy, or get my picture taken, but watching them have a good time made me have a good time. Jessie looked beautiful and so did her friends. What I liked the most is that everyone got along. The "rich" kids got along with the "poor" kids, and preps got along with the goths and emos. I was really happy that it all went well and there was no evil. We all got a break. We were finally home and we fell out of the truck. As soon as Jessie hit the ground, she ripped her shoes off and headed toward the house.

"I hear my bed calling me."

Jessie ran to the door, and I followed. She barged through the front door.

"How was it?" Toni looked up from her book.

"Great! I had so much fun." Jessie flopped on the couch. Rodney entered and shut the door behind him.

"Did you have fun?" Mike turned the television volume down and I took a seat next to Jessie on the couch.

"I did." Rodney took off his tux jacket.

"We went to Leo's before prom." Jessie smiled at Toni.

"You did? What happened!?" Toni laid the book she was reading down on the couch.

"Well he was definitely shocked at what he saw."

"And he mean mugged me the entire time." Rodney interrupted.

"He did?" Toni leaned in to listen.

"Yeah. He kept telling me how beautiful I looked and stuff. No big deal." Jessie shrugged.

"Everyone told Jessie that she looked beautiful. Jeremy was speechless." Rodney rocked back on his heels.

"True. I'm just that good." Jessie laughed.

"I'm glad you had fun." Toni kissed Jessie on her cheek.

"I had so much fun that I totally forgot about Leo." Jessie sighed.

"Good." Rodney said. "I'm going to get cleaned up and go to bed. I'm so tired." Rodney hugged Jessie then disappeared down the hall.

"Me, too. We'll talk tomorrow." Jessie got up, kissed her parents on the cheek, and we headed to her room.

Monday, Period 1: Art

Jessie entered the classroom with a huge smile on her face. She took her seat across from Leo. Leo didn't look up.

"Jessie, how was your weekend?" Shelby sat down with her supplies.

"Great. Prom was so fun. I liked dressing up." Jessie rested her head in her hands.

"You going to start wearing make-up?" David smiled at Jessie.

"I am." Jessie smiled. Leo looked up. "Cool" was all he said.

"I can't believe how great you looked, Jessie. I mean . . . really." Shelby nodded her head.

"Thank you. I try." Jessie shrugged.

"You did look amazing, Jessie. I should have taken you." David laughed.

"Ha, right."

"I heard you saw Jessie before prom." Shelby looked over at Leo.

"I did." Leo said bending a little piece of metal from another charm he was making.

"And?" David dipped his head to look at Leo.

"And, she looked really nice." Leo shrugged.

"Nice?" David rolled his eyes.

"Someone is regretful." Shelby hissed.

"Guys," Jessie sighed. "It's all over and we all looked good." Jessie laughed.

"Alright, dropping the subject." David cocked his head.

"Karla talked to me." Jessie said to Leo.

"And?" Leo didn't look up.

"She told me I looked nice and that was about it." Jessie shrugged.

"She's fake." Leo grunted.

"I know." Jessie sighed.

Period 4: Accounting

Jessie and I slowly walked to Accounting class.

"Jessie," we heard a voice say to us. We turned around to see Karla coming to us. I crossed my arms over my chest.

"Hey," Jessie said as she straightened the strap on her backpack.

"Did you have fun Saturday?" Karla began to walk with us.

"I did. You?"

"I thought it was okay." Karla laughed.

"Oh." Jessie said uncomfortable.

"Um, I wanna talk with you after school in the parking lot after everyone leaves." Karla stopped in her tracks and looked at Jessie. I saw hate flash across her eyes.

"Yeah, sure, that's cool." Jessie smiled.

I bet Jessie was thinking that she and Karla were going to be best friends again. *Guess again, Jessie.* I put my hand on Jessie's back.

"Cool. Well, see ya." Karla lightly hugged Jessie.

Jessie shook it off and entered Accounting class. We took our normal seats. I'm kind of glad school was coming to an end. The same thing over and over was making me bored.

"Jessie, I loved your dress," a group of girls came over to us that didn't normally talk to us.

"Thanks. You guys looked good, too." Jessie smiled.

Tiffany slummed through the door. I never noticed it, but she was starting to show.

"I'm so tired." Tiffany fell into her desk.

"You look tired. Why don't you go home?" Jessie asked.

"I might." Tiffany shook her head like she was trying to come back to her senses.

"I would."

"Is it a boy or a girl?" one of the petite girls asked.

"Girl." Tiffany sighed.

"Don't want a girl?"

"It's not that, but I was really hoping to have a boy." Tiffany weakly smiled.

"I understand." Jessie put her hand on Tiffany's shoulder.

"Well, I'm going home." Tiffany grabbed her belongings. "My stomach hurts." Tiffany put her hand up to her mouth like she was stopping herself from throwing up.

"I'll let you get my notes and I'll get your homework." Jessie reassured.

"Thanks, Jess." Tiffany walked out of the classroom.

"I feel sorry for her," one of the girls said to Jessie.

"Yeah." Jessie shrugged. Jessie's phone lit up with a text. It was Karla.

"Do not bring anyone with you. This is a personal convo." Jessie waited a while before she texted back.

"Well, I told Leo we would head to eat afterwards, but I will make him sit in the truck."

"Ugh, alright. But just him."

"Alright."

Jessie put her phone in her pocket and started copying the notes on the board. I looked toward the door and saw Anton standing there with a big, stupid grin on his face. This guy really irritates me. I folded my hands, laid them on the desk, and stared at Anton.

"Just to let you know, Tristan, I will see you after school in the parking lot." Anton laughed.

"I know," I said through clenched teeth.

"Aren't you afraid?" Anton moved in closer.

"Not hardly." I scoffed.

"Well, this battle has been long overdue." Anton licked his lips.

"I agree." I kept my eyes on Jessie.

"Good." Anton turned to walk away. "See you later, angel."

Anton laughed and headed out of the classroom. I took in a breath and exhaled. This was it. This battle is going to be the one that will finally rip Jessie and Karla apart.

Period 7: English 12

Jessie stood at the locker exchanging books. Leo crept up behind her then grabbed her hips. Jessie didn't flinch. I could tell she had too much on her mind.

"You okay?" Leo asked.

"Yeah. Karla wants to talk to me after school in the parking lot." Jessie closed one eye to see Leo's response.

"That's fine. I'll sit in the truck." Leo shrugged.

"She's being like super nice to me and I have no idea why." Jessie shook her head.

"I don't know, Jessie. What's that saying 'Keep your friends close and your enemies closer.'" Leo zipped up his backpack.

"I think you're right. God will give me strength. He always does." Jessie closed the locker.

"I guess." Leo shrugged.

"Trust me. He's got my back." Jessie smiled.

Jessie, Leo, and I headed to class. Jessie threw her backpack under her desk and took her seat next to Carrie. Leo lightly placed his backpack under his desk and took his seat in front of Jessie.

"So, I hear Karla wants to talk with you." Carrie looked over at Jessie.

"It's true."

"What do you think she wanted to talk about?"

"I don't know. Maybe this talk will be the end of our friendship for good." Jessie sighed.

"Well, let's hope." Leo turned around to face them.

"Come on. She and I've been through a lot and it's hard to just stop being friends with your best friend." Jessie defended.

"We get that, Jessie, but she's mean." Shelby entered the conversation.

"I don't care what you guys say, I know there's some good in her heart somewhere." Jessie looked at each of her friends.

"Yeah, Jessie, like waaaaaaay deep down." Justin laughed.

"Guys." Jessie narrowed her gaze at her friends.

"Sorry, Jess, we just want to make sure that you're going to be okay." Justin put his hand on Jessie's shoulder.

"I'm going to be fine."

"Did everyone enjoy prom?" Mrs. Lazarus asked as she entered the classroom.

"Yes," the kids that went said in unison.

"All you guys looked great. Leo, I didn't see you there." Mrs. Lazarus turned her attention to Leo.

"No. Proms not my thing." Leo laughed.

"Yeah, I saw Jessie walk in with this tall handsome guy and I was like 'What happened to Leo?'" Mrs. Lazarus joked.

"Yeah." Leo became uneasy.

"By the way, Jessie, you and your date looked simply amazing. All of you guys did." Mrs. Lazarus looked at the students.

"Thanks," they said in unison.

"Alright. Today, I'm going to let you guys finish those extra credit packets. Read the short story starting on page 598 and ending on page 614, and do the assessment questions at the end." Mrs. Lazarus clasped her hand together.

"Fair enough." Jeremy put his hand in the air.

Jessie and Jeremy didn't talk that much anymore. I really don't know what happened, but I have a pretty good guess. I think Jeremy realized that Jessie's heart was leaning toward Leo and he decided to give up and let Jessie go. It wasn't that they didn't talk at all because they did. They just didn't talk as much and flirted every once in a while. Jessie didn't seem to mind. No matter what Leo had put her through, he was still her number one guy.

"I can't believe I finished this all in one class period!" Jessie jumped out of her desk and walked toward the teacher's desk. Jessie placed the packet on Mrs. Lazarus' desk.

"Good job, Jessie. I see you got done before your partner in crime." Mrs. Lazarus pointed her head to Leo.

"I think he's got a lot on his mind." Jessie whispered.

"I see." Mrs. Lazarus went back to grading papers. Jessie stood there for a while then headed back to her seat.

"Well, that was fast." Leo said before Jessie got to her seat.

"What can I say? I just want out of this place." Jessie laughed.

"I agree." Leo flipped the packet back to the front and turned around to face Jessie.

"Everyone has been on my case about prom." Anger flashed in his eyes.

"I know. I keep telling people to be quiet, but they won't. It's getting on my nerves, too, because I have to relive the rejection." Jessie sighed.

"Rejection?"

"Leo, you rejected me."

"How?"

"You didn't ask me to prom. I figured like everyone else that you would take me." Jessie started to raise her voice. Her friends looked over at them.

"Jessie, you cannot be serious. Are you holding a grudge?"

"Leo, I have said this before. I am too lazy to hold a grudge." Jessie laughed.

"Look, prom is just not my thing. I would have taken you, but I couldn't bring myself to go."

"Leo, you are the one person I thought would want to come. You're all about school functions. You're my best friend and you should have been there for me." Jessie said almost crying.

I felt sorry for Jessie. I started to rub her back to try and calm her.

"Jessie, I'm sorry." Leo sighed.

"It's fine." Jessie shrugged. "Let's just put it behind us." Jessie smiled.

"Jessie, I don't want you to bottle this up and hate me." Leo stood up and tapped the packet against the palm of his hand.

"Leo, really, it's fine." Jessie managed a smile.

It was not okay. I knew she was not okay. She's cried almost every night since he rejected her about prom and she gets emotional about it every so often. Jessie doesn't show emotion unless it's anger and she was more hurt by this than angry. I'm also proud that she hasn't blown up on him. I noticed Jessie was starting to mature more and she really cared about what God thought about a lot of stuff. She told her friends and family that if God said "No", then she wouldn't, or "What do you think God wants?" She said stuff like that more and more every day. I think she was starting to realize what a big deal God was to her. I love it!

The class period went by rather fast. The students gathered their books and headed out of the classroom. Jessie, Leo, and the others stopped at Jessie and Leo's locker.

"Why are you guys hovering?" Jessie looked at Justin.

"We're not." Justin shrugged.

"Yes, you are." Jessie rolled her eyes.

"Jess," Leo grunted.

"Leo," Jessie grunted back. "Bye, guys." Jessie dismissed them.

"Fine, we're out. If you need me to pound her . . . you text me." Justin punched the palm of his hand.

"Ha, right." Jessie laughed as she put her books in her backpack.

"Bye." Shelby hugged Jessie.

"You act like she's going to kill me." Jessie laughed. Everyone stared at her with serious expressions.

"God's going to take care of me." Jessie smiled.

"He better." Justin called down the hall.

"Ready?" Jessie placed her hand on the locker.

"Yup." Leo then shut the locker.

Jessie, Leo, and I headed toward the school parking lot. The hallways were becoming more vacant along with the parking lot. Jessie noticed Karla's red Grand Am parked next to her truck. She and Leo took their time getting there. I saw Anton standing against Jessie's truck.

"Well, hello beautiful." Anton greeted me. I said nothing. My heart started to beat hard against my rib cages. I could feel my blood coursing through my body, and my teeth lightly chattered behind my lips in the language of Jehovah. Karla got out of her car and looked at Jessie with a smile.

"Here, if it gets too hot, roll the windows down or turn on the a-c. Jessie handed Leo her truck keys.

"Alright. Remember . . . God's got your back." Leo took the keys and headed toward Jessie's truck.

"Well hello, Jesus." Karla's voice rumbled with a dark discord.

"Judas." Jessie answered. "What's this all about?" Jessie laid her backpack on the ground. Anton walked up and stood next to Karla. I moved closer to Jessie.

"I think we need to talk about . . . well . . . our friendship."

"Karla, there is no friendship." Jessie let out a sarcastic laugh.

"Oh, Jessie . . . stupid . . . stupid Jessie." Karla leaned on the hood of her car. Jessie didn't say anything. She looked over to her truck and Leo was reading a book.

"So, do all Christians think they're better than everyone?" Karla pulled a cigarette out from behind her ear.

"Only some." Jessie simply said. I noticed the clouds rolling in and the sky turning a dark gray. The wind started to pick up.

"There's a storm coming." Jessie looked to the sky.

"Worlds are about to collide." Karla grinned. She cupped her hand over her cigarette and lit it. She took a drag and then exhaled. "Tastes good." Karla flipped the ashes into the air.

"Karla, what's this about?"

"I hope you die, Jessie." Karla hissed. Anton turned to smile at me. Thunder clapped in the sky.

"I rebuke those words of death." Jessie said through clenched teeth. I noticed her hands ball into fists.

"Rebuke those words of death? You act like God cares about you. If he did, you would have Leo in the way that you want him." Karla stood straighter.

"I don't have time for this."

"Oh . . . I think you do." Karla hissed. Her forked tongue slithered out of her mouth. Jessie pulled back, and I looked at Anton.

"Let it begin." He raised his hands up, summing up all of the evil. Demons of all sizes came from around the school. They ran and stood behind Anton and Karla. It started to rain and it slapped across our faces. I looked over to Jessie and Karla. They started to argue and, at that time, their spirits jumped out of their bodies. Karla's spirit jumped up in the air and expanded its big black wings and hovered in the air. Jessie's spirit did the same and kept its eyes on Karla's. Karla's spirit charged Jessie's causing them to fall to the ground. I grabbed my sword and headed toward Anton. The world felt like it stopped. The wind stopped blowing and the raindrops stopped in mid-air. Jessie and Karla stood there frozen. Their spirits fought one another. Jessie's spirit pulled out its sword and stabbed Karla in the wing. Anton blocked my sword with his. The battle was on.

"Tristan, you're an idiot. You think you're going to win this!?" Anton screamed at me. I didn't say anything. I yelled the warrior cry. Tens of thousands of angels came flying down to earth. They hit the ground and started fighting. No questions asked. I looked over at Jessie. At that time, Karla had punched her and she fell to the ground. Her spirit needed help . . . needed energy.

"Truce!" I called. I noticed Truce barrel through a group of demons and stand in front of me. We ducked as bodies flew over our heads.

"Tristan," he said almost out of breath.

"Take care of him. I'm going to Jessie. It's time." I nodded to Truce.

"You're sure?" he looked at me with intensity.

"Yes."

I nodded to him and then headed toward Jessie who was being beat badly by Karla. (It was their spirits that were fighting. In the natural, they were just fighting with words.) This was it. Jessie was going to need my help. I walked over to her as she laid on the ground. Jesaiah grabbed Karla from behind and pulled her wings back. She let out a yell as she fell to the ground. I knelt down to Jessie. Her long blonde hair was caked with blood, sweat, and rain.

A demon charged at Jessie.

"Ah!" she screamed. I heard squishing and a gasp for air and then a thud to the ground. I looked back and saw Jessie staring down at the demon she just killed and then to her bloody sword. I couldn't help but smile. She had to know that this was the battle that was going to end this friendship for good.

I had forgotten for a moment that she wasn't used to this. I grabbed the demon by his gigantic head and pulled him over me. His back slammed against the ground into a puddle and water splashed up and hit Jessie and me. I grabbed my sword, lifted it over my head, and penetrated the demon's chest. I put more force into it and my sword hit his heart. His heartbeat vibrated through my sword.

I looked over and three demons were punching and kicking her. She would throw her sword up ready to strike but one would kick her in the stomach causing her to crash to the ground. She fell into a puddle of blood and water mixed. I ripped my sword from the demon's chest and ran for Jessie. The demons started carrying her away. Four demons stood in front of me, so I couldn't get to Jessie.

"Truce, we gotta get Jessie," I called to Truce.

"She will be okay. Michael's on his way." Truce yelled. At that time, the demons started clawing at my face. I couldn't keep my eyes open. I heard Karla and Jessie in the natural still yelling at each other. The sound was very faint, but it could be heard. I looked to my right and saw Karla's spirit standing there glaring at me. The demons jumped off of me and headed toward other angels.

"Tell your God that He ruined everything!" she yelled at me. A growl surrounded her tone. I just stared at her and didn't know what to say. She charged at me, so I grabbed her by the throat and looked into her eyes. Hate looked back at me. I wanted to stab this girl with every fiber of my being but I knew that I couldn't. It was not my job. I dropped her to the ground and stared at her. Then a demon jumped on me and dug his claws into my back. He took his claws and ran down my back. I clenched my teeth in pain. I looked around and Jessie was nowhere to be found. I started to panic. I looked around even though the demon was still attached to my back. I started looking for Jessie and finally found her. She was standing in a circled surrounded by demons that she had slain. The demon that had been attached to my back was ripped off by Michael and killed.

"I'm going home, Karla. We're done." Jessie grabbed her backpack from the ground and headed toward her truck.

"Fine, Jessie, but remember this . . . I will always be in the back of your mind. You will never be rid of me!" Karla threatened. I looked to the heavens. We have already defeated her.

I don't know if Karla and Jessie will ever become friends again. That's for God to decide. Right now, they're from two different worlds that will always collide.

CHAPTER 21

The Last Day

Period 1: Art

Jessie busted through the classroom door. "It's the last day!" she yelled into the classroom as she threw her hand into the air. Cheers came from all over the room.

"Craig, I know it's the last day, but could you please not make an uproar?" Mrs. James asked.

"You're gonna miss me." Jessie smiled at her teacher.

"I think I will. I never had another student like you. I know that you're going to make a difference in this world. I'm not saying that just because you are my student. I really feel like you're going to make some major changes some day."

Mrs. James embraced Jessie. Jessie just stood there, not moving and not embracing back. She wasn't used to a teacher telling her that. All she ever heard was "I'm going to be surprised if you graduate," or "You're a slacker and a troublemaker," or "Your profession will probably be a street pharmacist." That's the stuff she was used to hearing. Yes, Jessie was graduating, but barely. She quit studying for a while and then had to hurry up and study with Leo just to get C's and D's. But that was it. She was still playing pranks on people, like the other day. We were sitting in Algebra 2 and Jessie sits behind Amy Dolman whom she cannot stand. Well, Jessie erased the problems she had gotten wrong, lifted the paper to her mouth, and blew the eraser shavings off into Amy's hair. I don't think she would ever stop doing that. She still switched the keys around on the keyboard, messing people up. She still grabbed people's books from their desk and put someone else's name in it, confusing the teacher on who had what book. That was Jessie, like her or leave her.

Jessie finally took her seat at the table with her friends.

"That was weird," Jessie stated.

"Yeah, but it was cool. I'm a better student than you ever were and no teacher ever said that to me." Leo grunted.

"That's why. The good students never make a difference. They're scared to," Jessie smiled.

"Right." Leo rolled his eyes.

"Good God! I can't believe it's the last day of senior year.' Shelby grew sad.

"I know. I keep feeling that I'm coming back next year, but I know that I'm not." Jessie exhaled.

"I know what you mean." Shelby played with the marble on the table.

"You still going to work on that project?" Jessie nodded to Leo. Leo was working on making a green stone shine.

"Yeah. It's for my mom." Leo shrugged.

"It's really pretty." Jessie commented.

"Thanks." Leo didn't take his eyes off of his project.

"I don't want it to end!" David yelled in tears. We all looked over at him. "I don't want to be without you guys! I want to see you guys five days out of the week." David leaned on Jessie and cried. Jessie rubbed his back.

"Wow! You're taking this hard." Jessie kept rubbing his back.

"I know. I can't believe high school is over with." David sniffled. "We have to leave. I really wanna stay in high school." David started to laugh.

"Not me." Jessie blurted.

"You hate school." Leo glared up at Jessie.

"Well, it shouldn't suck so much." Jessie shrugged.

"You made it suck." Leo drew in a breath.

"Leo, this is the last day we'll ever have this class together. I really don't want to ruin it with a fight." Jessie warned. Leo put his hands up in a motion to surrender.

Jessie and I sat in the art room not really saying much. It was a sad moment for her and her friends. This was the last day that she would ever have a class with them. Jessie looked at all of her friends and smiled. Leo looked up.

"What are you smiling about?"

"How much that I love you guys." Jessie smiled.

"Oh, I see. Well, I mean this is the last of it." Leo said.

"I know that." Jessie snapped. What was with this change of attitude?

"What the hell, Jess!" Leo caught the change, too.

"Never mind." Jessie shook her head.

Period 4: Accounting

Jessie sat in her seat next to Tiffany. She knew that the teacher wouldn't be doing anything today. What was the point? It was the last day of school.

"Wow! The last day of our senior year." Tiffany shook her head.

"I know. This is crazy. After this it's on to the real world."

"Man, Jessie, I never thought that you would be my best friend." Tiffany smiled.

"Same here."

"I mean, with Karla hating me and all."

"Well, now she hates the both of us."

"What made her hate you so much?"

"Well, I became a Christian and stopped drinking and smoking. I became friends with people that she didn't like and gained my old friends back." Jessie shrugged.

"She's stupid." Tiffany rolled her eyes.

"That's true!" Jessie laughed.

"Want to hang out after school today?" Tiffany shifted her body to face Jessie.

"Yeah, sure." Jessie agreed.

"Good. I need someone to talk to."

"Well, you know that I'm here for you." Jessie reassured.

"Thanks! That means a lot. Ever since I've gotten pregnant, not a lot of my friends ever wanted to hang out with me."

"Psh, that doesn't bother me. I will just be Aunt Jessie." Jessie chuckled.

"Sounds good to me!" Tiffany agreed. "You gonna miss high school?"

"Um, some of it I will, like seeing my friends and hanging with them in the hallways. But school itself I will not miss." Jessie shook her head.

"Yeah, I think I feel the same." Tiffany shrugged. "What about you and Leo?"

"What about us?" Jessie sighed.

"Think you guys will be friends after high school?"

"Yeah, for a little while." Jessie didn't look at Tiffany.

"What do you mean?" Tiffany dipped her head to look at Jessie.

"Look, I don't mean to be harsh, and I love Leo. You know that. But I don't see him being in my life forever." Jessie rested her head in her hands.

"I didn't know you felt that way." Tiffany rubbed Jessie's back.

"Yeah, no one does." Jessie laughed. "Everyone thinks we're going to graduate and get married. I'm sorry, but I don't see it happening. It breaks my heart, but when it's not there it's not there." Jessie explained.

"You don't think he'll always be in your life as just a friend?"

"I don't know, Tiff. If he does, it will be a miracle from God."

"I think you're just feeling this way because he hasn't asked you out or anything, but I think you guys will be together forever. It has to be that way. The whole earth will plummet if you guys depart. It just won't feel right." Tiffany laughed, trying to encourage Jessie.

"Maybe you're right. I'm just freaking out because high school is over with." Jessie laughed.

I think that that's how Jessie really felt, and a part of me thinks that she knew that that would probably come to pass. No one knows but God.

Jessie, a couple of friends, and I walked down the hallway to Sociology class. It was the last day of school, but they still had a pop quiz. So, she knew the students would all be there today because they could all use a boost on their Sociology grade. Jessie didn't see Karla. After what had happened, she would probably never see Karla again. Maybe at graduation, but she doubted it. Jessie and her friends took their seats and were ready for the pop quiz.

"Who gives a freakin' quiz on the last day of school?" Justin yelled.

"Mr. Neal," Carrie answered.

"After this, ya'll wanna skip to Steak 'n Shake?" Shelby whispered to the group.

"Yes. Maybe I can get Leo to come along." Jessie beamed.

"Yes, do that." Justin insisted.

"Get Allen and James." Carrie nodded to Jessie.

"Will do!" Jessie raised her hand to salute Carrie.

"Tiffany?" Shelby looked at Jessie.

"She and Amy are going to get their nails and stuff done," Jessie shook her head. "She told me after Orchestra. She and I were supposed to hang out, but it's 'whatever'."

"Alright. Should we skip the last day of school, though? I mean, it's the last day we're ever going to have class together." Shelby frowned.

"That's true." Justin sighed.

"And we all have the next class together." Carrie pointed out.

"Yeah. We can go to Steak 'n Shake after school." Justin suggested.

"I agree." Jessie chimed.

"I can't believe this is the last day of senior year." Danni sniffled.

"I know. We're not coming back." Carrie shook her head in disbelief.

"Yeah, it was so weird hearing them call over the intercom for the underclassmen to go to the auditorium to get their schedules set for the next year, and we didn't go." Jessie stared at her friends.

"Oh yeah, that was really weird." Justin tucked his pencil behind his ear.

"Wow, will everyone get into college?" Shelby looked around at her friends and then locked eyes with Jessie.

"No, I am not going. I told you that." Jessie said with frustration.

"Jessie, you have to go to college." Justin narrowed his gaze.

"You guys just watch. I'm going to show you that you don't have to go to college to be successful." Jessie nodded with certainty.

"How?" Shelby cocked her head at Jessie.

"I don't know. Be an author, start a business from scratch!" Jessie threw her hands in the air.

"You can't be an author, you're a D average student in English." Justin smarted.

"Um, spell check . . . duh." Jessie defended herself.

"No, you need to go to school for something that you know will benefit you." Carrie joined the argument.

"Well, thanks for believing in me." Jessie rolled her eyes.

"Jessie, we just don't want you to be a bum." Shelby hesitated.

"I'm not going to be a bum. You know what?" Jessie took a deep breath trying to calm herself. "It's students like me, the ones who didn't do good in high school, that make a difference and end up being successful." Jessie tore into them. "Why? Because I put my faith in God and not man. That's why! And if you can't handle and understand that, then maybe we shouldn't be friends. And I never said I was going to be an author. I'm saying it's something you can do without having to go to college!" Jessie yelled.

She started breathing heavy and her face was turning red. She was mad . . . really mad.

"Sorry, Jess. We didn't mean to make you mad." Shelby said just above a whisper.

"Well, you did!" Jessie glared at them.

"We're just looking out for you."

"Whatever. I'm over it." Jessie shot back.

The group stayed silent for a while. Awkward. I've never heard silence this loud. That's what it felt like. The silence was so loud it was unbearable.

Period 7: English 12

Well, it's the last period of the day . . . the last class Jessie was ever going to have in high school. Jessie was still not talking with her friends. I could understand why she didn't want to. They practically ganged up on her.

"Jessie, we're really sorry. We believe in you. We really do." Shelby broke the silence between them.

"It's alright. I know it's because ya'll care about me. I shouldn't have blown up." Jessie smiled.

"Good." Shelby nodded.

"Happy last day!" Leo busted into the classroom.

"I would have thought you would have hated this day." Jessie laughed.

"Heck no. I'm ready for the future!" Leo stood in front of Jessie.

"Me, too." Jessie fist pumped.

"Leo, Steak 'n Shake after school." Shelby informed.

"Yes, ma'am." Leo nodded. "Ride?" Leo squinted at Jessie.

"You know you're gonna ride with me. You don't have to ask." Jessie assured.

"I know, but it's polite." Leo stated.

"My babies are leaving me!" Mrs. Lazarus said as she entered the classroom.

"Awe, Mrs. L, we're gonna miss you." Jessie awed.

"I know. I'm going to miss you guys. I'm not just saying this. This is my favorite class." Mrs. L sniffled.

"Man, this makes me not want to leave." Leo grunted.

"You know, as much as I hate school, there are some things I'm going to miss." Jessie hung her head.

"Like me." Leo smiled.

"Ha! Yes. Like you." Jessie embraced him in a hug. Leo held Jessie, rested his face in her hair, and breathed her in.

"I'm really going to miss seeing you as often as I do now."

Jessie pulled back and looked up at Leo. Her hands wrapped around his waist. Leo's arms were wrapped around her waist and his hands rested on her hips. Jessie's long, blonde hair swayed back and forth as she spoke to Leo. Leo reached up and ran his fingers though her hair. *I didn't like this!* but Jessie seemed happy.

"Awe. I'm going to miss seeing that." Shelby awed at them. Jessie and Leo turned to look at Shelby.

"Oh."

Jessie realized what was going on and immediately pulled away from Leo. Leo's hand lingered in the air for a moment and then fell to his side. He caught Jessie's eye for a moment, but she looked away. Shelby glanced over at the group of friends.

"Oh my gosh. I'll say it. I swear!" Justin threw his hands in the air and Jessie looked over at Leo.

"Why didn't you guys ever date?" Justin crossed his arms over his scrawny chest and stared Jessie and Leo down. "We have been waiting for it all year and nothing happened. Quite frankly, I'm pissed." Justin blurted. Leo and Jessie started laughing.

"Yeah, what's up with this. We all know that you're meant to be together and now it's the end of senior year. We don't know what's going to happen in the future and . . . look? Ya'll aren't even together!" Carrie yelled.

"Whoa, chill out guys." Jessie tried to calm them.

"All year and nothing has happened. We know you guys like each other and I've held my tongue long enough." Justin defended.

"I have to agree with them." Shelby nudged Justin and nodded to Carrie.

"Oh, wow." Leo laughed, raking his fingers through his hair.

"Let's drop this right now." Jessie tossed her hair over her shoulder.

"Fine." Justin scowled.

"Well, sorry to disappoint you guys. Karla and I aren't friends anymore. I thought that would suffice you, but I guess not. I have to be Leo's girlfriend, too?" Jessie tugged at her navy blue t-shirt and stuffed her hands in her jean pockets.

"Yup!" they all said in unison.

"I'm done." Jessie laughed putting her hands in front of her.

"We're sorry. We just thought something would have happened by now."

"Hey, there's always the future." Leo butted in.

"Now you say something." Jessie threw her hands in the air.

"Maybe. We just didn't want to date . . . anyone in high school. Too much drama." Leo shook his head.

"Right!" Jessie agreed.

"Are you guys going to go out?" Shelby asked.

"Up to God." Jessie shrugged.

"What?" Leo looked over at Jessie.

"It's up to God." Jessie shrugged again.

"Right." Leo rolled his eyes.

"Don't start." Jessie bit off.

"I'm not." Leo raked his fingers through his hair.

"Do you do that when you're annoyed or being shy?"

"What?" Leo looked up at Jessie.

"Rake your fingers through your hair. You do that a lot. I've noticed it, You either do it when you're nervous, shy, or irritated." Jessie smiled.

"Ha! You know me better than I know myself." Leo laughed.

"Yeah, well, I pay attention."

"I notice when you get in trouble and don't want to laugh, you make it look like your picking something out of your teeth so you can get away with smiling because you think it's funny." Leo stated.

"Ha! Oh, my gosh. I never thought anyone would notice that!" Jessie laughed. She looked to the ground trying to hide that she was blushing.

"You do it when you like something someone says or does but don't want to admit it."

"Ha! Wow! You pay attention, too." Jessie laughed.

"Oh, I know tons of other things about you that you don't think I know."

"Well, same here, babe." Jessie smiled.

"Good afternoon, class, and happy last day!" the principal came over the intercom.

"I'm glad to see there were no senior pranks. So everyone that was supposed to graduate is going to graduate on time now. Just a few reminders. Bus 34 has changed to bus 87. Those that leave from the senior parking lot, please, if you would, be considerate of others . . . ."

"I can't believe we're done." Jessie shook her head.

"Same here." Danni chimed.

"Have a great rest of the day. Seniors, see you June eighth at two-thirty," the principal ended.

"Well, I will miss you guys." Mrs. L. settled in her desk.

"We'll miss you, too." Jessie said.

The bell rang. Jessie's senior year was over with. She and her friends hugged Mrs. L. and headed to the senior parking lot.

"We're free!" Shelby yelled. She ran down the hall, jumped up in the air, and clicked her heels together. The whole group laughed. As they turned the corner, they picked James and Allen up and headed toward the parking lot. We ran into Karla on the way there.

"Well, it's over," she scoffed at them.

"Yes ma'am." Jessie nodded. Leo put his arm around Jessie's waist. Karla noticed.

"We all know you own her." Karla rolled her eyes. "Well, Jessie, have a nice life." Karla flipped Jessie's hair up and then walked away. Jessie rolled her eyes and shook her head.

"Holy crap! She's irritating." Shelby grunted.

"No kidding."

We headed out the double doors. Out of nowhere we were bombarded with water balloons and silly string. The girls yelled and the boys laughed. They started grabbing balloons that didn't burst and threw them at people.

"You're dead!" Jessie chucked a balloon at Jeremy and hit his chest soaking his shirt.

"I got you, Jessie," Jeremy threatened.

"Oh, my god!" Amy Dolman yelled. We all looked to her. Our balloons were in hand and ready to be thrown.

"Some are full of pee!" she screeched.

The group looked at each other, dropped their balloons, and bolted to their vehicles. I looked back and Amy was crying in a puddle of pee. It was kind of funny.

"Hurry up!"

Jessie grabbed Leo by the arm. He was throwing balloons at anyone he could and started running toward Amy's truck. We looked back and her friends were dodging water or pee balloons. One came flying down and got Justin on his back.

"No! It's peeeeeee!" Justin screamed.

His scream resembled that of a girl. He fell to his knees in defeat. Carrie ran up behind him and retrieved him. They ran to her car and jumped in. Danni and Shelby were dodging balloons and jumping over those who had gotten hit.

"Shiiiiiiit!" Shelby jumped over a guy lying on the ground that got hit by a pee balloon.

Jessie fumbled for her keys. Balloons were flying all over the place. Jessie and I looked up and, at that time, a balloon crashed up against Leo's face. Leo's body tensed up. Jessie stared at him.

"It's water!" Leo screamed. "Let me in!" Leo screeched, looking behind him at the people throwing balloons.

Jessie climbed into her truck, reached over and unlocked Leo's door. Leo jumped in and slammed his door. Jessie rolled down her window to let some of the heat escape.

"Wait!" Allen yelled. Allen and James jumped in the bed of Jessie's truck. The truck slammed down.

"Whoa!" Jessie revved her engine.

Carrie raised her hand out of her window telling them it was time to go. We all sped out of the parking lot. My adrenalin was pumping. The pee balloons were gross, but it was high school and I wouldn't expect anything less. As we headed out of the parking lot, a giant green balloon was tossed into Jessie's truck. It hit Jessie's face, drenching her. Leo squinted at her and she looked over at Leo.

"Water!" Jessie yelled and fist pumped. Her whole side was soaked. Jessie's phone went off.

"Hello?"

"I told you I would get you." Jeremy laughed.

"That was you?" Jessie laughed. "Yeah. You definitely got me. My whole side is soaked." Jessie laughed into the phone.

"Who is that?" Leo asked.

"Jeremy. He's the one that threw the balloon in my truck." Jessie answered.

"Later, Jess." Jeremy hung up.

Jessie heard Allen and James yelling from the back of the truck. I couldn't help but laugh.

"I was gonna stay and throw some balloons, but I wasn't going to take my chances with the pee balloons." Jessie shook in disgust.

"I don't blame you." Leo laughed.

"Justin got hit by a pee balloon." Jessie slammed her hands on the steering wheel with laughter.

"Oh, I know. I saw it. He straight screamed like a girl." Leo and Jessie started laughing.

"Well, that's one way to end senior year." Jessie pulled her wet hair away from the side of her face.

"Jeremy got you good." Leo looked over at Jessie.

"Oh, I know. I'm so glad it wasn't pee."

"Hey!" Allen opened the little window at the back of the cab.

"James got hit by pee. "Allen laughed.

"Man, shut up apple head." James yelled.

"Ewww. We better take him home before Steak 'n Shake." Jessie cringed. "Can you text the others and tell them to meet there in like an hour?" Jessie handed Leo her phone.

"Sounds good," Allen said shutting the window.

"That was kind of fun." Jessie laughed.

"Yeah, I know."

"Gonna miss all them goobs."

Steak 'n Shake

"Who is the idiot that thought of pee balloons?!" Justin yelled as he sat down with the others.

"I have no clue. You and James were the only two that got hit." Jessie bit into a cheese fry.

"It was totally gross!" Justin put his beanie over his damp hair. "Where's David?" Justin asked.

"Got hit by a pee balloon. He's supposed to be here." Jessie said.

"No, he's spending the day with Kristin." Carrie shook her head.

"Oh." Justin lifted his head.

"Well, the pee balloons were funny but, yes, gross." Jessie laughed. Jessie sat and had a good time with her friends until Karla walked in. She looked over at us and then started walking toward us.

"Well, hello," she batted her eyes. They all rolled theirs.

"Oh, come on. It's the end of the year and we're never gonna see each other again." Karla whined.

"Good." Justin grunted.

"Shut up!" Karla glared. "So, Jessie, what's your plans after high school?" Karla turned her attention to Jessie. "I know . . . I know . . . move in with Leo, get knocked up, and be a freaking loser!"

Karla busted out in laughter. Her red hair was bouncing off of her shoulder, her Slayer shirt was moving in and out with the movement of her breathing. The group all looked around at each other.

"Leave, Karla," Leo threw his french fry back on his plate.

"Make me."

"I don't make trash; I burn it." Justin squeaked.

The group just stared at him. That was the oldest saying in the book. It came out when Jessie was in the first grade. I remember Marnie DeLaporte saying it to Sandy Sandberg when they got into a fight on who can climb across the monkey bars the quickest.

"Nice one, queer bait." Karla hissed.

"Why do you keep calling him queer?" Jessie folded her arms and rested them on the table.

"Because I don't like him.' Karla shook her head.

"Karla, leave." Leo demanded.

"No."

Leo stood up to face her.

"Leave. No one likes you." Leo stated.

Jessie looked up at Leo. Karla reached her hand back and drew it up to Leo's face. Leo caught her by the wrist. I looked from them to the others and then to Jessie. What on earth was going on? *Lord God, please deal with this.* I looked around to see if there were any demons and there were none to be found.

"I don't think so," he said threw clenched teeth.

No one said anything. I looked over at Jessie who was staring into her drink.

"Let go of me!" Karla pulled away from his grip. "Don't ever touch me!" she yelled, causing a scene.

Leo said nothing.

"I see how it is. It's come down to this!" Karla bent down and got in Jessie's face.

"You're worthless."

"I said go!" Leo pushed her away from Jessie. "I don't believe in putting your hands on a woman, but you just will not take a hint!" Leo yelled in Jessie's defense.

Karla stumbled back, looked at all of them, and then stormed out of the restaurant. Leo sat back down once he saw Karla pull out of the parking lot. The group stared at him.

"Leo, you didn't have to do that." Jessie sighed not looking up at him.

"No, Jessie, I did. She won't stop and you've told her plenty of times. I am not going to let her get away with it. High school is over with."

"I don't need you to protect me, Leo!" Jessie raised her voice.

"Are you sure about that!?" Leo yelled back. He shifted his body to face Jessie.

"Yes, I am. You're making things worse!" Jessie rested her head in her hands.

"Why are you afraid of her?" Leo grew soft.

He looked at the other friends. They shrugged, shook their heads, or sighed.

"I'm not afraid of her. 'Soft words turn away wrath,'" Jessie looked up at Leo.

"Jessie, I know you're spiritual but, if you're not going to take up for yourself, by God I will." Leo tapped his finger on his chest.

"Leo, let God take care of it." Jessie ran her fingers down the side of her glass.

"No."

"Leo!" Jessie yelled. "God is much scarier than we are!" Jessie said almost crying.

"Jessie, why are you making a big deal about this?"

"Leo, I'm not. I just want it all to go away." Jessie lowered her voice.

"Ignore it and it will go away?"

"Yes, Leo," Jessie argued.

"Sorry, Jess. You can do that but, if I'm around, she will not talk to you like that. You're doing the right thing with 'Vengeance is mine says the Lord', but I will not let it come to that. You're my best friend, you're a woman, and I will protect you from everything." Leo informed her.

"I am not an infant." Jessie looked up at him. Leo stared at Jessie for a while then broke the silence.

"Fine. Have it your way." Leo balled his hands into fists.

There was really nothing I could do. I agreed with Leo. I would want to keep Jessie from all the things Karla was doing, and I did for the most part. But Jessie was right. God needed to take care of this, and

He would. The rest of the time the friends talked about other things. Jessie and Leo barely talked, and Jessie finally got up.

"I'm going home. Carrie, can you take Leo home?"

"Yeah, babe, sure." Carrie smiled softly.

"Thanks." Jessie left a tip and we headed out of the restaurant. Leo didn't call for her.

Jessie and I jumped into her truck and headed out of the parking lot. She reached for her phone. There were three text messages—one from Rodney, one from Travis, and the last from Karla.

"If your bf touches me again, I will have him deported! Jessie closed her phone and rested it in the seat beside her.

"I am so glad high school's over with. Now, I just gotta figure out what God wants me to do." Jessie said aloud to herself. "Maybe I should go to ministry school."

Chapter 22

Graduation

Today is the big day. Jessie's graduating. Twelve years of school—done. I couldn't believe she's already graduating. I watched her as she talked with her family who were in the front room waiting for her to finish getting ready before she left to pick Justin up and head to the school. Emotion welled up inside of me, and I felt the tears of joy spring from my eyes. Jessie's all grown up. She's going to be going out into the real world. Were we ready for that?

"Jessie, you better get going." Toni said trying to hold back emotion.

"Don't cry, Mama, because I will." Jessie laughed. Jessie grabbed her cap and gown and headed toward her truck.

"See ya there!" Mike called to her.

I bolted out of the house with her. We jumped into the truck and headed toward Justin's house. We had to drive clear across town and then back to the high school. Jessie and I listened to music on the way to pick Justin up. I would be sitting with Jessie's family as we watched her accept this great accomplishment. I was so excited for her and her family. It took us all we had to get her to this day, but we did it. All of us, mostly Jehovah, couldn't have done it without him. Jessie pulled into Justin's driveway and honked twice. Justin ran out of the house with his cap and gown in hand. His purple gown flapped wildly in the wind. I moved back to the half cab and Justin climbed into the front seat.

"I can't believe we're graduating, Jess." Justin shut the passenger's side door and rested his cap and gown on his lap.

"Me either. This really is bittersweet." Jessie backed out of the driveway and we headed toward the school.

"Gosh, Jess, we may never see some of those people ever again." Justin rested his arm on the armrest.

"I know," Jessie sighed.

We finally got to the school. Hundreds of kids in caps and gowns stood outside taking pictures, hugging each other, and talking about how much they're going to miss high school. Even though they were glad to be out, they were still going to miss it. Jessie met up with the usual group of friends. She embraced each of them in a hug.

"This is it!" Frick said as he left Jessie's embrace.

"I know. Man, we've known each other for years." Jessie said holding back tears.

"Gonna miss it?" Shelby looked over at Jessie.

"I'll miss hanging with you guys, but school itself? No. I will not miss it." Jessie shook her head in certainty. I looked around as the kids started grouping up in alphabetical order. Jessie and I spotted Leo.

"Seeing him every day . . . that I'll miss." Jessie nodded her head toward Leo.

"Wow, I can't believe this is it." Leo said to them as he approached.

"You look great." Jessie hugged him.

"You, too." Leo smiled down at her.

"Jessie!" Jessie turned around to see her family yelling for her. She nodded to her friends and then left for her family.

"Where are you going to be?" Jessie's grandmother asked.

"The right side. Sit in row G. It will be the best view of me on the second balcony." Jessie pointed her family the directions in which they should go.

"I'm so proud of you!" Toni cried.

"Mama." Jessie sighed.

Jessie couldn't handle her mama crying. Even if they were happy tears, Jessie would cry if she saw her mama cry.

"Sorry." Toni said as she dabbed her eyes with a Kleenex.

Jessie looked at her family and smiled. Rodney, Ben, Aunt Indy, her other grandparents (Mama's parents), her other cousins, parents, brother, and Danny were all there. Jessie hugged her mama as they headed toward row G. Her grandmother stopped her before she headed back to her friends. She played with Jessie's purple and gold tassel for a moment and then placed her aged hands on Jessie's shoulders.

"Your grandfather would be very proud of you." Grandmother said holding back tears.

"I know. This is for him." Jessie said as tears filled her eyes.

"He's watching from Heaven."

Grandmother kissed Jessie's forehead, gave her shoulders a light squeeze, and then headed toward the other family members. Jessie stood here thinking about her grandfather and how she wished he could have been there. Her train of thought was broken by the principal.

"Alright, everyone. We're 'bout to start in twenty minutes. Take your places."

Jessie broke away from the memory of her grandfather. She finally found her spot in line and stood there waiting for them to announce that they were starting. I kissed Jessie's cheek and headed toward her family. I knew she would be safe if I left her. Jehovah gave me the okay. I found Jessie's family and made my way up to the bleachers where they were seated and settled between Jessie's grandmother, Craig, and Travis.

The lights dimmed and the graduation song played. The students filed in row by row holding candles. There were at least three hundred and fifty graduating with Jessie. The song ended and the lights came on. The principal took the stage.

"Well, you've made it," he echoed through the gym.

I looked around and saw people fanning themselves from the heat and little kids climbing all over the bleachers. I saw other angels of some of the students standing with their human's families. We started waving to each other and pointing down at our humans with pride. The principal was done talking and handed it over to valedictorian, Misty Montgomery. She stood behind the podium. She was average height with long, blonde hair, green eyes, curvy figure, and a sweet smile.

"Well, class of 2008, we did it!" she squeaked into the microphone. The graduation class grew into an uproar of cheers. The principal silenced them.

"Graduation is a time for us to say goodbye to being children and hello to being adults." Misty said into the microphone.

I felt my heart pounding with anticipation. I looked around at Jessie's family who were beaming from ear to ear. Misty finished her speech and the principal took over.

"We are now going to hand out the diplomas for the class of 2008!" the principal announced.

The gym grew into cheering from the students, families, and friends. Jessie looked back and smiled at Leo. He sat a row behind her and two seats down. He smiled back and nodded. The teachers got into a perfect line waiting to shake the hands of the students. The first row got up slowly and faced the aisle. They stepped out two by two.

"Alyssa Abe," the principal started.

It seemed like forever before they would get to Jessie. I kept my eyes on Jessie. She was shaking her leg up and down with nervousness and cheered for her friends as they accepted their diplomas.

"Freddie Crabtree," the principal boomed.

Jessie was just two people away. It was like it was lightning inside because of all the cameras that were going on. I heard mothers crying "That's my baby!" as their child grabbed their diploma and headed off the stage to retake their seats. I looked around the gym. My eyes were caught by the image in the balcony to the back of the gym in the center standing next to Truce. It was Mike, Sr. He came down to see his granddaughter graduate. My heart pounded with excitement. He stood with his arms over the rails. He wore blue jeans, a blue and white plaid t-shirt, and shiny black boots. He was thin with thick black hair and piercing baby blue eyes. He smiled at me.

"Jessica J. Craig," the principal announced.

I turned my attention to Jessie, clapped my hands, fist pumped, and hollered as loud as I could! All the other angels cheered for her. Her family roared with excitement. She grabbed her diploma, blew a kiss to her mama, and headed off the stage. I looked back at Mike, Sr. He was clapping and laughing, and his face was full of peace. He wiped a tear from his eye. As he looked upon his granddaughter and her big achievement, he looked back over to me and then to his beloved wife. Jessie's grandmother stood adoring Jessie as she took her seat with her diploma. I looked from him to her. He balled his hand into a fist and placed it on his heart. He nodded to me. I leaned over and kissed his wife upon her cheek, and I looked back to him. He reached his hand up to his forehead, saluted me, and nodded. Truce put his hand on Mike, Sr.'s shoulder and looked down at him. Mike looked down at Jessie and smiled. He nodded back to Truce, and then they disappeared.

Thank you, Jehovah, for letting him see this. I started to cry. I looked back at Jessie with my eyes full of tears.

"I take care of my children," I heard HIS voice say to me.

The graduation was finally coming to a close. The principal announced the last person. He took his diploma, hurried off the stage, and headed back to his seat. Jessie and her friends caught each other's attention and smiled. The last student took his seat. The class Song, "Free Bird", came on the surround system. It was the school telling the students goodbye. The students rose to their feet when the song ended.

"Well, class of 2008, you did it. Place your hands on your tassels. It is now time to make it official," the principal instructed. Simultaneously, the students moved the tassels from the left side of their caps to the right. After this, the gym filled with cheers of celebration. The students hugged one another, and they sprayed silly string at each another. The ushers started ushering the students out of the rows and into the hallway. They could go to the cafeteria to talk and hang out with each other for a little while. Jessie made her way to the hallway. The minutes I saw her go through the double doors I headed toward them. Now, I was back by her side where I belonged. Jessie met up with her friends in the cafeteria.

"Woo!" Jessie yelled as she saw them. "Man, we did it! We're outta here!" Jessie said in excitement.

"Pictures!" Toni called from behind Jessie.

Jessie and her friends stood in a horizontal line with their arms around each other. It was such a proud moment. The other parents had joined in the picture taking.

"I don't know which camera to look at!" Jessie yelled to the parents.

"Me either," Leo sighed. He and Jessie looked into the camera that Shelby's mom was holding. After the cameras had settled, Jessie looked around the cafeteria to see if Karla was around. Maybe, since high school was over with, they could squash the feud. Karla was nowhere to be found, though. Jessie shrugged it off and turned her attention to Leo.

"We gonna do something tonight?" Jessie asked. The cameras came back out and flashed viciously at the graduates.

"Yes," Leo said.

Leo put his arm around Jessie and smiled into her grandmother's camera. They shifted their bodies and turned to Leo's mom's camera.

"My face hurts," Jessie said to Leo through a smile.

"They're almost done," Leo said as he smiled at Carrie's sister's camera.

"I'm outta battery!" Toni called to Jessie.

"Good " Jessie raised her hand to her face and rubbed her cheek even though the other cameras were still going off.

"Hey, we all gonna hang out around six, right?" Shelby looked to the group.

"Yeah. Let's meet at the park." Jessie suggested. "That gives us five hours with family." Jessie shrugged.

All agreed and separated to be with their loved ones. Jessie and I walked over to the refreshment table and grabbed two Cokes—one for herself and one for Leo.

"Jessie, we did it!" Jeremy said as he approached us.

"Yes, yes we did." Jessie nodded.

She took her cap off and tucked it under her arm. Jeremy moved in closer. He looked at Jessie and then over to where Leo was standing with Allen and James.

"I always thought we should have been together." Jeremy tucked Jessie's hair behind her ear. "But I can't tell your heart what to do."

Jeremy gave Jessie a hug and then walked away. Jessie stood there shocked. She didn't move for a while.

"Jessie, you alright?" Rodney broke Jessie's train of thought. "Uncle Mike is waiting. He's hungry," Rodney laughed.

"Yeah. I'm going to give this to Leo and we can leave for dinner."

Jessie linked her arm into Rodney's and headed toward the crowd. She handed Leo his Coke.

"Well, boys . . . my family is taking me for lunch. I will see ya'll tonight."

Jessie hugged each one of them. Rodney, Jessie, and I caught up with the rest of the family. Jessie and I walked down the halls of Marion High School for the last time. Memories flashed before me like when she first stepped foot in this school, when she made all her new friends, and when she met Leo. As we made our way to the car, Jessie looked back at her old school. She was done. Bigger and better things awaited her. She was grown up now and her life was moving on. She sighed deeply and then climbed into Mike's truck.

Jessie and I hopped into her truck and headed toward Leo's house. She grew excited as she approached his house. She pulled out her cell phone and called him as she turned onto his street. We pulled in front of his house. He bolted out of the door with a brown sack with him.

"Food?"

"Yeah. I figured I'd at least bring something." Leo rested the bag on the floorboard and then put his seatbelt on.

"I can't believe we graduated." Jessie backed up onto the street.

"Me either, Jess." Leo sighed. "What's next?" Leo looked over at Jessie.

"I don't know," Jessie shrugged. Jessie's phone lit up from texts.

"Dang, Jessie. That was like seven texts in a row." Leo grabbed Jessie's phone that was lying on the ledge in front of her CD player. He scanned through. "They're all of our friends saying that they're there." Leo said. He then stopped on one that was from Karla.

"Karla texted you." Leo said as he looked up at Jessie. Jessie gripped the steering wheel.

"Read it to me, please." Jessie drew in a breath. Leo clicked the phone and opened the message.

"Alright," Leo sighed.

"Well, we graduated. Now I never have to see you and your two face again. Have a nice life, bitch! You're gonna be nothing but a lost cause.'" Leo read. Leo grew angry at the text.

"Don't you dare reply, Leo Gutierrez." Jessie stated as she turned onto the road that leads to the park.

"Jessie, you're just going to let her talk to you like that?" Leo slammed Jessie's phone shut.

"Yes, because I'm better than that and her power feeds from my anger. If I have no anger, she has no power."

"Well, then, can I say it? I will say it's from me. I don't like her treating you this way."

"Leo, I love the fact that you care about me, but it's really not that big of a deal. She's just blowing off steam." Jessie shrugged.

Jessie made it to the park and they cruised around trying to find their friends. They spotted Carrie's car and then the rest of the cars came into view. Jessie saw Shelby look up and smile. She parked her truck and we exited the truck. Leo shoved Jessie's phone in his pocket.

"I'm glad you guys finally made it." Shelby said as she ran over and embraced Jessie then Leo.

Jessie spotted Ellen sitting at the picnic table. Leo stood beside her with the paper bag.

"Here." Leo handed it to Shelby.

"Thanks." Shelby looked into the bag. "Yummy!"

Shelby walked over to the picnic table, grabbed the Chips Ahoy out of the bag, and ripped them open. Jessie looked over to Leo to see if he had seen Ellen. He did. He made his way over to her. They embraced in a hug and said congratulations on graduating. Leo then broke away and went to talk with the boys who were by the grill. Jessie and I were surprised. I looked down at her and saw a little grin creep across her face. She looked at her friends who were standing around talking and laughing and sharing stories about high school. I wrapped my arms around Jessie's shoulder and pulled her close to me. Jessie's attention averted to Leo.

"I hope he stays in my life forever." Jessie whispered to herself.

Jessie watched Leo as he raked his fingers through his black hair and laughed with the guys. She gathered herself and we made our way over to her friends. Jessie went for her phone that she thought was in her pocket, but it wasn't.

"Leo, have you seen my phone?"

Leo looked over to Jessie. "You probably left it in the truck," he called back.

Jessie shrugged and then turned her attention to her friends. Leo was keeping Jessie's phone with him because he knew that if Karla kept texting, it would just ruin Jessie's evening and he didn't want that.

"Jessie, remember the time we were in English class and the teacher was like 'Craig, you're late' and you just took her seat? Then Mrs. Lazarus said, 'You're always late. You were late yesterday' and Jessie said, 'Well, I'm on time then.' Jessie always was the one with the comebacks, always had an answer for everything." Shelby laughed.

"I can vouch for that." Leo called from the grill as he held his drink in the air.

"Ha, right." Jessie blushed.

"Carrie was the activist of the group." Justin blurted.

"I was not." Carrie laughed.

"You were, too. You were always organizing to prove your point." Justin put his arm around Carrie.

"Shelby was the whiner." Carrie blurted.

"Me!? Shelby sounded shocked and Jessie and the others laughed.

"Yes . . . you. There was always something wrong." Carrie teased.

"That's because there was." Shelby glared.

"Justin's the jerk." Jessie confirmed.

"Well, people should leave me alone."

Justin took a sip of his drink, glaring at the group from the top of the glass. I looked over at Leo, and he pulled Jessie's phone from his pocket. He turned his back to them. I wondered what he was doing. He closed the phone too quickly to be replying. I bet he was deleting her message. Good for Leo.

Being with Jessie and her friends was a blast. Slowly, people started to leave and then there was just the original group—Allen, James, Danni, Justin, Carrie, Jessie, Shelby, Leo, and David. They all sat around the picnic table, laughing and reminiscing about old times. Ellen Gray said her goodbyes. She hugged each of them and headed toward her car. Leo didn't move. He just said goodbye and continued talking with James and Allen.

"Wow, Leo. I thought you'd be all over Ellen." James blurted.

"Naw, she's not real enough. I learned that the hard way," he stated. Jessie was laughing and talking with the girls.

"Sometimes you just gotta wait for the best."

Leo looked over at Jessie as she talked and fellowshipped her friends. He smiled to himself. Allen and Justin exchanged looks and David kept his eyes on Leo. Jessie's phone went off. Leo turned his body away from Jessie and looked at it. Jeremy was calling. Leo opened and then shut the phone quickly.

"When did you get a phone?" Allen asked.

"Shhhh. It's not mine, it's Jessie's. Karla kept texting her mean things and I stole it for tonight so she wouldn't ruin Jessie's night."

"Well, that was nice of you." David smiled.

"I care about her." Leo shrugged running his fingers over the sweating Coke can.

"You love her?" Allen dipped his head to look Leo in the eyes.

"Ugh. Love is . . . ."

"Leo, what time do you have to be home?" Jessie interrupted.

"Doesn't matter." Leo smiled and then turned his attention to his friends.

"Well?" Justin crossed his arms over his chest.

"I don't know. Don't put me on the spot like that." Leo grew irritated.

The sun was now gone and the lights in the park turned on. It was close to nine o'clock. Jessie looked over to the table.

"I'm sooooo hungry. Let's go to Taco Bell," Jessie said to the group.

"No . . . Mexican food." Leo groaned.

"I want a cheese and potato burrito." Jessie whined.

"Jessie." Leo tilted his head.

"Fine." Jessie sighed.

"Steak 'n Shake." Shelby suggested.

All agreed. Shelby threw the pop cans away and the wrappers to the snacks that they had eaten. I really didn't see how these kids could have eaten. They ate only three hours ago and Jessie had gone to lunch with family.

"All I really want are cheese fries and a chocolate milkshake." Jessie rubbed her stomach.

"Me, too." Shelby laughed.

They all gathered in their cars and headed to Steak 'n Shake. Jessie searched around the truck for her cell phone.

"Leo, it's not here." Jessie looked up at him. He was standing looking at her.

"I know." Leo pulled it out of his pocket and handed it to her.

"Jeremy called and Karla texted like ten times."

"Leo, are you freaking serious?" Jessie looked at him from the other side if the truck.

"Yes, Jessie, I am. You were supposed to have a good time and, if I had let you talk to them, you wouldn't have."

Leo climbed into the truck and settled in. Jessie was still standing inside the door.

"If you let me?" Jessie crossed her arms over her chest.

"Yes, if I let you. You know you had a good time and I wanted that for you; therefore, I stole your phone." Leo looked at Jessie. Jessie climbed into the tuck and slammed her door shut. I sat in the half cab.

"Well, I can understand you not wanting me to talk to Karla." Jessie turned the truck on. "But why Jeremy?" Jessie looked over at Leo.

"Oh, I just didn't want you talking to him."

Leo reached over and played with Jessie's air freshener that hung from her rearview mirror. Jessie didn't say anything. She watched as the others pulled out of the park's parking lot and headed toward the bypass to Steak 'n Shake.

Everyone had a blast at Steak 'n Shake and they were extremely full from all the eating the entire day. Jessie pushed the empty plate toward the middle of the table.

"I'm so full." Jessie leaned against the wall. Leo laughed.

"Me, too. And I'm tired." Shelby looked at the time on her cell phone. "It's 1 a.m.," she announced.

"Oh, wow! I am about to head home." Allen took the last bite of his burger.

"Me, too." Jessie looked over at Leo. "If you want."

"Yeah, that's fine."

Allen nudged Leo, and Leo gave him a knowing look. James smiled at them. "What's going on?"

"Alright." Jessie grabbed her purse and stood up to leave. "Oh, here." Jessie left a three-dollar tip for the waitress. The rest pulled out their wallets and left a dollar for the tip. Leo got up and headed toward Jessie.

"See ya guys later." Jessie said as she hugged her friends.

She and Leo headed to the cash register. Leo paid for their meals and then we headed toward the truck.

"I had fun today." Jessie said as she settled into the driver's seat.

"Me, too, and I'm spent."

Leo rested his head on the head rest and Jessie started the truck. She waved bye to her friends and then pulled out of the parking lot. Jessie and Leo didn't say much on the way to his house. She pulled in front of his house and they sat there for a moment.

"Well, Jessie, we're graduated now." Leo rested his hand on hers.

Jessie looked at Leo's hand and then up at him. She slowly removed hers out from under his. Wasn't expecting that.

"I just hope we'll always be best friends." Jessie smiled.

"Jessie, you will always be my best friend, forever and always. I care about you a lot." Leo struggled to say.

"I feel the same about you, but things change after high school."

"Ha, I know. You'll always be my best friend even if, God forbid, we never see each other again." Leo shoved his hand into his pocket.

"Here. I made this for you," said Leo.

Leo turned the little lights on that were under Jessie's review mirror. He held a necklace charm made from a green stone. Jessie smiled.

"It's beautiful. I thought you said this was for your mom." Jessie looked up at Leo.

"Ha. My mom's favorite color isn't green."

Leo handed the charm to Jessie. It was held together by the metal that he had cut out into an oval and welded a metal ring around it that held the stone together. It was really pretty and very thoughtful.

"I didn't get you anything." Jessie sighed.

"I don't care." Leo laughed.

"I want to do something for you. I wanted someone to do something for you without you thinking you had to do something in return. You already do a lot for your family and friends. I see the little things you do for them and no one else notices. I see how loving you are with them." Leo explained.

I looked over at Jessie, waiting for a response.

"Oh well. Thank you." Jessie said holding back tears.

"You're welcome. Trust me, Jess. You've come a long way from what you used to be. I'm proud of you." Leo leaned over and embraced Jessie with a hug. They held each other for a moment and then he broke away.

"I better get inside." Leo turned to face his house.

"Alright. Thanks again. I will talk to you tomorrow probably." Jessie wiped the tear from her eye.

"You bet. Be safe, Jess."

Leo got out of the truck and headed toward his house. Jessie watched as he went inside. He gave her a wave and then we headed toward Jessie's.

CHAPTER 23

Searching For Answers

It was the middle of July now. Jessie still hung out with her friends almost three times a week, maybe more. Jessie was watching as her friends slowly bought stuff for college. She and her dad sat down and decided that Jessie was going to ministry school. I was surprised and happy at the decision. Jessie just hasn't broken it to any of her friends.

"I'm going to break the news to my friends when we hang out." Jessie looked over at Mike.

"Good for you. Don't let them change your mind, especially Leo." Mike narrowed his gaze at her.

"I got this." Jessie held her hand out in front of her.

"Alright." Mike nodded.

"How do I tell them?"

"Just be, like, 'I'm going to ministry school'. They already know you're spiritual." Mike shrugged as he flipped through the channels on the television.

"I got that. How am I going to tell them that I'm moving to South Carolina?"

"Juice, you're making this harder than it is. Just tell them 'I'm going to ministry school and it's in South Carolina'. That's all you have to say, and then let them digest it." Mike looked over at Jessie.

"I guess. Leo's going to be so pissed." Jessie sighed.

"Why? You're getting out of this God-forsaken town and going to make something of yourself." Mike shook his head. I had to agree with Dad.

"I know, but he doesn't want me going . . . what . . . fourteen hours away." Jessie stood up and looked down at her dad.

"Jessie, it's going to be fine." Mike reassured.

"Let's hope." Jessie pulled her hair back into a pony tail.

Jessie and the rest of the group sat around Carrie's in-ground pool talking.

"I'm so hot!" Carrie fanned herself.

"Get in the pool." Justin suggested as he threw a beach ball at her.

"I'm about to jump in. I'm freakin' burning up." Leo stood up and walked to the edge of the pool.

"He gonna take his shirt off?" David leaned in and asked Jessie.

"Ha, probably." Jessie huffed.

And he did. He tossed it to Jessie to place on the table. Jessie couldn't take her eyes off of him.

"Oh, my gosh. I didn't know he had a body like that." Jessie looked over at her friends. Leo stood by the pool revealing his pecks, the start of a six pack. I think that's what the girls called it.

"Oh my . . . ." Jessie put her hand over her chest.

"Woo. If I wasn't hot, then I am now." David fanned himself with his hand.

The girls started laughing. Leo dove into the pool. Jessie searched the pool looking for him. He came out of the water with his long, black hair soaked.

"I think I need something to drink." Jessie got up and headed to the kitchen through the back door.

"She's in love." David smiled at Shelby and Carrie.

"I know." Shelby took a sip of her Pepsi.

"Where did Jessie go?" Leo looked up at them.

"Drink." Shelby held up her Pepsi can.

"Okay," Leo said and then hit the beach ball to Justin.

"Turonomo!" Allen and James yelled as they cannon ballad into the pool. The force of their massive bodies hit the water, throwing Leo and Justin to the other side of the pool.

"Ouch." Justin slammed against the pool. He grabbed his rib. Leo held on to the side of the pool.

"They're too big for that." Justin glared.

Leo couldn't help but laugh. I looked to the friends around me who had gotten hit by some water, also. Jessie came from the kitchen and took her seat at the patio table with David, Shelby, and Carrie.

"Jessie, this is killing us. Leo and you have got to be like dating and not telling us." David rested his head on Jessie's shoulder.

"Nope. Neither never asked, and I don't want a long-distance relationship." Jessie didn't look at them. David looked up at Jessie.

"Wait. What?' Carrie rested her arm on the table waiting for a response.

"I don't want a . . . ."

"We heard. Is Leo going to Mexico?" Shelby asked.

"No." Jessie laughed. She was about to tell them. *Lord, give her strength.*

"Then what?"

"I'm moving to South Carolina." Jessie shifted her body to look at them. They stared at her for a moment and then looked at each other.

"That's like forever away." David whined.

"No, it's not." Jessie scoffed.

"Jessie, why?" Shelby asked.

"I'm going to ministry school in South Carolina. I feel that's where I should be." Jessie shrugged.

"I mean, we're happy for you, but I don't' want to see you go." David said fighting tears.

"I know, guys, but there's texting and email, facebook, and all that stuff. We'll always keep in touch." Jessie smiled.

"I don't like this." Shelby shook her head and then looked to the boys in the pool.

"You told Leo yet?" Carrie asked.

"No." Jessie looked down.

"He isn't going to be happy." Shelby noted.

"I know." Jessie sighed.

"When you going to tell him?" David asked.

"I don't know. Soon. I leave August twentieth." Jessie blurted.

"Jessie! That's like a month from now." Shelby's eyes grew dark.

"I know. I didn't know how to tell you guys."

Jessie started to tear up. I put my arm over her shoulder and rested my head against hers.

"You need to tell Leo, like tonight." David bobbed his head.

"I will." Jessie sighed.

"Good." Carrie said.

Jessie looked around at her friends. She knew that she had put a sour mood on the day.

The boys got out of the pool and headed to the patio furniture where the girls and David were.

"I feel better." Leo said as he pressed the towel up to his wet hair.

"Good." Jessie laughed.

"My rib hurts!" Justin glared at Allen and James.

"Why are you mad at us?"

"If your fat asses wouldn't have cannon balled and thrown me into the pool, I wouldn't have cracked a rib." Justin grew furious.

"You're such a drama queen." Allen rolled his eyes.

"No. I'm pissed." Justin glared as he ran the towel over himself.

"Man, this summer has been great. Oh, I got that job in Peru." Leo looked over at Jessie.

"Oh, good. I'm happy for you." Jessie beamed.

"Yeah, I'm going to save for my own place, or try to. I would need a roommate."

Leo coughed out and then looked at Jessie. The group looked at Jessie. She shot them a dirty look and they backed off. *And what was he implying. Jessie doesn't move in with guys. No, she gets married and then lives with a guy. That's it. No moving in without a wedding band, and we need the wedding band FIRST!*

"This has been a good summer so far." Carrie smiled and then gave Jessie a stern look.

"Oh, my gosh." Jessie grunted. "And I'm about to ruin it." Jessie didn't look at her friends.

"How so?" Leo nudged Jessie to hand him his shirt. Jessie grabbed his shirt and handed it to him.

"What's up, Jess?" Justin asked rubbing his rib.

"I'm moving to South Carolina." Jessie blurted.

Welp, she did it! No one said anything. Jessie slowly looked up at Leo. He looked down at her. His face was stern and eyes were fixed on Jessie.

"Wow, Jessie, that's pretty far away." Justin let out a deep breath. He placed one hand on the back of Jessie's chair and leaned on it.

"I know, but I really want to go to that school." Jessie looked behind her at Justin.

"Jessie, I hate to see you that far away but I'm happy for you, too." Justin shook his shaggy brown hair out of his face. He leaned his scrawny pale frame against Jessie's chair.

"Thanks, Justin." Jessie smiled.

"I'm not happy." Allen crossed his arms over his huge frame.

"Us either." Shelby looked over at Jessie. Leo didn't say anything for a while.

"Well, she's gotta do what she's gotta do."

Leo slipped into his shoes. He wasn't happy about it and he was doing a bad job of hiding it.

"You don't . . ." Carrie looked over at Leo.

"Jessie and I can talk about it later." Leo gave Carrie a stern look.

"Yes, sir." Carrie widened her eyes and looked over at Jessie. Jessie closed her eyes and sighed.

"Jessie, South Carolina is really far away." Allen stated.

"Drop it." Leo looked up and glared at Allen.

"Sorrrrrrry."

"Well, not to change the subject but . . . Leo, if I wasn't gay then and, after seeing you in that pool, I am now." David said laughing. He was the only one that did. They all just looked at him. I rolled my eyes.

"David," Leo sighed, "that's flattering and all, but shut up." Leo pinched the bridge of his nose.

"Well, sorry." David bobbed his head.

"Fine." Leo put his hands on his hips. "I'm tired." Leo looked at Jessie. We both knew that he wanted to leave and talk about Jessie moving to South Carolina.

"Um, I'll take you home." Jessie got up and grabbed her stuff.

"See you later." Shelby hugged Jessie.

"See ya." Jessie hugged her friends.

"I support you, Jess." Justin kissed Jessie on the cheek.

"Thanks, babe." Jessie smiled and then pulled from his embrace. Leo was already at the gate waiting on Jessie.

"He's pissed," David whispered.

"I know." Jessie frowned and then headed toward the gate.

Jessie, Leo, and I got into the truck and sat in silence.

"When were you going to tell me?" Leo looked over at Jessie.

"I don't know." Jessie rested her head against the steering wheel.

"Or were you just going to up and leave and not say goodbye?" Leo growled.

"Like you did sophomore year when you went to Mexico!" Jessie jerked her head up to look at Leo.

"Don't throw that in my face." Leo warned.

"Why, Leo?" Jessie started to cry. "Do you have any idea how hurt I was. You broke my heart and you haven't stopped breaking it since!" Jessie yelled.

Oh, Lord, please help us. I looked over at Jessie. I felt like this all needed to come out into the open. I then sat back and listened.

"Are you kidding me? I broke your heart one time." Leo pointed his finger up. "When I went to Mexico and didn't tell you, that's it." Leo grew angry.

"You cannot be serious! What about Ellen and all that stuff? Leo, we got into several fights our senior year and all those times you broke my heart."

"Oh, and you didn't break mine!?"

"I never broke your heart. Not like you broke mine."

Jessie started to cry. I hated to see her like this. Tears stung the corner of my eyes.

"Damn it, Jessie!" Leo punched his window.

Jessie and I flinched. *There was no need for that. My spirit was getting irritated.*

"Why are you so mad?" Jessie's voice grew soft.

"I don't know!" Leo looked over at Jessie. Her breathing picked up.

"There has to be a reason why you just all of a sudden became an ass!" Jessie slammed her fist in the seat.

"I'm an ass?! Look at you, Jessie. You're . . . ugh . . . never mind. I'm going to shut up before this gets brutal." Leo looked forward.

I noticed Jessie's hands start to shake. She was really mad, her face was red from crying, and her make-up was running. I looked to the right and saw her friends peeking out from the gate.

"Leo, I cannot have you being mad at me just because I'm leaving for South Carolina." Jessie sniffled.

"I don't care, Jessie. Maybe my life will be better." Leo cocked his head.

Jessie balled up her fist and struck Leo's face. I flinched at the action. Everything grew quiet . . . ."

"Get out of my truck. Allen can take you home." Jessie said through clenched teeth.

"And you want to go to ministry school." Leo looked over at Jessie.

Leo climbed out of the truck. He looked down at the floorboard, picked the item up, and chucked it at Jessie, hitting her in the neck. I looked down and it was the glass that they had taken from Jessie's house. It wasn't a plastic glass; it was glass. My temper started rising. Jessie tried to dodge the glass, but it hit her. He grabbed her neck and she looked at Leo. Leo slammed the door shut and walked toward the group of friends. Jessie started her car and headed toward her house. I crawled into the passenger's seat. I looked at Jessie. Her face was so full of sorrow and hurt.

"How do I always screw things up!" Jessie slammed her hand against the steering wheel. I watched as her temper flared.

"I hate him! He makes me feel like dirt."

Jessie rolled to a stop at a stoplight. She wiped her hand with the sleeve of her summer jacket. She looked in the mirror on the sun visor and straightened her hair and make-up so her family wouldn't ask her questions.

It's now August fifteenth. Five more days and Jessie was leaving for South Carolina. She saw all her friends but Leo. I sat with her at night as she cried because of Leo. I didn't want her to leave without saying goodbye to him. Jessie never told her family about the fight that they had gotten into. She didn't even say that Leo was never there when she hung out with her friends. Most of the time she would say that she was just hanging with the girls. I could tell she really missed him. Today was a beautiful day. It was hot out but it was a beautiful day nonetheless. Jessie and I sat on the porch as she read. Her phone lit up from a text message.

"I heard you were going to ministry school. What a joke."—Karla.

Jessie just looked down at the text, closed the phone, and continued reading. She picked up her phone and searched for Leo's name. She found his name, took a deep break, and clicked send. I heard it ring three or four times but no answer. Jessie pulled the phone from her ear and sighed.

"I ruined everything," she said out loud.

She placed the phone on the little table beside the wicker couch and continued reading. I watched as two doves chased each other, a woman walked her dog, and a group of kids rode past on their bikes. I looked down at Jessie's phone that was ringing. It was Leo's ring tone. Jessie looked down but didn't answer it. *Answer it!* She kept her eyes on it until "missed call" flashed on the screen. I looked at her and then back at the phone. She couldn't be serious. It rang again. Jessie looked down at it and decided to answer it.

"Hello?" she answered coldly.

"What did you want?" Leo asked.

"I guess to tell you that I'm really sorry for what I did and that I'm leaving in five days and I want to say goodbye to you." Jessie blurted. Nothing was said for a while.

"I forgive you and I'm really sorry, too." I heard him answer.

"Good." Jessie let out a sigh of relief.

"Yeah."

"We're all hanging out tonight. Would you like to join?" Jessie asked.

"No. I will see you before you go."

"Oh, okay. Well, I leave Friday." Jessie informed.

"I will see you then." Leo's words drifted. I noticed Jessie's eyes starting to tear up.

"Bye," Jessie said and then hung up.

Jessie sat around the pool with her girlfriends talking about life and drinking pop.

"So what happened with you and Leo that night? You still haven't told us and it's been like a month. He hasn't talked to any of us either." Shelby raised her hand to her forehead to block the sun.

"I don't wanna talk about it." Jessie splashed her feet in the water.

"Jessie, we're your best friends. We need to help you." Carrie grunted.

"Fine!" Jessie threw her hands in the air. "We were sitting and talking. Well, he gets mad and punches the window on the passenger's side door window. We yelled and then he said that maybe his life would be better if I would have left and that's what . . . ." Jessie sighed with tears filling her eyes. "I punched him in the jaw." Jessie slowly looked up at her friends. They were all looking at Jessie shocked.

"Jessie, you punched him?" Shelby tightened the strap on her bikini top.

"Yes, I hit him." Jessie looked away from her friends. "He made me mad. You know me and Leo. We do this stuff all the time. Remember in Art class when he shoved me into the cabinet and then I got all mad and pushed him up against the wall choking him with my forearm?" Jessie stated. *I remember that.*

"Jessie, maybe you guys should take a year or so off from each other." Danni suggested.

"No, I can't live without him in my life."

"Jessie, that's insane!" Carrie argued.

"He feels the same because we talked on the phone today. We made up and he's going to be here to say goodbye to me when I leave." Jessie smiled.

"You guys kill me." Danni shook her head.

"What can I say?" Jessie shrugged and smiled.

"Woooo!" we heard a male voice yell. Out of nowhere, Allen, James, David, and Justin burst through the side gate and headed toward the pool.

"Ah, don't get me wet!" Carrie yelled as she grabbed her beach towel.

The boys jumped into the pool splashing water all over the girls. The girls laughed hysterically.

"You guys are retarded." Jessie got up from where she was sitting.

"We love you, Jessie!" the boys said in unison. Jessie laughed.

"I love you, too!"

"Hey, Jess." Jessie turned around. Leo was standing in front of her.

"Oh, Leo. Hi." Jessie said nervously.

"I couldn't wait to see you." Leo raked his fingers through his hair.

"You're nervous." Jessie smiled. Leo looked up at Jessie resting his hand on the back of his neck.

"Leo, we've been through a lot together. It's okay." Jessie reassured.

"I guess I just don't want to see you go." Leo exhaled. I looked to the other friends who were staring at them.

"Let's go into the kitchen and make some pizza." Carrie suggested.

"Good. I'm starved." Justin jumped out of the pool and headed toward the back door. They all followed. I stood beside Jessie.

"Leo, I wouldn't leave if I didn't have to." Jessie walked closer to him.

"You don't have to go." Leo laughed.

"Yes, I do." Jessie cocked her head at him.

"Ah."

Leo pulled Jessie into a hug. Jessie rested her head on his chest. I know it may not be God's plan, but they act like boyfriend and girlfriend. I do not understand why they don't just go out! You have no idea how frustrating it is! I moved closer to Jessie. I wanted to pull her away from this before someone's heart seriously gets broken.

"Well, unless I had a good reason to stay."

Jessie pulled away and looked up at him. Leo's eyes filled with regret. He looked at her with so much intensity that my heart started pounding in my chest.

"Jessie, you need to do what God told you to do. I know that God means everything to you." Leo's eyes searched her face. I knew that wasn't the answer Jessie wanted to hear.

"Well, we better get inside with the others."

Jessie pulled away and headed for the back door. Leo stood there with his arms still in embrace mode. I shook my head and followed Jessie.

The group of friends like always had a blast together. I noticed Jessie would stop and look at her friends. I knew she was thinking about how much she would miss them. Jessie and the girls cleaned up while the guys, of course, watched.

"Well, I'm heading home." Jessie announced.

"Can I get a ride?" Leo looked over at Jessie.

"Ha, yes." Jessie laughed. She reached over Justin and grabbed her purse and keys.

"Five more days, Jessie." Justin reminded.

"I know. Love you guys."

Jessie hugged each of her friends. Leo and Jessie headed out the door and to the truck.

"Bye," they called after us. I walked alongside Jessie. I felt nervousness and anxiety coming from her. Leo and I climbed into the truck and Jessie followed. She looked over at Leo.

"Well, say goodbye to my truck. She gets sold tomorrow." Jessie started her truck.

"Why?" Leo turned to look at Jessie.

"She can't make the trip to South Carolina. It's cool, though. My dad and I bought a 1998 Toyota Camry. It's white with four doors. Better than this." Jessie scanned her truck.

"Well, you're already to go then." Leo smiled. Jessie pulled out of Carrie's driveway and turned onto the bypass.

"We're picking it up on the drive down there. We gotta go through Tennessee anyway." Jessie shrugged.

"What are you doing for the next four days?"

"Well, I'm going to finish packing, sell the truck, spend time with family, and then leave."

"Right." Leo said coldly. Jessie ignored the comment.

"James and Allen are getting a place together." Jessie changed the subject.

"Good." Leo kept his focus on the road. Jessie turned onto Leo's road.

"Well, I will see you Friday." Jessie pulled up to Leo's house.

"Bye."

Leo got out of the truck and headed toward his house. Usually, Jessie waited for him to be sound in his house, but she took off without waiting. She sped down the bypass.

"He irritates me!" Jessie yelled into the truck. I quickly looked over at her.

"God, if this isn't going to work, please show me." Jessie prayed.

"What do I do? . . ."

CHAPTER 24

Onward Christian Soldier

It's August 25th. Jessie's just finishing up putting her boxes in her dad's truck. The day is beautiful and not as hot as the day before. Jessie's stuff is almost loaded. She looks at her phone. There were no calls from Leo. Her friends were supposed to be here any minute. She had to leave by 1 p.m. and it was already noon. Jessie sighed as she heaved a box into the truck. Jessie and her other family had had a goodbye dinner last night and she got to say goodbye to her grandmother, cousins, and aunts last then.

"That's the last of it!" Travis yelled from the front door.

"Good." Jessie shut the tailgate and walked over to her brother.

"That's them." Jessie pointed to three cars.

They had finally come to say goodbye. Jessie had food ready for them in the kitchen. She figured she could feed them and fellowship before she left. One by one the cars piled into the driveway.

"I'm gonna miss you!" David came running up to Jessie embracing her.

"Hey, it's not time for goodbye yet." Jessie chuckled. "Hey, David, this is Bubby. Travis, this is David." Jessie introduced them.

"Hey, how are ya?" Travis shook David's hand. Everyone piled out of the cars and headed to Jessie's house. Leo came walking up.

"I'm here if you need me." Travis kissed Jessie on the head and headed toward her parents who were trying to look busy outside. Travis stopped and talked to Leo for a while. He looked back at his sister and headed toward her parents.

"Hey, Leo." Jessie hugged him.

"Hey, Jess." Leo hugged her back.

"I have food in the kitchen for you guys." Jessie smiled.

"Great! I'm starved." Justin bolted to the kitchen.

"He's always hungry." Shelby laughed.

They all made their way to the kitchen. Justin already made a sandwich and had ten cookies on his plate. They all took a seat around the table or on the counter.

"So, how long will it take you to get there?" David asked as he bit into a chip.

"Um . . . we're going to split it up—ten hours today and four tomorrow." Jessie rubbed her pinky.

"Wow, South Carolina. Well, at least one of us is getting out of Marion." Allen leaned against the counter.

"Think you'll live there permanently?" James lifted himself off of the counter and headed toward the fridge.

"I don't know. I guess if I really like it." Jessie shrugged. Leo didn't say anything. He was too focused on downing his sandwich.

"Think you'll meet anyone there?" Shelby blurted. Leo choked on his food and then looked up at Jessie.

"Um . . . I will meet a lot of people." Jessie smiled at Shelby.

"No. She means a boyfriend. I mean, you're a good-looking single woman." Carrie shrugged. Her short brown hair was bobbing on her shoulders.

"Oh, I don't know. Could be. There's going to be a whole new pool of boys." Jessie laughed.

"Yeah, but that doesn't mean anything." Leo shook his head and placed his plate on the table.

"I think you'll meet someone." Shelby shot a dirty look at Leo who returned it.

"Well, I'm going just for God. If I get a guy along the way, then good. If not, that's okay, too." Jessie looked over at David.

"Sounds good to me." David reached over and wrapped his arm around Jessie's waist.

"I'm coming to visit you." Justin shrugged.

"Holy crap . . . road trip." Allen looked at all of them.

"Ha, guys, I'm not even gone yet and you're already coming to see me." Jessie laughed and rested her arms on David's shoulder.

"We already miss you." Carrie smiled.

She got up and gathered the empty plates from the others and threw them away. The rest started helping clean up the kitchen.

"I can't believe you're leaving me!" Justin threw his arms around Jessie and rested his head on her shoulder.

"Ah, Jusy." Jessie rubbed his back.

Jessie's nickname for Justin sometimes was Jusy. She's been calling him that since the eighth grade.

"Well, we've been best friends since the eighth grade." Justin pulled himself up to look at her and stuck out his lower lip.

"Ah, I love you." Jessie reached up and kissed him. It wasn't a long, drawn out kiss. Just a kiss between good friends.

"You have soft lips." Justin laughed.

"Thanks." Jessie laughed.

Justin walked toward the fridge with the other guys, who stood there with their mouths gaping open. Jessie turned to the girls and David.

"Yup, she kissed me. Yeah, it was a little peck and was totally friendship, but she kissed me. Sucka!" Justin laughed and pointed at Leo. Leo rolled his eyes.

"Just friends, though." Leo stated.

"So. I don't see you getting a kiss." Justin crossed his arms over his thin frame.

"When I kiss Jessie, trust me, it's gonna be more than a peck." Leo glared at Justin.

"So, you're gonna kiss . . ."

"Hey, guys, my dad just called from outside. It's almost one and I gotta get going." Jessie interrupted.

"No!" David started to cry.

"Oh, you guys are starting college next week and it's going to be like I never existed." Jessie laughed.

"No." Justin shook his head. Jessie, the others, and I headed toward the truck.

"Call me whenever you want and text me every day." Shelby said choking back tears. Shelby pushed her bangs from her face.

"I will and same to you." Jessie hugged her.

"We love you. We got you this." Carrie reached into her oversized purse and pulled out a gift and a card.

"Ah . . . I didn't get you guys anything." Jessie started to cry.

Jessie's parents and brother were waiting in the truck. Jessie opened the gift. It was a picture of all of them hanging out by the pool. They had decorated the picture frame. It had glitter and stickers and said "Best Friends" across the top of it.

"Read the card in the car." Carrie patted Jessie's hand.

"Oh, okay." Jessie looked up at her friends.

I felt my throat tightening. She had known these friends for four years. They grew together, they loved together, they fought together, they laughed together, and they watched as some drifted. They did everything together. I saw Leo standing at a distance from the group. Jessie tugged at her All-American Rejects t-shirt and flipped her long, blonde hair over her shoulder.

"Juice." Jessie's dad called out the truck window.

"Alright, guys." Jessie looked back at her dad and then to her friends. "This is it. Till Thanksgiving." Jessie lowered her gaze at them.

"Yes. We're going to miss you." David started crying, causing the girls to cry.

"Please, guys, you have got to stop. It's not like we're never going to see each other again." Jessie hugged each of them and kissed them on the cheek.

"We love you." Carrie blew Jessie a kiss on the way to her car.

"Jessie, if you don't get a boyfriend, get at me." Justin called as he walked to Carrie's car.

"Will do." Jessie laughed.

"Wow! I still can't believe you're leaving us."

Allen bent down and hugged Jessie. She embraced him and was engulfed by his massive frame. The moment choked me up. Even I was going to miss these kids.

"Bye, Jess," said James.

James hugged Jessie and kissed her cheek. Then he and Allen headed to their car. Shelby hugged Jessie one last time and then headed to her car with David. David had already hugged her several times. Leo stood at a distance.

"We better hurry." Leo walked up to Jessie. His hands were in his pockets, his white "wife beater" exposed his muscles, and his long, black hair rested below his shoulders.

"Yeah." Jessie sighed.

"Uh." Leo choked out. *Lord, give him strength.* I crossed my arms over my chest and rested my head in my hand.

"You know I'm going to miss you." Leo raked his hand through his hair.

"I know, and I'm going to miss you." Jessie looked up at him.

"You call me if you need me." Leo reached out and grabbed Jessie's hand.

"I will. Same to you." Jessie laughed.

"I know." Leo laughed nervously.

I looked toward the friends in the car. They all stared at them.

"Here. I wrote this for you. Please don't open it till like you're at least two states away." Leo handed Jessie an envelope with her name written on the front.

"Oh, okay." Jessie looked at the envelope and then up to Leo.

"I love ya, Jessie." Leo exhaled.

"I love ya, too." Jessie hugged Leo. They kept their embrace for a while.

"I gotta go." Jessie said through tears.

"I'm having a really hard time letting you." Leo pulled her closer.

We needed to wrap this thing up. It was getting too intense even for me.

"Jess." Dad called. *Thank you, Dad!*

"Alright." Jessie said to Leo.

"Alright." Leo looked down.

"Be safe. I'll be waiting for you." Leo smiled at Jessie.

"Leo." Jessie sighed.

"I don't care what you say. I will." Leo dipped his head to look into Jessie's eyes.

"Alright." Jessie laughed. "Bye, Leo."

"No, I like 'See you later' better." Leo laughed.

"Alright. See you later."

"Later, Jess." Leo bent forward.

Oh no! He was going to kiss her. I held my breath. My heart started beating fast. Jessie turned to the side and embraced him in a hug. I let out my breath. I couldn't believe she did that.

"I'm going to miss you," she said in his neck.

Leo pulled away, looking at her with confusion probably because we all knew that's what she was waiting for, for four years! I can't say that I'm disappointed. She needed nothing standing in her way of what God had planned for her.

"Later, Jess." Leo dropped his hands from her waist.

"Later." Jessie nodded.

Leo looked for a moment and then turned toward the car. Everyone, even Jessie's family, was staring at them. Leo turned around and waved to her and then got into the back seat of Allen's car. All of her friends waved to her. Jessie and I stood there watching her friends pull out of the driveway and drive away. Jessie looked over at her dad's truck and took a deep breath.

"That was just sad." Toni said from the front seat.

"Yeah, I know." Jessie started crying.

"It's okay, sis." Travis hugged Jessie.

"I know. I gotta read this card." Jessie opened the envelope to the card. It was homemade by one of Jessie's friends on the computer. It had "Best Friends" in bold blue letters with a purple background, and it had a different picture of them all on the front. There were butterflies all over the front. Jessie opened the card and read it aloud to her family.

"Best friends are hard to come by. When you find a true friend, never let go. We love you Jessie!" Jessie said through tears. They all wrote a little something.

"Jessie, you will always be one of my best friends. You're kind and compassionate and always there for me! I love you!—Shelby"

"I love the fact that you have an answer for everything and a joke every time someone is sad. I'm going to miss seeing you, Jessie.—Carrie"

"Oh, my gosh. I didn't know Christians could be so cool and accepting of my gay-ness (lol) until I met you. Thanks for making me feel loved no matter what the circumstances. Love you—David."

Jessie looked over at her brother. "Dang, Jessie, they're really going to miss you." Travis looked at the card and then to Jessie. Jessie read off the rest.

"Even though you and Leo always had a thing, you were supposed to be with me. lol Love ya, Jess. Gonna miss ya.—Justin"

"Me and Applehead have the same thing to say. WE LOVE YOU!—James and Allen"

"Jessie, I'm going to miss you . . . your laugh, smile, the way you love to argue with me. Gonna miss it all. Much love.—Leo"

"That's all he wrote?" Toni said with disappointment.

"No." Jessie pulled the envelope out from her back pocket. "This is what he's got to say." Jessie looked over at Travis.

"Oh, wow. I wonder what it says." Travis widened his eyes.

"Ha! He doesn't want me to read it till I'm at least in Tennessee." Jessie shrugged sticking the envelope back in her pocket. She stared at the card and then placed it back in the envelope. Jessie let out a sigh and rested her head against the headrest. I sat in the middle of her and Travis and leaned back and rested my head on her shoulder.

Tennessee

I couldn't believe we were already in Tennessee. One more state and we'd be in North Carolina, but I think that Jessie's dad wanted to stop and rest in Tennessee. Tomorrow we would go through North Carolina and then hit South. The place where Jessie's school was was maybe two miles from the North Carolina border. Her aunt's house was only four hours from Jessie's new school. Jessie hadn't awakened since she got in the truck. Her dad didn't want to stop and eat till they got to her aunt's, which was okay. They had eaten sandwiches before they left.

"Jessie, we're almost to Aunt Georgia's house." Travis lightly shook Jessie. Jessie slowly woke up.

"Really?" She looked over at Travis.

"Really." Travis smiled.

"I'm starving." Jessie blurted.

"Us, too." Toni grabbed her stomach.

"We're going to eat at Georgia's. It's only an hour away." Mike sighed.

"I guess." Jessie sighed and then looked out the window. She grabbed her phone from her purse and checked. She had eleven text messages from her friends. She went through replying with a smile.

"Hey, we're in Tennessee. You going to read Leo's letter?" Travis looked over at Jessie.

"Not yet." Jessie said not looking up from her phone.

"Can I?

"Uh . . . no." Jessie laughed.

"Alright." Travis sighed.

Jessie closed her phone and sighed. Leo hasn't called yet. I remembered when she first met him in Biology 9. He was sitting by himself looking over papers. His hair was shorter then. She looked at him like he was the most beautiful thing she had ever seen. I actually remember her saying that *"he's the most beautiful thing I've ever seen"*. I remember all their fights from freshman year all the way to senior year and, well, the summer after that. I'm going to miss them being together. There are sometimes when I wish I was a human and I could put Leo in his place after some of the things that he's done to Jessie, but all I could do was pray. I wonder how close they were going to be now that Jessie was going to be in South Carolina.

"We're here," Travis said as they turned on to Aunt Georgia's road.

That was a fast trip. It was a very silent trip. I felt for Jessie. She wanted to do what God wants for her, but I knew that she wanted to stay back and be with her friends . . . with Leo. Jessie and her family climbed out of the truck and met Aunt Georgia at the front door. Georgia was a peaceful woman. She was tall, a little on the heavy side, long gray hair, piercing green eyes, and very homey. She was cute. She embraced each of them. We entered the house and were engulfed by the smell of roast, potatoes, rolls, macaroni and cheese, and more. It smelled so good. Jessie headed straight to the table.

"Hungry, Jess?" Georgia laughed.

"Yes, ma'am, and tired." Jessie smiled weakly.

"You slept the whole way." Travis blurted.

"I'm just tired." Jessie shrugged. Everyone else took their seats at the table.

"Are you ready for college?" Georgia looked over at Jessie, passing her the macaroni and cheese.

"Yeah, kind of nervous. I already miss my friends." Jessie chuckled.

"I understand. Did you leave a guy behind?" Georgia so bluntly asked.

I looked up from where I was sitting on the couch. The living room was connected, so I could see them and I had a clear shot of Jessie. Jessie's jaws tensed up and she wore a scowl.

"No." Jessie answered as politely as she could. "Why would you ask me that?"

Jessie's family all looked at one another and then to Jessie and Georgia.

"I don't know. It just seems like you would. I feel your heart breaking." Georgia bit into a roll.

"Your vibes are off because I didn't leave a guy behind." Jessie laughed.

"Okay." Georgia shrugged.

I looked around the house and saw pictures of Jessie's family all around the walls—her immediate family and extended family.

"Well, you're going to like the Camry. I haven't driven it in a while, but everything should be good." Georgia smiled at Jessie.

"Cool." Jessie returned the smile.

Jessie and Travis helped Georgia clear the table and they set out the ice cream.

"Let's play cards." Georgia suggested as she placed the ice cream on the counter to get a little softer before she started dishing it out.

"Okay." Travis turned to the desk that was by the front door. He grabbed a stack of cards.

"I'm not really in the mood for cards." Jessie sighed and then headed to the couch and sat next to me.

"Oh, Jessie, you need to get your mind off of stuff." Aunt Georgia walked over to Jessie and patted her knee.

"No, I really don't want to." Jessie sighed.

"Jess, come on, Bullshit isn't the same without you." Travis grunted.

"Travis, watch your mouth." Toni yelled from the back room.

"Ma, it's the name of the game." Travis called.

"I don't care. You could have said bull crap." Toni argued. Travis rolled his eyes and looked over to Jessie.

"I don't want to play that." Jessie sighed. "Let's play kemps." Jessie got up from the couch.

"I'm down for that," Mike said as he entered the house with the duffle bags. He dropped them on the floor by the couch.

"We playing cards?" Mike looked at Travis holding a deck of cards.

"Yes, sir." Travis smiled and then looked over at Jessie. Jessie slugged over to the table with the rest of her family.

Card playing went well into the night. They laughed and yelled but mainly laughed. I think it took Jessie's mind off of her friends and Leo. Jessie had to go to sleep, though, and that's when the wheels in Jessie's head turned the most.

"Well, I'm off to bed." Jessie put her card s in a neat stack and placed them in front of her.

"Good idea." Georgia yawned.

"I will see ya'll in the morning." Jessie rubbed her eyes and then headed to the bedroom we would be staying in.

"Night, hun." Georgia called. Jessie didn't answer.

We entered a white room with a twin bed and a night stand. Jessie climbed into bed. She opened her phone, texted all her friends goodnight, powered her phone down, and then went to sleep.

South Carolina

Jessie woke up at ten o'clock a.m. Her eyes opened wide as she looked around the room.

"Oh, my gosh. I'm going to my college today," she said nervously. "I wanna go back. I need Leo." Jessie shivered.

I got up from the end of the bed, walked over to her, and stroked her hair. She stopped shivering. I knew that she was nervous, but I knew God was going to take care of her. I would be there to protect her. Jessie got out of bed and headed toward the smell of pancakes.

"Hey, college girl." Mike announced to Jessie.

"Yeah." Jessie slumped into the kitchen chair next to her brother.

"You excited?" Travis bit into a sausage link.

"Yes and scared." Jessie shook her head.

"It's going to be okay," Mike smiled from across the table.

"Yeah." Jessie stared into her empty plate.

"You and I will be in your Toyota, and your mom and Travis will be in my truck." Mike declared.

"I gotta drive the interstate?" Jessie looked up at her dad.

"Yes."

"I can't do that." Jessie said with fear in her voice.

"Yes, you can. I'm going to help you."

"Mike, you know that won't work. You and Jess have very little patience with each other." Toni chimed.

"No, we're going to be fine." Mike rolled his eyes at his wife's comment.

"I guess." Toni's eyes widened.

The breakfast went slower than usual. I think it was because no one wanted to see Jessie leave, and Jessie didn't want to leave. Jessie finished breakfast and headed back to the room that she was staying in. She sat on her bed and looked out the window at the birds. She grabbed her phone on the nightstand and powered it up. She had gotten all the goodnight texts back from her friends. Leo still hasn't called. Jessie closed her phone and rested it on the table. She walked to her duffle bag, pulled out some clothes, and then headed to the bathroom. I sat on the edge of the bed waiting for her to get ready.

"Alright, you guys. Be careful and, Jessie, live it to the fullest." Georgia embraced Jessie.

"Thanks for everything." Jessie hugged.

"You're welcome." Georgia held Jessie out at arm's length and smiled. "You're going to do great."

Georgia kissed Jessie on the cheek. Jessie smiled and then headed toward to her new car. I climbed into the back seat. It was actually really roomy and comfortable. It was better than that half cab in her truck. The rest of Jessie's family said goodbye to Georgia and then got into the vehicles.

"Alright, Juice, here we go." Mike patted Jessie's hand.

"Yes. Here we go."

Jessie pulled out of the driveway. She followed her dad's direction on how and when to get on the interstate. We were coming off the off ramp when a semi-truck came up beside us.

"We're gonna die!" Jessie jerked the wheel pulling the car away from the semi.

"Juice! You cannot do that! You will kill someone!" Mike grabbed the handle above the door.

"Sorry. It scared me." Jessie breathed heavily.

"Just go." Mike sighed.

"I didn't mean to. I swear he was going to hit us."

"He knows what he's doing. You, on the other hand, do not." Mike shook his head.

"Sorry." Jessie rolled her eyes.

"So, are you missing Leo yet?" Mike bluntly asked.

"No." Jessie lied.

"I don't believe you."

"What's there to miss, Dad?" Jessie argued.

"Juice, I'm not stupid. I know that you really like him."

"Doesn't matter." Jessie switched lanes.

"I'm proud of you going to this school and doing what God has told you." Mike looked over at Jessie.

"Yeah, well, I don't want to happen what happened to me in my junior year." Jessie laughed.

"Me either." Mike admitted.

I sat in the back seat listening to them talk. It would be four hours until we got to our destination. I leaned back in the seat and relaxed. Jessie did a really good job of driving for her first time on the interstate. She would tense up every time a semi-truck came up beside us. Jessie and Mike talked about anything and everything—from friends to God, to the future to Leo and the family. I noticed Jessie's nerves ease when she leaned back in her seat and drove.

Time was going by fast and we were fifty miles from the South Carolina border. I was starting to get anxious and wanted to see what this place was like.

"Dad, do you think I should be this far from home?" Jessie looked over at her dad for the second that she could.

"Yes. You're going to be fine. Did you ever read Leo's letter?" Mike asked.

"I haven't' yet." Jessie shook her head.

"You might need to." Mike looked intently at Jessie.

"No. It's cool. I will later, after I get settled in my dorm."

"Alright. If that's what you want." Mike shrugged.

Jessie looked into the rearview mirror at her brother and mom in her dad's truck behind them.

"She did good driving that truck for as short as she is." Jessie laughed.

"Yes, she did." Mike laughed.

We were close to the South Carolina border. I drew myself closer to my window anticipating the sign that welcomed you to the state.

"We're almost there." Mike grew excited.

"Yes, we are." Jessie tried to seem excited.

"This is going to be great, Juice." Mike kept his focus forward.

"I know. God's going to take care of me." Jessie smiled.

"Yes, He will."

"God's got my best interest at heart."

There it was—the "Welcome to South Carolina" sign. I could see it from a distance.

"Oh, we're almost 'bout to cross over." Mike laughed.

What was that under the sign? I squinted my eyes at the black mass that stood below it. I couldn't see it quite yet. It was still at a distance. I pulled my body closer to the window. The sign came closer and so did the shadow below it. My skin tensed up. My stomach jerked. My spirit grew irritated as I looked at the black figure. Below the South Carolina sign, with a wicked smile across his face stood . . . Anton.

Dad, I would like to thank you for all your support and tough love when it came to writing and publishing Tristan's story. I would also like to thank you for being a dad that was always there for my brother and I and never leaving Mama. You've always worked hard and had a job to support your family. You're amazing dad. I love you.

Mama, Thank you for always being there for me when I needed you and loving me even when it was hard you're amazing, gorgeous and the sweetest person that I know. I love you so much.

Bubby (Travis), No matter where life takes us you will ALWAYS be my best friend. You've been there for me since day one. You tend to be overprotective but with the world the way that it is. I'm starting to see why. I am proud to be your little sister. I love you so much!

Grams, Even though we don't always see eye to eye and you always warn be about things in life, even when it seems like I am not listening. Trust me. I am. I appreciate your wisdom. I love you.

Cousin Rodney, You were never a cousin to me but more like a brother. I always have fun when I'm around you and you always make me laugh. You are very important to me. I love you.

Martin Geppert, My artist. Thank you for sharing your amazing talent with me. You are awesome, beautiful and full of life. God smiled on me when he brought you into my life and now I can't picture my life without you.

I saved the best for last . . .

Jonathan Geppert. My best friend and spiritual soul mate. Thank you for your contribution to the book. But above all thank you for being my friend, listening to my hopes, dreams and vision and being a part of them. Thank you for putting up with me because we both know I can be difficult at times. I love you and I'm glad God gave me you.